A MORTAL TERROR

A MORTAL TERROR

A Billy Boyle World War II Mystery

James R. Benn

Published by Soho Press, Inc.
853 Broadway
New York, NY 10003

Maps used with permission of the U.S. Army, Center of Military History.

Library of Congress Cataloging-in-Publication Data

Benn, James R.
A mortal terror / James R. Benn.
p. cm.
ISBN 978-1-56947-994-0
eISBN 978-1-56947-995-7
1. Boyle, Billy (Fictitious character)—Fiction. 2. World War,
1939-1945—Italy—Fiction. 3. Soldiers—Crimes against—Fiction.
4.Americans—Italy—Fiction. 5. Serial murder investigation—Fiction.
I. Title.
PS3602.E6644M67 2011
813'.6—dc22
2011018081

This book is for—
Camille
Claudia
Emma
Luke
Nathaniel
Noah
Oliver

The future.

swift there came
a mortal terror;
voices that I knew.

The Epic of Hades, Book II, Actaeon

PART ONE

Switzerland

■

CHIASSO, SWITZERLAND
SWISS-ITALIAN BORDER

January 1944

CHAPTER ONE

KIM PHILBY OWED me one. I'd helped him out back in London, and he told me to ask if I ever needed a favor. Well, now that I needed one, I didn't hesitate. I wanted to be there when—not if, when—Diana Seaton returned from her mission.

Philby was the only person who could make that happen, so I was glad he was in my debt. As head of the British Secret Intelligence Service's Mediterranean operations, he controlled all the spies, saboteurs, and agents operating in neutral nations and behind enemy lines from Portugal to Turkey. That included Diana Seaton of the Special Operations Executive, who had been sent into Rome, disguised as a nun, to establish contact with a pro-Allied circle within the Vatican.

How do I, a lowly lieutenant, know all this? Because Diana Seaton is the love of my life, and I worry about her day and night. A lot of people worry about each other in this war, but unlike them, I can do something about it. I work for General Dwight David Eisenhower, which gives me access to secrets out of the reach of most colonels and many generals. The fact that in private I call him Uncle Ike doesn't hurt either. It allows me to get involved with men like Kim Philby. When Philby called two days ago to tell me he was good for the favor I'd asked, Uncle Ike gave me a five-day leave and told me to stay out of trouble. I'm going to Switzerland, I told him, how much trouble could there be in a neutral country?

As I stamped my feet on the station platform, trying to keep warm, I thought I might have been off the mark. It was cold, and the sun was casting its last feeble yellow rays sideways from the west. I watched the German and Italian border guards, about fifty yards away, their frosted breath trailing like plumes as they walked. Chiasso is a border town, and the railroad runs right through it. The platform stretches from the station on the Swiss side south to the Italian border, marked by a customs house and crossing gate. Philby and I had been waiting an hour, nervously watching the train halted behind the gate, still on Italian soil. Diana was on board, or so I'd hoped, until a half dozen men in leather trench coats entered the train, and a platoon of German soldiers with submachine guns surrounded it. The black locomotive released a sigh of steam from its boiler, as if straining at the leash for the final stretch.

"Gestapo," Philby had said. "Not to worry. She has good travel papers, signed by the German general commanding rail transport in Northern Italy."

"The Gestapo can sniff out phony papers, no matter how good."

"Oh, they're the real thing, old boy," Philby said, clenching his pipe between his teeth. "This general is quite the churchgoer, especially since he arranged for the transport of several thousand Italian Jews."

"To where?" I knew the Nazis were rounding up Jews everywhere, and shooting a lot of them. But I didn't know where they kept transporting them to, or why. It didn't make sense when they needed railroads for troops and supplies, but then nothing in this war made much sense.

"To those camps in the east we keep hearing about. This old general began to feel guilty, more so after we landed in Italy. He let it be known he'd be glad to do a small favor for the Vatican now and then."

"Isn't it dangerous to give him Diana's name? Or whatever name she's using?"

"Yes, it would be," Philby said absently, as he knocked the ash from his pipe and jammed it into his coat pocket. "That's why she's coming out with a group of twenty nuns. Didn't want to tell you the details before now, you understand."

"Sure, security. Lot of that going around."

"The cover story is that they're being sent to a convent outside of Zurich, to relieve crowding in the Holy See. Solid on all counts. Look there," he said, pointing to the train. A rush of black leather exited, accompanied by shouted orders. The troops surrounding the train trotted to their vehicles. The Italian border guards stood back, melting into the shadows, mere spectators on their own soil. Two burly Gestapo men stepped down from a train car, holding a civilian by his elbows, guiding him to the waiting sedan. The civilian looked around, his head swiveling wildly as he sought some way out. He dug in his heels, but the two goons carried him easily. Then he dropped, as if he'd fainted. One of the Germans pulled back his leg to give him a kick, and all of a sudden the prisoner was up, pushing his tormentor and twisting free. He ran along the train, his arms pumping, and leapt from the platform, hitting the ground hard, rolling and coming up at a run, limping as one leg threatened to give out. Pistol shots cracked and gray dust kicked up at his feet. Then an MP40 submachine gun sounded, the harsh burst slamming into his back. He took another two steps, perhaps not realizing that death had burrowed into muscle and bone. His momentum propelled him forward, almost in a cartwheel, until his body fell limply across the track. The sigh of steam flowed from the locomotive again, a mournful sound that seemed to apologize for the sudden death of a passenger so close to his final destination.

The Germans pushed the Italian border guards forward, ordering them to retrieve the body. As they grabbed the fellow by his feet and pulled, they left a streak of crimson that pointed, like an arrow, to the Swiss side.

"Lucky fellow," Philby said. "That was at least quick."

"One of yours?"

"No. Some poor bastard on the run. Deserter, maybe. Probably betrayed by some other chap looking to save his own skin. Here we go," he said as the gate was raised and the train finally lurched forward, its giant steel wheels rolling over the bloodstains as it left Nazi territory.

The train arrived at the platform, and lights switched on above us as the sun gave up and set below the looming mountains. To the south, a blanket of darkness settled over occupied Italy, where the blackout was complete, not a glimmer allowed to guide Allied bombers. The Swiss side seemed gaudy in comparison, bright lights shining on gray pavement and orange tile roofs. Maybe I'd gotten used to the blackout in London, but the glare of streetlights and lamps was blinding. I shaded my eyes and strained to see into the compartments as they rolled by, the train moving slowly until its caboose was safely on neutral ground.

The compartment doors opened, and the passengers spilled out with a mix of nervous chatter and ashen faces. Some looked like businessmen, others refugees. Wartime travel to a neutral country provided for odd traveling companions. Then I saw them, two cars down: a procession of black habits, led by an older nun. They wore cloaks against the cold and white wimples encased their faces, their black veils prohibiting sideways glances, their eyes focused on the ground at their feet.

"Hold," Philby said in a low voice, placing his hand on my arm. "Don't say anything. We don't know who may be watching the station."

I saw her. Not her face, but her walk. Nothing could hide that confident swing of her shoulders, the aristocratic posture, the determined steps. It was Diana, her head bowed a fraction less than the others. The nun in the lead said something in Italian, and they turned to enter the open doors of the station. Diana glanced up, looking in all directions. Her eyes met mine and flashed wide for a split second, then disappeared as she assumed the obedient, demure posture of a nun following her abbess.

Philby and I fell in a few steps behind them as I watched for signs of anyone trailing us. I pulled my hat brim low over my eyes, blending in with the crowd, while trying to spot anyone who didn't. I was in civilian clothes, and if it hadn't been for the threat of German agents in similar attire, not to mention the blood on the tracks, I might have talked myself into enjoying this Swiss interlude. Instead, I saw everything with suspicious eyes, not trusting that anyone was who he said he was. I wasn't, Diana certainly wasn't, so how could we assume we were surrounded by harmless Swiss neutrals?

We trailed the procession of nuns out onto the street. They walked up the Corso San Gottardo, each clutching a small black suitcase, dodging the pedestrians strolling along the thoroughfare. Wind whipped at their cloaks and veils, the black fabric snapping like flags in a parade. Passing restaurants and shops with unaccustomed light spilling out into the street, the nuns made a beeline for the Chiesa di Santa Maria, a bronze-roofed church in a small, park-like setting. Trees surrounded two buildings to the rear, and I guessed this was where they'd be staying. As they entered the church, Philby guided me down a narrow side street, where a gray sedan sat idling. We got in the backseat and the driver took off without a word, circling around to the rear of the church. The car stopped and Philby got out, holding the car door open. A church door opened, the light from inside briefly framing the silhouette of a nun, who dashed to the car and slid into the backseat. Philby slammed the door and got in the front, a split second before the driver accelerated and sped along the gravel drive and out onto the road.

"Billy," Diana said, glancing toward Philby, her eyes showing a curious mix of surprise, joy, and fear. "Why are you here? Is something wrong?"

"Nothing wrong, my dear," said Philby. "I simply owed Lieutenant Boyle a favor and brought him along to see the sights."

"Then you *have* been busy since I last saw you," Diana said to me, her face relaxing. We'd last seen each other in Naples, a month ago, before an assignment from Uncle Ike cut our time together short.

"Yes. I asked if I could tag along when your mission was finished. I never thought you'd be brought out so soon."

"It was . . . sudden," she said. Her voice wavered, and I thought tears welled up in her eyes, but she regained her composure in an instant, running the rosary beads she wore through her fingers. "What's the connection?" Diana asked in a low voice, nodding toward Philby.

"It's a long story."

"They all are," Diana said, as she took my hand in hers and gazed out the window. She rubbed the moisture away and stared at the traffic, the streetlights, the glow from windows—all the signs of normalcy that had become so abnormal in these years of war. She blinked rapidly as the tears returned, and one dropped onto the back of my hand.

"Are you okay?" I asked.

"Long and sad," she said. "Every story is so long and so sad." She gripped my hand until her knuckles turned white. We drove on through the peaceful streets in silence broken only by the sound of muffled sobs.

CHAPTER TWO

THE HOTEL TURCONI was located just north of Chiasso. It sat atop a hill at the start of a wave of foothills and high ridges cresting the Alps themselves. It was a small place, perfect for knowing who your fellow guests were, and for watching the winding road that led up from the border town. When we'd first checked in, the owner nodded to Philby like a long-time customer, the kind who liked to be left alone. He didn't blink at our passports, both Irish, and reserved a table in an alcove for our meals, set apart from the other diners. Our papers and our names were phony, but the money Philby handed over wasn't. I hoped he wasn't stingy with the king's pound notes, since I didn't like the idea of German agents paying us a visit while we slept.

The owner himself served us. Wild mushroom soup and roasted duck breast with apples, washed down with a couple of bottles of Merlot Bianco—from his cousin's vineyard, he was proud to tell us. It beat dining in London, with all the rationing restrictions, even though Diana was still dressed as a nun.

"Why don't you change?" I asked as our host cleared the dishes and Philby fired up his pipe. "Do you need clothes?"

"Kim," Diana said. "Didn't you tell him?"

"Tell me what?" I wanted to know.

"The mission isn't over," she said, lowering her voice. "I needed to report something in person, so I asked to come out. I'll go back as soon as I can."

"I will be the one to make that decision, my dear," Philby said in his best professorial tone. "That's why I didn't tell Boyle. I'm not sure myself if you should go back. First, I need to hear what was so important, and how you came to learn of it. The Germans are great ones for playing games, and it could be false intelligence designed to draw out an agent, forcing you to take the sort of intemperate action you did."

"This is not the sort of intelligence they would plant," Diana said. "And I am not intemperate." She drank her wine and set the glass down hard, punctuating her statement.

"Very well," Philby said, shrugging his acceptance. "We can discuss the matter later, in private."

"No," Diana said. "This is not something to be hidden away and kept secret. Billy does work for General Eisenhower, after all." She made it sound like Philby was an idiot, not her spymaster boss.

"And I am in the business of managing secrets," Philby said. "Not broadcasting them before their usefulness can be determined."

"I saw a report from the bishop of Berlin, Konrad von Preysing," Diana said, ignoring Philby, who refilled his wine glass and eyed her with faint amusement, as if she were a precocious child on the verge of misbehavior. "It was sent directly to the pope, and one of his secretaries typed a copy . . ."

"If you insist on proceeding, move on to the facts," Philby said. "There is no need to detail your sources for Lieutenant Boyle." It was a way for him to assert his authority while allowing her to continue.

Diana waited for a heartbeat, then nodded. "Kurt Gerstein is an *Obersturmführer* in the SS. A lieutenant. He joined the Nazis in 1933, but quickly became disillusioned and spoke out against their anti-religious policies. For his involvement with various Christian youth groups, he was thrown out of the party, severely beaten, and briefly imprisoned for anti-Nazi activities."

"So how did he end up in the SS?" Philby asked, an eyebrow raised in disbelief.

"In early 1941, his sister-in-law died in a mental institution."

"Nazi euthanasia?" Philby asked.

"Yes. At that point, Gerstein became committed to acting against the regime. He apparently decided the best way to do that was from within. A few months after her death, he joined the SS. Either they didn't check his records, or his technical skills made them willing to overlook them. He had an engineering degree, and had completed his first year of medical school. So they brought him into the Technical Disinfection Department of the SS."

"What, do they clean garbage cans?" I asked, wondering where all this was leading.

"No. They are in charge of disinfecting the clothes of all the Jews they kill. Jews, Gypsies, Communists, opponents of the regime, anyone who is sent to the extermination camps."

I'd read about the concentration camps, where enemies of the Nazis were sent, and I knew the SS and the Gestapo had no qualms about shooting whomever they wanted. But this felt different. A whole structure dedicated to extermination? It was bigger than wanton slaughter, beyond evil, beyond believing. Everything I'd read or seen in newsreels about the Nazis made me angry. This made me sick.

"We know the Nazis have treated the Jews terribly," Philby said. "As they have many others. We know many die in the camps in the east, but extermination? Surely they use them for labor, and many die, but you can't mean wholesale slaughter?" Philby's normally suave demeanor faltered for a moment as he took in what Diana was describing.

"The Technical Disinfection Department also provides a gas called Zyklon B. It is used in gas chambers, in large quantities," Diana said, her lips compressed, as if the words were too terrible to let loose into the world. "Kurt Gerstein is in charge of the delivery of Zyklon B. He delivered large quantities to a number of camps in Poland, including a huge complex of camps at a place called Auschwitz."

"Unbelievable," Philby said, and I couldn't tell if he simply did not credit Diana, or was stunned at the enormity of what she was telling us.

"In 1942, he visited several concentration camps, including Belzec, in Poland. While he was there, he witnessed the gassing of three thousand Jews. This was what he had joined the SS for. To gather evidence of outright extermination. He described what he had seen to the Swedish diplomat Baron von Otter, and the papal nuncio in Berlin, Father Cesare Orsenigo, as well as to the bishop. All promised to send word to London, and each did. When nothing but silence came of that, Bishop von Preysing wrote directly to the pope."

"Diana," Philby said, leaning forward to whisper to her. "Are you sure this chap isn't mad? Surely I would have heard of such a report coming from Berlin. Perhaps he had an attack of conscience and fabricated the worst he could imagine."

"You don't understand," Diana said. "What do you think is happening in these camps? Gerstein witnessed it all, the trains coming in, the few able-bodied separated to be worked to death, all the rest ushered into the gas chambers. They have them marked as showers, to disinfect for typhus. Jewish trustees tell them to fold their clothes and leave them on benches, to remember where they left them. Then they enter the chamber and the doors are locked behind them. The Zyklon B is dropped through vents in the ceiling. In twenty minutes they open the doors and pull out the dead. They pry the gold from their teeth and incinerate the bodies."

"The very Zyklon B that Herr Gerstein so thoughtfully provided?"

"Yes. So that he could witness what was being done. So he could tell the world. But so far, the world hasn't listened." She slammed the table with the flat of her hand and her glass fell, staining the tablecloth with wine before it rolled off the table and shattered.

Philby sat in silence, haunted perhaps by visions of mass killing, or worried that he hadn't been privy to reports smuggled out of Nazi Germany. Finally he stirred enough to chastise Diana about overreacting to Vatican gossip and to tell me to keep quiet about what I'd heard, and then left the table.

"What do you think, Billy?" Diana said, now that we were alone. I knew Diana was counting on me to believe her, to back her up. I squirmed in my seat, trying to find the words she wanted to hear, but I didn't know what to say. It was all so insane, it was hard to come up with a logical thought. Then I remembered Sammy.

"I had a friend in high school, Sammy Vartanian. He was Armenian, and his father used to curse the Turks for killing over a million Armenians in 1915. I'd never heard of it, and I figured maybe Sammy's old man was off his rocker. So I looked it up in the encyclopedia. Sure enough, there is was. The Armenian Genocide. I figure if something like that happened a few decades ago, and I never heard of it, then you could be right. Besides, I believe in you."

"I'd heard talk among Jews we have hidden in Vatican City, but I thought it might be nothing more than rumors. Not the deportations and shootings, all that is well known. It's the sheer scale of it all. Like a giant assembly line of death."

"But you believe this report from Gerstein?"

"Yes. It all checks out. Bishop von Preysing vouches for him, and he's completely reliable. He's been anti-Nazi and quite outspoken about it, unlike most other German bishops. And thank you."

"For what?"

"For believing in me." Diana reached her hand toward mine, and her skin held an electrical charge. I pulled away, looking around to see if anyone had seen this Irish civilian hold hands with a nun. Diana blushed, the red flush stark against the white surrounding her face.

"Let's go," she said, and I followed her up the stairs, aware of the movement in her hips beneath the black cloth. My heart was beating fast, and I wondered if I should feel guilty about desiring her so soon after discussing the fate of millions. Then I wondered if I was going to hell for lusting after a nun, even a phony one. That made my heart beat even faster, but I didn't have time to decide which to worry about, since we were in front of Diana's door. Guilt and hell were pretty much the same thing in my upbringing, and I knew I could never explain this situation to a priest and ask for absolution.

"Listen," I said, as she turned the key in the lock. "I'll understand if you want to be alone, you know, after your long trip and all."

Diana eyed me, then the hallway. It was empty. The only sounds were those drifting up from the restaurant two floors below. She pressed her body against mine, her face warm, her eyes half closed, her lips moist as we kissed. Our arms encircled each other, and I tasted the sweetness of her mouth and the saltiness of the tears that streaked her cheek. I reached for the unlocked door, pushed it open, and we entered like two dancers in tune with the music of longing. I kicked it shut as Diana pulled the white coif from her head, letting her long hair loose. She carefully removed the cross she wore around her neck and the rosary beads from her woolen belt, placing them on a small table by the gable window. Then she removed her scapular—the black apron draped over her shoulders—and covered them with it.

"I've missed you," she said, kicking off her shoes and wiping a tear away.

"Is that why you're crying?" I asked, taking her in my arms, feeling warm flesh beneath the nun's habit and trying not to think about all the real nuns I'd known. This was not the time for visions of Sister Mary Margaret.

"I don't know. It's everything. The war, the innocent deaths, all the lives ripped apart. It's too much to bear. I don't want to think about it anymore, at least not now."

We struggled out of our clothes, not wanting to separate for a second, eager to release our bodies from the confines of belts and buttons. I laughed when Diana pulled off her tunic, half expecting all the saints in Switzerland to barge through the door.

"What's the matter, haven't you ever seen a nun undress before?"

I laughed some more and Diana giggled as the pile of clothes by the side of the bed grew, layers of her undergarments mixing with my civvies, until we were under the duvet, basking in the warmth of our flesh on a cold winter night, safe from the murderous conflict that threatened from all points of the compass. The world had shrunk down to the two of us in this room. The war had burned away all the petty arguments, all the ill will that we'd let come between us. There were no questions about tomorrow or the next day, no expectations of the future, no wondering what would become of us. Fear, blood, and death had washed us clean, leaving only what survived, or what had burrowed deep into our hearts, as far from the danger as it could go and still be remembered. We caressed each other, coaxing those memories out, letting them breathe the air of joy and freedom before we put them away again.

We laughed, but I can't say we were happy. We made love, but it was desperate and burning hot, as if we were keeping evil at bay by the very act. We cried, but our woes were so small that I was ashamed of the tears. We held each other, and knew it would not last.

We slept, but could not rest.

CHAPTER THREE

THE NEXT MORNING, he was waiting for us. A young guy, his face smooth and pink. He sat at our alcove table, pulling at his shirtsleeves to best display his gold cuff links. I squeezed Diana's hand and stopped before he saw us. I watched as he sipped his coffee, resting his hands just so, allowing the gold to sparkle. A leather briefcase was on the chair next to him. His hair was brown and wavy, his expression bored, his fingers manicured. He'd been out in the sun, most likely on a ski slope. He had the healthy, athletic look of a college boy, and the well-tailored look that came from a rich daddy. His eyes weren't on the other guests or the entrance. He didn't even notice us a dozen steps away. He sipped his coffee and looked at his copy of the *Neue Zürcher Zeitung*, the major Swiss daily newspaper. Probably checking his stocks.

"Let's go back," I whispered, pulling Diana by the arm. She wore a silk blouse and tweed skirt from the clothes that had been provided for her and the sensation was appealing.

"Why? Because that boy is at our table?" She stood closer to me as we edged against the wall. Feeling the smooth silk against her skin, I hated the thought of leaving her so soon.

"He's from the embassy. It can only be trouble."

"How can you be sure?"

"He's American. He's not an agent, unless he's in disguise as a Harvard twit. He's too young to have any clout, which makes him a messenger boy. And messages from embassies are like telegrams—always bad news."

"All right," Diana said in a low voice, her face close to mine, close enough to feel the heat of her breath on my cheek. She backed away and I followed as she took the stairs. Two at a time.

SUNLIGHT STREAMED IN, warming us as we huddled under the white duvet.

"Do you think he's still down there?" Diana asked.

"Yeah. He's probably knocked on my door a couple of times by now. If he's got half a brain he'll start asking questions and figure out I'm in your room."

"Perhaps Kim will shoot him. Or have him shot, more likely." She laughed, and it sounded like wind chimes on a warm spring day. But it was winter, a war winter, and this hidden moment with a bit of sunshine was all we had. It was enough, I decided, and laughed along with her, until we lay exhausted and the sun rose higher in the morning sky, leaving the room in a gloomy chill.

Dressed again, we went down to the restaurant. It was nearly empty, with no trace of the messenger boy. The waiter brought coffee to our table and said the young man had gone off to look for me. He smiled and Diana blushed.

"I hope they don't have microphones in the rooms," Diana said as the waiter left.

"Could they?" I asked, and then saw she was trying to hide a laugh. "Make a nice souvenir," I added, trying to cover up.

"Mr. McCarthy?" It was the embassy kid, looking at a photograph and checking it against my face. It took me a moment to remember that was the name on my Irish passport.

"In the flesh," I said, and Diana gave an abrupt laugh, her hand covering her mouth as she looked away. "Please join us."

"I'm sorry, but I need to speak to you in private."

"Unnecessary, as I'm sure Mr. Gallagher has told you." That was Philby's cover name.

"Very well," he said, taking a seat and waving off the approaching waiter, probably having had his fill of coffee. "Julian Dwyer, Assistant Commercial Officer, American Embassy."

"Sorry we missed you earlier," I said.

"How do you know I was here earlier?"

"Because I saw you and figured you were bad news. So we skipped out."

"My time is quite valuable, Lieutenant Boyle," he said, whispering my name and rank in a hiss.

"No it isn't. There's not much commerce these days between Switzerland and the U.S. And the fact that you couldn't find me and you stand out like a virgin in a whorehouse means you're not a spy operating under diplomatic cover. I bet you just graduated from Harvard or one of those snobby schools and daddy got you a posting so you wouldn't have to associate with the lower classes and dress in khaki."

"Yale," Julian said, sounding offended more by the Harvard remark than anything else.

"I'm not a college football fan, so it makes no difference to me. It boils down to the fact that you're the only guy they could do without up in Bern and not insult whoever sent the message to be passed on to me. You dress well, I'll give you that."

"Billy," Diana said, placing her hand on my arm. I was getting steamed, and poor Julian was the perfect target. It wasn't his fault, but he was right in front of me, and I never liked his type much anyway.

"It was my grandfather, not my father," Julian said. "Six-term congressman. And I have a punctured eardrum, not to mention flat feet, so khaki was never in the cards. But I would look good in it."

"Okay, Julian, sorry. But I'm not wrong, am I? About bad news?"

"I guess you would call it bad news," he said, eyeing both of us. "Your orders, Lieutenant Boyle, are to proceed immediately to Naples, Italy. I've booked you on a flight from Zurich to Lisbon tonight. From there you'll travel to Gibraltar and then via military transport to Naples."

"Tonight?"

"Yes. The orders came from London. From a Colonel Samuel Harding."

"Thanks, Sam," Diana said, with an edge of bitterness.

"I still have three days of leave," I said, knowing it was futile.

"Sorry. I have the orders right here, along with a file," Julian said, popping open his briefcase.

"I believe you," I said. "It's got to be important if Colonel Harding sent it. My leave was approved by General Eisenhower, so if he's overruling that, he's got good reason. Have you read the file?"

"The file is for you," Julian said.

"Right. It's not sealed, so stop making believe you haven't looked at it. This has got to be the most interesting thing that's happened since you got here."

"Not quite as interesting as some of the Swiss girls I've met skiing at Gstaad, but you've got me dead to rights. You're sure?" He nodded to Diana.

"Spill, Julian. She's got higher clearance than either of us."

"There have been two murders in Naples," Julian said. I could see the eagerness in his eyes. He was excited, and I was sure this bit of cloak-and-dagger was the high point of his life.

"Only two? Must've been a slow night."

"Both U.S. Army officers. First guy was found in the 3rd Division bivouac area at Caserta, outside Naples. Lieutenant Norman Landry. Found behind a supply tent, his neck snapped. The other officer was Captain Max Galante, M.D., of Fifth Army medical staff. He was found the same night, outside headquarters at Caserta, strangled."

The waiter came to our table with a tray of warm rolls, butter and jams. Conversation ceased as he laid everything out. As soon as he was gone, I buttered a roll, not knowing when or where my next meal might be.

"Forgive me for asking, Julian," Diana said, flashing him a warm smile, "but terrible as these murders are, they don't seem to warrant your presence here. Why the orders from London? Fifth Army must have plenty of military police to sort this out."

"Like the lieutenant said, I'm only the messenger. But there is something here that may explain it. Pictures of the bodies." He pulled two black and white photos from the file, face down. "They're a bit gruesome."

"Gruesome is par for the course," Diana said. "Let's see them."

They weren't pretty. Lieutenant Landry was on his back, head lolled to one side. His field jacket was open, and his .45 automatic was still in his holster. His hair was curly, and a splash of freckles decorated his cheeks. He looked young—too young to be leading men into combat. A canvas tent was visible in the background. A piece of paper appeared stuck in his shirt pocket. As if in answer to my unspoken question, Julian laid the other photo on top. It was a close up.

"The ten of hearts," I said.

"A brand new card," Julian said. "No other playing cards were found on him."

"You read this pretty carefully," I said.

"There wasn't much else to do, waiting for you."

"Okay, okay. What about the other guy?"

"Meet Captain Max Galante," Julian said. Captain Galante was older, late thirties maybe. Stocky, dark haired. His throat was heavily bruised, his eyes bulging, the terror of death still on his face. Landry probably died instantly. This guy didn't. What looked like a playing card stuck out from his shirt pocket as well.

"Don't tell me," I said.

"The jack of hearts?" Diana asked.

"Yes," Julian said, laying down the close up as if he were dealing a poker hand.

"When did this happen?" I asked.

"The bodies were found yesterday morning. As soon as Fifth Army put two and two together, they sounded the alarm. German agents, Mafia, Italian Fascists, they're seeing them all behind every rock."

"There must be a lot of nervous majors, not to mention colonels and generals," I said.

"From the cables in the file, I think it's a general who sounded the alarm. But he probably got a major to do the work. Count in the British, and there are probably a thousand majors within five miles of Caserta Palace. And they're all worried it will be them next."

"No one else killed?"

"Not since we got that report last night in the diplomatic pouch from London."

I leafed through the paperwork. Orders to proceed without delay to Naples and report to Major John Kearns at Fifth Army HQ. Maybe he didn't like the odds. Maybe he knew Harding and called in a favor. There were more photos of Galante. I guessed that once the MPs realized there was a link between the two murders, they paid more attention to the crime scene. Close-ups of the neck, front and back.

"Interesting," I said.

"What?" Julian and Diana said at the same time, leaning in to study the photo.

"The killer used a lot of force, and the good doctor fought back. These bruises and abrasions go up and down the neck, as if Galante struggled to get away. You can see the thumbprints where the killer squeezed. There's also a bruise here at the base of the neck, from the excessive pressure."

"So the killer was angry? Probably not uncommon," Julian said.

"Look at Landry," I said, placing that photo next to Galante's. "No signs of a struggle. His pistol still in his holster. This killing was quick, professional. No sign of anger."

"Two murderers?" Diana said.

"Maybe. Or two entirely different reasons. Can't really tell much, but it's something to look into. The cards could mean something, or be nothing at all."

One of the photographs was a long shot, taken several steps back from the body. Galante lay against smooth gray boulders bordering a pool of water. It looked familiar, the waterfall and the sculpture of a pack of dogs bringing down some guy with antlers on his head. Not the kind of thing you forget.

"I've been here," I said. "These are the gardens in back of Caserta Palace. The palace is at the top of a hill, and the gardens, fountains, and waterfalls go on forever, down the hill at the rear."

"The Fountain of Diana must be beautiful," Julian said, looking at the photo.

"Huh?"

"Oh, I see," Diana said. "Diana and Actaeon, right?"

"Exactly," Julian said.

"Is that somewhere in the file?" I asked.

"No, it's nothing about the murder. Just a bit of Greek mythology, the kind of thing you pick up at Yale. Or one of the fine English schools, I'm sure," he added, smiling at Diana.

"Okay Yalie, explain it to the one of us who didn't pay attention in public school."

"Diana was the virgin goddess of the wild places. One day she and her maidens were bathing in a forest stream. Naked. Actaeon was out hunting with his pals. They'd bagged their share of stag, and he was heading back with his pack of hunting dogs when he saw Diana. He was stunned by her beauty, but she could not allow a mere mortal to tell the world what he had seen. So she turned him into a stag, and his own dogs hunted him down and tore him apart."

I studied the picture. Galante, dead in front of the sculpture that told a story of death from thousands of years ago. What had he seen in his last moments? Not the beauty of a goddess.

"When do we have to leave?"

"We should go now."

"Give us half an hour."

Diana and I walked along the road, arms wrapped around each other. I didn't have to apologize. It could have been Kim Philby sending her off suddenly as easily as Julian Dwyer coming for me. We'd both donned our coats without speaking to spend our last few minutes outside, under blue skies. It was quiet away from the hotel, a farm on each side of the road, cowbells sounding from a hillside pasture.

"I thought you might want to tell Julian about Kurt Gerstein and the camps," I said.

"I'd rather be with you. He's not a bad sort, really, but it would be beyond his grasp."

"What do you think Kim will do?"

"About Gerstein's information? I don't know. He seemed at a loss, which is unusual. I want him to send me back, but I think he's upset about me coming out for this. He'd rather have hard information about troop movements, that sort of thing."

"Be careful," I said. "Of him and the Germans."

"Good advice. It's not bad, you know, inside the Vatican. We're safe there."

"Okay," I said, knowing that anything else would only get Diana angry and me worried.

"You be careful, too. This seems like an odd business, with the playing cards. What do you suppose the killer is up to?"

"Sowing confusion? Or maybe it all makes sense to him. Or them. I'll be careful, I promise."

"Okay," she said, echoing my own words, and probably my thoughts, as we leaned into each other. "I'll only ask one thing."

"What's that?"

She stopped and turned to face me. "That whatever happens, to either of us, you keep a place in your heart for me. Always. Don't ever forget I love you."

I couldn't speak. I held her close. I stared into the blue sky, drinking in the distant and near beauty, filling that space in my heart that was already feeling the claim of the war on it, the draw of the dead waiting for me, their stories, their desires, their final moments. I felt Diana's cheek, her skin cold in the mountain air, like the sheen of ice on a pond in December.

CHAPTER FOUR

I SHED MY civilian clothes in Gibraltar, and transformed from an Irish businessman into a piece of military cargo. I was tossed in the back of a B-24 Liberator making an early morning run to Naples, carrying mail, a couple of war correspondents, a congressman, and me. A supply sergeant had met me at the airfield with a duffle bag full of government-issue duds and a .45 automatic. The congressman had come on board with a fifth of bourbon, and shared it with the reporters in hopes they'd mention his name. I didn't work for anyone who bought ink by the gallon, and he wasn't from Massachusetts, so the bottle didn't come my way often. I settled in on some mail sacks. B-24s weren't built for passengers, and there was damn little room in the narrow fuselage.

As they boozed it up, I read through the file Julian had given me. The initial report about Lieutenant Norman Landry was brief, the kind of cop shorthand I was used to. Perfunctory, describing the physical condition of the body, but little else. The kind of report a patrolman might write up after finding a drunk knifed in a doorway off Scollay Square at three in the morning. Dutiful scribbling doomed to the unsolved file, unless the victim turned out to be a Cambridge boy or a Beacon Hill gent.

Landry's death was attributed to the usual "person or persons unknown" with no speculation as to why someone had snapped his neck. A doctor from the 32nd Station Hospital had listed cervical fracture as the cause of death. I could tell as much from the angle at which Landry's head canted on the ground. He had been killed in a bivouac area near San Felice, a small village about five miles from headquarters. His regiment was resting and refitting there after being pulled out of the fighting along the Volturno Line, where he was one of thousands of GIs. A report from the MP noted that Landry had been popular with his men, a platoon he'd led at Salerno and on the road to Cassino before they were pulled off the line for rest outside of Naples. The fact that he'd survived, and that his men liked him, told me two things: he was a good soldier, and he led from the front. Lots of platoon leaders get killed quickly. Others who survive do it by staying behind their men. If Landry's men, especially the veterans, liked him, then he wasn't one of those.

The last person to see him alive, other than his killer, was Lieutenant Kenneth Dare, the chaplain attached to Landry's battalion. I wondered if it had been a social call or if something more serious was bothering Landry.

The photographs showed the ten of hearts clearly. In the close-up, it was easy to see the card was brand new, clean and crisp. It must have come out of a new deck and gone straight into Landry's pocket. Maybe the ten of hearts was his good-luck charm, who knew?

The report on Captain Max Galante was more detailed, not surprisingly. Even before the MPs got the playing-card connection, this murder had been a priority. Captain Galante was a medical doctor assigned to the Fifth Army headquarters staff at Caserta. He got noticed, if not for his rank, for his proximity to the high and mighty. General Mark Clark, commander of Fifth Army, and his boss, British General Harold Alexander, of Fifteenth Army Group, both called Caserta Palace home, along with a passel of rear-area brass.

The MP's report included the duty roster from the 32nd Station Hospital, where Galante worked. He'd gone off duty at 1800 hours, and planned to meet two other doctors for dinner two hours later, at eight o'clock civilian time. The other doctors rented an apartment in town and paid their rent in rations, which their landlady cooked for them. Galante never showed.

The hospital and the apartment were on the south side of the palace. A hand-drawn map was paper-clipped to two photographs; the first showed the hospital and the tree-lined boulevard with the palace at the end. The second photo, according to the map, was taken from the opposite side of the palace. Gardens and walkways sloped gently downward, over a mile of it all, leading to the end where the statues of Actaeon and Diana stood against the backdrop of a water-fall. That gave me the basic layout, but no answers about why Galante ended up at the far end of the gardens.

I went through the photographs again studying the position of the body. While it appeared that Landry had been left where he fell, Galante's body looked like it had been laid out, tucked alongside the rocks that bordered the pond fed by the waterfall. Had he even been killed there? From what I could tell from the photos, there were no scuff marks in the grass, no telltale gouges of earth where a heel dug in during a struggle. But I had no way of knowing for sure; whoever took the shots hadn't bothered to show the surrounding area, away from the body and the pond. Within the pond were the two sculptures, one of Diana and her maidens, all aflutter at Actaeon seeing her naked, and opposite was poor Actaeon with the head of a stag, being killed by his own hounds. Death and beauty sharing the same tranquil spot. Was Galante killed by one of his own? Had this spot been chosen for some reason other than its seclusion?

The jack of hearts stuck out of Galante's pocket, just as the ten was positioned in Landry's. Side-by-side shots of the two cards, front and back, showed that they were from the same pack—or at least the same kind of pack—and apparently unused. Probably no finger-prints. Maybe Galante and Landry had been in a card game together and kept souvenirs. Maybe they'd won big, and a killer, or killers, had decided to grab their cash.

All I knew for sure was that I had two stiffs waiting for me at Caserta, not to mention all the self-important brass throwing their weight around, demanding protection. The two cards were a flimsy connection, and the different ways the bodies had been left to be found didn't seem like the work of the same killer. I gave up thinking about it, and wished I had a drink.

The plane lurched as we hit some turbulence, and the file containing the photographs fell to the deck. A close-up of Galante's head and neck sailed farthest, ending up on the congressman's toes.

"What the hell is this?"

"A guy who didn't share his booze," I said, grabbing it from him before the reporters got too interested. The aircraft shifted sideways in heavy winds as the pilot descended.

"It's all gone," he said, slurring it into one barely understandable word. The newspapermen moved away from him as he swayed in his seat, his face gone pale. I grabbed the files and moved as far away as I could just as the bomber hit another pocket of turbulence and the congressman vomited his share of the bottle into a bucket.

A few hours ago, I'd been looking forward to a day with Diana, strolling down a peaceful country road, and hoping for at least one more night together. Now, here I was, the stink of bile and whiskey in the air, hoping this crate would land in one piece so I could search for a card-carrying killer. The air had grown colder, and I shivered as one of the reporters made his way over to me, balancing on the narrow gangplank.

"Phil Einsmann," he said as he sat. "International News Service."

"Lieutenant Billy Boyle." We shook hands. "You're not going to be sick, are you, Phil?"

"No worries. I've flown worse than this. Combat mission over Germany a few months back, and I wish I'd had a bottle for that one."

"I didn't know correspondents went on bombing raids," I said.

"They don't, anymore. A few months ago, the Eighth Air Force decided to train a handful of reporters and send them on a few missions, to get the story out for the folks back home. We've been in ground combat, so they figured why not? Be good press for the flyboys. So they train about a dozen of us. How to adjust to high altitudes, parachuting, even weapons."

"You actually volunteered?" I asked, thinking that air travel was bad enough without flak and tracer rounds shredding the aircraft.

"Yeah, crazy, huh? Some joker starting calling us the Writing 69th, and it stuck. They chose a few of us for the first mission. Me, Walter Cronkite from United Press, this kid Andy Rooney from *Stars and Stripes*, Bob Post from the *New York Times*."

"I think I remember hearing about Post," I said.

"Yeah," Einsmann said. "The one thing they didn't think through was the bad press if one of us got it. Post was killed over Germany. His B-17 blew up midair. Our first mission was our last. I'll tell you, if Bob hadn't been killed, I don't know if I could've gone back up there. I've never been so scared."

"Get a good story?"

"Best thing I ever wrote. Making it back in one piece focuses the mind wonderfully."

"You and your pal headed to Naples?"

"I'm going back, believe or not. I was supposed to go to London. I left last night, and when I got to Gibraltar there was a cable from the home office. Return to Naples. Caserta, actually. I was billeted near Fifth Army headquarters. Something must be brewing."

"News to me," I said, and we both laughed at the unintended joke.

"Does that photograph have anything to do with why you're headed to Naples, Lieutenant Boyle?"

"Call me Billy, everyone does. And I'm going to Caserta, too. Maybe I can give you a lift. You and your pal."

"He's the competition, Reuters, and he's on his own. You're pretty good at not answering a question."

"Used to be a cop, so it's second nature to ignore reporters."

"Hmm. An ex-cop, first lieutenant, traveling way above his pay grade, with pictures of what looks like a strangled officer. You know they bumped a colonel to make room for the congressman?"

"How come they didn't throw you off instead?"

"Billy, I've found that the promise of a mention in a news story works wonders with all sorts of people."

"Including the noncom in charge of the flight manifest," I guessed.

"Sergeant Randolph Campbell, of Casper, Wyoming, soon to be

mentioned in a little piece about Americans stationed at Gibraltar."

"Based on your extensive research there."

"Yep. Two hours on the ground. Talked to Randolph and a bunch of other guys. Dateline Gibraltar: the unsung heroes who keep men and material moving in the Mediterranean Theater. Sounds good, doesn't it?"

"Yeah, and I'm sure Randolph's mom will think so, too."

"See, you can answer a question! So fill me in on the dead guy."

"I can't, Phil, sorry."

"Listen, Billy. You're headed to Caserta, so that's obviously where the killing took place. I've been there more than a month, I know the place inside out. Odds are I'll get the dope on this guy before I change my socks. And I really need a clean pair."

"Okay," I said, deciding he had a point. It had been a while since I'd been to Caserta, and Galante's death was probably the main topic of discussion at the palace anyway. It might be interesting to hear what Einsmann had to say about it. Plus, there was no reason to mention Landry. "The name is Captain Max Galante, M.D. He was strangled two days ago—no, three days ago—his body was found two mornings ago."

"Where was he killed?"

"Not sure, but his body was found next to that pool with the statue of Diana and the guy who got eaten by his dogs. You know it?"

"Actaeon. That's a ritzy neighborhood," Einsmann said.

"How so?"

"Engineers just finished building bungalows for generals, pretty close to that fountain. Tennis court and dance hall too. Seems like the palace is too run-down and drafty for the big brass, so they ordered up a little complex for themselves. The CO of the engineer unit wrote up an official complaint, saying his men came over here to win a war, not build vacation homes for generals."

"You gotta love an idealist. How close to the fountain?"

"A stone's throw if you have a good arm, but there's trees and shrubs bordering the place."

"You didn't hear anything about this? You were still there when the body was discovered." It was odd that a newsman wouldn't be all over a juicy story like this, even if the censors would probably keep it under wraps.

"I went down to Naples for a couple of days there before flying out. Painted the town red with a couple of guys from the BBC. You said Galante was a doctor?"

"Yeah, he worked out of the hospital near the palace."

"Must be the 32nd Station Hospital. I've interviewed lots of boys there. Nurses, too," he said with a raise of the eyebrows.

"I bet. Ever run into Captain Galante?"

"Name doesn't ring a bell, but I paid more attention to the female staff. CID, that's the new Criminal Investigation Division, right? Are you CID?"

"No."

"Who do you work for, then?"

"Listen, this has to be all off the record, okay?"

"Sure, Billy. If there is any news in this, I might follow up with you, but that's got nothing to do with this conversation. Strictly background."

"Okay. I work for General Eisenhower. Actually, I work for Colonel Sam Harding, who works for the general. He sent me down here to investigate."

"Well, well. My boss turns me around and sends me back to Italy, and your boss sends you down here to check on a dead doctor. There's more to this story, Billy. I mean, it's terrible that Captain Galante was killed, but people are killed every day in this war."

"Where is your boss?"

"London."

"I can't see how he found out, or even if he did, why he'd send you back. This is small potatoes, Phil."

"Maybe," he said, eyeing me. "Are you Ike's personal cop?"

"Sort of," I said. "It's a long story." I told him the whole thing, about how the Boyles viewed this war as another alliance with the British, who were seen as the real enemy in my strongly Irish Republican household. About Uncle Frank, the oldest of the Boyle brothers, who was killed in the Great War, and how Dad and Uncle Dan didn't want to lose another Boyle in the second round. A few political strings were pulled, and after Officer Candidate School I was sent down to Washington D.C., where I was supposed to sit out the war in safety, on the staff of an obscure general laboring in the War Plans Department.

It had been a great idea. Mom was related to the general's wife, and we'd met him a few times at family events. So it was Uncle Ike whom I went to work for, and he jumped at the chance to have an experienced investigator on his team when he was chosen to head U.S. Army forces in Europe, back in 1942. It had been quite a surprise to us all.

I left out the part about my not being all that experienced. I'd been promoted to detective, sure, but with the Boyles, the Boston Police Department was sort of a family business. Especially when Uncle Dan sat on the promotions board and Dad was a lead homicide detective.

Of course I made detective; I'd just needed a little more time to actually learn the ins and outs of detecting. A little more on-the-job training with Dad would have gone a long way. But Emperor Hirohito had other ideas, and I ended up on Uncle Ike's staff, trying not to make a fool of myself. Because if I did, I knew I'd end up as one of those lieutenants leading an infantry platoon with a life expectancy of weeks, if not days.

Some things are better left unsaid.

PART TWO

Caserta, Italy

CHAPTER FIVE

WE'D LANDED AT Marcinese airport, between Naples and Caserta, where a jeep and driver were waiting. I'd let Einsmann tag along, leaving the drunken congressman and the Reuters reporter on the tarmac looking lonely and confused. We dropped Einsmann off at a cluster of tents pitched on the south lawn of the palace, and he and I agreed to meet up later at the officer's bar.

The driver parked near the side entrance, had me sign for the jeep, and took off. A light mist began to fall and the palace loomed against the gray sky, large and formidable. I could see the gardens descending on the north side, but the rain obscured the distant fountains. I turned up the collar on my mackinaw and ran inside.

When I'd last been here, the town had just been captured. The palace was a mess, everything of value looted or destroyed. Now it hummed with activity, spruced up as purposeful men and women in the uniforms of half a dozen nations and services scurried along, a few like me pausing to gape at the high gilt ceilings. I worked my way to a desk at the base of the main staircase, where a corporal sat at a desk, directing traffic. I asked him where I could find Major John Kearns, and he pointed to a chart behind him, which contained a layout of the building.

"G-2, third floor, quadrant two," he said, and then went back to his paperwork. The diagram showed all five floors and four sections of the building, each with its own courtyard. I figured out where I was and spotted the rooms allocated to Fifth Army Intelligence. I took the staircase, got lost a couple of times, tripped over communications wire strung across a hallway, watched a rat scamper out of an empty room, and finally found a door with G-2 painted above it. I knocked and entered. The room was cavernous, with a row of deep-set windows at the far side. Maps were mounted on the walls, desks pushed together in the middle, telephone line strung like a clothesline above my head.

There were three noncoms in the office. One staff sergeant and a master sergeant ignored me, leaving it to a corporal to handle stray officers. The corporal looked at me, one eye squinting against the cigarette smoke that drifted from the butt stuck in his mouth. He went back to the photograph he was studying through a magnifying glass, looked up again a few seconds later, and finally spoke when it was apparent I wasn't going away. "Help you, lieutenant?"

"I'm looking for Major John Kearns."

"What's your business, sir?" The corporal leaned back in his chair as he spoke, while the two sergeants stood and moved to opposite sides of the room, one of them resting his hand on the butt of his automatic.

"That's between me and the major, who asked me to come here. Ease up, fellas, I'm not carrying a fifty-card deck."

"You'll have to excuse us, Lieutenant Boyle," said a voice from a narrow hallway at the far end of the room. "The boys are a little overprotective these days. Come on in." I caught a glimpse of a tall, lean figure as he disappeared into the shadows. The noncoms relaxed, but watched me in a way that made me nervous to show them my back.

The hallway was dark, paneled in wood that gave off a musty smell of rot and centuries of dust. It opened into a large room with a fireplace big enough to stand in and windows ten feet high. Marble pillars flanked the windows, and the arched ceiling was painted with scenes of Roman soldiers and pudgy women in white flowing gowns.

"Quite a place, isn't it?" Kearns said, gesturing for me to sit. He had high cheekbones and close-cropped hair with a hint of gray creeping in. He wore a .45 in a shoulder holster and looked like he was on friendly terms with it. He took his place opposite me at a long table strewn with maps and glossy black-and-white photographs, a confusion of shorelines, mountaintops, and gun emplacements. I didn't think the question really needed an answer, so I nodded and waited for him to explain things.

"How's Sam?" he asked.

"Fine, Major. You know him well?"

"Sam Harding and I were in the same class at West Point," he said, holding up a hand to show me the West Point ring. "We were roommates." He went silent, as if that explained everything. Maybe it did.

"How did you come to ask for me to be sent here, sir?"

"Sam and I got together a few times in Naples, when he was still in Italy. He told me about you. Said you weren't half bad at snooping around."

"That's not something I've heard from him very often," I said. Never was more like it.

"No, you wouldn't. But like I said, we go way back. Even though he had a few drinks in him, I knew he meant it. Tell me he was right."

"Snooping is easy. Finding a murderer is another thing, especially when there are thousands of guys within a few miles, all heavily armed and trained to kill."

"I need you to find this guy, Boyle. Find him and stop him."

"What about the military police? CID? I'd think the new Criminal Investigation Division would be all over this one. Solving it would make the guy in charge a hero."

"Make, or break. There's no guarantee CID can close the case. I want someone on the job who's got nothing to lose. Find the guy or not, you go back to London when it's over. Work with CID, but you get this killer before he deals another card."

"How is G-2 involved? Is this an intelligence matter?"

"Everything is, until I understand what's behind it. Right now, I don't know if this is a German agent, a stay-behind Italian Fascist, or someone who wants a promotion the easy way. And I don't like not knowing. CID is not under my jurisdiction, but you are. Understood?"

"Sure, Major, I understand that. What I don't get is what's so damned important that you needed to pull me in. Do you have any reason to believe you're next?"

"We have more majors here than we know what to do with, Boyle. As a matter of fact, I worry more about some trigger-happy major plugging the next poor slob who taps him on the shoulder to ask for a light. But that's my worry. I've got two things I want you to worry about." Kearns leaned forward, folding his arms on the table, his head inclined so that he stared at me with his eyeballs nearly rolled up. I waited ten, fifteen seconds, and then knew it was up to me to ask.

"What two things, sir?"

"One, finding the killer. Two, what I'll do to you if you ever again suggest that I called you here for my personal protection." He nodded toward the hallway. "Corporal Davis has your billeting information and will tell you where CID is. Ask for Sergeant Jim Cole. Now get out."

I did, thinking that he and Harding must have gotten along well at West Point.

The corporal gave me billeting papers and directions to CID. Quadrant one, second floor. As I climbed the stairs, I wondered about Kearns and his attitude. Not that I didn't care about anybody—major, private, or civilian—being murdered. But there were murders everywhere, not to mention deaths in combat, and the mass killings going on in occupied Europe. All over the continent, people were being shot, strangled, gassed, knifed, bludgeoned, and poisoned. Some because of who they were, others because of the uniform they wore, and often because someone they loved—or once had loved—lost his or her temper in a rage of jealousy and possessiveness. Death was everywhere, commonplace. So why was I here? Kearns didn't impress me as the kind of guy who needed a bodyguard flown in, and I knew Harding wouldn't have cooperated if that were what he'd wanted. Maybe he wasn't too worried about dead majors or even dead colonels. Maybe it was the ace of hearts that kept him up at night.

As I navigated the maze of hallways and descended a marble staircase, I counted officers. By the time I found CID, I'd given up counting majors after a dozen. There'd been six lieutenant colonels and four full bird colonels, three brigadier generals, and one major general. All within five minutes. Brigadiers were the lowest-ranked generals, and there were probably plenty within Fifth Army HQ, as well as those with the divisions and brigades. A major general, with two stars, was just below the exalted level of three-star lieutenant general. The only one of those I knew around here was General Mark Clark, Fifth Army commander. And maybe his boss, 15th Army Group commander General Harold Alexander, but I wasn't certain of his exact British rank.

As I entered the Criminal Investigation Division office, I considered the possibility of an operation aimed at assassinating Clark or Alexander. It would have answered the question of why Kearns and G-2 were involved, but it didn't make much sense otherwise. If it were a German plot, why would they announce their intention by starting with junior officers? It didn't add up, and I decided to wait until I learned what Sergeant Cole had dug up before I tried out any theories.

CID had a string of rooms, connected by a passageway running along the outer wall. Each was decorated in a different color, the paint peeling and curling off the walls. The first room housed military police, and one of the snowdrops—so named for their white helmets—sent me two rooms to the right. I shivered as I walked past the tall windows, feeling the damp cold seeping through. Rain splattered against the glass, which rattled as the wind gathered up and blasted the casements.

The next room was long and narrow, with two rows of desks facing each other. On the walls, mirrors in fancy frames were set into panels, reflecting what light there was into each other, except for the gaps where the glass was missing or shattered. With his back to a busted mirror, a sergeant stood over a desk covered in playing cards.

He wore his field jacket buttoned up, probably against the breeze that seemed to run through the high-ceilinged room. He scratched absently at his chin, appearing to be lost in thought.

"Sergeant Cole?"

"Jesus!" His eyes widened in surprise as he took a step back, then recovered. "Sorry, Lieutenant, I guess I didn't notice you walk up."

"You are Sergeant Cole, CID?"

"Yes sir, I am. You must be Lieutenant Boyle? Major Kearns said to expect you." Cole sounded worried, as if I were here to fire him. His eyes darted about the room.

"That's me. What have you got here, Sergeant?" I pointed to the cards on the desk, but kept my eyes on Cole. He was jumpy, and I had to wonder if he was hiding something, or hiding from someone.

"Do you know the details of the case, Lieutenant? How the bodies were found, with playing cards?"

"Ten and jack of hearts," I said. "I read the files."

"These are the originals," he said, opening a drawer and taking out a small manila envelope. "No fingerprints, and they seem brand new."

I slid the cards out onto my palm and studied them, lifting each by the edge. They were crisp and clean all right. No soft edges from repeated shuffles, no bend in them at all. The backs were red, the usual swirling vines pattern that you never paid much attention to. I put them back and handed the envelope to Cole.

"Trying to match them?"

"Yes sir. As you can see, it's a common deck. I was able to buy the same kind, with blue or red backs, at the post exchange in Naples, and get them for free at the Red Cross center or at the hospital."

"The same hospital where Captain Galante was stationed?"

"Yes, the 32nd Station Hospital. Why do you ask?"

"How long have you been in CID, Sergeant?" I asked as I took a seat. He lit a cigarette and sat, taking his time with the answer, fiddling with his lighter.

"I'm fairly new. About a month."

"Were you an MP before?"

"No."

"Cop before the war?"

"No."

"Fair to say then that you've got a lot to learn. Let's start with this: Asking why I want to know something is a waste of time. An investigator needs to know everything about a case, everything that has the slightest connection. You never know when something is going to fit in later on. So explore every angle. Don't ask why, because I don't know why. By the time we know that, the investigation will almost be over. Make sense?"

"Yes sir, it does."

"You have any problem working with me on this, Sergeant Cole?"

"No sir."

"How about your commanding officer?"

"Captain Bartlett, sir. He's in Naples, working on a black market case. He said to cooperate with you." Cole looked at the doorway, as if he expected Bartlett to return and check on him.

"Okay, good." It sounded like Bartlett was not eager to dive into this one. He was giving me a rookie and leaving it in my hands. If I failed, it was all on me. If not, as soon as I was gone he'd claim the credit. Cole seemed oblivious. "What else do you have?"

"Not much, sir. Landry was well liked by his men. No trouble from that quarter. He took good care of them, if you know what I mean."

"Unlike some other officers?"

"I don't mean any offense, sir."

"Don't worry, Cole, I'm not all that big on officers above lieutenant myself," I said with a smile that was meant to put him at ease.

"Some officers, you know, they look out for themselves first."

"So I've heard. What about sergeants?"

"Harder to get away with it," Cole said. "Everyone sees what a sergeant does. His men, his superior officers. If he screws up, it makes his lieutenant look bad, then his captain, and before too long he's in big trouble."

"Landry's sergeants are a good bunch?"

"Sure. Steady guys, you know?"

"Any of them make Landry look bad? Did he make life miserable for any of them?"

"Lieutenant Landry wasn't like that. He got his guys out of scrapes when they had too much to drink, and in the field he was always up front with them."

"Sounds like a stand-up guy," I said.

"So why would someone want to kill him?"

"Good question, Cole. Any of his men have a theory?"

"No, nothing."

"What about Galante?"

"What about him? He was a doctor, he helped people. Killing him makes no sense."

"Unlike Landry?"

"No, I didn't mean it that way." Cole shook a fresh cigarette out of a pack and lit it from the stub of the other one. His hand shook, the faintest of tremors sending ash onto the playing cards on the desk. I sat back and waited as he crushed the first butt out in an ashtray. A wisp of smoke curled up from it, but Cole didn't notice. He inhaled deeply, and blew smoke toward the ceiling, his politeness a good cover for not looking me in the eye. I didn't speak.

"What I meant was, why would anyone kill a doctor? There are plenty of captains around here. Why pick one who actually helps people?" His voice had a tinge of panic to it, as if the thought of anyone who'd murder a doctor was too much for him to bear.

"Sergeant Cole, what did you do before you were assigned to CID?"

"I was with the Third Division. Squad leader, after Sicily."

"Been with them long?"

"Since Fedala," he said, and brought the cigarette to his lips with his left hand. The right sat on his lap, out of sight. Fedala was the invasion of North Africa, fourteen months ago. That had been a long haul, being shot at by the Vichy French, Italians, and Germans along the way.

"Let me guess," I said. "You got your stripes because you were the only one of the original squad still standing."

"You learn something by staying alive, can't deny that," Cole said, as if he were confessing a mortal sin. "All the other guys—killed, wounded, captured. I lost track of dead lieutenants, and saw four sergeants killed before they promoted me. Replacements kept coming, most getting it pretty quick. Not much I could do about it either. They'd panic, forget everything I told them, run around when they should stay put, stay put when they should advance. They weren't ready."

"Were you? At Fedala, fourteen months back?"

"Hard to remember. That was a lifetime ago." He lit another butt, unable to hide his shakes. He gripped his left arm with his right hand, over the stripes, as if he'd been wounded.

"After Sicily they made you squad leader. Then Salerno."

"Then Salerno. Then the Volturno River crossing. That's where I got hit. Shrapnel in my leg."

"Not a million-dollar wound," I said. Not bad enough for a stateside ticket on a Red Cross ship headed westward.

"Nope." Cole smoked with a determination that was impressive. He didn't talk with smoke flowing out of his mouth like some guys. He savored each inhale and exhale, as if the burning tobacco held the kiss of an angel.

"Anything else I should know?"

"Nope. What are you going to do next?" Cole was a cross between nervous and relieved. Relieved that I was here to tell him what to do, and nervous that he might have to do it. Buying up playing cards seemed to be his limit.

"Find where I'm billeted, dump my stuff, and get some sleep. I've been in the air more hours than I care to count." I wanted to meet Einsmann and see what he'd found out, and there was no reason to take Cole away from his cards and smokes. I handed him my billeting papers and asked him how I could find the place I'd been assigned.

"On the Via Piave?" he said when he looked at the address. "Jesus, that's Captain Galante's apartment!"

CHAPTER SIX

KEARNS HAD APOLOGIZED, saying that the corporal was supposed to have told me. Space was at a premium, and his idea had been that I might as well be given that bunk, where I could talk to the two doctors who shared the apartment. It did have a certain logic, but I wondered what Galante's pals would think of it. Their feelings weren't high on Kearns's list, so I headed out of the palace to meet my new friends and interrogate them.

I swung the jeep out of the parking area and onto the Via Roma, watching for the turn Cole told me would take me to the Via Piave, a side street of relatively intact structures, two- and three-story stone buildings, most closed off by large iron gates or strong wooden double doors leading into a courtyard. Halfway down the street, two homes were destroyed, heaps of blackened rubble still spilled out onto the roadway. The rain was falling harder now, and the smell of charred timbers and ruined lives filled my nostrils. Through the gap where the houses had been I saw a row of B-17s lined up, their giant tail fins shadowed against the darkening sky. Except for when weather like this grounded them, it was going to be a noisy neighborhood.

I found the building, its masonry decorated by a spray of bullet holes. Most centered around one window on the upper story where hinges held the remnants of wooden shingles. A sniper, maybe, drawing fire from every GI advancing up the street, as they edged from door to door, blasting at any sign of movement, not wanting to die from the last shot of a rearguard Nazi. Or a curtain fluttering in the breeze, catching the eye of a dogface who empties his Garand into the window as the rest of his squad joins in, excitement and desperation mingling with sweat and noise until all that remains is the smell of concrete dusk and nervous, jumpy laughter.

I parked the jeep in the courtyard and turned off the engine. Rain splattered on the canvas top, reminding me of distant machine-gun fire. I took a deep breath, telling myself this was way behind the lines, and there would be no snipers lurking in third-story windows. Wet as everything was, I swore I could smell concrete dust in my nostrils. Shaking off the memory, I grabbed my duffle and took the stairs up to the main door. I was about to knock when it opened and a short, stout, gray-haired Italian woman unleashed a torrent of language at me, beckoning me in with one hand and pointing to my feet with the other. I didn't need to understand Italian to get it. I wiped my wet boots on the mat and hung my dripping mackinaw on a peg. She must have decided I passed inspection, and led me down a hallway into a kitchen, allowing me on the tile floor as she pointed to another room beyond. I wanted to linger and savor the smells coming from the pots on the stove, but the old woman had her back to me, busy with whatever was cooking.

"You must be Boyle," said a figure in an armchair, seated before an old coal stove. I was glad of the warmth, and stood close, rubbing my hands. He watched me, folding the newspaper he'd been reading, as if he thought I might be of greater interest. He was a British captain, the Royal Army Medical Corps insignia obvious on his lapels.

"You were expecting me?"

"Yes. We got a note that you'd be taking Max Galante's room. Terrible thing, him getting it like that. Bradshaw's the name," he said, extending his hand. "Harold Bradshaw."

"Doctor Bradshaw?"

"Oh, please. Leave the doctor and military business out of our little home, will you? There's enough of that outside these walls. Hope that doesn't spoil things for you, Boyle. Sit down, why don't you?"

"If I wasn't taking a dead man's bed, I think I'd feel at home here," I said, settling into another chair drawn near the fire. "I hope you don't mind."

"Not at all. Can't say I knew Galante all that well, and this is war, isn't it? Still, one hopes for a quick bullet on the field of battle, if one has to buy it. Not a brutish attack by one of your own."

Bradshaw packed a pipe and fussed with it the way pipe smokers do. He was in his forties, with a bit of a paunch and receding hairline. His uniform was worn and wrinkled, and I guessed this was about as much spit and polish as the army was going to get out of him. I stretched my legs and let the stove warm my boots.

"You're both doctors at the same hospital, and you lived together, but you didn't know him well? How come?"

"What's your concern with this, Boyle?"

"They didn't tell you I was investigating the murders?"

"No," Bradshaw said as he blew out a plume of smoke. He admired the coals for a moment before continuing. "Only your name and that you were to be billeted here. So you're with the American CID?"

"Working with them. I'm curious about your remark, if you don't mind me asking." I figured the best way to interrogate Bradshaw was to keep it casual, pal to pal after a tough day at work.

"Not at all. Galante kept to himself. There were four of us here, all medical men. Two American, two English. We work long hours, not much time for socializing. And at my age, not the same inclination as the younger lads."

"There are two other doctors living here?"

"One, at the moment. Stafford got transferred, then Galante got himself killed. That leaves Wilson. Captain Jonas Wilson. Yank, like you."

"Was he any friendlier with Galante than you were?"

"Well, I wasn't unfriendly. The way you put it makes it sound like I disliked the fellow. No, he was pleasant enough company. He and I often chatted at meals. We all tried to arrange our schedules to be here for dinner. Signora Salvalaggio can work wonders with any kind of ration. Even bully beef."

"The lady in the kitchen?"

"Yes. She lives downstairs. Keeps house for us, cooks and cleans. We all pool our rations and share with her, pay her a bit as well."

"Is Captain Wilson here?"

"Not yet. Should be soon, though. You're welcome to stay and eat with us, but if it's going to be a regular thing you'll have to throw in your share."

"Thanks. Not tonight. I have to meet someone. Is there anything else you can tell me about Captain Galante? Did he have any enemies you know of?"

"He never mentioned anyone. He was transferred to the hospital only a month ago, hardly time to generate a blood feud."

"Where was he before the transfer?" That was something that hadn't been covered in the file I'd been given.

"An infantry division, part of the medical battalion," Bradshaw said. "Can't recall which one."

"You really don't know much about the man, do you?"

"Hardly a thing, Boyle. We didn't work together at the hospital. I specialize in skin conditions, or at least I did in civilian life. Here I deal with trench foot, frostbite, burns, that sort of thing. Galante was a surgeon, but he was also interested in shell shock. Nervous exhaustion. He'd talk a blue streak about it if you let him." There was something disapproving in Bradshaw's voice.

"You're not as interested?"

"I served as a private in the trenches back in '18. Saw enough shell shock to last a lifetime. Didn't want to talk about it." Bradshaw held the pipe stem in his mouth with grim determination and looked away from me, out the window, into the darkness.

"Did Galante talk about anything else? Interests?" I knew the topic of shell shock was closed, but I didn't want Bradshaw to clam up totally.

"He knew Italian history, and spoke some of the language. Chatted with Signora Salvalaggio now and then. About what, I have no idea. I recall that he was intrigued by the Royal Palace. Quite a place in its time, I'm sure, but a drafty flea-ridden ruin now."

"Fleas?" I resisted the urge to scratch.

"Fleas and rats. Never go near the place if I can help it. Ah, here's Wilson."

Bradshaw introduced me to the other doctor, telling him I was with CID. Close enough.

"Are we suspects?" Wilson asked as he took a seat and lit a cigarette. He was younger than Bradshaw, but not by much. Dark hair, thinning. Dark eyes, glancing at Bradshaw, who only grunted.

"Where were you the night he was killed?"

Wilson's eyes widened. Apparently his question had been a joke.

"Here, I think. We had a lot of casualties in from the Liri Valley that day. We all worked late. Bradshaw and I were both back here by eight o'clock or so. Galante never showed, but that was normal for any of us. We often sleep at the hospital if needed. After dinner, I sacked out. We're not really suspects, are we?"

"Listen," I said. "Most investigations are about ruling people out. I'm sure no one thinks of you as suspects, or they wouldn't have me staying here. Were you close with Galante? Friends?"

"Friendly," Wilson said, relaxing into his chair. "Not pals. He hadn't been here long, and like I said, the hours can be long."

"So the 32nd Station Hospital does more than care for calluses on the backsides of HQ types?"

"Fair amount of that," Bradshaw offered. "When you get this many generals in one place, you tend to see a lot of normal ailments, the type of things you'd see in peacetime. Colds, influenza, gout, bad back, the list goes on."

"A lot of them would like their own personal physician too," Wilson said. "But we get a lot of battle casualties brought in from the line. Wounds and illnesses. We've had over a thousand cases of trench foot, not to mention frostbite."

"Worse among you Americans," Bradshaw said. "Your army needs better waterproof boots. The way it rains around here, your chaps end up living in constant mud in the mountains."

"Could Galante have been at the palace to treat a general?" I wanted to get the conversation back to the main topic. Shortage of winter gear was a whole separate crime.

"Maybe," Wilson said. "Hasn't CID checked that already?"

"I'll check tomorrow. I only got in today, so I need to get up to speed."

"From where?" Wilson asked.

"I was on vacation in Switzerland," I said.

"Just what we need, a joker. Come on, I'll show you to your room."

The room was spare. One bureau with a washstand. One narrow bed. One small table and chair. One light hanging from the ceiling. One window. I tossed my duffle on the floor and sat on the bed. The springs creaked. The room smelled faintly of dust and stale air. I went to the window and opened it, despite the weather. I leaned out and lifted my face to the cold rain, hoping it would help me rally against the tiredness that was creeping through my bones. It was fully dark now, the B-17s on the airstrip lost in the gloom. I heard a jeep start up and saw headlights casting their thin glare on the rain-slicked road. Time for me to go too. Drinks at the palace. What a war.

CHAPTER SEVEN

I GRABBED A meal at the officer's mess at the palace. Not the senior officer's mess, which I had first mistakenly blundered into. I knew something was wrong when I saw the white tablecloths set with gold-trimmed porcelain and crystal glassware. GIs wearing white jackets carried trays of broiled steaks and other delicacies to tables graced by elderly colonels and generals who looked more like businessmen at a hotel than soldiers not far from the front. I'd backed up to the doorway, not wanting to draw attention to my silver lieutenant's bars. I watched the diners, staff officers most likely, and wondered what they wrote home about. The atmosphere was muted, soft and swanky, the hefty clink of real silverware on porcelain somehow reassuring.

GI waiters crossed in front of me, taking orders, clearing dishes, pouring wine looted from only the best cellars. I saw one guy trip, a little stumble, losing his balance enough to send his load of plates crashing down. It was loud, the tile floor sending echoes of shattering sounds across the room. Heads rose from beefsteaks, irritated at the interruption. Turning to leave, I noticed another GI huddled in a corner, hidden from the diners by a sideboard that held glasses and dishware. He gripped the sideboard with one hand, pulling himself up, the other hand held over his heart. His face was white, his mouth open as he gulped in shallow breaths of air.

"You okay, buddy?" I asked as I took his elbow.

"Yeah . . . yes, sir, I'm fine. The noise, it surprised me, that's all. I'm fine." He stood, embarrassment flushing his face red. At least it gave him some color. He tossed me a weak smile and left, glancing around guiltily in case anyone else had noticed.

There were no fine tablecloths in the officer's mess. The food was warm and filling, even if I had to serve myself, and I didn't linger. But there was plenty of lingering in the room that served as the officer's club. A bar was set up beneath a towering gold-relief sculpture of an angel holding a scroll, with two doorways twenty feet high on either side. The floor was inlaid marble, with plush carpets set out in the seating areas to keep the noise down, but that did little to drown out the chatter that rose from every corner of the room. It was a lively bunch, officers of all ranks, nationalities, and services, with a liberal sprinkling of WACs, ATS, and other females, some wearing decidedly civilian outfits. Those ladies were surrounded by senior officers, guys who wouldn't be questioned about their choice of female companion.

I saw Einsmann and he nodded to an empty table at the far end of the room. I got a whiskey at the bar and joined him.

"How are things, Billy?"

"Better for some than others," I said, raising my glass in a toast and glancing at the brigadier general with a woman who looked like a movie star on his arm.

"You got that right," he said. "This war is a real racket for some guys."

"I saw the senior officer's mess upstairs. Talk about easy street."

"I ate there a couple of times. Nice thing about being a reporter is that when the brass wants to butter you up, you eat well. You know the chef they got up there worked at the Ritz in New York?"

"He should've brought over his own waiters. Those GIs dressed up in white jackets are lucky they aren't paid in tips."

"Better than white coats," Einsmann said with a sharp laugh.

"Why do you say that?"

"They're all convalescents from the hospital. Bomb-happy, you know what I mean? They got the jitters all the time. Somebody figured it was a good job for them while they waited to go back up the line."

"Interesting choice of occupation," I said.

"How so?"

"Waiting hand and foot on senior brass, watching them devour steaks, knowing they're the guys ordering you into the mountains, to live on K rations in a muddy hole. Must be great for morale."

"I never thought about that. Could be a story in it, Billy."

"Everybody's got a story," I said, not certain where Einsmann might be going with this. Some of those convalescent boys had had it tough, and I didn't want an overeager newshound making it tougher. "Did you find out anything about what I told you?"

"Not much, Billy. Word is Galante was kicked upstairs, sent to the 32nd Station Hospital because he didn't get along with a senior officer on the 3rd Division staff."

"Galante was with the 3rd? That's the same outfit Landry was from."

"Yeah, but he was with the Medical Battalion. Unless Landry had been wounded, chances are he wouldn't run into him. There are probably over twelve thousand guys in the 3rd Division right now, especially with all the replacements coming in."

"Okay, so what was the problem?"

"Shell shock, or nervous exhaustion, whatever they're calling it these days. Galante had his own ideas about treating it, and he clashed with a colonel named Schleck. Seems Schleck doesn't buy the whole concept, and blames any GI's failure of nerve on poor leadership."

"Combat fatigue," I said, recalling what I'd heard back in London. "They're calling it combat fatigue now."

"Yeah, well, there's plenty of it going around, whatever the moniker. The boys in the 3rd Division have been at it since North Africa. I wrote a piece about them a month ago. They hit the beaches at French Morocco, then ten months later in Sicily. Then more landings at Salerno, fighting along the Volturno River and up to Cassino. They finally got pulled out of the line a couple of weeks ago."

"Is that why they're here, to rest and refit?"

"Who knows? Maybe the brass is fattening them up for the kill. Me, I don't know how the infantry does it. It's one thing to fight the Germans in this terrain. It's another thing to live up in those mountains, with the rain, cold and knee-deep mud. But to do both at the same time? No wonder some guys go off their rocker."

There wasn't much to say about that. I tried to imagine what it was like, winter in the high Apennines; Germans dug in behind every ridgeline, trying to kill you while you worked at not freezing to death. Yeah, no wonder. I sipped my whiskey and tried not to think about the guys who were up there right now, dying. There were times to think, and times to drink. If you knew which to do when, you might stay sane. I took another sip, then slammed back the rest of the booze, waiting for the warmth in my belly to spread while visions of cold and wet GIs faded from my mind.

They didn't. As Einsmann and I gabbed, about the war, the women in the room, the brass, all the usual bull, I knew they were out there. I'd been there too, not as high as in those mountains, but out in a foxhole with cold water pooled at the bottom, hot lead flying above, and the cries of the wounded all around. I could see it now, even as I watched Einsmann return with a couple of fresh glasses, and for a moment it felt like there was no time at all, but simply here and there, the bar and the mountains, and I could as easily be in one as the other. I must be tired, I thought, too much travel. We talked, and drank, and the noise of the conversations in the room rose into an incessant buzz as it grew more crowded. I could barely make out what Einsmann was saying and had to lean closer when I heard him mention ASTP.

"What did you say about ASTP?" My kid brother Danny was in the Army Specialized Training Program back home. He'd enlisted as soon as he was eighteen, and the army put him into ASTP after basic training. It was a program for kids with brains, sending them to college for advanced courses while keeping them in uniform. The idea was that they'd graduate as officers, keeping the army supplied with second lieutenants as the war went on. It was tailor-made for Danny; he was a bright kid in some ways, but he was too young to have any common sense about staying alive. A college campus was the safest place for him.

"Working on a story about it," Einsmann said. "The army is pulling most of those kids out of college."

"Why?"

"They're short on infantry replacements. The brass figures it doesn't make much sense to keep those boys in college when they need bodies now. They pulled over a hundred thousand of them out, about two-thirds of the program."

"When did this happen?" I'd had a letter from Danny a month ago and he hadn't mentioned a thing about it.

"Few weeks ago. There's a transport landing in Naples tomorrow with the first batch for Italy. Most are going to the 3rd. I'm going down there to interview some of them. Then I'll follow up in a few days when they've been assigned to their platoons. Ought to be interesting."

"My kid brother is in ASTP, but I guess I would have heard if he'd been called up. I can imagine these veterans giving college boys a cozy welcome, especially since they've been sitting out the past few months on campus." I hoped Danny wasn't among this bunch. They'd have a hard time before they ever got to the front.

"I figure that's what will make it interesting," Einsmann said. "Word is some noncoms think the ASTPers will have a monopoly on promotions when they hand out new stripes. Especially the Southern boys."

"Everything will probably smooth out once they get up on the line," I said. *Yeah, it'll be peachy up there, one big happy family united by butchery and misery.*

I saw Major Kearns making his way through the crowd, with two *Carabinieri* officers in tow. They both wore dark-blue dress uniforms, with the flaming grenade emblem of the Italian national police on their service caps.

"Lieutenant Boyle," Kearns said, after a nod of greeting to Einsmann. "This is *Capitano* Renzo Trevisi, and *Tenente* Luca Amatori. Capitano Trevisi is in charge of the local Carabinieri garrison."

"Billy Boyle," I said, standing to shake hands.

"Pleased to meet you," Trevisi said in heavily accented but precise English. He looked to be about forty, with a thick, dark mustache, a slight paunch, and a friendly smile. "If I can be of any assistance, I am at your service. Major Kearns has told us of your investigations. I do not think there is any civilian involvement in this unfortunate matter, but please ask should you require anything."

"Thank you, Capitano, I will."

Trevisi spoke in Italian to his lieutenant, who had been silent during the exchange in English. I heard Galante and Landry's names mentioned as he gestured to me. "Tenente Amatori will provide whatever you need if I am not available. *Buona sera.*"

"Interesting," Einsmann said as they moved off.

"What?"

"I've never seen Italian officers here before, army or Carabinieri. I wonder what's up?"

"Well, the Italians are on our side now. They have a combat group fighting near Cassino, and most of the Carabinieri are loyal to the new government. Stands to reason they'd show up at HQ sooner or later. Plus there have been two murders."

"Yeah," Einsmann said. "But the killings are an army matter. No way they'd let the locals in on that unless they needed them for something."

"Well, not my problem," I said as I watched Kearns and the two Italians huddled in conversation. Maybe it was somebody else's problem, maybe not. I decided I had enough to worry about without adding Italian cops, and got back to the subject of Galante.

"This Colonel Schleck, who got Galante transferred out. Where do I find him?"

"Personnel section, 3rd Division HQ, over at San Felice."

"I'm headed there tomorrow. I'll see what he knows."

"What can he tell you? I doubt he killed Galante because they disagreed about combat fatigue."

"No, but if he had it in for Galante, he had to know him, right? You can't have a beef with a guy and not get to know him, even if it's only his weaknesses."

"And Galante's weakness might tell you about who killed him?"

"It's all I have right now," I said.

I finished my drink and made my way out of the room, passing a group of colonels and women in low-cut dresses. The colonels were flushed and loud, their lips smacking with drink and lust. The women laughed, a harsh, high laugh that echoed off the marble floor and stayed with me as I stood in the rain, looking toward the invisible mountains to the north, where men shivered, suffered, and bled.

CHAPTER EIGHT

SAN FELICE WAS a fair-sized village, or at least had been before the fighting passed through. Now it was a fair-sized pile of rubble, with the few intact buildings housing the 3rd Division staff. In front of a burned-out church, a water pipe stuck up from the ground, a spray of water gushing into the air. Women and children with buckets were lined up, eager to haul the fresh water home. At the base of the pipe, a gleaming white stone arm lay on the ground, its fingers gracefully pointing to the sky. Debris and masonry cascaded from the buildings into the street, making it hard to tell where the outline of homes and shops had been, but it was obvious this had been the piazza, the center of the village. Now it was crammed with shattered stone, a line of black-clad women, and American military vehicles.

I found G-1, Personnel, on the ground floor of a two-story school that was missing its roof. Colonel Raymond Schleck was seated at a desk near a boarded-up window, a tin bucket catching drips of rainwater from the ceiling. Files were stacked in wooden boxes all around him, and two clerks at the other end of the room pecked at typewriters, making piles of forms in triplicate, some nearly a foot high. They had the grimly bored look of men who knew there was probably an easier way to do this job, but also understood it had to be done the army way.

"Colonel Schleck?"

"See one of my clerks, Lieutenant, I'm busy." Schleck cranked a field telephone, barked a few quick questions into it, listened, and slammed it into its leather case without comment. He crossed off names on a list and consulted a personnel file. Without looking up, he spoke again. "You still here?"

"Yes sir. I need to speak with you about Captain Max Galante. I'm afraid one of your clerks won't do."

"And who the hell are you to tell me what won't do?" Now I had his full attention. I showed him my orders. He gave them back, frowned, then waved in the general direction of a chair.

"You've heard Captain Galante was murdered?"

"Yeah. Tough break. I lost a good platoon leader too. Landry. What can I do for you, Boyle?"

"Tell me about Galante. You two had a disagreement, right?"

"You think I killed him because of that?" He gave a small chuckle and shook a Chesterfield from a crumpled pack. He lit up and tossed the match into the bucket.

"You had him transferred out of the division, so I doubt there'd be a reason to kill him. But what did you think of him?"

"I thought he worked hard, and was sincere in his beliefs."

"Listen, Colonel," I said. "It's nice not to speak ill of the dead, but that doesn't help me find who killed Galante and Landry."

"Okay," Schleck said. "He was a snotty prig who thought he was smarter than everyone else. I mean it when I say he worked hard, but he had a bad attitude."

"About combat fatigue?"

"Listen, Boyle," Schleck said, sitting up straight and pointing his nicotine-stained finger at me. "You start telling these boys that all they have to do to get out of the line is to go on sick call with the shakes, pretty soon you'll have empty foxholes all across these damn mountains. You can be damn sure the Krauts don't believe in combat fatigue."

"You think it isn't real?"

"I don't say there isn't something to it. But Galante and I differed on the cause. In my book, there's only one way to explain why one unit, on the line as long as another, has a completely different rate of combat fatigue cases."

"What's that?"

"Leadership, Boyle. At every level, from generals to second lieutenants. That's what makes the difference. Poor leadership leads to excessive cases of nervous exhaustion, or whatever the shrinks call it. In a unit with good leadership, the cases are fewer. When the men trust their officers, they have confidence, and that keeps them going."

"But it still happens, in every unit."

"Some men are cowards. It's unpleasant, but it's true."

"Was this the reason you had Galante transferred out?"

"It was on my recommendation, yes. We needed to send a message, that there was no easy way out of combat duty. Galante was always trying to ease the burden on the men, with all good intentions, I'm sure. But the fact is, it's a heavy burden they face. It's not fair to them to make believe it's anything but."

"Okay, I get what the beef was about. You described him as snotty. Why? Because of his attitude?" I understood the difference of opinion. But the use of "snotty" spoke to something deeper, a disdain that made me suspicious.

"Holier than thou, by a mile."

"You also said he was a prig. What does that have to do with anything?"

"Nothing. That's just me spouting off. He liked art, Italian history, that sort of thing. He preferred to spend his off-duty hours chatting with the locals and visiting museums. He wasn't much of a poker player or drinker."

"He wasn't the only guy to visit a museum over here. Did he think he was better than you?"

"I didn't say that. He just didn't pass the time like most guys. We do have a few other oddballs who keep to themselves, but they do their job and don't get anyone hurt."

"You make him sound dangerous," I said.

"He was. He got an entire squad killed."

"How?"

"Ask Sergeant Jim Cole. He's one of your CID buddies, isn't he? Now get the hell out. If you need anything else, see my assistant, Major Arnold, next office. He will cooperate as required, but I don't want to see you step foot in my office again."

That was that.

MAJOR MATTHEW ARNOLD wasn't in, and his clerk said he was busy organizing the new replacements. I showed him my orders and told him to inform the major I might have questions for him. The clerk said everyone had questions for Major Arnold, like how many replacements would they get, and were any experienced men coming in. I got the impression I was everyone's lowest priority.

I thought about Cole not saying anything about knowing Galante. That made me suspicious. If Galante did get a squad wiped out, then there would be plenty of guys looking to even the score. Maybe Landry was involved? But why hadn't Schleck told me more, and why hadn't anyone else mentioned it? I hoped the guys in Landry's platoon could explain things. I drove out of the village, toward the 7th Regiment bivouac area, following the signs as they led me along roads that were little more than dirt tracks soaked from recent rains. Heavy trucks plowed the mire in both directions, splattering my jeep with thick, yellowish Italian mud.

I drove until the road turned into a field, churned into a thick ooze of ankle-deep mud by countless wheels and thousands of GI boots. Beyond was a sea of tents, rows of olive drab stretching in every direction. I gunned the jeep before I got stuck, and parked on a patch of high ground in a line with other vehicles. As I got out, my boots sank in the muck, and it began to rain. I turned up the collar of my mackinaw and ran, as best I could, to the rows of tents marked 2nd Battalion, Easy Company.

Within the tent city, planking had been set up between rows, and the going was easier. There were mess tents, medical tents, supply tents, assembly tents, and command tents. The smell of wood smoke hung in the air, as small tent stoves tried to beat back the wet chill.

Around the perimeter deuce-and-a-half trucks backed up to the large supply tents and disgorged crates of food, ammunition, and all the other necessities of life and death. Communication lines were being strung throughout the encampment, wire parties carrying spools of the stuff, unreeling it through their leather-glove-clad hands.

"Third Platoon?" I asked a corporal weighed down with bandoliers of M1 ammo.

"Follow me," he said. After a couple of turns, he nodded to a small two-man tent. Then he left, distributing the bandoliers to neighboring squad tents. I pulled aside the tent flap, wondering if a new lieutenant had been assigned yet to take over Landry's slot. Two-man tents were usually reserved for officers.

"Close the damn flap!" I did, and wiped the rainwater from my eyes. "Lieutenant," a voice added as an afterthought.

Seated on one cot was a staff sergeant, cleaning his Thompson submachine gun and giving me the eye. Across from him a second lieutenant fed pieces of wood into a small stove. Between the two cots and footlockers, cases of supplies, the stove, and the two guys, there wasn't much room.

"Looking for someone, Lieutenant?" the staff sergeant asked.

"Is this 3rd Platoon? Landry's outfit?"

"Landry's dead," he said. "This here is Lieutenant Evans. He has the platoon now."

"Andy Evans," the other fellow said. He had an eager smile, a fresh face, and shiny lieutenant's bars on the collar of his wool shirt. We shook hands, and I introduced myself to both of them.

"Gates," was all the sergeant said. He was no more than a couple years older than Evans, but all the freshness was long gone from his face. He worked intently on reassembling his Thompson, the scent of gun oil rising from his labors.

"Platoon Sergeant?" I asked, pointing at his stripes, three chevrons and a rocker.

"Yeah," Gates said. His eyes narrowed as he glanced at Evans, and back to me with the faintest glimmer of interest. "You assigned to us?"

"No," I said. "I'm here to investigate the murder of Lieutenant Landry."

"I hear he was a good man," Evans said. He'd understood what Gates was getting at and was trying to assert his authority. Problem was, he wouldn't have much pull with a veteran like Gates until he survived a few days in combat without getting anyone killed for no good reason.

"Good or bad, he's dead," Gates said, wiping down the assembled Thompson. "Not much we can do about it."

"Let me guess," I said, taking a seat on Evans's cot, glancing at the red hair sticking out from under his wool cap. "They call you Rusty."

"Yeah. Since I was in short pants. What do you want, Lieutenant?"

"To find out who murdered Landry. You want justice for him, don't you?"

"Andy," Gates said, ignoring my question. "Be a good time to check on the men, see that they got a full load of ammo."

"Good idea," Evans said, as if he'd been about to do just that. He put on his helmet and field jacket and left, looking happy to leave this talk of his predecessor behind.

"Justice," Gates said. "You look like you been around enough to know there's no justice up front."

"The murders didn't happen at the front."

"No, but sooner or later your number's up. At least Landry went out clean and dry. Odds were he wouldn't last much longer anyway. Good platoon leaders seldom do. Lucky guys and cowards have a better chance. Sorry, but I can't get all worked up over it. I've seen too many come and go to care how they get it."

"That's a helluva attitude," I said.

"It's the way it is. If I can help you, I will. But I have my hands full right now with this platoon and a green second louie. They're getting ready for something, and it's going to happen soon. They pulled us off the line a few weeks ago, gave us clean uniforms, hot showers, good food, and plenty of passes. Not to mention replacements. There's something brewing, and it ain't good news, let me tell you."

"Why do you say that?"

"You ever get good news in the army?"

"You have a point. What do you think of Evans?"

"Nervous. Eager to show he's got what it takes. He got transferred in from a supply outfit in Acerra. At least he ain't right off the boat. He'll screw up, then either figure things out or get himself or us killed. The usual."

"Landry figured things out?"

"Yeah. He came to us from battalion staff. He knew some of the guys, didn't have to prove anything. Made sure we had hot chow when he could, never volunteered, kept his head in a fight. Can't ask for much more."

"Except not to get killed in bivouac. Any idea who had it in for him?"

"Not a clue. No one, really. He must have seen something, or ran into someone who had a secret. Someone who knew how to break a neck."

"Who found the body?"

"Don't know. Some private from the transportation company, I heard. It was stashed behind a supply tent."

"Stashed? Why do you say that?"

"I went over there as soon as I heard. Landry was next to the tent, and a set of guy wires ran above his legs. He couldn't have fallen there. So someone stashed his body, out of sight."

"Makes sense. Can you show me?" The photo I'd seen of Landry hadn't shown the lower part of his body, so I'd missed the fact that he'd been placed there. And Cole hadn't mentioned it. Was he a rookie at this, or did he have something to hide?

"Come on," Gates said with a sigh. He donned a poncho, his helmet, and slung his Thompson, barrel down, over his shoulder. We headed out into the rain. The supply tents were at the edge of the area, a double row, back to back. There was just enough space between the guy wires from each tent to walk without tripping over them. The ground was soaked, but it hadn't been ground up into mud yet.

"It was dry when he was found," I said.

"Yeah, we had a clear spell for a while. It's been raining off and on since. You looking for anything special?"

"No, just trying to get a feel for things. I saw one photograph, but it only showed his upper body. You're right, he wasn't killed here. So someone had to carry him from someplace else."

"What difference does that make?"

"Don't know yet. Maybe he didn't want the body found until he got to Galante."

"I heard his body was sort of hidden too. Tucked away by those fancy fountains."

"Rusty, for a guy who doesn't care about this investigation, you seem to know a lot about it."

"Not much else to do around here but clean weapons and listen to scuttlebutt. You seen enough?"

"Yeah," I said, looking down the long row of tents, a back alley of olive-drab canvas. Landry had been killed somewhere close and hidden here. It had to be close. It took some nerve to snap a man's neck and then carry him when you could be seen at any moment. Even in the dark, you could trip over a tent stake, create a racket, and be done for. I didn't have a good feeling about this.

"Let's get out of the rain," Gates said.

CHAPTER NINE

WE SAT IN the mess tent, clutching mugs of hot coffee as rainwater dripped from our clothes. Gates wiped his Thompson down and leaned it against the bench.

"Not everybody here goes around armed," I said.

"Not everybody here has been around since Tunisia, Sicily, and Salerno. I notice you keep your .45 close at hand."

"You never can tell," I said. "Especially in my line of work."

"That's what I tell the men. If you're always loaded for bear, the bear won't win. It's got to become a habit, if you want to stay alive."

"Evans hasn't picked it up yet," I said. He was a couple of tables away, playing cards with three other lieutenants. Not a weapon among them.

"No. He says it's safe here." He shook his head at the futility of explaining things to officers, and sipped his coffee. "He hasn't fired a weapon since he's been in Italy, so you can't blame him. Too much."

"Do you know Sergeant Jim Cole?"

Gates's eyes flickered for a second. "Jimmy Cole? Sure. He's over at CID now, right?"

"Yeah, he's working this case with me. How about Captain Galante? Did you know him when he was with 3rd Division?"

"Knew of him," Gates said. He looked away at nothing in particular.

"What did you think of him?"

"I think he's dead, and I have the living to worry about. Now I have a question for you."

"Okay."

"Do you think I killed them?"

"That's not how it works. If I could—"

"Do you think I killed them?"

I looked at his hard eyes. I looked at his strong arms, and at his weapon close by. He held ready violence like a whip at his side.

"I don't think so. But I've been wrong before."

"Fair enough," Gates said. "You want to talk to the other sergeants?"

"Sure," I said. "But tell me about Cole and Galante first."

"No need for that. Come on." Gates rose, and I followed him out of the mess tent. I knew I wasn't going to get anything more out of him about Cole, but I didn't know why. Rusty Gates was hiding something, but I didn't think it was murder. He was a deadly killer, yes. But everything he did was about surviving. He wanted to live, and he wanted his men to live. Landry had been a good platoon leader, and there was no percentage in seeing him dead. But as I told Gates, I'd been wrong. Dead wrong.

The rain was heavier now, and we dashed along the plank boardwalks to a tent in the Easy Company area. Gates held the flap as we entered, and the warmth from a glowing tent stove was welcome. Crates of supplies were stacked to the rear, and next to the stove a table was set up, with three noncoms lounging around it. Two lanterns hung from the ceiling, shedding light on a stack of cash, empty bottles, cigar butts, and other debris from what looked like a long night of poker.

"Game busted up, boys?" Gates asked.

"Yeah. Flint finally cleaned the padre out. He was the big winner all night, and when he caved, the other guys left. Couple of corporals from Baker Company, they shoulda quit hours ago. Who's this?" A stubby hand gripping a smoldering cigar waved in my direction.

"Lieutenant Boyle. He's looking for whoever killed Landry and Galante. He wants to talk to you guys."

"Call me Billy, fellas. Everyone does. Who made the killing?"

All three of them looked at me, mouths agape. "I mean, who was the big winner?" I pointed to the pile of scrip.

"That'd be me, Billy. Amos Flint."

"Flint has Second Squad," Gates said. "Louie with the stogie there has First Squad, Stump the Third."

I shook hands with Flint. He had a ready grin, but who wouldn't, after raking in all that dough? He had startlingly blue eyes, and was neatly attired in a chocolate-brown wool shirt, usually reserved for officers. He had the satisfied calmness of a winner who'd known he'd win all along.

"Louie Walla, from Walla Walla," the cigar-chomping sergeant said as he extended his callused hand. "Last name is Walla, and I'm from Walla Walla, Washington. How 'bout that?"

"Amazing, Louie," was all I could say. Louie was short, with black curly hair, a raspy voice, and an easy grin wrapped around his cigar.

"Don't mind Louie, he gives everyone that speech," the next sergeant said. "Marty Stumpf. They call me Stump, on account of the Kraut-sounding name." Stump was sandy-haired, with high cheekbones and eyes that didn't seem to miss a thing.

"Yeah, if we called him Stumpf up on the line, one of his cousins might answer," Flint said, and they all laughed at what sounded like a familiar joke. Stump rolled his eyes.

"You guys answer Billy's questions. I'm going to pull Evans away from his bridge party. Weapons inspection in one hour. Have your men ready."

"Aw, Rusty, we been up all night," Louie said.

"Yeah, and look where that got you. One hour," Gates said as he left.

"He's right," Flint said to the others. "We gotta stay on our toes, and show the rookies what's what." The other sergeants groaned but did not argue.

"Anybody have an idea about who might want Landry dead?" I asked, watching their eyes for the downward glance, the rapid flicker, anything that would signal hesitation, the censoring of thought into words.

"Nobody south of the Bernhardt Line," Flint said, referring to the name the Germans gave to their current main line of defense, stretching across the Italian mountains south of Monte Cassino.

"You got that right," Stump said. "Landry was one of the best."

"That's what everybody says," I said. "Funny that he got murdered. What do you think, Louie?"

"I think I'd like to get my hands on whoever done it. Now we got ourselves a ninety-day wonder for a platoon leader, like to get us all killed if he ain't smart enough to let Rusty run things."

"I think Billy is asking what we think about who might have killed him, Louie," Flint said. "Not about his replacement."

"Yeah, sure. Well, no one had a beef with him that I know of. He was real good to us, on the line and off. Kept the MPs off our backs, that sort of thing."

"He a big gambler?"

"No," Stump replied, and the others shook their heads in agreement. "No more than the average Joe. Helps to pass the time. But he didn't owe anyone, I'm pretty sure."

"You think that's why the ten of hearts was left on him?" Flint said. "Like a warning not to welsh?"

"No, you don't kill a guy who owes money, unless it's to make an example."

"Hell, if the Lieutenant needed dough, any of us woulda been glad to cough up what we had," Louie said. "We all looked out for each other. I woulda given the shirt off my back for the guy. Saved my life just a coupla weeks ago. Pulled me outta the way of a Kraut 88. Took the arm off a guy not twenty yards behind us. And Flint, he saved Landry's life more than once, right?"

"Yep," Stump said. "He plugged that Kraut officer we thought was dead. He was about to put a slug into Landry's head. Flint shot him from fifty yards out, square in the back of the head."

"Nice shooting," I said.

Flint shrugged. "Lucky. I was just hoping these guys would hit the dirt. The guy only had a Walther."

"Worked, didn't it?" Stump said. "I dove into a shell hole filled with mud. I would have shot that sonuvabitch just for getting me wet. Landry gave that Walther to Flint, and he sold it to some headquarters weenie for a load of booze when we got sent here." He grinned.

"Yeah, there's no percentage in carrying a Kraut pistol," Louie said. "You get captured, especially by the SS, and they take exception."

"Don't like it much myself," Flint said. "Finding a Kraut carrying around anything from our boys." There were murmurs of agreement, and I knew I was in the presence of hard men, men who knew how to survive, to put away mercy until another day. Kinder men than them were buried in graveyards for hundreds of miles behind us.

"You guys have any trouble with the military police?"

"Naw, nothing that you'd call trouble," Stump said. "We ain't had time to get into any real trouble. A few twelve-hour passes that got us as far as Acerra, a town about an hour south. It ain't much, but it's still in one piece, so it's the best place to go if you can't get to Naples."

"Landry go down there much?"

"A few times, sure," Flint said. "We saw him having dinner with some other officers at a café, that sort of thing. He and I had to go down there the night before he died, as a matter of fact. One of the men in my squad started a fight, broke up a joint pretty bad. We had to square it with the locals."

"What kind of joint?"

"The kind with booze and broads," Louie said, grinning as he clamped the cigar in his mouth. "We didn't want the MPs to declare it off-limits, so we took up a collection, fixed things with the owner."

"Landry knew it would be better all around to keep things quiet," Flint said. "Give the boys a place to blow off steam, and keep a good soldier out of the stockade. All it took was a wad of occupation scrip."

"No hard feelings with the locals?"

"No," said Flint. "And even if there were, no civilian could make it in here, never mind get the drop on Landry." He was right. I'd had a flicker of hope that this could be traced back to a barroom brawl, but it didn't add up. This killer was in uniform, invisible to everyone around him. A strong, experienced killer.

"You all know Landry a while?"

"Yeah," Stump said. "He was with battalion staff when I got transferred in, back in Tunisia. Landry brought Louie with him when he got the platoon just before Sicily. Flint's been around the longest, since Morocco, right?"

"Yep," Flint said. "Not many of us left from back then."

"Any other sergeants in the outfit?" I asked. "Assistant squad leaders?"

"We *was* the assistant squad leaders," Louie said. "We got promoted due to sudden vacancies opening up. Ain't enough noncoms to go around, so no more assistant squad leaders. Just a bunch of green replacements."

"We're supposed to have twelve-man squads," Flint said. "We each have two or three experienced men, but none ready for corporal's stripes yet. Plus about a half-dozen replacements."

"Are you getting any of the ASTP replacements coming in?" I asked.

"Them college boys? Be more trouble than they worth," Louie said, crushing out his cigar.

"Aw, you never know," Stump said. "Keep an open mind, will ya?"

"My kid brother is in ASTP," I said, unexpectedly bristling at Louie's insinuation. "I think he'll do alright if it comes to that."

"No offense, Lieutenant," Louie said. "You know how it is with replacements."

"Yeah, I know. Tell me, did any of you know Captain Galante?"

"He patched me up once," Flint said. "Got a piece of shrapnel in the calf, and he took good care of it. Let me lay around the hospital for a couple of days, with all those pretty nurses. He was a decent guy."

"That's what I heard too," Stump said. Louie agreed.

"Any idea who'd want him dead?"

"No," Stump said, looking at the others, who shook their heads. "He wasn't like a lot of the other officers. Didn't drink a lot, kept to himself. Didn't you tell me, Flint, he had a thing for Italian art?"

"Yeah, right," Flint said, snapping his fingers. "He told me all about the fancy artwork they have in the churches here. I don't remember the names of the artists, but he knew them all. He knew all about Italian royalty too. Me, I didn't even know they had a king over here until he fired Mussolini. King Victor Emmanuel, it was. Galante told me all about them, how the royal family used to have fancy dance balls right here in Caserta, in the palace."

"A real bookworm," Louie said.

"Louie, you got no class," Stump said. "Billy, you got any other questions? We gotta go get our boys ready for inspection. Everybody gets a pass into town once we're done."

"Just one. What about Jim Cole?" There was silence, and three sets of eyes looked everywhere but at me. "What's the big secret?"

"Nothing," Stump said. "Cole's a good guy."

"Yeah, leave him out of this," Flint said. "Let's go."

Louie shrugged, and they all stood.

"Don't you feel bad taking all that dough from the padre?" Stump said.

"I'm going to give it back, most of it anyway. For some worthy cause," Flint announced with a grin. "I just wanted to hang onto it for a while, make believe it was mine."

"Who's the padre?"

"Father Dare," Flint said. "Regimental chaplain."

"Last guy to see Landry alive," Stump said.

"Not counting the guy what killed him," corrected Louie Walla from Walla Walla.

THE RAIN HAD let up, so as the three sergeants went to organize their squads, I walked back to where Landry's body had been found. Smoke mingled with the fog and dressed everything in a dull, damp gray. I stood in the narrow pathway in the rear of the supply tents, an alleyway bordered by stakes and ropes from the tents on either side. I planted my feet where the killer must have stood to drop Landry's body, and saw how he must've had to drag him by the collar to get him under the guy wires and up against the tent.

Where did you come from? I thought as I looked around. How

far did you carry him? Why did you bring him here? I went back to the boardwalk and looked in every direction. More tents, more open space. Was Landry killed in a tent? No, then he could have been left there. I walked in front of the supply tent, and noticed the tire tracks in the mud. Trucks had been bringing in supplies constantly, backing up to the supply tents for easy unloading.

Here, Landry was killed here. In between trucks parked for the night. No, not for the night, just for a while. That's why the killer had to move the body, if he didn't want it found right away.

But why did he need the body not to be found? Why hide both bodies in places that only delayed their discovery? To show someone else? To frighten someone—a major, maybe? Or was it simpler than that? Maybe he had to go get a deck of cards. If that was it, then the cards were an afterthought.

So what if they were? That and a nickel would get me a phone call.

I shivered, mostly from the chill creeping up my boots, but also from the presence of murder. Here, on this meaningless patch of dirt, a man's life ended. The air was different here, choked with mist, as if the specter of violence oozed from the ground. I looked around, feeling I was being watched, trying to pick out a pair of eyes focused on me and this patch of dirt. Nothing but GIs hurrying back and forth, killing time while waiting to be killed.

Maybe Landry would have been dead anyway in a week, maybe two, when they went back to the line. But that made those two stolen weeks all the more precious. Some bastard had taken that from him, and I was going to make sure he paid for his sins.

Before he added to them, I prayed.

CHAPTER TEN

"I WAS WONDERING when you'd pay me a visit," Father Dare said as he invited me into his tent. He had his gear laid out on his cot, and was stuffing his field pack with thick wool socks. A communion kit lay open, the brass chalice gleaming from a fresh polish. Rosary beads lay curled on the wool blanket. "Have a seat, Lieutenant Boyle."

"How'd you know I was here, Father?"

"Word travels fast, especially about the dead," he said, as he sat opposite me in a folding camp chair, surrounded by stacks of hymnals. He sighed, leaned forward, and looked straight into my eyes. "How can I help you, son?"

Father Dare was maybe thirty or so, hardly old enough to call me son, but with the silver cross on his collar and the paraphernalia of the church all around him, I let it slide. He was a tall guy, with dark hair and thick eyebrows that almost met when he furrowed his brow. His eyes were bloodshot, likely from the night of poker and cigar smoke.

"No one else has been much help," I said, unsure of exactly what I hoped to learn here. "It's pretty much the same story everywhere. Lieutenant Landry was a good man, an officer the men could count on. Well liked. Captain Galante didn't get along with Colonel Schleck and got himself kicked upstairs to the hospital at Caserta. He kept to himself, didn't seem to bother anyone other than Schleck. What can you add to that?"

"That about sums it up. Landry was solid. Galante was a good doctor, I saw him in action many times. Are you Catholic, by any chance?"

"Yes, I am."

"I thought you had the look of the altar boy about you. Am I right?"

"Yes, sir. Back in Boston. How can you tell?"

"Oh," he shrugged. "I'm not really sure. Something in the eyes. A great disappointment at the ways of men and God. It comes from youthful adoration dashed on the rocks of death and despair. I see it in you, son. It's clear the war has marked you. Have you been to confession recently?"

"Thanks, I'll pass for now." Not that I thought a chaplain could be a suspect, but until I figured out who was who, I preferred to keep my deepest and darkest to myself. "The war has marked everyone, don't you think?"

"Yes. Some more than others. The sensitive ones, the ones who had ideals, they have it the worst."

"Who does best?" I asked.

"The boys who had nothing, who were used to tough times. Not that sudden death and dismemberment are easy to take, but anyone who's been hardened by life has a thicker skin, if you know what I mean. But sooner or later, it gets to everyone. It's just a matter of time."

"Is that what Captain Galante thought?"

"That every man has his breaking point? Yes, he did. That's what didn't sit well with Colonel Schleck. He didn't like the idea that all the men under his command would break in time. I think it made him feel too responsible. It was easier for him to insist that some men are cowards, and the rest have to be led by example."

"Just as long as I'm not the one to lead them."

"No one likes being responsible for other men's lives. I'd bet you have been, and the experience didn't sit well with you."

"Really, Padre, I'm okay. I don't need to tell it to the chaplain."

"Well, I'm here if you need me. For a while, anyway."

"Pulling out soon?"

"The signs are all there. Plenty of supplies, extra socks, and ammo. Good food, replacements coming in. Not hard to figure. It pays to be ready."

"From what the noncoms tell me, things have been pretty rough for your outfit."

"Yes," Dare said, looking right through me for a fleeting moment, as memories danced just out of his field of vision. "Rough. There seemed to be no end to the minefields, machine guns, and mortars." He kept looking into that middle distance, the place where the mind's eye sees everything it wants to forget. Finally he rubbed his eyes and sighed. He stayed quiet, and I wondered if he were praying.

"Sorry," he said, standing. "We lost a lot of men before we came off the line after Monte Cesima. Took the starch out of my collar." He forced a weak smile. "The men get torn up horribly. I never imagined there were so many ways to be wounded and still live. I work with the litter bearers mostly."

"It's hard to imagine there's someone living in the midst of this carnage and committing murder," I said, trying to bring Father Dare back to the present.

"Evil exists in the world, we know that to be true," he said. "It saddens me, but comes as no surprise. This person must have a tortured soul. Perhaps the exposure to so much violence has released demons that might have stayed buried in peacetime."

"That's generous of you."

"No, not generous—realistic. Being a man of God means that you also have to accept the devil for what he is. Why wouldn't the prince of darkness haunt a battlefield, probing for weaknesses, uncovering what lies beneath our civilized exteriors?"

"I was a cop in civilian life. I found the reasons for murder were more mundane. Love and money usually topped the list."

"Don't you think it takes the devil to turn what once was love into murderous intent?"

"Maybe," I said, not wanting to get into a theological argument. My money was on the devil within us, not the guy with horns and a pitchfork. "Did Landry or Galante have any problems with love or money?"

"There's little time for love of the kind you mean. Lust can be satisfied for chocolate or cigarettes, I understand. I have no idea what Landry may have done while in town, but I know Captain Galante was not the type to pursue lust. He was a not a lighthearted man. He took his responsibilities seriously. Any free time he had he spent studying Italian culture. He loved the language, the history, everything about it."

"So I've heard. The only guy he seemed to antagonize was Colonel Schleck."

"The colonel does his job the best way he knows how. So did Galante; he just didn't care whose feathers he ruffled. Can't say why. No one really knew him well. There was another chaplain, a rabbi, who he got along with, but he was wounded in Sicily and shipped home."

"Galante was Jewish?"

"Yes, he was. Does that matter?"

"I don't know. Maybe some guy said something, you know, 'dirty Yids,' that sort of thing. And Galante took offense." I tried to sound like I neither approved nor disapproved of the term, so I could go along with the good Father whichever way he went.

"Some people aren't too used to Catholics either, but they don't murder them. Landry was Protestant, I believe. I never heard anything about remarks directed against Galante's religion."

"I'm trying to find a way to look at this, Father. So far, there's no reason I can find for anyone to do more than pin a Good Conduct Medal on these guys."

"Yes, I understand. It's a bit like my line of work, isn't it? People seem to be fine on the surface, but it's their eternal soul that I worry about. It takes some digging to find out the truth about a soul."

"Sounds like you didn't dig anything up on Landry or Galante."

"No, and I'm not keeping anything from you. Neither took confession with me, or shared confidences. Perhaps they were what they seemed."

"What about Sergeant Jim Cole?" I was getting a little tired of people singing the praises of the living and the dead. I needed to hear their secrets, not their eulogies. "Did he do his job?"

"He did," Father Dare said, not meeting my eyes. He stood and began taking things out of his field pack and repacking them.

"Past tense?"

"I'm sure he's doing a good job at CID as well."

"When was he transferred out of the division?"

"After Monte Cesima, about a month ago."

"Why?"

"Jim Cole is a good man. He was one of the most selfless leaders you'd ever hope to find up on the line. He never asked a man to do what he wouldn't do, or hadn't done a hundred times. Night patrols, taking the point, it didn't matter, he was always there."

"Was he in Landry's platoon?" I couldn't believe Cole would leave that out if he was, but I was beginning to wonder what he had left out.

"No, he was with 1st Platoon."

"But same company? Did he know Landry and his men?"

"Damnation, Boyle! Of course they knew each other. There weren't but a few dozen who'd been with the outfit that long. Everybody knows everybody, except for the replacements, until they're dead or veterans."

"What happened to Cole, Padre?"

"Leave him out of this."

"I've been told that before."

"Then I don't need to say it again." He threw a few decks of cards into his pack. He had a cardboard box full of them.

"Where do you get the playing cards?"

"Quartermaster. Chaplains are morale officers, among other things. I'm issued sports equipment, cards, that sort of thing. I don't think there will be much time for baseball when they ship us out."

"Do you usually play poker with the enlisted men?" Chaplain or no, it was frowned upon for officers and men to gamble together.

"All the time, Lieutenant Boyle, all the time. They're a lot more fun than most of the officers, who never let me forget I'm a priest. And I love poker. I cleaned up at the seminary." He grinned, and I couldn't help taking a liking to him.

"But not tonight."

"No, Flint won big. I can read most people. It comes with the profession, and it's useful in poker. But Flint is different. Bluffing or holding four aces, it's all the same on his face. Unreadable. The best damn poker player in the platoon."

"They asked him if he was going to give the money back. Why?"

"It's sort of a tradition. If I win, I use the money to help out any boys who need it. Problems at home, that sort of thing. Sometimes for the local children, if we're in a village. When I lose big, the winner will usually pass some scrip back to me."

"Like tipping the dealer."

"Sort of. Word got around it was good luck, so my private good-will fund is never entirely depleted."

"Pretty creative, Padre. Did you play cards with Landry?"

"A couple of times. He didn't like to gamble with the men under his command. Said he didn't want any of them owing him money."

"Because someone might question who he chose to take point?"

"I think so," Father Dare said. "It's strange, though. He'd gamble with a captain or major who might send him to his death, but he wouldn't play with an enlisted man whom he might have to give the same order to. Doesn't really add up, does it?"

"It makes sense to the army," I said, giving up on understanding the logic of military rules. The padre gave a short snort of laughter and continued with his packing.

"How was Landry the last time you saw him? Was there anything unusual?"

"Not that I recall. Of course, everything here is unusual when you know you're being fattened up for the kill. Everyone is a bit jumpy."

"Anyone in Landry's platoon a big loser? I mean in hock to another guy?"

"Louie. I'm sure he's introduced himself to you."

"Louie Walla from Walla Walla."

"That's Louie. He owes a few guys money from cards and craps. He won't have much left next payday, but he's good for it. Anyway, that couldn't be a motive. He didn't gamble with Landry."

"No, I guess not. What about Stump and Flint?"

"Stump's been up and down at cards, and he stays away from the craps games. Flint usually wins, like I said. He's got a good poker face. Otherwise, he's the life of the party, a real charmer most of the time."

"Most of the time?"

"He's also got a temper, but you don't see it too often. I heard he got into a fight with three Italians in town and laid them all out."

"What was it about?"

"No idea. A woman, a bottle, who knows? The boys don't go to museums when they get a pass. They wander around, eat and drink, look for women. It doesn't always put them in the best neighborhoods." He stopped stuffing wool socks into his pack and sighed, shaking his head. "Listen, for all their faults, they're a good bunch. They just like to blow off steam once in a while."

"You ever been to that joint in Acerra? The one where one of Flint's men had a fight?"

"That's where Flint took on the three locals, from what I hear. Bar Raffaele on Via Volturno. And no, I haven't been there. A chaplain would definitely put a damper on things for all concerned. Now let me finish getting my gear together so I can catch some shut-eye. Unless you need spiritual counseling."

"Thanks for your time, Father." As I rose to leave, he pulled a .45 automatic from his duffel and loaded a magazine into it. "I thought chaplains were men of peace."

"We are. Trouble is, we're at war. The Geneva Convention allows medics and litter bearers to be armed, in order to provide protection for the wounded. Sometimes it's necessary to guard the flock. You know what it's like in battle, I expect. Men are on edge, their fingers on the trigger, waiting for the next threat, the next person trying to kill them. They don't always see the red cross on a helmet or that a man is down and wounded. All they see is the uniform, and the threat it implies."

"You think you're going to stop a berserk German with a Schmeisser submachine gun with that?"

"I may be a man of God, but I don't plan on being a martyr. I'll do what I have to do to protect those under my care."

CHAPTER ELEVEN

THE AFTERNOON WAS dark and gloomy as I sat in a line of military traffic, inching along in my jeep. We had to pull over for a truck convoy heading into the 3rd Division bivouac area. Men, artillery, and supplies flowed along the mud-caked road, nearly bumper to bumper. Something was happening, but in true army fashion, I'd be the last one to know if all my suspects shipped out to parts unknown.

I needed several things. I needed to know if the division was shipping out soon. I needed to see where Galante's body had been left. And I needed help. I needed Kaz. Kaz would be an extra set of eyes and ears, not to mention someone smart enough to figure out what was going on. I needed Lieutenant Baron Piotr Augustus Kazimierz.

Kaz had been my best friend since I got shipped over here in 1942. He'd been on General Eisenhower's staff as a translator, mostly as a courtesy to the Polish government-in-exile. Kaz was the last survivor of his family, alive only because he'd been studying in England when the Germans invaded Poland. His entire family had been killed, wiped out by the Nazis as they eliminated the educated elite of the country. Kaz wanted to serve, but a heart condition had kept him out of uniform. He finally talked his way in, as a translator for Uncle Ike. He was a skinny, bookish kid, and the idea was he could work in an office and do his bit.

Kaz's father had seen what was coming, and deposited the bulk of the family fortune in Swiss banks. As a result, Kaz was filthy rich. Rich enough to permanently keep a suite of rooms at the Dorchester hotel in London, the same suite where he and his family had celebrated their last Christmas together. I bunked with Kaz when I was in London and felt the ghosts of his past life drift by us in the ornate high-ceilinged rooms. One of those ghosts was Daphne, the love of Kaz's life. Sister of Diana Seaton. Maybe that's why I worried about Diana so much. I didn't want to become scarred like Kaz.

Kaz wore a physical scar as well. An explosion—the same explosion that had killed Daphne—had ripped his face from the corner of one eye down to the cheekbone. The injury and the loss had changed him. For a long time, he hadn't cared whether he lived or died, and I felt it was my job to keep life interesting enough for him to hang around. Lately, he'd turned a corner. He'd begun working out, building himself up, but for what I didn't know. All I did know is that he had more brains than ten other guys put together and wasn't afraid to use the Webley break-top revolver he wore. I could use both kinds of firepower. I decided to radio Colonel Harding and ask for Kaz to be sent down from London.

The column finally passed and the traffic moved along, toward Caserta. I ran through the leads I had to follow. Pay a visit to Bar Raffaele in Acerra and see what the scuffle was all about, and why Landry and Flint went down there to pay damages. Find out whom Louie owed his next paycheck to. Go back and find Major Arnold, Schleck's second-in-command, and see if he'd be more talkative. Ask Sergeant Jim Cole why he didn't tell me about knowing Landry and Galante. An infantry division is a big place, about fourteen thousand guys at full strength. He should have mentioned it, even if it was only a coincidence. He didn't, and I wanted to know why. I also needed to find out how Galante had gotten a squad killed, and why Cole was supposed to know about that. Maybe it was just a rumor that Schleck glommed onto, but if true, it would be a motive for revenge. Then ask the same question around the 32nd Station Hospital, and see what Galante's colleagues had to say.

It was a lot of legwork, and none of it might end up being important. But it gave me the illusion of being on the right track, and I might get lucky and stumble onto something I'd recognize as a clue. After an hour of stop-and-go traffic, I parked in front of the Caserta HQ and went to see Major Kearns. My plan was to send the radio message to Harding, then look at where Galante's body was found before it got too dark. Then Cole, then chow, and onto the officer's club to practice my interrogation skills at the bar. It was a good plan, except that it didn't hold much promise in terms of solving the murders.

"Billy!" A familiar voice echoed in the hallway leading to Kearns's office.

"Kaz," I said, turning to find him behind me. "What are you doing here? I was on my way to radio Harding to ask for you."

"He sent me immediately, but we had aircraft trouble and I was stuck at Malta for a day. It's good to see you, Billy." We shook hands warmly, both of us glad to be working together again. As usual, Kaz looked perfect in his tailored British battle dress uniform, complete with the red shoulder patch with "Poland" inscribed in bold letters. His blue eyes shone eagerly behind his steel-rimmed spectacles, and as usual the Webley revolver was at his hip.

"Do you know what's going on here?" I asked.

"Yes. Colonel Harding briefed me in London, and I saw Major Kearns twenty minutes ago. He told me to find Sergeant James Cole in CID, and that he'd tell me where you were. But he wasn't in."

"I'm glad you're here, Kaz."

"As am I," he said. We stood in silence for a heartbeat, the bonds of mourning, suffering, and hardship still strong—so strong that there were no words for it, none that I understood, anyway.

"Let's take a walk," I said, putting my arm around Kaz's shoulder. "I haven't seen where Captain Galante's body was found yet. Then we'll look for Cole." We walked through the gardens, beautiful even with tents and vehicles marring the landscape. A waterway led from the palace down the gentle slope to the Fountain of Diana and Actaeon. As we drew closer, the formal gardens became wilder, and smooth marble gave way to rough stone, creating the effect of entering a wilderness.

"Apparently the major was lured here," said Kaz. "One wonders why he was placed in this particular location."

"Out of the way?"

"Surely. But why was that important?"

"I don't know. Not a lot about this makes sense."

"Ah," Kaz said as the final pool of water came into sight. "Diana and Actaeon. You know the story?"

"It was explained to me," I said. "Guy got turned into a stag for daring to look at a naked goddess, then got ripped apart by his own hunting dogs." A small waterfall descended over moss-covered rocks, between two sculptures. Diana on one side, covering her nudity, and Actaeon on the other, being brought down by hounds. It was an oddly private place, sunken from view, surrounded on three sides by trees and shrubs. Not a bad place to stash a body. "I saw this place once before, but I'd forgotten how hidden it was."

"The report said Galante's body was laid out at the wall of the pool," Kaz said.

"Over here. There are still some chalk marks," I said.

"Interesting," Kaz said. "He's facing Actaeon."

"So?"

"Perhaps nothing," he said, squatting down to get a corpse-eye view of the fountain. "It just strikes me as odd. This is a public place, although hidden from view until you come upon it. I don't think the killer's objective was to hide the body, at least not for very long."

"Right," I said. "He could've put it in among the trees and shrubs. That would have bought him more time."

"I wonder if this placement was a statement."

"What kind of statement?"

"That Captain Galante had seen something, as Actaeon had. Something that must be kept hidden from human eyes. Once he'd seen it, his fate was sealed."

"Listen, Kaz, this is a nice quiet place, a good place for a killing. The murderer brings Galante down here under some pretense, strangles him after a short struggle, then rolls his body next to that wall. Short and sweet. No mythological psychiatric mumbo jumbo."

"Perhaps, Billy. I admit to a weakness for the old myths. The killer might also." I looked at the statues, and thought about my father telling me there was no such thing as a coincidence.

"You might be right about Galante being killed because he saw something. We have to find out what." This was why I needed Kaz, to help me see what was staring me right in the face.

"What do you make of the playing cards?" Kaz asked as we trudged back to the palace. The sky was darkening with low, gray clouds rolling in.

"It could be part of some crazy game. Or it could be to throw us off the scent. Maybe these two guys were the only targets, and by using the ten and the jack, he's got us worrying about the next victim instead of focusing on Landry and Galante."

"It could have been just one of them, with the second man killed to confuse us."

"I'm confused enough as it is. The only thing I've found out is that Cole held something back from me. He's only been with CID a short time. Before that he served in the 3rd Division and knew everyone in Landry's platoon. They all refuse to talk about it, as if they're protecting him. Colonel Schleck, who runs Personnel for the division, says Galante got a squad killed, and that Cole knows all about it."

"Do you think it's true?"

"Schleck seems convinced. What's more important is why Cole held that story back, especially any relationship he had with Galante."

"If Galante was somehow responsible for an entire squad being killed, that could be a strong motive," Kaz said.

"Yeah, and I wonder if any of those guys were Cole's buddies."

"Let us find the sergeant," Kaz said, "and discuss this with him."

"Maybe after we get some chow. I'll fill you in on my Swiss vacation."

"Switzerland? How . . ."

"What's going on over there?" I said, interrupting Kaz and

pointing toward the palace. To one side, among the jeeps, trucks, and ambulances lined in neat rows, a growing mass of people was gathering, many of them pointing to the roof of the palace. We hurried closer, curious as to what the hubbub was all about. GIs, officers of all ranks, nurses, and civilians began to jostle us, eager to get closer to a break in the endless routine of headquarters work. No one seemed to know what was happening, but no one wanted to miss it.

Vehicles were started and headlights lit the wall of the palace. Lights went on in windows as they were thrown open and heads peered out, looking up, then down at the crowd, then up again. The sun had begun to set, and the roof, a full five stories up, blended into the dark gray sky. The headlights only made it worse with their bright angled glare. Someone found a searchlight mounted on a truck and switched it on. A harsh white light played across the building, and I could see people in the windows covering their eyes, turning away. The beam darted back and forth until it caught a pair of boots dangling from the edge of the roof. Then the full form of a GI, his hand shielding his eyes. Even at that height, with the mask of an outstretched palm covering his face, I knew we'd found Sergeant Jim Cole.

I raced up the stairwell, looking for a way to the roof. Kaz was right on my tail, keeping up as we hit the fourth floor. Not too long ago, he would have stopped, gasping for breath halfway up. I didn't know if his heart could take it, but I figured Kaz was more interested in living what life he had than worrying about dying.

One more floor, and we found Kearns at the base of a narrow set of stairs, with a couple of MPs keeping the curious at bay. "It's Cole," he said.

"Yeah, I saw him. What happened?"

"You tell me. He came to see me this afternoon, looking for you. Next thing I hear, he's on the roof. What did he say to you?"

"Nothing, I just got back from 3rd Division."

"Well, get up there and talk to him, dammit! Bring him in, Boyle."

"Yes sir. I'll need some rope."

"You're going to tie him up out there?"

"No. It's for Kaz. Tie it around his chest and anchor it to the stairs. Then send him out. I may need something to grab onto and it'd be nice if it stayed put." Kearns sent an MP and I took the metal stairs, holding onto the thin rail as the walls narrowed and ended at a small wooden door. I opened it and had to duck to squeeze through.

It was windy. Windy and dazzlingly bright, as the searchlight caught me square in the eyes. I stumbled back, grabbing for the door, but it had shut in the wind. I grabbed air, slipped, and felt myself sliding down a section of roof, panicking in my near blindness. My leg jammed up against a low wall, but my head kept going until it hit granite. It hurt, but not as much as the idea of falling. The searchlight moved on.

"I've been thinking about shooting out that light," Cole said, his voice even and low, eyes on the crowd below. We were on a flat section of the roof, a narrow catwalk at the corner of the building. Above us the roofline sloped into the night. Below us, a long fall to hard ground. A knee-high wall was all that separated me from air. It did less for Cole. He sat on it, his boot heels dangling into space. A .45 automatic rested in his hand, and he gestured with it lazily toward the searchlight.

"I'll do it for you," I said, hoping for a chance to establish a common bond. I untangled my legs and stood. Or more accurately, leaned against the roof, as far from the edge as possible.

"Don't come any closer," Cole said.

"Yeah. Or else you'll jump. Pretty obvious. What's with the gun? Can't make up your mind which way to check out?"

"What? Why'd they send you out here anyway, Lieutenant, to crack jokes?" He still didn't look at me.

"No, I'm serious. I was a cop back home, saw my fair share of suicides. Usually they picked one method and stuck to it. Did you have a plan when you came up here?" One thing my dad taught me is that it's a rookie move to tell any jumper that this too shall pass, you'll feel better in the morning, that sort of stuff. It's likely he's already heard it, and it didn't stop him from climbing to the top of the highest thing he could find. Sometimes a person would jump just so he wouldn't have to listen to another idiot lecture him. No, best thing was to go right at him, ask him what he planned to do. It let him know you took him seriously, that you knew he was in pain. Then, maybe, he might talk.

"The gun is for anyone who tries to stop me," Cole said, finally giving me a quick glance.

"Listen, if you think I'm going to grab you and let you wrestle me off that ledge as you make your swan dive, you got another thing coming. This is as close as I get. Tell me what happened today."

"Today? What do you mean?"

"You didn't come up here yesterday. Or the day before. Not that I know of, anyway. So what got you on this ledge today?"

"You wouldn't understand. You couldn't, or you'd be up here yourself. I keep seeing them. Especially the little girl. I see her in my dreams, and she's alive. She's holding her doll, like kids do, you know? Then I wake up, and I know she's dead. I can't go on any longer, I can't." Cole spoke in a deliberate, slow voice. The voice of a man who was sure of himself. This wasn't a cry for help; this was a guy in the last moments of his life. I needed to get him thinking in a different direction.

"Why were you looking for me today? Was it about the case?"

"It's nothing. Meaningless."

"Come on, Cole, help me out. If you jump, I'll be all alone on this investigation. Tell me what you know." What I knew was that this wasn't the time to ask about dead squad mates from the 3rd Division.

"I don't know anything. Except that nothing matters, no matter what you do. You try to do good, but it turns evil. You try to save lives, but you end up taking them."

"This is war, Cole."

"Innocent lives. I can't forget them. He won't let me. I can't carry this any longer." He thumped his chest, once, then again, harder. "It'll never go away, never."

"Who won't let you?"

"He was my friend," Cole said, his voice breaking. "I see it in his face, see everything all over again." He began to sob now, rocking back and forth on the ledge. I reached out to steady him, but his gun hand was up in a flash. "Don't touch me!" His face was contorted in agony as tears streamed down his cheeks.

"Okay, okay. Just tell me, Cole. Who are you talking about?"

"Everybody wants something, don't they? You do, the army, the Krauts, you all want something. Answers. Blood. Promises. But I've got nothing left to give. I'm going crazy, I can't take it anymore. I don't want to see that face for the rest of my life. I see that doll too, a rag doll in a red dress. Even when I'm awake, I see it. I don't want to live like that. I can't."

I heard a noise behind me, and hoped it was Kaz.

"Shoot the light," I said. "Shoot the damn searchlight!" It was all I could think of.

"There's people down there. Are you nuts?"

"You're a combat infantryman, Sergeant Cole. You telling me you can't hit a big, blazing searchlight dead center at this range?"

"What do you care?"

"You're the one about to kill yourself, so what do *you* care?" It was like daring a kid to break a window back home. *What are you, chicken?* I heard the door move on its hinges.

"Okay," Cole said, taking the dare. "But first, in case someone shoots back, I have something to give you." He reached into his pocket, and tossed a double strand of pearls into my hand. Pearls? Smooth white pearls. I was dumbstruck.

"What's this?"

"You're the detective," he said. He stood, balancing his weight, and raised his arm, aiming the .45 at the searchlight. A murmur rose up from the crowd, and I hoped it covered the sound of Kaz coming through the door.

It didn't. I leapt, but Cole saw my move and sidestepped away from me. I came down hard on the edge of the granite wall, Kaz hanging onto my legs, the breath knocked out of me. I looked up at Cole, surprised at how agile he was, and tried to think of what to say.

"Don't jump." It was all that I could come up with, and it came out in a wheeze as I gulped air.

"I'm not going to," he said, and took another careful step away from me, sliding his feet along the narrow ledge. He raised the automatic and placed the muzzle under his chin. He didn't move as the searchlight played over him and the crowd below gasped. He stood, rock solid, until the slightest movement of his finger shattered the night with a sharp noise, blood, and bone.

CHAPTER TWELVE

"WHO WAS THAT up there?" Phil Einsmann asked. He'd been coming upstairs as Kaz and I headed down, and he turned to descend with us. He handed me a handkerchief, and I must have looked at him dumbly because he made a rubbing motion. I ran the handkerchief across my face and it came away red-streaked. I've never gotten used to the tremendous power of the human heart, and I don't mean its capacity to love. I mean as a pump. The last mechanical function at the moment of death by violence, the release of crimson as if the body is leaving its final mark upon this Earth. And on anyone who happens to be close by.

"It's not a story, Phil. Not one his folks back home need to read, anyway."

"I'm not asking as a reporter, Billy. I have a lot of friends here. Who was it?"

"Jim Cole. Sergeant with CID. Did you know him?"

"No, not really. I heard he was new with CID, saw him around, but those guys are a tight-lipped bunch. What set him off?"

"Hard to say." I meant it.

I handed Einsmann his handkerchief, but he told me to keep it. Couldn't blame him. I introduced him to Kaz, and then left him to go to CID. I didn't feel like talking right now, and Kaz could tell. He took the handkerchief and wiped the side of my neck. The top of my jacket was covered in tiny dots of drying blood, and I hoped it wasn't too noticeable. We walked among people filtering back to what they had been doing before the crazy sergeant shot himself on the roof. Shaking their heads, telling each other it was unbelievable, the poor guy must have been off his rocker. All the things people say to put as much distance between their own lives and the suddenness of death.

That was one of the terrifying things about being on the line. There was so little distance. Death was all around you, and not just during combat. It could be a mine where you didn't expect it, a sniper shot, or a random shelling. It's why you lived in a hole in the ground, getting as much distance as possible between yourself and the rest of the world.

I found myself standing in front of the door to CID. Staring at it. Kaz was standing by, patiently. I rubbed my eyes, shook my head, and wished I had a hole to crawl into.

"We don't have to do this now," Kaz said.

"Yeah, we do. I don't want anyone going through Cole's stuff. Might be a clue there." I put on my cop face and opened the door.

An MP sat at his desk, a cigarette smoldering between his fingers. "Jeez, Lieutenant," he said, shaking his head. "Can you believe it?"

"Did you see it?" I asked.

"Yeah, we were trying to keep people back. That shot. The blood. I couldn't believe it was Jim."

"Was he acting strange at all?"

"No more jumpy than usual. He spooked easy. But I never figured he would kill himself. Jesus."

"Did you see him leave here?"

"Yeah, I did. He went into his office, then came out a few seconds later. He must have gone straight to the roof. Jesus."

We left the MP and went into the office Cole shared with the other CID investigators. It was empty. Cole's desk was clean as a whistle except for the white phosphorus grenade set square in the middle of it.

"What is that?" Kaz asked, stopping short of the desk.

"It's a new kind of grenade. M15 white phosphorus." I walked around the desk and studied it. The safety lever and pin were both securely in place. It was about the shape and size of a beer can, painted gray with a yellow stripe around it. "When it bursts, the phosphorus makes white smoke, good for cover. It also burns incredibly hot, thousands of degrees, I've heard. It's used for taking out pillboxes or fortifications, if you can get close enough."

"Why would a CID agent have one?" Kaz asked.

"No reason at all," I said, opening the two drawers on the side of the desk. The playing cards Cole had shown me were there, along with forms, pencils, an empty holster, and an Armed Services Edition paperback—*Deadlier Than the Male*, by James Gunn. I flipped through it and two photos fluttered to the floor.

One photo was of Cole standing in front of the Caserta Palace with two people. One of them looked like Captain Max Galante. That was a surprise, but not as much as the other.

"This is Signora Salvalaggio, Galante's former cook and land-lady," I said. "What was Cole doing with them? For that matter, what was Galante doing with her?"

"We can ask her tonight," Kaz said. "I am billeted with you."

"Good, because she doesn't speak English," I said, as we studied the other photo, which was much more worn at the edges. It showed three GIs, arms around each other, weapons slung over their shoulders and wine bottles in their hands. It looked like a hot and dusty summer's day. Sicily, maybe.

"That's Cole, on the left," I said. "And Sergeants Louie Walla and Marty Stumpf. Third Platoon. Let's find these guys. It's time for secrets to be told."

We asked the MPs on duty about the WP grenade. No one had noticed it, or seen anybody bring it in. I carefully put it in my jacket pocket and we headed for the jeep. On the main floor I spotted Father Dare, and he made a beeline for me.

"Is it true? Cole killed himself?" He looked stunned, his eyes wide with hope that I'd tell him it was all a mistake.

"Yes, Father, I'm sorry to say it is. I'm heading out to find the other sergeants now. Anything you want to tell me about Cole before I do?"

"I wasn't there, Lieutenant. Better let them tell you," he said. "You don't have to look far, they're all over at the NCO club. Passes were cancelled, so they drove over here to have a few beers. They told me about Cole."

"They saw it happen?"

"Yes, Rusty told me. They were walking to the NCO club when they saw all the commotion. Was that you up there with Cole?" He glanced at the stains on my jacket, then locked eyes with me. "What did he tell you?"

"Not nearly enough. Where's the NCO club?"

"Across the way from the main entrance there's a row of Quonset huts. It's marked, you can't miss it."

"What were you doing here, Father?"

"I came for a good meal at the officer's club. I have a feeling we're pulling out very soon. More replacements came in today; we're almost back to full strength. I think I've lost my appetite, though. Good night, Lieutenant."

"Good night, Father. I'm sorry."

Father Dare walked away, looking distraught.

"Isn't the clergy supposed to comfort others?" Kaz asked.

"Yeah," I said. "What do you make of a poker-playing padre who carries a .45?"

"You can be religious and still wish to defend yourself. And to gamble."

"No law against that. Listen, while I talk with these guys, will you ask around and find out if there's an armory in this joint, or nearby? Some place where they have M15 WP grenades?"

"Do you think it had anything to do with Cole's suicide?"

"I don't know. It could be evidence from some other case, for all I know. See what you can find, and we'll meet at the officer's mess and compare notes."

IT'S NOT UNHEARD of for an officer to grab a drink or a meal at a NCO club, but as a courtesy he's expected to ask permission of a senior noncommissioned officer present. I spotted Rusty Gates and figured a platoon sergeant was senior enough.

"Mind if I join you fellows for a while?" Gates was sitting with Louie Walla from Walla Walla, Flint, and Stump. It was a subdued crowd. "Be glad to buy a round."

"You just bought yourself a chair, Lieutenant," Flint said, making room at the table. Gates gave me a nod, then signaled to the bar for five beers.

"Call me Billy, fellas. I was a cop back home, and I still turn around and look for my father when someone calls me lieutenant."

"You're in the family business, then?" Flint said.

"Until the war, yeah."

"Looks like you're still keeping your hand in," Stump said. "Asking all those questions."

"And I've got more. That's why most cops don't have a lot of friends outside the job. Always asking questions, it tends to get on people's nerves."

The beers came, and I waited to see who would say it, if anyone would. I held onto my bottle, half-raised in a toast.

"To Jim Cole," Gates said. They all repeated his name, then we clinked bottles and drank.

"Was that you up there with Cole?" Louie asked, gesturing with his beer bottle to the rust-colored stains on my jacket.

"Yeah. Major Kearns thought I should try talking him down. You guys saw it all, right?"

"We did," Gates said. "Now I suppose you want to know the whole story?"

"Yep. And why you all held back."

"It was for Jim," Louie said. "We was doin' him a favor, god-damn it."

"It's okay, Louie, it's okay," Gates said. "Flint, tell Billy what happened."

Flint took a long draw on his beer, set it down hard, and pursed his lips. He shook his head before beginning, as if he wondered if this was a good idea. "I was assistant squad leader. Cole was my sergeant. He came over from First Platoon after we lost a couple of guys. He knew what he was doing; he'd been with the company longer than anyone."

"Since North Africa," I said.

"Yeah. That had started to bother him. You know, with so many guys killed and wounded, and not a scratch on him. He kept saying his number was up, it had to be."

"Everybody worries about that," Gates said. "That wasn't the problem."

"Right, right. The problem was Campozillone," Flint said. He gulped the rest of his beer. "It's a little village near the base of Monte Cesima. The division was advancing on Mignano, and we had to clear Campozillone of Germans. It was a small place, but it over-looked the main road. It was on a hill, with a big stone church at the top, like a lot of these villages."

"Good place for an observation post," I said.

"Yeah. Landry and the rest of the company stayed on the main road while Third Platoon hustled up this dirt track. The village had taken an artillery barrage the night before, and we hoped the Jerries got the message and cleared out. When we got there, it was all narrow streets, like switchbacks, heading up to the church. The buildings were real close together, made from white stone, like granite. Solid."

"Them switchbacks were perfect for an ambush," Louie said.

"Yeah. It was real quiet at first. Some buildings were piles of rubble. Others were fine. It was hard to tell if they were homes or shops or what. They were all shuttered up. So we keep going, checking out alleyways and side streets, advancing up toward the church. No sign of Germans or civilians."

"It was hot," Stump said. "I remember sweating. Hot for November, even in Italy."

"Hot," Flint agreed. "We were almost to the church, and it seemed like the Germans might have pulled out after all. There was a set of steps leading up to the road, so we took them, our squad. The others went around the bend in the road, and we went up the steps, figuring to save time."

"It wasn't a bad move," Louie said. Everyone nodded their agreement.

"Then the Krauts opened up. Machine gun in a cellar window, at the head of the steps. They had the road and the steps covered. We lost two guys right away. One, MacMillan, had been with us a while. The other was a replacement, I never got his name."

"We was pinned down," Louie said. "Stump and me. Rusty was with us. We had one guy wounded, out in the middle of the street, but we were all holed up in doorways, nowhere to go."

"We started lobbing grenades," Flint said. "But they'd miss the window and bounce away. Some of these buildings had real narrow basement windows, and that's where the Krauts set up. Like a pillbox. The building between us and the Krauts was nothing but rubble, which blocked all the entrances on our side. We couldn't get at them."

"Bishop was out in the street, hit pretty bad in the legs," Gates said. "They left him alone, hoping one of us would try to get to him."

"We was screwed," Louie said.

"What happened?" I asked.

"The MG42 stopped," Flint said. "A few rifle shots, then they were gone. The medics got to Bishop, and we kept going. But now we knew they were probably setting up somewhere between us and the church. Everyone was mad. We wanted to get those bastards. Mac and Bishop, plus that kid—it got us all pissed off. You know how it is, when one minute you're so scared you just want to get into the deepest hole you can find, and then something happens, your blood's up, and you're doing something that might get you killed. It was like that. We moved up, hugging the walls, watching for those basement windows, waiting for shutters to swing open and the MG to open up again."

"We were all jumpy," Stump said. "Lots of firing at shadows."

"Our squad was in the lead," Flint said. "Cole took point. We were about fifty yards from the church, only one more switchback to go. I was looking at the bell tower, watching for snipers. I heard Cole say something and saw him point to a building at the top of the road. The roof had been caved in, but the rest of it was intact. It had stone steps leading up to the front door, and two small windows with bars on them on either side of the steps."

"I heard him yell for covering fire," Gates said.

"Yeah, then everyone started shooting. He ran toward the building, and I followed, shooting and yelling. We were all a little crazed, you know? Cole was screaming about the basement, that he saw movement, and to fire at the windows. I did, and as we got close, he pulled out a WP grenade, one of those new M15 gizmos, you know? And I figure, good idea, even if he misses, some of that Willie Peter will spray into the basement and fix those Krauts good. So he throws, and Jesus, it was a beautiful shot. The windows were a bit high off the ground, which made it a little easier, but it sailed in there perfectly. You saw it, Louie, wasn't that a shot?"

"Right between the bars," Louie said. "Cole had a helluva arm."

"Flint," Gates said in a low, quiet voice. "Tell Billy what happened."

"Well, we took cover. You know that stuff flies everywhere and burns like the devil. But when it went in, we moved up, covering the door, figuring Krauts might come spilling out."

"But there weren't no Krauts," Louie said, helping Flint along. I felt the weight of the grenade in my pocket, as well as the weight of what I knew was coming. I thought about the fact that someone had left this grenade on Cole's desk hours—or minutes—before he'd decided to kill himself.

"No. Smoke was pouring out, and inside was a white-hot glow. We heard screams. We got to the window, and there was this guy, this Italian. He was on fire, his back was blazing. He had a little girl, he must have shielded her from the blast, and he was trying to push her out between the bars, but he couldn't. Cole grabbed at the girl, but he came up empty. Except for a rag doll she'd been holding."

"It was a whole family," Gates said. "Father, mother, couple of kids. They'd evidently taken shelter during the bombardment. When the roof caved in, it blocked the stairs to the basement. They were trapped."

"Cole just stood there," Stump said. "Holding that rag doll. And I mean he stood there, looking into that burning basement. We couldn't move him."

"We found those Krauts," Louie said. "They was hightailing it outta the church, four of 'em, makin' for an olive grove. We'd split up, a squad on either side of the church. Soon as they saw us, it was *kamerad, kamerad*. But we wasn't in the mood."

"What happened with Cole?" I thought about pulling out the grenade and plunking it down on the table, but I didn't know what that would tell me. If one of these guys put it on Cole's desk, he might expect it. The rest would think I'd lost it.

"Landry came up with some medics and they checked him out, but he wasn't wounded. Flint brought him to the aid station, just to give him a rest," Gates said. "Since he wasn't hurt, they didn't know what to do, so Father Dare took over and took care of him for a couple of days. The padre brought him back, and he seemed okay. Quiet, not out of his head or anything. So we think everything is back to normal, that he got over the shock. We're closer to Mignano now, and the next morning we shove off to occupy another hill. I left Cole's squad in reserve, but we come up against a farmhouse with a bunch of Krauts holed up in it. I needed Cole to move his squad down an irrigation ditch to get closer, so I send him out. It's good cover, and they get close, but they stay in the ditch. I crawl down there to see what's the problem, and everyone's looking at Cole, waiting for the order. But he won't move, won't speak. So I gave the squad to Flint, and we took the farmhouse. No casualties."

"Did he say why he froze?"

"He said he just couldn't do it anymore," Flint said. "He was okay as soon as he got away from the shooting. But he said there was no way he could ever go up on the line again."

"He wasn't shaking in his boots or anything. He just said he couldn't do it no more," Louie said.

"It wasn't like some guys who try to talk their way out of it," Gates said. "He was ready to take whatever the army dished out, but he sure as hell was not going up on the line ever again."

"Fourteen months, since Fedala," Stump said. "That's how long it took. Fourteen months and one morning in Campozillone."

"We got Father Dare to talk to Captain Galante," Flint said. "He'd just been assigned to the hospital here, and we knew he was an okay guy. If Colonel Schleck ever found out about Cole freezing, he would have transferred him to another company and court-martialed him if he didn't fight. We didn't want that to happen."

"Schleck claimed Galante got a squad killed," I said. Now that everyone was in the mood to tell the truth, I wanted to get as much out of them as I could.

"Bullshit," Gates said. "That wasn't Cole anyway. It was another old-timer from Dog Company, couldn't get out of his foxhole. Said he'd be dead if he did. Guy had the Bronze Star and two Purple Hearts, so he wasn't goldbricking. Galante pulled him off the line and that very day his squad got caught in the open. The Bonesaw cut them to pieces."

"So Galante got Cole transferred to CID?"

"Yeah," Gates said. "That's how it went. Cole was fine knowing he still had a job to do, but that he was off the front line. But we figured no one needed to know the whole story. No reason to embarrass him."

"You all were okay with that? No one felt left in the lurch by Cole?"

"There but for the grace of God," Gates said, to nods all around.

CHAPTER THIRTEEN

"THERE ARE NO arms or weapons storage in the palace," Kaz said as we settled in at the officer's club. Neither of us had felt like eating, so we went directly to drinking. "There is a rule against carrying grenades within headquarters, but it is not well enforced."

"Who'd want to go up against some guy fresh from the line?" I enjoyed the vision of a mud-encrusted, filthy GI, grenades hanging from his web belt, M1 slung over his shoulder, as he sauntered through the palace, scaring the pants off clerks and typists, not to mention the residents of the fancy mess hall upstairs. He would seem to be from another world, a wraith who lived underground and only came out to kill or die.

"The rule was made after a major posed for a photograph, kitted out like a combat soldier," Kaz said, grinning. "Apparently he had political aspirations, and wanted a picture to impress his future constituents. Somehow he managed to pull the pin, then dropped the grenade and ran. The photographer threw it into a latrine, which thankfully was empty. The ensuing odor and destruction brought about the regulation against grenades as fashion accessories."

"So the WP grenade probably came from a combat outfit."

"Or it could have been stolen from a supply depot," Kaz said.

"Basically we'll never know. Hundreds of people were in and out of this place tonight. All of Cole's sergeant pals, his padre, CID staff, even those Italians," I said. I cocked my head in the direction of two Carabinieri officers in their dark-blue uniforms.

"Billy, the Italians are fighting on our side now. The First Motorized Combat Group performed admirably around Monte Cassino. They took heavy causalities."

"Yeah, I heard about that. It's just that Italians have done more shooting at me than I like. Takes some time to get over that."

I finished my whiskey and got refills for both of us. I filled Kaz in on Cole's story as I'd just heard it. When I was done, Kaz got the next round. We drank in silence; any words we might say would only seem trivial.

"What do we do now?" Kaz finally asked.

"What do you know about pearls?"

"What has that to do with anything?"

"Excellent question," I said, leaning in closer. "There wasn't time to tell you before, but Cole gave me something before he shot himself. Pearls." I withdrew the necklace from my pocket, keeping it balled up in my fist. I passed it to Kaz under the table. "No one knows about this, so keep it out of sight."

"Did Cole say anything?"

"You're the detective."

"Billy, this is—"

"Lieutenant Boyle, is it not?" I hadn't noticed the two Carabinieri approach our table, but I was glad to see Kaz had, as his empty hand emerged from his jacket pocket.

"Yes," I said. "Capitano Trevisi, this is Lieutenant Baron Piotr Augustus Kazimierz." I remembered the captain from when we met the other night, but I drew a blank on the lieutenant by his side.

"Renzo Trevisi, at your service. Baron, this is Tenente Luca Amatori."

"Please join us," Kaz said, with a slight bow and a graciousness I would not have pulled off.

"Thank you," Trevisi said. "We do not encounter many titled personages here, other than military, that is." He spoke English well but with a thick accent, and slowly, so it took a second to realize he had made a little joke.

"Ah, yes. My title is a minor one from the Polish petty nobility. I was about to tell Lieutenant Boyle about the Italian House of Savoy, and the grand balls held in this very palace."

"King Umberto and the great Queen Margherita of Savoy did reside here," Trevisi said. "I am from this very town, and remember as a child watching their carriages parade through the streets. It was magnificent. Such a pity Umberto was assassinated."

"At least it prevented Margherita from staying on the throne. She was a notorious Fascist supporter," Luca Amatori said. His English was rapid and perfect. He was younger than Trevisi, and he had the impatient look of a guy who was tired of agreeing with his superior officer.

"Now Luca," Trevisi said, in a weary parental tone. "Many of the wealthy and the aristocrats wanted stability after the last war, and they weren't alone."

"You're not a fan of royalty, Tenente Amatori?" Kaz asked.

"On the contrary, Baron. I have the greatest respect for King Victor Emmanuel. He ordered the Carabinieri to arrest Mussolini, after all."

"Yes, the Carabinieri were not great supporters of Fascism. The king felt safe to call upon us when it was time to get rid of *Il Duce*. Mussolini," Trevisi clarified, for our benefit. "Old habits, you know. We had to call him that for so long, it is difficult to change."

"Certainly," I said, as I noticed Amatori glance away, his knuckles white where he gripped the chair. I decided it was time for a change of topic. Murder was safer than politics. "Does your jurisdiction extend to Acerra, by any chance?"

"Yes," Trevisi said. "Does this involve your investigation?"

"Perhaps. We need to find an establishment that caters to soldiers. Liquor and women, nothing fancy from the sound of it."

"Are you looking for a recommendation?" Trevisi asked, one eyebrow raised in conjecture.

"No, Capitano," Kaz said. "I believe Billy is looking for a specific establishment, in connection with the investigation."

"We have a name," I said. "Bar Raffaele."

"*Capisco*," he said. "Tenente Amatori would be glad to accompany you. Tomorrow? Perhaps he could meet you here in the morning."

Luca Amatori was happy to guide us through the fleshpots of Acerra, mostly to get away from his boss, as far as I could tell. We made our arrangements, more drinks arrived, and we toasted to victory. I could picture Trevisi making the same toast with schnapps not too long ago.

"We interrupted your discussion of the palace in the last century, I think," Trevisi said. "Little is left of its former grandeur. You should have seen it before the turn of the century. *Era bello*."

"Yes, I was about to tell Billy about Queen Margherita. A very elegant woman, a patron of the arts, she revitalized the Italian court, made it fashionable. She held balls and parties that became famous all across Europe."

"People loved her," Trevisi said, nodding his approval. "They called her the Queen of Pearls."

"I'd guess all queens like pearls," I said, trying to sound casual.

"Oh, but Margherita loved them. She wore huge strands and had many different necklaces. She was renowned for her pearls," Trevisi said.

"Wasn't there a theft at one point?" Kaz asked.

"Yes, back in the 1890s. She and the king held an anniversary ball here at Caserta. As I recall the story, a small box containing a three-strand necklace was stolen from her dressing room. It was never recovered, and apparently has never turned up. The Carabinieri chief resigned in disgrace. Very unfortunate."

"You have an excellent memory, Baron," said Amatori. "I haven't heard that story since I was a child."

"I was a student before the war. One tends to accumulate bits of information."

"Indeed," Amatori said. "And you, Lieutenant Boyle? Were you a student in America?"

"Not for long," I said. "I was a police detective."

"Ah, a fellow officer of the law! Of course we will assist you in every way possible," Trevisi said. We had another round to toast our cooperation, then finally parted ways.

"THE QUEEN OF Pearls?" I said as we got into the jeep and Kaz tossed his bag into the back. It had started to rain, a steady, incessant spitting that sounded like drum rolls on the canvas top.

"As I was about to tell you when your Italian comrades showed up. Billy, if Sergeant Cole had these, there may be more. Perhaps he found them in the palace and was being blackmailed. Or threatened by an accomplice?"

"I don't think that's why he jumped. What happened in Campozillone caused him to jump."

"But why this particular night? That was months ago, and as you said, he'd found a place in CID where he could still be useful." Kaz turned up his coat collar against the blowing rain. "You know that I have thought about it," he said in a softer voice.

"Yeah, I do." I placed my hand on Kaz's shoulder for a moment. There was nothing left to say.

"There were times I missed Daphne so much. I missed everything. My family, my way of life, my country. When things got difficult, as they did in London recently, it was a temptation."

"An end to all your problems."

"Yes, that is the answer for some. But for me, it seemed like defeat. They would finally win, those who took everything from me. So we must think, who won with Sergeant Cole? Who defeated him, months after that dreadful incident?"

"He said he couldn't forget the innocent lives he took. *He won't let me* is how he put it."

"Who was he talking about?"

"He didn't say. Only that it was a friend, and that he could see it all in his face, see everything that happened."

"Someone from his unit, who reminded him of that day. Someone he'd felt close to, and now his face only reminded Cole of what he had done."

"Maybe," I said, turning a corner and sending up a sheet of water that drenched the hood. "Or he had a friend who was a jewel thief on the side. Right after he said that, he handed me those pearls. It was the damnedest thing."

"Could the pearls have anything to do with the murders?"

"I don't know. Maybe Cole found the queen's pearls. All I know is I've had too much to drink and it's been a long day. We're almost home."

"In good weather it must be difficult to sleep," Kaz said, looking out over the B-17s lined up on the airfield across the road. He was right. When the skies cleared, they'd be revving engines and flying overhead all day.

"Good weather? What's that?" Right now GIs in the mountains were huddling in trenches, caves, dugouts, wherever they could find cover from shrapnel and storm. Roads were turning into mud pits that could suck a heavy truck down to its axles and stall a Sherman tank. Sunny Italy. I'm sure it existed in some other time and place, but not in this winter of 1944.

Signora Salvalaggio greeted us at the door, watching as we hung up our dripping coats and stamped the wet from our boots. I assembled some of the few Italian words I knew and attempted an introduction. "*Salvalaggio di Signora, questo è il Tenente Baron Piotr Augustus Kazimierz.*"

"*Il barone? Da che la famiglia la sono?*"

"*Siamo discesi dalla casa principe di Ryazan,*" Kaz broke in. "*È un piacere incontrarla, Signora.*" He made a little bow as he took the old lady's hand and kissed it. She accepted it without surprise, and graciously escorted us through her kitchen and into the living room. Before I had time to ask Kaz what the exchange was all about, Captains Wilson and Bradshaw were on their feet and I made another round of introductions. The heat from the coal stove was a relief after the cold rain.

"Welcome, Lieutenant," Bradshaw said. "We had a message from Major Kearns this morning that another investigator would be taking the spare room. Haven't found the murderer, Boyle?"

"Not yet," I said, pulling my chair closer to the stove. "We'll probably be at the hospital tomorrow afternoon, asking the staff about Doctor Galante. Anybody there he was close to?"

"I saw Galante talk more to our landlady than anyone at the hospital, outside of medical business anyway," Wilson said. "They were always chatting in Italian. Galante said he liked the practice."

"An odd duck, that one," Bradshaw said. "Not to speak ill of the dead, but he did keep to himself, more interested in artwork and Italian history than anything else. I believe he said he was Jewish, so I wonder what the fascination was."

"His family was Italian," Wilson said. "He once told me he hoped to get to Rome when it was liberated, to see his mother's birthplace. Her family emigrated at the turn of the century. According to him, she was descended from one of the oldest Jewish families, been around since Roman times."

"Any idea what he and the signora talked about?"

They didn't. I wondered why I cared, as the warmth from the coal fire seeped into my body.

CHAPTER FOURTEEN

THE NEXT MORNING I found Kaz in the kitchen, seated at a worn wooden table, drinking espresso as Signora Salvalaggio hovered over him, filling his tiny cup and laying out a plate of cheese and bread. He'd told me last night that she knew of the clans of Poland, and had asked him which princely family he was descended from. I didn't even know that there were princely families in Poland, so this old landlady had a leg up on me.

"*Buon giorno*," she said, placing a cup of steaming, thick coffee in front of me. It tasted strong and sweet.

"*Molto buono*," I said.

"Billy, are you becoming a student of languages? I didn't know you'd learned Italian," Kaz said.

"Picked up a few sentences, that's all. Hard not to."

Kaz spoke to the signora, pointing at me, and they both laughed.

"You two became pals pretty quick," I said, smiling to let her know I could take whatever Kaz had dished out.

"Signora Salvalaggio used to work at the palace, as a seamstress. She understands the distinctions of European royalty, even the minor nobility. She is very well educated for a woman of her time. She knew Queen Margherita personally."

At the mention of the queen's name, I thought the signora stood a little straighter, as if the memory of her royal service brought back the posture of her youth. For a moment, I saw her as that younger woman, not a gray-haired lady in the typical black garb of the elderly. Taller, dressed in finery at the court, with smooth skin and glossy black hair. Her dark eyes met mine, as if to say, yes, I was once beautiful, can you believe it? She smiled, and returned to tidying up the kitchen. I wondered if she'd been around when the pearls were stolen, and if she might be able to help us identify what we had. Maybe she'd recognize the queen's pearls, or might know if these were cheap imitations.

"I wonder if she was there when the pearls were stolen," I said.

There was a crash, and Signora Salvalaggio stood with her hand to her mouth, a glass shattered at her feet. "Have you found them?" Her voice trembled, as if she were on the verge of tears, the precise English a shock to us both.

"Signora, please sit down and tell us what you know," Kaz said, as he pulled out a chair. "*Per favore.*"

"Do you have them, the pearls?" Her voice was now insistent. Kaz glanced at me and I nodded. He took the pearl necklace from his jacket pocket and placed it on the table. She gasped, and reached for them, but stopped herself. "The last time I saw that necklace, I dressed the queen myself and put it around her neck. It is the same clasp, the same length. It is the queen's."

"Signora Salvalaggio, I had the impression you did not speak English," I said. "You are quite fluent." I didn't know which surprised me more, her perfect English, or her claim about the pearls.

"I did not let the Germans know I spoke their language either," she said. "There is nothing to be gained by idle conversation."

"Yet you spoke with Doctor Galante often."

"Yes. He was cultured, and from one of the ancient Roman families, even if he was a Jew. The *Italkim*, they call themselves. He understood the nature of things."

"He appreciated Italian culture, the language and history."

"Yes. Not many men in the army do. Any army. They use the palace as if it were a barracks." She spit out that last word.

"Tell us about the pearls, Signora," Kaz urged her with a gentle hand laid on her arm.

"I was a seamstress, but it was not a commoner's position," she said, waving her hand as if dismissing a servant. "I came from an old family, honorable but impoverished. My husband had died one year after we married, from the cholera, and I almost succumbed myself. The queen heard of my plight and brought me to Caserta, to be in charge of her gowns—sewing, repairing, and altering. Oh, you should have seen them! Silk, velvet, satin, gold embroidery, nothing was too precious to go into her gowns. 'Inspire the popular imagination,' that's what she used to say about her gowns and jewelry. She saw it as her duty."

"What happened to the pearls?" I asked.

"It was on Their Majesties silver wedding anniversary, in 1893. She wore a long parure of rubies with this short three-strand pearl necklace. It was a grand party, the emperor and empress of Germany, the queen of Portugal, the grand duke and duchess of Russia, so many of Europe's finest were there." Her eyes were focused on a distant memory of the old century, long-dead aristocrats dancing in the now rat-infested palace. Meanwhile, I was trying to figure out what a parure was.

"When did they go missing?" Kaz asked, in a whisper.

"That night. I was supposed to put all the jewelry away, it was a sign of the trust the queen had in me. But I rushed through it, since I had fallen in love with a young man, a lieutenant, like you two gallant gentlemen." She smiled, and looked away, a faint blush showing on her wrinkled cheeks. "He was waiting for me downstairs, and in my hurry I left the necklace in its black lacquered box on a table in the dressing room. It should have gone in a locked armoire, where I'd put it many times before. But the heart is always in haste, at least for the young," she sighed.

"What happened?"

"In the morning, the lacquered box was gone. When I last saw it, all the guests had departed, and very few people left the palace after that. Because of all the royalty gathered, there were guards on all the doors throughout the night."

"Except for you and your lieutenant."

"Yes. The Carabinieri suspected us, of course. We were questioned for days. We had walked through the gardens under the moonlight. It was beautiful, and I had no way of knowing it was the last truly happy night of my life."

"You lost your position?" Kaz asked.

"Yes. For my negligence. And my lieutenant was transferred to Sicily, in disgrace. I never saw him again."

"No one else was questioned?"

"The others were all too exalted to be questioned. But the theft made the guests nervous, and they all left the next day. I was somehow always certain it was waiting to be found. Where was it?"

"I don't know. It was given to me."

"Ask the person!" It was an order, and in the set of her face I could see her lineage. Impoverished and disgraced, she still had the aristocratic bearing, the readiness to issue orders that commoners must obey.

"He's dead. He shot himself moments after he handed me the necklace."

Signora Salvalaggio crossed herself. "That such beauty could ruin so many lives," she said, shaking her head.

"Did you stay in Caserta to search for the pearls?" Kaz asked.

"Back then, I had no such thought. I had nothing, no family left, no place to go. I walked into town and looked for work. A good seamstress can always find employment, and I did. Not sewing fine gowns, but it kept me alive. I often wondered where the pearls were, and if the Carabinieri had their eye on me. If they did, I disappointed them. I never ran off with my fortune."

"But now you have been vindicated," Kaz said, gathering up the necklace. "We can tell the authorities."

"Ha! Do what you wish. It does not matter. Who is left alive to remember a theft in 1893? The old king and queen are both dead. The Carabinieri headquarters was destroyed in the fighting; any records they had went up in flames. I am simply an old seamstress with her stories of grand balls, lost love, and other ancient memories. Please, take it away."

"Did you tell Doctor Galante all this?" Kaz asked as he carefully swept the necklace into his pocket.

"Not at first. But the *dottore* was so interested, he flattered me with his attention. Foolish for an old woman, I know. I found myself telling him the story, describing the rooms, where the nobles and servants slept, where the jewels were kept. He would come back and tell me about what he'd seen and how the rooms looked. It was all so sad to hear, but at the same time, it brought back memories of the good times, before the pearls cursed me."

"He never found anything?"

"No. I believe he would have told me if he had. We had become friends, of a sort. A lonely man, more of a scholar than his colleagues, and an old woman with a sad but interesting story. Will you find who killed him?" Her lip trembled, and I knew that she had valued Galante's friendship. A cultured man, who respected her and her stories of royalty and palace balls.

"That's why we're here," I said, sounding confident but avoiding a direct answer.

"It wasn't over the pearls, was it? Please, no."

"There seems to be no connection," Kaz said. I wasn't so sure.

"Did you know another American, Lieutenant Norman Landry?"

"No," she said. "I know very few soldiers, only those they send for my rooms and cooking. But I do know the priest, *Prete* Dare."

"How?"

"He came to visit *Dottore* Galante. Twice. Once he dined with him. Your American priests are very different from ours, I think."

"Father Dare is one of a kind. Did he know about the pearls?"

"I don't know. I never heard the dottore speak to him about it."

"What did they talk about?"

"Nothing I recall. Other soldiers, the war. The dottore spoke often of *sgusciare la scossa*, you know?"

"Shell shock," Kaz said. "Combat fatigue."

"Yes," she said. "I did not know these terms, but Dottore Galante explained them to me. It was his life's work, he said, to learn about this. He was very annoyed with some officer who kept him from it, and had him sent to work at the hospital."

"Did he and Father Dare speak about this?"

"Yes. When he came for dinner, it seemed the padre was asking his opinion about soldiers they both knew. But I did not pay attention to names. American names are so strange to me, especially the names soldiers use."

"What do you mean?"

"What is the word? *Soprannome?*"

"Nicknames," Kaz supplied.

"Yes, yes. It makes it so difficult to understand, especially with the Americans. One of the men they talked about, he had a French name, at least to my ears. And there was something about a ridiculous town he was from. They always laughed when they said it."

"Louie Walla from Walla Walla?"

"Yes!" She slapped her hand on the table. "The dottore was worried about him. Why, I cannot say. I was too busy preparing *la Genovese.*"

"Were the other doctors at the dinner?"

"No, they were both working. I think Dottore Galante wished to dine alone with Il Prete."

"*La Genovese?* Is that the Neapolitan beef and onion ragout?" Kaz's concentration on the case had apparently been broken.

"Yes, Barone. I will make it for you, if you can find some good meat. Not horse meat, although it will do in a pinch," Signora Salvalaggio said, with a conspiratorial smile.

"Why do they call it *la Genovese*, if it comes from Naples?" I asked.

"A mystery," she said, with a shrug.

A real mystery. Priests and doctors, suicide and murder, hidden pearls and Willie Peter grenades. Nothing made sense, nothing connected. I drank the last of the espresso, now gone cold, the harsh taste gritty and sour on my tongue. Kaz and the signora chatted on about cooking while all I could think of was who was going to be dealt the next card.

Then I recalled seeing women in Sicily, squatting at the side of the road, their knives slicing into the bodies of horses killed in the German retreat. The animals were still in harness, flies buzzing around their eyes, as the Sicilian women butchered them and carried slabs of flesh home, blood staining their shoulders. I watched Signora Salvalaggio, and wondered what she might be capable of. To what lengths would she go to recover her honor? Or the pearls?

CHAPTER FIFTEEN

"WHAT SHOULD WE do with the pearls?" Kaz asked as we drove to the palace to pick up Luca Amatori, our Carabinieri guide for our trip to Bar Raffaele in Acerra.

"I'm not sure," I said. "I wish I knew if they were a dead end or a connection to the murders. There might be some percentage in letting it slip that we have them."

"Meaning a fair chance that someone will try to kill us for them. I'd prefer a different plan, Billy."

"Well, that wouldn't have worked anyway. If word got out, CID would want us to turn in the pearls. They'd sit in a locked file somewhere until a colonel with a key decided to bring home a souvenir. No sense in letting that happen."

"What would you do if this were Boston?"

I wanted to say, *Whatever the patrol sergeant said to do*. My experience as a detective was limited to the few weeks between my uncle calling in a few favors on the promotions board, and the attack on Pearl Harbor. Before that, I'd been a beat cop, working different parts of the city, and helping Dad out when he needed a few extra bluecoats at a crime scene. Dad was a homicide detective, and it was his plan to bring me up in the family business. It was a good plan, but the war had gotten in the way. Instead, I said, "It's not the same. I doubt we'd ever find a dead queen's pearls in Boston."

"What about one of the old Boston families? The Brahmins, as you call them. You find jewelry from a theft that happened fifty years ago. The original owner is dead. The family is stupendously wealthy. No one is pursuing the case. What do you do?"

I took a corner harder than I needed to, sending Kaz rocking in his seat. Only fair, since he was putting me in a corner too.

"You forgot the old family retainer, living a life of shame."

"What if there were one?"

"I know some cops who'd split it with her. Not many. A few would turn it in, a few would keep it for themselves."

"What about the rest?"

"My dad always said you couldn't trust a guy who was either too honest or too crooked."

"I don't understand," Kaz said.

"I didn't either, at first," I said. It was hard to explain. "Okay, for example. There was a fire, a few years before the war, in Mattapan Square. Big two-family house, four-alarm blaze in the middle of the night. Everyone got out, and the firemen kept it from spreading to the neighbors, but the building was ruined, had to be torn down before it caved in on itself. So the next day, I'm there with a few other cops to keep the onlookers at a safe distance while the wrecking crew takes it down. There's a fire truck too, in case anything's smoldering under the debris."

"Are there any Boston Brahmins in this story?" Kaz asked.

I responded with a hard stop at an intersection, but he'd braced himself for it. "Wait. There was an attic, used by the two families for storage. But it used to be an apartment, back before the turn of the century. No one remembered who'd lived there, or where they went. When they pulled the front of the house down, a wooden crossbeam came loose and hit the ground, rolled right into one of the workers. Broke his leg. So we push the crowd back to make room for him, and as we're standing around while the firemen rig a stretcher, a cop named Augie Perkins notices a coffee can sticking out from the horsehair lathing on a section of interior wall.

It was from the attic. Stuffed full of fives, tens, and twenties, all rolled up tight."

"Why leave money inside a wall?"

"You'd be surprised what you find hidden in old houses. Lots of people don't trust banks or their relatives, so they keep money hidden. Trouble is, they don't tell anyone, and end up taking their secret to the grave."

"Who owned the house?"

"I'll get to that. The lid was off, and Augie sees that there's a ton of dough in that can, and he thinks no one else sees it. So he eases over, kneels down to tie his shoe, pulls it free, and stuffs it under his jacket."

"But you saw him, right?"

"No, a pal of mine did. Joe Leary, one of the firemen. He waits until the worker is loaded onto the ambulance, and the crowd breaks up. Then he clocks Augie good, opens his coat, and shows the rest of us what he'd taken."

"And you arrested him?"

"No. Joe told us the building was owned by a rich guy named Frederick Perkins. Almost a Brahmin. Good enough for one of them to marry his daughter, and his money, anyway. We weren't in a hurry to give him a tin can of cash he never knew about. So there's ten of us, not counting the guy with the broken leg. Joe suggested we split it thirteen ways."

"Why thirteen?"

"A share for each of the families that were burned out, one for the guy with the broken leg, and the ten of us. Even Augie, but we had to cut him in, just to keep him quiet."

"It sounds like an admirable plan."

"Except for Teddy Booker. Augie was the greedy one, and Teddy was the too-honest one. He threatened to turn us all in if we didn't give the money to the owner of the property. Joe threatened to bash him one, too, but Teddy didn't give in. He took the money, and reported both Augie and Joe for pilfering."

"What happened?"

"No one would speak to Teddy after that. They called him By-the-Book Booker. He quit the force and moved to Chicago. Augie and Joe lost their jobs. Frederick Perkins got a can of cash, had a heart attack two weeks later and died."

"And the moral of the story?" Kaz asked.

"Like my dad always said, don't trust anyone too honest or too crooked. They'll both get you in hot water."

"I still don't know what we're going to do with the pearls. But at least now I know not to give them to Augie or Teddy," Kaz said.

"Which do you think Luca Amatori is?" I said, as we pulled onto the gravel driveway leading to the palace to pick up our escort and former enemy.

"I think we'll find out more without his boss around," Kaz said. "Capitano Trevisi didn't seem to think much his Tenente's opinions."

"*Buon giorno*," the Carabinieri lieutenant said as he walked to the jeep. He was right on time. Kaz got in back and the lieutenant thanked him.

"After enduring Billy's driving, you might not thank me, Tenente."

"Please, call me Luca. We are all lieutenants, yes? It would be tiresome to hear of it constantly."

"Certainly, Luca. Call me Kaz, which is Billy's version of Kazimierz."

"Been stuck at *tenente* long?" I asked as we shook hands.

"Stuck? Yes, and at war also," Luca said, pulling his blue service cap down tight on his head. "It has been a long time since we have known peace. Here, take this turn for Acerra," he said as we came to the main road. We drove south, past horse-drawn carts loaded with firewood, blackened ruins, the odd intact farmhouse, and fallow winter fields, sodden from recent rains. The weather was clearing, low gray clouds tumbling across the sky, making way for the sun and the bombers that would follow.

"Have you been stationed at Caserta long?" Kaz asked, leaning in from the backseat.

"No. I was transferred here with others from my battalion, two months ago. We had been in Yugoslavia, but returned to Italy with the armistice. I think we are about to be sent somewhere else. We have received new arms and supplies, and there are many rumors."

"Not the first time I heard that. Any idea where?"

"No. No one tells us anything. We wait, we patrol, and we do what we can against the black market, but it is hopeless."

"Do you have much trouble with GIs?"

"Yes, but we can do little about it. Only the military police and your CID may arrest your soldiers. We work closely with them, but it is understandable that they take care of their own in a foreign country."

His words made sense, but I could tell from his tone that it bothered him. It would bother any good cop, so I liked that about him. "Any scuttlebutt about where you're going?"

"Pardon me?"

"American jargon," Kaz said. "Rumors, loose talk."

"Ah. We will be flown into Rome after American paratroopers take the airport. Or, that we will land on the beaches west of Rome with our own San Marco Marine Regiment. We are going to protect the pope, we are escorting the king into Rome, take your choice. They all involve fantasies of heroics and reclaiming our national honor. I suspect the reality will be somewhat less glamorous."

"Rome is not that far away, maybe a hundred and twenty miles. It's not impossible."

"Except for the Germans dug in along the Bernhardt Line, and on Monte Cassino, it would be a pleasant drive," Luca said. "Although machine guns do spoil any outing."

"A seaborne landing does make sense," Kaz said, more usefully. "To go around them."

"I'll be sure to tell General Eisenhower next time I see him," I said. Getting to Rome sounded fine to me. Maybe I could go along and find Diana.

"If only generals would listen to lieutenants," Luca said.

"This general will. Billy is his nephew. We are attached to General Eisenhower's headquarters," Kaz said, with a touch of pride in his voice.

"Really?" Luca looked like he had a hard time believing we worked for Uncle Ike.

"Yeah, really. Now tell us what you know about Bar Raffaele."

"How can I say no to the nephew of General Eisenhower himself? The bar is run by a pimp named Stefano Inzerillo. He took over a bombed-out building, cleaned it up, put in a rough bar, a few tables, and serves terrible wine at high prices, which soldiers are willing to pay."

"The women?"

"Inzerillo is smart. He does not employ them directly, and they do not use his premises for their services. He has kept out of trouble, and probably pays someone not to declare the place off-limits."

"But he did have trouble recently, according to the men in Lieutenant Landry's platoon. He made them pay for damages."

"I had not heard. Inzerillo has at least two men at the bar at all times to prevent fights."

"Bouncers?"

"If you mean men who will break an arm or a kneecap, then yes."

"Thugs," Kaz said.

"Yes, thugs," Luca said, nodding his head. "If anyone caused damages, they must have been damaged themselves. Inzerillo is not one to be caught unawares."

We drove on, passing a crumbling castle perched on a hilltop, surrounded by olive trees. Destroyed in another war, centuries ago, Luca informed us. It was nice to know we weren't responsible for every ruined building in sight.

"Billy," Kaz said from the backseat, "there's a jeep following us. It's been there since we left the palace, hanging back."

"I see it," I said, checking the rearview mirror. With the canvas top up, it was hard to tell who or how many were in it. "You sure it's following us?"

"Either that or they left for Acerra right after us."

"There is an AMGOT office in Acerra," Luca said. The American Military Government for Occupied Territories ran government functions in areas that had been liberated. "I've made the trip on several occasions with American officers in a jeep. Nothing unusual about it."

"Keep an eye on it anyway, Kaz." At that moment, two jeeps came around a curve and passed us in the opposite direction. A common enough sight, as Luca said. I drove on, past olive groves, the trees with their silvery leaves in straight rows, marred by the occasional shell hole and shattered, blackened trunks.

We followed Luca's directions into Acerra, winding through narrow streets, past a walled castle, complete with moat and drawbridge, where American and British flags flew next to the Italian banner. That had to be AMGOT. We entered a neighborhood of even narrower streets. Clothing hung from lines strung between buildings, adding odd traces of color to the dingy and shadowed roadway. Shops and homes were shuttered, and only a few civilians were on the street, eyeing us with indifference, suspicion, fear, or avarice, depending on their intentions. I was pretty sure that covered all the bases in this part of town.

We pulled over in front of a building with a gaily painted sign announcing this was Bar Raffaele. The sign was the nicest thing on the street. Empty wine bottles, cigarette butts, and other debris littered the sidewalk. The sour smell of spilled wine mingled with the tang of urine and rotting garbage.

"Welcome to Acerra," Luca said.

"Reminds me of certain parts of Boston," I said. "Scollay Square, right outside the Crawford House, for instance. Makes me a little homesick, almost."

"It makes me ill," Kaz said. He pounded on the locked door. "I hope it smells better inside." There was no answer.

"*Aprire, aprire!*" Luca thundered, hammering on the door with the butt of his pistol. "*Carabinieri!*"

I heard the creak of doors and shutters opening all around us, as people risked a look at the commotion. I turned around and they all shut, no one wanting to take a chance on being seen and dragged into an unknown situation.

"Carabinieri? *Italiano?*" came a voice from behind the door. It sounded fearful and weak, not what I was expecting.

"*Si, aprire ora,*" Luca said, and the door cracked open far enough for a bloodshot eyeball to peer out at us. It flickered at each of us, growing wide as it lit on me. Luca said something calming in Italian, and the guy finally undid the chain lock and opened the door.

He was holding a sawed-off shotgun. But that wasn't what surprised me. It was his face. Ugly purplish-red bruises covered it. His other eye was swollen shut, and he winced as he stepped back, the shotgun pointed to the floor.

"*Posare il fucile,*" Luca said, in a tone that I would have recognized in any language, coming from a cop. *Put the gun down.* He did. "*Che è successo a lei?*"

"Who is the *Americano?*"

"A friend. Now tell us, what happened to you?"

Inzerillo steadied himself with one hand on a chair, then eased himself down into it. Broken ribs. I could tell by the way he moved, and by the sharp intake of breath between clenched teeth. Two fingers were taped together on one hand, probably broken. His knuckles were about the only part of him that wasn't bruised, meaning that he hadn't even gotten a good punch in.

"You were beaten by someone who knew what they were doing," I said, walking around the table to look at Inzerillo from all angles. "Somebody who took his time, who wanted to inflict as much pain as possible, and still leave you conscious. He broke your fingers, cracked your ribs, worked on your face, but didn't hit you in the head. Or your mouth, so he wouldn't have pieces of your teeth in his fist. A connoisseur of pain, a man who enjoyed his work."

"I fell down the stairs," Inzerillo said in his thick accent. If he could have moved his face more, he would have sneered.

"A man who might come back," I said.

"When did you fall down these stairs?" Luca asked him as he holstered his pistol and then removed the shells from the shotgun.

"Last week, I don't remember. *Venerdì?*"

"Did anyone see you fall down the stairs last Friday?" Luca asked. Inzerillo shook his head. "Where were your men, your bodyguards?"

"Ask them, if you can find the bastards!"

"What was the argument about?" I asked.

"I told you, I fell down the stairs. Am I under arrest?" He sounded hopeful.

"No, Signor Inzerillo," Luca said with a sigh. "We have nothing to arrest you for. Clumsiness is not a crime. Gentlemen, do you have any other questions?"

"Talk to us off the record, Inzerillo," I said, pulling up a chair and sitting across from him. The stand-up interrogation was not going to work, so why not try the one-guy-to-another technique? "We know a GI did this to you. Just tell us what you know about him and we'll keep it quiet."

"I do not know you," Inzerillo said. "So I don't trust you."

"He is the nephew of General Eisenhower," Luca said. Inzerillo rolled his eyes. The eye I could see, I should say.

"Were these the damages Lieutenant Landry came back to pay for?" I said, gesturing at his face and hands.

"The lieutenant never paid me for anything."

"You knew Landry?"

"Sure. He has a favorite girl. Always trying to get her to quit, but she makes too much money. I think she breaks his heart."

"What about a doctor, Max Galante? Or an army priest, Father Dare?" The chaplain had said he never came here, but a pistol packing priest deserved a bit of distrust.

"We have a doctor who takes care of the girls, but his name is not Galante. And priests do not come here, thank God. What is Landry going to pay me for?" The wheels had started to turn in his beaten, larcenous head.

"One of Sergeant Flint's men broke up the place?"

"No. Only I have been broken."

"Falling down the stairs." He nodded, as if I'd finally figured it out. "You know Landry's sergeants? Gates, Flint, Stump, Walla?"

"Louie Walla from Walla Walla," Inzerillo said. "Louie likes to have fun. Sure I know them, I know many GIs. It is my job to help them relax, to enjoy *vino* and *amore*."

"What you sell here is not fit to be called either," Luca said. "Come, he is not worth our time."

"You sure you won't let us help you?" I asked, giving it one last try. He laughed, coughed, and winced again.

"Thank you for your cooperation, Signor Inzerillo," Kaz said. "It will be duly noted in our report."

"What do you mean, *Inglese?*"

"I am Polish, Signor, but I do wear the British uniform proudly. What I mean is that we will report to the Army Criminal Investigation Division, and to the Third Division headquarters, that you have fully cooperated and an arrest of the soldier who attacked you is imminent."

"Huh?" Inzerillo said, trying to follow Kaz. "*Imminente?*"

"Yes, imminente. You should probably give the Signor his shotgun shells back, Tenente. He may need them."

"No, you wouldn't. It is a death sentence, and I am an innocent man!"

"I doubt that," Kaz said. "Innocent men have nothing to hide."

"*La santa madre di dio,*" Inzerillo said softly. "Talk to Landry. He will tell you."

"You don't know?" Luca said.

"Know what?"

"He is dead. *Assassinato.*"

It was a rookie move to tell Inzerillo that Landry was dead. He hadn't picked up on the past tense when we'd mentioned his name; his English wasn't that good. Luca was more of a military man than a detective, so he didn't get that if Landry knew whatever Inzerillo was trying to keep covered up, and Landry had been killed, Inzerillo would see the same thing might happen to him. Kaz's ploy had been a good one, but after hearing Landry had been murdered, Inzerillo clammed up tight. There was nothing to be learned from him.

We left Inzerillo's neighborhood behind, gladly, and took Luca's suggestion to stop for lunch off the main piazza. The Trattoria La Lanternina was a different world. Clean sidewalks, delicious smells from the kitchen, tablecloths, and several Carabinieri at their midday meal. Any joint where bluecoats ate was okay by me. Luca stopped to chat with two officers and we grabbed a table.

"Friends of yours?" I asked when he joined us.

"Yes, we served together in the Fourteenth Carabinieri Battalion. I haven't seen them for months. Tell me, was this trip worthwhile?"

"It was," I said, before Kaz could say anything about Luca blowing our chances with Inzerillo. No point in showing him up. "We know that Landry knew something about what happened to Inzerillo, and was killed a day later. There might be a connection."

"But no connection to Doctor Galante," Kaz said. "He showed no recognition of that name."

"Still, it's interesting. And why did he deny that Flint and Landry went to see him? All the sergeants agreed that they had."

"Maybe Landry went to see that girl he liked. Maybe that's where the money went," Kaz said. "Perhaps Inzerillo was afraid to admit there had been a fight, in case he would be closed down."

"Could Landry and Flint have beaten him like that?" I wondered aloud. "Maybe he harmed the girl, and they took it out on him."

"Or your Lieutenant Landry was insanely jealous of this prostitute, and killed her," Luca said. "And then her family attacked Inzerillo and killed the lieutenant."

"You don't really believe that, do you?"

"No, but with no evidence, it makes as much sense as your conjectures."

"I'll talk to Flint and see what he says. I'll bet the girl fits in somewhere. Any chance of finding her?"

"A prostitute, yes. A specific prostitute, never. If anything did happen with Landry, she will have disappeared. If not, she would not allow herself to be found by the authorities for obvious reasons."

"Well, I don't know of anything else we have to go on. Luca, if you hear of anything else from Inzerillo, please let us know. Kaz and

I will check out the hospital and see what the staff has to say about Galante."

Luca ordered as the waiter delivered a decanter of wine. "Since we spoke last night of Queen Margherita, I thought you should taste the dish named after her. Pizza Margherita. It is said that she scandalized the court by eating pizza bread from street vendors when she visited Naples. It used to be sold plain, rolled and eaten by hand. The story goes that she noticed the poor eating it and ordered a guard to bring her one. She loved it, and the people of Naples appreciated her for noticing their native food. A chef created a pizza dish in her honor, using tomato sauce, mozzarella cheese, and basil leaves, to represent the colors of the Italian flag: red, white, and green."

"Quite a lady," I said. "Pearls and pizza." Kaz nearly choked on his wine.

The pizzas were good, thinner than I was used to from the North End, but tastier. The place was crowded, and I was glad to see normal life returning to this little part of Italy.

"What was it like in Yugoslavia?" Kaz asked Luca as we relaxed after the food.

"Garrison duty, mostly boring. A few times we went out with the army to hunt for partisans. We never found them, which was frustrating, since they could always find us when they wanted to. We lost men on guard duty, throats slit. Terrible."

"Did you have a hard time with the Germans, when the king declared the armistice?"

"No. There were no *Tedeschi* in our area. The Carabinieri stayed loyal to the king. Other units did as their commanders told them. Some even joined the partisans to fight the Germans. It was a difficult time."

That was that. I got the impression Luca didn't want to talk about it, and I wondered if he had friends or family who had gone over to Mussolini's puppet state in the north.

"Boring, frustrating, difficult," I said. "You add terrifying and you pretty much sum it up for all of us, Luca."

No one disagreed.

CHAPTER SIXTEEN

THE 32ND STATION Hospital was buzzing. It was a complex of buildings that might have been Italian Army barracks from a couple of wars ago. Outside of the headquarters building, a line of ambulance trucks, their sides painted with huge red crosses, pulled into the central square. Doctors, nurses, and orderlies spilled out of half a dozen buildings, unloading stretchers and directing the wounded to different wards. The patients were all bandaged and wearing army-issue pajamas; these weren't fresh casualties, but transfers from evacuation and field hospitals closer to the line.

At the same time, GIs were loading a pair of trucks parked next to the dispensary, as a nurse with a clipboard checked the inventory while talking with a doctor. He wore a wrinkled white lab coat, a major's gold leaf, and a neatly trimmed mustache. He looked like the guy we'd come to see.

"Excuse me, Major Warren?"

"I'm a little busy, Lieutenant. See the adjutant if you're looking for a buddy, or Ward 13 if you've got the clap." He spoke without looking at me, and went back to reviewing the inventory with the nurse. She wore the army-regulation white dress and blue cape, which looked snazzy, but wasn't very useful closer to the front lines, where nurses wore whatever army fatigues they could scrounge.

"It's about Captain Galante, sir."

"Listen, Lieutenant," he said, turning to face me. "I've talked to

CID and gave them a statement. I don't have time to go over that again, so check with them. Some sergeant was here, I forget his name."

"Sergeant Cole?"

"Yeah. Talk to him, I'm busy."

"He's dead, sir. He killed himself."

"Jesus! Was that the guy who shot himself on the palace roof?"

"Yes sir. I just need a few minutes of your time."

"Perhaps I can assist with the supplies, while the doctor speaks with my friend?" Kaz said to the nurse. She was pretty, but I knew Kaz was going to interrogate her while I talked to the doctor. Major Warren agreed, and led me to his office. The sign above the door read Chief of Medical Services.

"Sorry if I barked at you, Lieutenant, but I've been up to my eyeballs in work today, starting before dawn." He fell into the chair behind his desk and I sat across from him, waiting as he lit up a Lucky. His desk was stacked with patient charts, an overflowing inbox, and an empty outbox. "Accident on the road from Naples. A truckload of replacements—ASTP kids—goes over an embankment. Broken bones, lacerations, the usual for a road accident. Poor bastards hadn't been off the boat for a full day yet, and they're all banged up already."

"I hear there's a lot of replacements coming in," I said, trying not to think of my brother Danny and worrying if he was headed for trouble.

"Indeed. Some of us have been told to get ready to move out. There's a big push going on somewhere, that's for sure. Now, what can I do for you?"

"I need to ask some questions about Doctor Galante that Sergeant Cole may not have asked. Did he frequent prostitutes?"

"Galante? That's a good one, Lieutenant. He probably never even thought about it. I never heard him speak about much of anything except medicine and Italian culture."

"You're sure? This won't be part of any official report, in case you're worried about his family finding out."

"I'm sure. Have you talked to the doctors he roomed with? Wilson and Bradshaw?"

"Yes, they didn't really know him well. Ships passing in the night. Galante was transferred from Third Division. You know anything about that?"

"Just what I heard. He got into a dispute with a colonel and got booted upstairs. He wasn't happy about it, I can tell you that."

"You all must work hard, but this place does look pretty comfortable."

"It is. Long hours every day of the week, but clean sheets and decent food every night. A far cry from battalion aid stations near the front lines. The Luftwaffe bombed us once, but that's as close as we've come to real danger here."

"What was it that Galante didn't like?"

"He wanted to work on combat fatigue cases. Exclusively. He was almost a bore on the subject." He looked at me shrewdly. "You probably know that's what the beef with the colonel was about. Sending him here was a real punishment. We don't treat psychiatric disorders. We have dentists, physical therapists, surgeons, even a dietician, but no psychiatrists."

"So what happens to combat fatigue cases?" I sensed that there had been no love lost between Warren and Galante, especially on this topic.

"We don't often get casualties direct from the front. Like the boys who just came in, they've already been patched up and sent here for further treatment. They have to be actually wounded to be sent here." He crushed his cigarette out.

"What's your opinion on combat fatigue?"

"Not sure. I'm a surgeon. If I can't cut it out or sew it up, I'm at a loss. I know some cases are sent back to headquarters to do menial work. Seems sort of pathetic."

"I agree. I've seen the waiters in the senior officer's mess."

"But Galante's theory seems weird too. A hot meal, change of clothes, a good night's sleep, and then *wham*, back to the front."

"Isn't that what you do? Patch them up so they can go back as soon as they're able?"

"That's what Galante said. I guess the difference is some of the brass don't mind GIs in a hospital bed if they have holes in them, but they don't like the idea of able-bodied men getting a rest from combat."

"Able-bodied, yes. But what about their minds? Their spirits?" I thought about Jim Cole. No surgeon could ever cut out the memory of that basement, remove the guilt, and patch it all up.

"Like I said, I cut, I stitch. And I do a damn good job of it, as well as running this place. I've seen the inside of men's bodies, I've operated on the brain more times than I like to recall. But I never saw evidence of a spirit in there. Sorry. I wish I had." I wasn't so sure he was. Anyone who looked for the soul between bits of bone and blood didn't know what they were looking for.

"Did Galante have professional differences with another doctor over this? Anything more than a medical disagreement?"

"Far as I know, his serious disagreements were all with the brass at Third Division. We may debate medicine here, Lieutenant, but we're usually too exhausted to do much about an opposing opinion. But there is someone you should talk to. Doctor Stuart Cassidy. He's in Radiology, but he's the closest thing we have to a shrink. He interned with a psych department in Chicago, I think. He and Galante were friendly, as far as that went with the late doctor." Major Warren made a call, and told me to hustle out to the trucks that were being loaded. Cassidy was one of the doctors being transferred to parts unknown.

I found Cassidy sitting on the tailgate of a truck, leaning against his duffel bag. He looked young for a doctor, with wavy blond hair and an easy smile. Behind him the truck was loaded with medical supplies, stretchers, blankets, cots, and rations.

"Taking a trip, Doctor Cassidy?"

"I am, Lieutenant. Naples harbor is all I heard. You know anything about what's happening?"

"Not a clue," I said, introducing myself and giving Cassidy the short version of the investigation. Like everyone else within twenty miles, he knew about the murders and the suicide. "Anything you can tell me about Max Galante would be helpful."

"Max was brilliant," he said, without hesitation. "Too brilliant, maybe, for his own good."

"What do you mean?"

"I happen to agree with his ideas about combat fatigue. Other units are using the same approach, and it's working well. But Max was so sure of himself that he didn't suffer fools gladly. Sometimes he forgot he was in the army and didn't hold his tongue. It's a problem with us doctors. We think we're gods, but the army has other gods who outrank us."

"Like Colonel Schleck, Third Division."

"Right. Him and his assistant, Major Arnold. Max made a big stink about how they were incompetent Neanderthals for not taking combat fatigue seriously, as a disease. If he'd been more diplomatic, he'd probably be alive today."

"You're not saying there's a connection?" Did Cassidy know more than he was letting on?

"Not—I just mean he would have been with his unit, and wouldn't have run into whoever killed him. Is there a connection?"

"Not that I can see. If every guy who ran afoul of incompetent Neanderthals got killed, there wouldn't be anyone left to fight this war." Cassidy gave a knowing laugh. "Anything going on in Galante's personal life that might have gotten him in trouble?"

"Can't see it," Cassidy said. "He spent time reading medical journals, when he could get them. Visited museums when they weren't bombed out. He liked his landlady, said she was helping him improve his Italian. He couldn't wait to get to Rome, poor guy. His family hailed from there, went way back to Roman times, according to him. Other than that, I can't think of a thing."

"Did he ever mention Sergeant Cole?"

"Sure. He got him transferred to CID after that incident in Campozillone. He was worried about him."

"Any guys from his old outfit come to see him here?"

"Yeah, Landry, the other guy who got killed. He and Galante got on well. I know Max went to their bivouac at least once. Cole dropped by a couple of times after he started at the palace." That was the first link I had between the two victims, not to mention Cole.

"Do you think Cole was unbalanced? Did Galante think he should have been hospitalized?" I wanted to know more about Galante and Cole, and anyone else he knew in Landry's platoon. Like the killer, maybe.

"No. Not in the way you mean. We call it Old Sergeant's Syndrome. Unofficially, of course."

"What's that, some sort of combat fatigue?"

"It's more than that. According to current thinking, combat fatigue can be dealt with by rest and a short period of relative safety. But for those men who have fought and endured for long periods of time, there finally comes a point at which they become fatalistic. They're usually sergeants, because simply by surviving for months in battle, they've been promoted. In most cases, they are the only man left of their original squad, if not platoon."

"So hot chow and a cot won't do it for them?"

"Nope. You can send them back on the line, but they'll just tell you they know their number is up. They become ineffective as leaders, see themselves as dead men. They've reached the breaking point, and if placed in danger, they simply can't function. And remember, these are men who, by virtue of their survival, have won citations and been praised for their bravery. Like Sergeant Cole. The incident in that village just hurried along what was about to happen. The wonder is not that he succumbed to it, but that he endured so long."

"What's the treatment?" I asked, starting to think about Cole, and what strings Galante had pulled to watch over him, or what regulations he'd broken. Who else knew about that?

"Well, that's the good news. All that's needed is to remove these men from immediate danger, and to give them something useful to do. They still want to serve, so any position off the line makes them feel useful. Once the threat of death in combat is removed, they become healthy again, especially if they have a job to do. CID was perfect for Cole."

"But you said Galante was worried about him." Or maybe he was worried about what Cole knew. Was there a reason Cole ended up in CID, working in the palace, where he'd have a chance to search for pearls?

"Yeah. What happened in that village produced a burden of guilt that was unusually strong. It must have weighed on him more than we thought."

"Well, it could have been something else entirely," I said, wondering again about the pearls and what part they played in this. The truck engine turned over, and Cassidy jumped down, hoisted the tailgate, and we shook hands.

"Good luck, Lieutenant. I hope you catch the guy. Gotta run."

"Keep your helmet on and your head down, Captain." I liked Cassidy, and hoped he wasn't headed into dangerous territory. Sometimes keeping your head down just wasn't enough.

I watched the trucks leave, with Cassidy and another doctor as passengers and enough gear and supplies for more casualties than I wanted to think about. Replacements, doctors, Naples harbor, leaves cancelled. It was obvious that a force was shipping out, but for where? They could be headed to England for all I knew. Or maybe southern France. Or Rome, who knew? Was that why Diana had to get back so quickly? No, don't let it be Rome, I prayed silently. I don't want her in the midst of a battle. And don't let Danny be one of the nameless replacements either. I decided I should find a church and send up some prayers before it was too late.

"Billy," Kaz said, strolling out of a nearby ward. "What is wrong? You look lost."

"Just thinking. About Diana, and my kid brother Danny." I told Kaz about the ASTP program being curtailed, and how some had been among the replacements flowing in. I told him about the accident, and that I wanted to be sure Danny wasn't among the injured.

"Come, I will ask Edie to check," he said.

"Edie?" I said as I followed him.

"First Lieutenant Edie Embler, of Long Island, New York. She is an operating-room nurse, and is heartbroken over the departure of Doctor Cassidy. But I will console her, if we ever solve this case."

"Will you now?" I was glad to hear it, but I didn't want to act like it was a big deal, so I needled him a bit. He ignored me.

"Edie," he said when he found her. "Could you put my friend's mind at ease, and check the names of the young men from the truck accident? He is worried his brother could be among them. Humor him, please."

"Sure, Piotr. What's the name?" Edie had a faint trace of freckles across her nose, and curly black hair pulled back and stuffed under her white cap.

"Danny Boyle," I said, as she grabbed a mimeographed sheet from a pile on her desk.

"Boyle," she said, tracing her finger down the list. "No, not a Boyle among them. Feel better?"

"Yes," I said, but I didn't. I couldn't shake the feeling of dread that hung over me. Was it Diana I was worried about? Danny? I felt connected to both, and certain that one of them was in danger.

"Edie," Kaz said, "tell Billy what you said about Captain Galante."

"He had an argument," she said. That got my attention. "The day before he was killed."

"With who?"

"I don't know his name. He was an infantry lieutenant, I could tell."

"How could you tell?"

"You just can. The way they carry themselves. It sounds funny, but I just know. He wasn't pretending at anything. And he wore the Third Division patch, the blue and white stripes. Probably a platoon leader."

"What were they arguing about?"

"I don't know, but the lieutenant wanted help with someone, or something, I don't know. I wasn't really paying attention. Captain Galante finally agreed to help him, and then he left in a big hurry."

"Help him how?"

"He just said, 'Okay, okay, I'll do it.' That was it."

"Thanks, Edie. And thanks for checking the list."

"No problem. You two boys come back if you need anything."

I said we would, but I knew she meant Kaz. I think she was already consoled.

"That was interesting," I said to Kaz as we drove up the main road to the palace. "Had to be Landry. Who or what were they arguing about?"

"And did it have anything to do with who killed them?"

"Right. There has to be a connection there, to a person or persons unknown, or to someone we know. Inzerillo, Cole, who else?"

"Didn't Signora Salvalaggio say that Galante and Father Dare discussed Louie Walla?"

"From Walla Walla," I said automatically. "We should talk to Louie and the other sergeants. They held out before, protecting their pal Cole. Maybe they're protecting somebody else now."

"Landry? Perhaps he asked for help for his prostitute girlfriend. Perhaps she needed medical care."

"Hmm. That would explain the argument. Galante was a straight arrow. He probably drew the line at brothels."

"Or was drawn into one," Kaz said. "Do you think we should try to find her?"

"It would eliminate a whole lot of questions if we did, either way."

"Without Luca, perhaps we could persuade Inzerillo to tell us where she is," Kaz said. His voice was harsh, and I knew he meant business. Kaz had been a gentle soul when I first met him, but now there were times when his intent was as grim as the scar on his face.

I remembered my first meeting with the sergeants of the Third Platoon, and the discussion about carrying captured souvenirs. Neither side liked finding evidence of how their comrades' bodies had been looted. In the same breath that they condemned the Germans for mistreating captured GIs with German sidearms, they'd all but admitted doing the same.

Mistreating prisoners, or shooting them? I didn't know, but I knew that in most units there was always one guy you didn't detail to escort prisoners to the rear, if you wanted them to survive the journey. Hard men, I had thought at the time. Damned hard men, I thought as I turned the wheel and drove in the direction of Acerra, determined to get to the bottom of something in this cursed investigation.

CHAPTER SEVENTEEN

WE SMELLED THE smoke from the center of town, and I had a bad feeling. Another bad feeling, on top of all the others. Black smoke churned above the rooftops ahead, and if I didn't know where I was going, I could have used it as a beacon. Vehicles clogged the road near Bar Raffaele, and we left the jeep to walk the last hundred yards. A long flatbed truck marked *Vigili del Fuoco* stood in front of Bar Raffaele, two hoses attached to a large cylindrical tank pumping water onto the building.

The bar wasn't the only thing burning. A U.S. Army truck in front of the main entrance was engulfed in flames, its burning tires producing most of the black cloud we'd seen from a distance. More smoke billowed out from the two windows, both partially blocked by the truck, which had been pulled up against the door, blocking the exit. Firemen tried to get near the windows but were driven back, gasping and coughing. We followed two of them down an alleyway, to the rear of the building that housed the bar. Empty bottles and rotting garbage were piled against the wall beneath a pair of windows, iron bars set into the masonry, probably to discourage thieves. One wooden door was set low, down a short flight of steps. A torrent of flame gushed up from the door, and I could make out a jerrycan at the base of the steps.

"Truck up against the front door, and a can of gas ignited at the back door," Kaz said.

"He must have seen us," I said, realizing I could scratch Jim Cole off my list of suspects.

"Who?"

"The killer. He saw us here and decided not to take a chance on Inzerillo staying quiet. But he knows Inzerillo's guard is up, that he's barricaded himself in there. So he uses it against him."

"Cunning," Kaz said as we stepped out of the back alley and went around the front. There, the flames had died down amid the swirls of acrid black smoke, and the fire truck pulled out to circle around the block. Kaz spotted a Carabiniere talking to onlookers and approached him as I tried to get a look inside. The wreck of the truck was too hot to get close to, and all I could make out was a gray haze inside the building. No telltale smell of burned flesh, but no sound of movement, no cries for help. The heat or the smoke must have gotten him. In his weakened condition, he couldn't have moved fast enough to escape.

"He says witnesses saw the truck pull up alongside the entrance, but paid little attention," Kaz told me. "Two of them saw an American soldier take something from the truck and walk around back. It was common knowledge that Inzerillo dealt in the black market, so it was not seen as unusual."

"Could they indentify the GI?"

"No. He wore a helmet and had his collar turned up. They can't say if he was an officer or enlisted man. Both claim not to have seen the fire start, front or back. The Italian officer says they are scared to talk, that if a tough bastard like Inzerillo could be killed, no one is safe."

"I think that was part of the message."

"It worked. These people look genuinely frightened. Should we check the truck?"

"No, it's probably stolen. He used the spare gas can for out back, then probably lit a rag stuffed into the fuel line. Hoofed it back to his vehicle, and was gone before the local fire brigade got here."

"There's only one piece of good news in all this," Kaz said. "He hasn't played the queen of hearts yet. Perhaps the cards were a feint, to distract us."

"Or maybe he had loose ends to tie up before he moved onto bigger and better things. Let's get back," I said. I didn't think much of Inzerillo, but I didn't like him added to the list of victims either. He was a loose end, and now no one would have to worry about him unraveling. I should have seen this coming. I should have seen Cole's death coming, for that matter. I don't know what I could have done about either, but that didn't stop me from feeling responsible.

As we turned to leave, the Carabiniere whom Kaz had spoken to called him over and I watched as they talked, the conversation growing heated at the end.

"What was that about?" I asked as we walked back to the jeep.

"He asked if we had a vehicle to tow the truck away. He thought we were from the AMGOT headquarters in town. When I said we were not, he began to ask what our interest was with Inzerillo. I told him it was part of an investigation that Lieutenant Luca Amatori was involved in. He didn't like that answer."

"He probably didn't like being kept in the dark, especially since the investigation involved an Italian civilian. Can't blame him."

"No, it wasn't that. It was the mention of Luca's name. He called him a Fascist, and a friend to the Nazis."

"Strange," I said as I started up the jeep. "The Carabinieri aren't known for Fascist tendencies. And Luca didn't come across as a Nazi sympathizer."

"Would you, after the king deposed Mussolini and the government went over to the Allies?"

It was a good question, and I gave it some thought as we drove back to Caserta, even though I couldn't see how it had a damn thing to do with our card-dealing killer and the murder of Inzerillo. But I did wonder what Luca had done to deserve the contempt of a fellow officer, to generate so intense a disdain that it would be brought up to a stranger, an outsider. Maybe it was nothing, some guy with a beef, spreading rumors about Luca. I didn't want to know. I had problems of my own.

* * *

WE DROVE TO the 3rd Division bivouac area. I wanted to see who had been where this afternoon. But the going was slow, the roads crammed with long convoys of trucks, all headed east, toward Naples and its big harbor. Huge GMC deuce-and-a-half trucks, some pulling artillery, most crammed with GIs huddled together on the open bench seats. Ambulances, flatbeds with Sherman tanks, and jeeps overflowing with soldiers and gear, some so top-heavy I was surprised they made it around the next bend. It was a constant flow of men, so many that it seemed we must have emptied out entire towns and schools to get all these soldiers, all these anonymous clean-faced boys, their hands clenched around the barrels of their M1s, heads bowed low against the wind, as if they were murmuring their nighttime prayers.

There was little traffic in the opposite direction, but we were held up at every intersection. As we came to the outskirts of Caserta, a flight of P-40 fighters flew over, heading for a landing at the Marcinese airfield. One plane trailed the others, smoke rhythmically sputtering behind it.

"Do you think he'll make it?" Kaz said, following the P-40's progress.

"He's close, he should," I said, and glanced upward. The puffs of smoke stopped and the aircraft hung in the air for a moment, then began a lazy twirl straight down, as if a giant hand had swatted it out of the sky. There was no evidence of a pilot trying to regain control, nothing but dead weight descending to a stony field where it blossomed into a fireball, a final violent eruption of flame and smoke marking the spot.

We drove on.

An hour later we pulled into San Felice, home of the 3rd Division headquarters. I wanted to quiz Colonel Schleck and Major Arnold about their disagreement with Max Galante over combat fatigue. From what Doctor Cassidy told me, it had been more personal than professional. Maybe they'd also tell me how much longer the division was going to be around. I had a feeling it wouldn't be for long.

The bombed-out school that served as headquarters had its own fleet of trucks parked outside, tailgates down and GIs loading them up with boxes and crates of whatever it was you needed to run a division HQ. Typewriters, carbon paper, and Scotch were high on the list.

We parked the jeep and worked our way inside amidst the heavy lifting.

"You back again? Boyle, wasn't it?" Colonel Schleck growled, heading out in full battle gear. Grenades hung from his web belt, Thompson submachine gun at the ready, helmet on. You might have thought the Germans were right outside the door.

"Still is, sir. I wanted to talk to you and Major Arnold if I could."

"You can't. We're pulling out, and Arnold is AWOL. If you see the bastard, shoot him. My clerk is still in the office upstairs. Talk to him if you need anything. You find that killer yet?"

"No sir. The whole division pulling out?"

"Headquarters is staging to Naples, that's all I can say." And that was all he did say. He got in a waiting jeep, signaled with his hand like a cowboy at a cattle drive, and a small convoy of trucks followed him.

"Interesting fellow," Kaz said as we headed to the G1 office. "I'm not surprised he doesn't believe in combat fatigue. He looks like he's enjoying the war."

"Some guys do. They get rank and privileges they never had in civilian life, and if they're just behind the front lines, in a headquarters outfit, they wear combat gear and get their picture taken to show the folks back home. I'll bet a lot of them will get into politics after the war."

"I fear for your nation," Kaz said, as we entered the office. Boxed files were stacked everywhere, and a corporal with his sleeves rolled up was pulling sheets from a typewriter, separating the carbon paper from the duplicates, as he looked up.

"Sorry, Lieutenant. No more replacements, we're all sold out."

"I don't want replacements—"

"Well, if you don't like the ones you got, sorry, can't do anything about that either. Those ASTP kids are wet behind the ears, but we gotta take what we can get."

"No, no, listen. I need to talk to Major Arnold. Colonel Schleck said he was AWOL?"

"Lieutenant, you got a complaint about the guys in your platoon, lodge it with me. It's better than bothering the officers. What's the beef?"

"No beef, Corporal. It's a murder investigation."

"This war's murder. You mean the guy with the cards? Thought that kinda died down, so to speak." He laughed at his own joke.

"Corporal," Kaz said, in a low and even voice. "Tell us where Major Arnold is or the killer may start working the deck in the other direction. An eight of hearts would do quite nicely for you."

"I've heard guys say they'd kill for my job, but no one ever threatened me outright," he said, and again laughed at his little joke. We didn't. "Okay, okay. This morning we got the last truckload of replacements in, right off the boat, twenty ASTP kids to farm out. The colonel was eager to leave, so he told Major Arnold to handle it. He tells me to pull the list of platoons still short on guys. Problem is, there's been trouble in some squads. The ASTP guys hang together, the noncoms resent them since they come out of college and the officer program, you know how it is. It ain't easy keeping everyone happy."

"Does this story lead to Major Arnold anytime soon?"

"Yeah. So the major wants to place these kids one per squad, figuring they'll fit in better if they have to buddy up with a non-ASTP guy. See?"

"Sure," I said, not really caring about the psychology of replacement handling.

"So he takes my lists, and has the driver take him to the bivouac area, and doles out the kids, one per squad, where they're needed most. Takes him an hour or so, then he comes back here. Tells me he's going to his tent to square away his gear, and I ain't seen him since."

"Why did Schleck say he was AWOL? He told me I could shoot him if I found him."

"The colonel sent for him, sent runners everywhere. To his quarters, back to the bivouac area, but nobody could find him. Colonel Schleck is a man of little patience."

"Did he have much patience for Max Galante?"

"At first, he tolerated him 'cause he was a good doctor and he worked right up front. But when he started pestering the colonel about nervous exhaustion or whatever, that did it. Colonel Schleck does not believe in it, therefore it doesn't exist, so Galante got his walking papers."

"What was Major Arnold's opinion of Galante?"

"His opinion was that his immediate superior is correct in all things. Makes it easier to get through the day around here. Which reminds me, I got to get everything packed and shipped to Naples. Anything else I can do for you?"

"Where is Major Arnold?" I asked, one hand on his shoulder in a fatherly gesture, the other hand on the butt of my .45 automatic.

"Honest, I don't know, Lieutenant. He should have been back long ago."

"Is there something about the major you're not telling us?" Kaz asked. "Some place he might go? A woman, perhaps?"

"No, he wouldn't disappear for a dame. The only thing I can think of is that he's a real souvenir hound. He's always trading with the dogfaces. Nazi knives, pistols, flags, all that junk. He's a teetotaler, so he has his officer's liquor ration to swap with. The boys love that."

"So he's off hunting souvenirs?"

"No need to, the guys come to him. But he might be packing them up and shipping them home. Check the field post office. It's a busy place, he might have gotten held up."

"You didn't mention this possibility to Colonel Schleck?"

"The major and I get along. I'm no snitch."

"Okay, just tell me this. Who might get a pass today to go into Acerra? Or have business there?"

"All passes were cancelled last night, and I don't know of any official reason for anyone under the rank of general to go to Acerra. That's AMGOT territory. We got guys going to Caserta all the time, but that's usually for headquarters errands. No one minds a quick stop once business is taken care of, since it's so close, but for Acerra you'd need a pass, and there ain't none."

The corporal gave us a description of Major Arnold and we headed to the field post office, looking for a short, wiry officer with curly brown hair and parcels tucked under each arm. He wasn't there, and no one remembered him coming in. We decided to check his tent, and if we didn't find him there we'd move on. Where to, exactly, I wasn't sure.

Officers' tents were pitched in a field behind headquarters. It was high ground, free of mud, a good deal for guys who didn't rate a real roof over their heads. There were four rows, each marked with the occupant's names and a wood-slat walkway.

I opened the flap and called the major's name, but no one was home. He kept the place neat, his cot made, books and papers stacked on a small folding table. His gear was all there. Footlocker, carbine, field pack. The insert tray from the footlocker was on the cot, shirts precisely folded. In one corner sat two wooden boxes, a hammer and nails and a roll of twine perched on top of them.

"Souvenirs?" Kaz asked, testing one of the lids. It came up, and revealed Nazi daggers, belt buckles, a black SS officer's cap, iron crosses, and other medals.

"Check the other," I said, studying the rest of the area. There had to be some clue as to where Arnold was. It looked like he had stepped out in the midst of packing and never returned.

"It says fragile," Kaz said. Arnold had marked the contents as china. Kaz opened it, and there were four plates, wrapped in newspaper. Beneath them was a Nazi flag, the black swastika on a field of blood red. "What's this?" He unfolded the flag and a Walther P38 pistol fell out.

"Major Arnold could get himself in trouble. It's against regulations to mail weapons home."

"There are two magazines as well," Kaz said. "But at least the pistol isn't loaded."

"He was probably banking on the post office being too busy to ask questions, with everyone pulling out. I don't even know how much attention they pay anyway. I heard a story about a sergeant shipping a jeep home, one part at a time."

"Impressive," Kaz said. "Should we look further for the major, or is this a dead end?"

A dead end. A missing major. I looked again at the footlocker, and pushed it with my boot. It was heavy, and I had that real bad feeling again. I'd been sidetracked by the fire, and hadn't thought about the next victim since then. There was a padlock in the latch.

"Why is this locked, if he hadn't finished packing?" The tray, its compartments filled with shirts, sat on the cot.

"Perhaps he has his valuables inside?" Kaz sounded hopeful, but it was that false hope, the hope you feel when you go for an inside straight. Brief, insubstantial, useless. I took the dagger from Arnold's souvenir box and began working the latch. The footlocker was plywood, not built to withstand a steel blade. I dug around the top latch, loosening the screws until I could pull the latch free. I hoped that all I'd end up with was a chewing out from a superior officer for destroying his footlocker, but that was inside-straight thinking. I lifted the top, and the only card I saw was the queen of hearts, stuck between the dead fingers of Major Matthew Arnold.

He was short, which was a good thing. He was on his side, knees to his chest, hands up to his face, as if at prayer. The card stuck out from between two fingers, the red heart at odds with the pale face of the dead major.

"Strangled," I said. "Strangled and stuffed in a box. Why?" His neck was bruised and the blood vessels in his eyes had burst.

"It had to be a major," Kaz said. "The odds were it would be one from the Third Division, since the first two victims had been."

"No, I mean why stuffed in a box? The killer didn't hide either of the first two bodies. Galante was tucked against a wall, but he was in plain sight. Why hide the third victim? It's not the same pattern."

"To delay his being discovered?"

"Has to be. In order to give the killer time to get away. Which means he was seen by someone, and he needed to put time between that and the discovery of the body."

"We should go back to division headquarters," Kaz said. "Report and contact CID."

"Not yet," I said, shutting the footlocker. "Let's go."

"It's more important that we find out where the GIs in Landry's platoon have been today," I said as I gunned the jeep down the muddy road to the bivouac area. "It all started with him and it has to go back to him. Galante, Cole, Inzerillo, they all connect to Landry and his men. If we reported the body now, we'd be tied up for hours with CID and filling out reports. We'll go back as soon as we talk to Sergeant Gates and get an accounting of where his men have been."

"I suppose Major Arnold is in no hurry," Kaz said. Traffic was light, and I was glad we hadn't stumbled straight into the entire Third Division pulling out. I turned into the churned-up, muddy field and drove to the same small rise I had before, claiming what dry ground I could. Before us was the bivouac, rows of olive-drab tents of all sizes, with vehicles loading and unloading supplies around the perimeter, just as before. But there was something different.

"Those are British trucks," I said. The men unloading them were British. Not a Yank in sight. As we drew closer, I noticed a pile of white-painted signs at the end of each row of tents. Signs for units of the 3rd Division, no longer needed.

"Has the Third Division pulled out?" I asked a British sergeant leading a work detail of Italian civilians. Brooms, shovels, garbage cans, wheelbarrows. I guess more than ten thousand GIs can leave a fair-sized mess.

"Whoever the Yanks were, they've gone," he said. "Got to clean up for our lot to move in tomorrow. Can I help you, Lieutenant?"

"No," I said. "I doubt it."

I walked along the perimeter until I saw the signpost, lying on the muddy ground. 2nd Battalion, Easy Company. Soon I found the tent where the poker game had been in session. Third Platoon territory. Everything was cleared out, nothing but folded cots and the debris of a departing unit. Empty wine bottles, mostly. Crumpled paper, odds and ends that men had accumulated when in camp but tossed out as unnecessary when they were on the move, back to the sharp end.

Garbage cans had been placed along the wooden walkway, but not enough to handle the last-minute discards. The one in front of the poker tent was overflowing with bottles, broken crates, and other indefinable rubbish. On top was a single tan leather glove, holes worn through the fingertips, the kind the wire crews had been wearing when I first came here.

"This is what he wore," I said to Kaz. "Leather gloves. A new pair would give enough protection."

"You mean whoever beat Inzerillo?"

"Yeah. I wanted to check the knuckles to see who'd been using their fists. But leather work gloves would do the trick." I tossed the glove back on the pile, and wondered if that new pair, complete with bloodstains, might be at the bottom of the can. It would prove the connection I was certain of, so I tipped the can over, glad that the British sergeant and his work crew weren't in sight.

I moved stuff around with my boot, but didn't see another glove, bloodstained or not. Out of the corner of my eye, I did catch something red poking out of the mess. It looked familiar, as if I ought to know what it was.

"What is it, Billy?" As soon as Kaz spoke, I knew exactly what it was. A rag doll in a red dress.

CHAPTER EIGHTEEN

I WATCHED AS CID agents searched Arnold's tent, knowing they'd come up empty. I had. The rag doll was in my jacket pocket, and I was keeping quiet about it for now. Without Gates and the others to confirm it was the same doll from the girl in the basement, it didn't mean much as evidence. Even then, it was only my word that Cole had said he'd seen the doll, in his dreams and while awake. I had thought he meant he saw it in his mind's eye, but now I knew different. Someone had kept that rag doll from Campozillone, someone who wanted to spook Cole, to terrify him, to push him over the edge. Or was it to control him, keep him dependent?

He was my friend, Cole had said. *I see it in his face, see everything all over again.*

A friend, a buddy from 3rd Platoon, who kept the memory fresh, the wound open. Manipulating Cole, keeping him under control. For the pearls? Were they wound up in the killings, or was it something less sinister? Looting went on all the time; maybe this was just a higher class of loot. Who wouldn't scoop up a pearl necklace found hidden behind a wall or in a drawer with a false bottom? It was like the house on Mattapan Square. Original owner long gone, no questions would be asked. But had Cole stumbled on it, or had someone told him where to look? What difference would it make? Maybe a life-and-death difference. I tried to make sense of what I knew for certain.

Cole and Inzerillo, dead. No evidence they knew each other. One a suicide, the other beaten up and then burned. His death could have been a Mafia hit for all I knew.

Landry, Galante, Arnold, dead. Ten, jack, queen. All killed up close, the same calling card left on their corpses. They all knew each other to some extent. Arnold must have processed Cole's transfer at Galante's request; I doubted Colonel Schleck would have approved it.

The rag doll bothered me. Or was I reading too much into it? Maybe Cole just couldn't take it anymore. Maybe seeing his pal, whoever it was, was too much of a reminder. Maybe the pain was too much to bear. Maybe Inzerillo antagonized a mafioso, or didn't pay a debt. First a warning, then the torch. Maybe Cole found the pearls on his own, by accident, and had no idea of the story behind them. Maybe. But the rag doll was real, in a place where it shouldn't have been.

If all those maybes held water, then I had less to go on than I thought. Three dead officers, with the king and ace waiting to be dealt. A colonel and a general. Did the killer have them picked out already? Or was it simply a target of opportunity? If the killer was in the 3rd Division, it made sense that he'd have more contact with 3rd Division officers than anyone else.

If, maybe. I didn't have much to go on. The only good news was that colonels were not as easy to come by as more junior officers.

Arnold's body was carried out on a stretcher. Luckily rigor mortis wasn't fully established yet, probably due to the warmth in the closed footlocker.

"We have to find out where Third Division is headed," I said to Kaz as the stretcher passed us. They loaded it into an ambulance, which drove off at a sedate pace, no sirens, no rush for the late Major Arnold.

"No one knows, or admits to knowing," Kaz said. "I found several officers packing their gear, and they all claim ignorance."

"It shouldn't be hard to find an entire division. The front line is about thirty miles north. If we follow the main road, we should catch their tail soon."

"But Colonel Schleck said they were staging to Naples. That's due south."

"That might mean the coast road north from Naples, or the harbor. They could be shipping out to England for all we know."

"We should report to Major Kearns," Kaz said. "He may be able to tell us."

"Not that we have much to report. I'm sure he's heard about Arnold by now. I'm sure every colonel and general at the palace has."

We made a stop in San Felice, figuring it might be worth it to search Arnold's office desk and files, unless his corporal had packed everything up and shipped out too. We were in luck. There was still a skeleton staff at 3rd Division headquarters, the corporal included. Most of his crates and boxes were gone, but he was still on duty, clacking away on his typewriter.

"You've heard about Major Arnold?" I said.

"Yeah, word travels fast. You really find him in a trunk?"

"We did. In his tent. Did he mention meeting anyone there?"

"Nope. But if it was souvenir trading, he wouldn't have. He made it clear he preferred things on the QT."

"We found two boxes of souvenirs, ready to be shipped home. Including a Walther P38."

"Jeez. You ain't supposed to send Kraut pistols to the States, are you? Where is it now?"

"It's evidence, sorry."

"What a waste. The major, I mean."

"Yeah. It's important that we find out where the division is going. Do you know, or can you find out?"

"You think the Red Heart Killer is one of us? That's what they're calling him, I heard."

"Yeah, catchy. I asked you a question."

"Sure. I mean, no, I can't. They got this thing locked down tight. If we were going back up on the line, we'd all be there by now. But they're staging everyone on a staggered schedule. Naples is all I know. Maybe we're going to be garrison troops, that'd be nice."

"I don't think that's in the cards," I said, disappointed that no one laughed. "Tell me, do you remember paperwork on Sergeant Jim Cole, transferring him to CID?"

"Sure I do. Doc Galante came in, waited until the colonel was gone, and spoke to Major Arnold. He knew Schleck would never go for it."

"But Major Arnold did?"

"Yeah, no problem. Routine stuff."

"We're going to search the major's desk, okay?"

"Be my guest," he said, pointing to the far corner. "I ain't packed it up yet."

I sat at Arnold's desk as Kaz wandered about the room, looking through paperwork stacked up on a table, ignoring the corporal's stares. There were half a dozen personnel files on top of the desk, all new second lieutenants who had just transferred in from stateside. They weren't suspects, and they were safe, at least from the card-dealing murderer. The Germans would probably get half of them within days, most of the rest within weeks. I put the files aside.

Mimeographed orders from the division chief of staff were stacked by date, the latest directing Arnold to await transport to Naples until the rest of the headquarters unit arrived there. All the others had to do with the mundane daily routine of any HQ. Boring, repetitive, useless.

I went through two drawers and found nothing of interest. Forms in file folders, lined up alphabetically. In a bottom drawer, under a copy of *Stars and Stripes*, was something more interesting: a Luftwaffe forage cap, filled with wristwatches, rings, and a few German pay books. *Soldbuch*, they called it. It contained a photograph of the soldier, his unit, rank, that sort of thing. I dumped the lot onto the desk.

"The major collected those books," the corporal said.

"And he had a nice sideline in watches too. Taken from the dead, stripped from POWs. Interesting guy." I flipped through one Soldbuch, looking at the photo of a young kid who could have been wearing any uniform. I didn't like looking at war souvenirs. It made me think of some fat Kraut pulling my wristwatch off.

"I'm not seeing anything here but evidence of a tidy mind and an acquisitive nature," I said.

"Billy," Kaz said. "You should look at this." He held a clipboard, one of six hung from nails on the wall.

"Those are replacement lists," the corporal said, "the latest batch. I ain't had time to file them away yet."

"What?" I asked Kaz. His finger pointed to a list of names, and traveled down three from the top. A column of serial numbers and names.

BOYLE, DANIEL P., PVT.

"What is your brother's middle name?" Kaz asked.

"Patrick," I said. I felt sick as I said it, and leaned on the table for support. "Daniel Patrick Boyle."

"Hey, you found a relative?" the corporal asked. "Lucky guy."

"Is this the ASTP group you were telling us about?" I pointed to the clipboard.

"Yeah. Those are the replacements Major Arnold brought out. Before he got it."

I'd been hoping for that inside straight to come along, and how did I finally manage to beat the odds? By having my kid brother show up and join a division about to end up in combat, if my guess was right. Replacements were flowing in to Caserta, filling the ranks after other replacements had been killed, wounded, or captured. I traced the line with his name on it to the right, past numbers that meant something to the army and nothing to me, until I came to his unit. Private Daniel P. Boyle had been assigned to the 3rd Division, 7th Regiment, 2nd Battalion, Easy Company, 3rd Platoon.

Right in the goddamn middle of not only the shooting war, but my investigation.

KAZ DROVE US back to Caserta. I was in a daze, unable to get my mind off Danny. The plan was to report to Major Kearns and find the 3rd Division. I was certain of two things: my kid brother was headed for trouble, and the Red Heart Killer was going to strike again.

Kearns was busy, so I waited outside his office while Kaz went to check on something he said was bothering him. A lot of things bothered me, so I didn't ask what it was. I watched messengers, aides, high-ranking officers, British airmen, and a couple of civilians scurry in and out of the Intelligence section, everyone in a hurry. I bet none of them gave a hoot about my kid brother and all the other green kid brothers heading up to the line. I was upset, and the more I watched them, the more I wanted to deck one of them, just to see how they liked it. But I held back, because of the two MPs on duty outside Kearns's door, and because while I knew it would be satisfying, it wouldn't help me find Danny.

"Boyle," Kearns said, appearing in the open doorway. "Get your gear and be back here in one hour. We're shipping out."

"We, sir? Where?"

"You'll drive with me to Naples. We're joining VI Corps staff."

"Third Division is part of VI Corps, isn't it?"

"Yes," Kearns said. "That's why you're coming with me. I've been transferred, and you need to find this killer. Something big is about to happen, Boyle, and we can't have one of our own gunning for the brass. One hour, you and Lieutenant Kazimierz."

"You've heard about Major Arnold then?"

"Me and every GI, Italian, and Brit within ten miles. The damn Krauts probably know by now."

"Where are we going?"

"That's top secret. You'll know when you get there. Now hustle, goddammit."

He was steamed, so I hustled out of sight. I waited for Kaz, who showed up twenty minutes later. I told him what Kearns had said and we beat feet to the jeep and made for Signora Salvalaggio's. We grabbed our gear and said our good-byes. The signora promised to cook la Genovese for Kaz when he returned, and gave him a curtsy that wouldn't have been out of place at the palace, a lifetime ago. She didn't ask about the pearls, and I was glad, because I had no idea what we were going to do with them.

"What were you doing, back at the headquarters?" I asked Kaz as we drove to meet up with Kearns.

"Asking around, about the Fourteenth Carabinieri, the unit our friend Lieutenant Luca Amatori served with. I was curious, after the reaction of the officer in Acerra."

"What did you find out?"

"The unit served primarily on the island of Rab, off the coast of Yugoslavia. As concentration camp guards."

PART THREE

Anzio Beachhead

CHAPTER NINETEEN

FOR THE HUNDREDTH time in this war, I sat in a jeep at a crossroads, watching a convoy of trucks crossing an intersection ahead of us. Worrying. Everyone was worried, about getting killed or wounded, about fear and what your buddies thought of you, about trench foot and the clap, about chickenshit officers and insane orders, about *Schu*-mines and what your girl back home would do when she heard you were alive but minus your private parts.

Everyone worried, everyone sat, everyone waited. But now I had a new worry. My kid brother. When Dad would get mad at Danny and me, he'd say that if he could put the two of us in a sack and shake it up good, he might end up with one son who was smart enough to stay out of trouble, and strong enough to get out of it when it came looking. Trouble was, Danny was a skinny kid, smart enough in class but just plain dumb anywhere between home and school. I was always stronger than most, but I used up all my smarts before I got to the schoolhouse door. We'd come home with our fair share of black eyes and pants torn at the knee, usually as a result of trouble Danny got into and I got him out of. Or in deeper, he claimed. I wondered if he had any idea how deep this trouble was.

I got tired of worrying and watched the scenery instead. On the left, a drainage ditch was filled with sluggish water, and beyond that a ruined farmhouse sat crumbling into the earth as weeds and vines worked their way through the masonry. On my side, an open field sloped gently away, down to a long green patch where water flowed, a real stream, not a ditch, maybe with frogs in the warm weather. Maybe fish. What did they fish for in Italian streams? I didn't know, but the memory of springtime at the grassy edge of a stream came back to me, and I wanted to run through that field, feel the sun on my neck, scoop up fresh cool water and splash my face.

A line of pine trees ran up to the road, forming a neat border to the side of the field. In the field itself withered brown plants and faded grasses hung on, and occasional rock outcroppings provided a shape and contour that gave the land its own definition. This was a place that people knew well, perhaps by name, a natural field where sheep could graze, kids could play, and lovers could go for a walk. I spotted a flat limestone rock that would be great for a picnic, and a tall one that would be perfect for shade in the summer.

I wanted it to be summer. I wanted to be in the field, exploring it with the intensity of a child, the barely remembered sense of discovery and awe that a new place, a new object, a new sensation could bring. I closed my eyes and saw Danny and me running through a field much like this one, racing for the stream, splashing in the water and laughing without quite knowing why, or caring. It seemed, in that moment, that the field encompassed everything good, life at its best. Nature, youth, innocence. This field, and all the ones in my memory, held life.

I opened my eyes. Above, a bird glided high across the sky, circling the field. A hawk. No, it was a falcon, a peregrine falcon. As he turned, the sun lit his blue-gray wings, a dead giveaway. A hunter on any continent. A flutter caught my eye, far beneath the soaring falcon, and I knew if I saw it, he saw it even more clearly. He tucked in his wings and dropped in a fast, steep dive, heading straight for a blackbird lazily making for the trees, about ten feet off the ground. The falcon hit the blackbird, hard, claws outstretched and wings wide, braking before the momentum brought them both to ground. A flash of dark feathers, and it was all over. The falcon carried his limp prey to the flat rock, set it down, and began to rip the bird apart. The falcon paused and gazed in my direction. Maybe he was worried we were a threat. Maybe he was telling me to get a grip, or reminding me that the field was death as well as life.

As the column moved through the intersection, I did not look back.

THE ROAD WAS ours the rest of the way, two hours straight to the Naples docks. The column snaked through the narrow streets leading to the waterfront. On each corner, Italians sold bottles of wine, fruit, and anything else GIs would fork over cash or cigarettes for.

"Major," I said, leaning forward as the driver weaved the jeep between crates of supplies and lines of American and British soldiers. "Can you tell us now where we're headed?"

"Not until we board ship. It's all top secret, not to be revealed until we are sequestered from the civilian population. We can't take a chance on Fascist spies getting word to the Germans."

"Okay," I said. Next to me, Kaz shrugged. We could wait. The traffic stalled, and we bought some oranges from a skinny young girl doling them out from a burlap sack. Following her was a short, pudgy guy with a thick black mustache, selling postcards. He held a stack in his grimy hands, fanning them out for all to see.

"Naples harbor, Anzio. Good-a luck, boys. Nice-a women in Anzio. Post-a cards, Anzio, Nettuno here." He kept up his singsong pitch. Army security, you gotta love it.

"Anzio. That's about a hundred miles north of the German lines, Major," I said.

"Yeah, well, I guess the cat's out of the bag already. We ship out in the morning, hit the beach the following day. Anzio and Nettuno are two seafront villages about a mile apart. The idea is to get behind the Germans and cut off their supplies from Rome. Something along those lines."

"Something?" Kaz said.

"We'll talk when we're on board," Kearns said. He seemed to be in a bad mood. Maybe it was finding out our target was common knowledge, or the vagueness of the battle plan, or the fear that a colonel and a general would get their necks snapped. None of these things made me happy either.

As we entered the harbor, MPs waved trucks to their unloading areas, and after a quick check of Major Kearns's orders, we were directed to the main wharf where Liberty ships and landing craft of all types were lined up, taking on men and the machinery of war.

"Here's our ship," Major Kearns said. "The USS *Biscayne*, command vessel for the invasion. You'll be traveling with the brass. General Lucas is on board."

"And a number of colonels and other generals, no doubt," Kaz said.

"Yep, so keep your eyes peeled and don't get in the way."

We followed him up the gangplank and a swabbie showed us where to stash our gear. Kaz and I had a cabin about the size of a janitor's closet with two double bunks. Plenty of room, as long as the four guys didn't all get out of their bunks at once.

Up on deck, we gazed out over the five-inch guns on the bow and watched the parade of troops boarding vessels all along the waterfront. LSTs had beached themselves beyond the wharf, their bow doors dropped onto flat rocks where GIs used to sunbathe and fishermen had dried their nets. Now, Sherman tanks backed in, their engines growling as they slowly made their way onboard. Shouts and curses drifted up from the ships as the traffic jammed up on the docks.

"What do you know about Anzio?" I asked Kaz.

"In ancient times it was called Antium. Both Nero and Caligula were born there. Actually, that is where Nero was when Rome burned and he famously played his lyre. He had a summer palace in Antium, and Rome is only forty miles away; the sky must have glowed with the flames. I hope we shall get to see the palace ruins."

"I bet there will be plenty of ruins. Just not all two thousand years old. What about Caligula? Wasn't he the crazy one?"

"A bloodthirsty killer, a megalomaniac, yes. But Nero was no prize either. He had his own mother killed for plotting against him."

"Both sons of Anzio," I said.

"Ironic that we are pursuing a killer, perhaps a madman, to that very place."

"Is he a madman? It seems he has a plan, of sorts. The playing cards, plus the murder of Inzerillo, pushing Cole to suicide. These aren't sudden or random. They're deliberate, linked in some way we can't yet understand."

"Billy, we don't know for certain that Inzerillo's killer is the same man."

"It's a good bet. His joint was frequented by the Third Platoon, Landry was mixed up with some girl there, and we have conflicting stories about damage done. Somebody's hiding something, and I think that has something to do with Inzerillo being silenced. What I don't see anywhere is a motive. For any of this."

"Caligula was a madman, but he managed to run an empire. Being insane doesn't mean one is out of control. It is another way of seeing the world."

"So our guy has his own set of rules?"

"Yes, rules that make sense to him. Perhaps he views us as out of step with reality."

"Being in the army, it would be hard to keep to your own rules, your personal sense of reality."

"It is difficult, maintaining individuality in such a large organization that demands obedience and discipline."

"Yeah, it's hard enough for guys like us," I said. I felt I had the thread of an idea, but didn't know how to put it into words. "But our Caligula, he'd have a real hard time of it, wouldn't he?"

"Are you getting at his motive?"

"Maybe. I've been trying to think of the usual motives. Greed, passion, revenge. But what if it's beyond that? Something we can't imagine, but that he desperately needs to cover up?"

"That would mean the victims all knew something. Something that got them killed."

"A lieutenant, a captain, a major, a pimp, and a sergeant. What did they have in common, and what did they know?"

"Perhaps we should be asking which colonel and which general have something in common with them," Kaz said.

"We're not going to get a senior officer to admit knowing a pimp. And Captain Galante wasn't really part of Landry's Third Platoon crowd."

"But Landry and Galante were connected. They knew each other from before Galante was transferred to the hospital at Caserta. Sergeant Cole was transferred to Caserta courtesy of Captain Galante."

"I can see some connection there," I said. "But I don't see how it all hangs together, and where it's going. I keep thinking we have to go back to the beginning, that there's something we got wrong from the start."

"Like what?" Kaz asked.

"Wish I knew, buddy, wish I knew." We stood in silence, feet up on the rail, watching the activity on the wharf. It was a nice day, maybe mid-fifties, a hazy sky and calm waters. A good day for watching a parade. A bad day for solving mysteries.

"Look," said Kaz, as he pointed to a column of blue uniforms advancing along the wharf. Carabinieri. About a hundred, maybe more, marching in good order, packs on their backs and rifles slung over their shoulders. They halted before the Liberty ship next to us and began to file aboard, their boots clanging against the metal gangplank. Lieutenant Luca Amatori brought up the rear, giving his boss, Captain Trevisi, a snappy salute before he followed his men up. It was hard to make out at that distance, but I got the impression Trevisi was as glad to stay on shore as Luca was to leave him there. At the top of the gangplank, Trevisi saluted again, and leaned on the deck, just as we were doing, watching the massive preparations.

"I didn't have a chance to ask you about Luca and the concentration camp," I said. "What did you find out?"

"I spoke to a friend on the staff of British Army Intelligence, a fellow Pole. He had a file on Lieutenant Amatori. Our friend Luca was posted to the island of Rab, in the Adriatic, off the coast of Yugoslavia. The Fourteenth Carabinieri Battalion was charged with guarding a concentration camp there, mainly for Yugoslav civilians suspected of partisan activities. Mostly Slovenes and Croatians, often entire families if they were thought to have helped the partisans."

"He did say something about partisan activities," I said, reluctant to change my opinion about the likable Luca.

"Yes, but the Italian and German anti-partisan sweeps were particularly brutal, and more than a thousand died of starvation in the camp itself. It held more than fifteen thousand prisoners, many housed only in tents, even in winter. Men, women, and children, including about three thousand Jews."

"What happened to them?"

"The story is not quite clear. There are references to complaints made to Rome by the commander of the Fourteenth Carabinieri Battalion, protesting the treatment of Yugoslavs. The Jews, all Yugoslavian, were treated much better than the partisan prisoners. Apparently the Jews, having not been part of the partisan movement, were viewed as being in protective custody."

"But in a concentration camp."

"Yes, the Fascist government did put them in the camps, in Italy as well as Yugoslavia. Some were worse than others, depending on the whim or politics of the commander. When Mussolini fell, the new government ordered the Jews released, but gave them the option of staying in the camps, in case they feared being rounded up by the Germans."

"That's a hell of a choice."

"Indeed. A few hundred joined the partisans to fight, others fled to partisan-held territory. But about two hundred were too old or sick to be moved. The Germans took over the camp and transported them to another camp in Poland. Auschwitz, I think it was."

"Auschwitz? Diana mentioned Auschwitz, and another camp in Poland, Belzec."

"The Germans seem to prefer Poland as their killing ground," Kaz said. "Belzec was the first camp set up, but Auschwitz has grown into a huge operation. I wrote a paper detailing what is known about it while I was in London with the Polish government-in-exile. Three main camps, over twenty-five satellite camps. Inmates are put to work on war industries, and often worked to death."

"It may be worse than that," I said. The warm sea breeze on my face felt odd, as if nothing of beauty or any pleasant sensation should intrude upon these words. I told Kaz everything Diana had told me, and watched his face harden with disbelief, horror, anger, and all the emotions I had gone through. It couldn't be true, that was the first response of any sane person.

"Oh my God," Kaz said. "Witold Pilecki."

"Who?"

"Captain Witold Pilecki, of the Polish Army. In 1940, he volunteered as part of a Polish resistance operation to be imprisoned in Auschwitz."

"That's one brave guy, or a fool."

"Many people thought the latter, especially after his reports were smuggled out. The underground delivered them to London. He talked about the mass killings, and requested arms and assistance to free the prisoners. His request was never granted. He was thought to be exaggerating, either deliberately or as a result of conditions in the camp. His report stated that two million people had been killed there, during a three-year period. He simply was written off since no one believed the numbers he was reporting."

"What happened to him?"

"He escaped, last April. I think he must be with the Home Army, the Polish underground."

"Three years in hell, and no one believes him."

"Does anyone believe Diana?"

"I do. But I don't think Kim Philby did. Or he didn't want to. Or couldn't."

I watched Luca Amatori on the deck of the Liberty ship next to us. He was enjoying the sun and the breeze, maybe feeling he was part of some grand plan, helping to liberate another piece of his homeland. Did he ever think about the two hundred sick and elderly Jews he left behind on Rab? Did they ever disturb his sleep? What else did he do, hunting partisans in the mountains of Yugoslavia, that might haunt him at night?

There was so much evil in this war. Maybe Luca was a good man, maybe not. Maybe he had been a good man once, before the shooting started. Before the hard choices. That's how evil made its way in this world. Not with a devil's face, as the nuns taught us. It slithered between the cracks, caught decent people off guard, dragged them along until they were in too far. Then it made them into something they never thought they could ever be.

Had our killer, our Caligula, once been innocent? Had evil snuck up on him, or was it an old friend? Death was everywhere. Soldiers and civilians, the grim and the meek, they were all drawn into this killing machine that sucked in souls from the front lines, the air, the water, from quiet homes far from the fighting. Why should some fool be allowed to feed the machine more than it demanded? That trumped evil in my book.

A column of GIs passed below us, and I saw Danny's face, glasses on his freckled nose under a helmet that looked way too large. I started to cry out, but it wasn't him. The kid didn't have his walk, and the set of his shoulders wasn't right. Somebody else's kid brother.

I covered my face with my hands and prayed. Prayed for Danny, for his innocence, even harder than I had prayed for his life. It seemed so precious.

When I looked up, Kaz was gone. Probably in search of better company. There was a flurry of salutes on the deck below, and I figured it had to be senior brass coming aboard. It was Major General John Lucas, commander of VI Corps and this whole damned invasion. He pulled himself up the steel stairs—ladders, I think the Navy insisted on calling them—huffing a bit as he made it to the upper deck. He turned and addressed the crowd on the lower deck, mostly correspondents and headquarters types. I saw Phil Einsmann waving and I waved back, but he was trying to ask the general a question, not flag down a drinking buddy. He got the general's attention and shouted above all the others.

"General Lucas, any comment on where we're headed?"

"It's top secret," Lucas said, and then waited a beat. "But no one told the street vendors, I hear, so I'll tell you what you already know. It's Anzio."

That got a laugh among the reporters, and a halfhearted cheer from the officers. General Lucas looked amused, like a banker at a Rotary Club luncheon who just told a joke. He had a stout banker's body and gray hair. He didn't look like much, but I'd heard he'd been a cavalry officer on Pershing's Punitive Expedition into Mexico, and then wounded in the Great War. There had to be some fire left in the man, but he was keeping it tamped down, as far as I could see.

"Are you headed for Rome once you're ashore?"

"Are you going to attack the Germans from the north?"

"What strength do you have?"

These and a dozen other questions were shouted out while Lucas signaled for quiet.

"Now that you're all on board and under armed guard," he said, to another round of polite laughter, "I can answer your questions. My orders are to secure a beachhead in the Anzio area and advance upon the Alban Hills. We expect the enemy to put up a stiff resistance and respond rapidly with reinforcements. Therefore, the primary mission of VI Corps is to seize and secure the beachhead. I have the British First Division, the U.S. Third Division, and other attached troops, including Rangers, paratroops, and British Commandos. We're going to give the Germans a surprise, I'll tell you that."

"What about after the beachhead?" Einsmann shouted. "Are you going to take the high ground?"

"The Alban Hills are nearly thirty miles from the beachhead. We're not going to rush into anything. We can't afford to stick our neck out and make a mad dash for the Alban Hills, or Rome, or anywhere else. Seize, secure, defend, and build up. That's what I aim to do. Thank you, gentlemen."

General Lucas ascended the ladder to the bridge deck, his corncob pipe stuck into a corner of his mouth. I wasn't exactly a fan of "Old Blood and Guts" George Patton, but it struck me that I'd rather have a general like him leading an invasion than this paunchy, grandfatherly figure.

"Billy, what are you doing here?" Phil Einsmann said, working his way to my corner of the deck. "I thought you'd still be in Caserta, tracking down the Red Heart Killer."

"Is that what you press boys are calling him?" I was sorry he'd been given such an interesting nickname. He didn't deserve it.

"It's catchy. I filed a story, but I doubt the censors will release it. Not good for morale back home. You didn't answer my question."

"Habit. I like reporters, I just don't like telling them anything."

"Hell, Billy, I already know about Major Arnold and how you found him stuffed in his own trunk. There hasn't been another killing since then, has there?"

"No. And I'm not taking this sea cruise for my health."

"So you think the killer is someone in the Third Division?"

"I didn't say that. Lots of other guys making this trip."

"Okay, okay. I'll tell you something, though. Lucas is not happy with his orders. He thinks he's being hung out to dry. He's got two-plus divisions and they're landing him on a flat plain with mountains almost thirty miles away. The orders from General Clark are pretty vague. Did you pick up on that? To 'advance upon the Alban Hills.' What does that mean—take them, or approach them?"

"Could be either."

"Exactly. If Lucas fails, Clark can blame him whichever way it goes, for not taking the hills or for advancing too rapidly. Lucas is between a rock and a hard place, without enough troops to do the job."

"Is that why you were asking him what his plans were?" "I was hoping to get him riled up, so he'd say something worth printing."

"I think it's been some time since he's been riled."

"That might be a damn good thing, Billy. A lack of rile could keep some of these boys alive."

"Where did you hear all this?"

"Not everybody clams up in front of reporters. It's easy to get stuff off the record. On the record and past the censors, that's another thing. So level with me, Billy, off the record. About the murders."

"I wish there was more to tell. Yeah, I think it's someone in the Third Division. Someone who knew the victims. Someone who had a reason to kill them. Did' you ever meet a guy named Stefano Inzerillo? He ran a dive called Bar Raffaele in Acerra." I didn't mind trading information with Einsmann, especially since he'd probably not get word one past the censors.

"You used the past tense, Billy. I take it he didn't sell his business and move?"

"He's moved on to another location. Did you know him?"

"I know the joint."

"Not a spot for high rollers; not like the officer's club at the palace. What were you doing there?"

"Billy, I took you for a man of the world. What do you think? It wasn't for the fine wine. How did Inzerillo get it?"

"Someone beat him up pretty bad, so he barricaded himself in his bar. Some guy, a GI most likely, set the place on fire."

"Jesus. Anzio could be a rest cure after all this."

"Did you ever see Lieutenant Landry there?"

"The first victim? I don't know, never met him. Couldn't tell you. I did see Sergeant Cole there once though."

"I thought you said you didn't know him."

"I knew who he was. I only said I hadn't spoken with him since he got transferred to CID. Father Dare told me he helped get Doc Galante to wrangle a transfer for him. Wait a minute—it would have been Major Arnold who did the paperwork on that. Was Cole's suicide part of this?"

"Off the record, I'd call it murder."

CHAPTER TWENTY

THERE HAD BEEN fireworks in the night, and I'd finally understood what "the rockets' red glare" meant. There were no bombs bursting in the air, but the shoreline took it on the chin. To the north, Anzio and Nettuno glowed a dull orange as smoke-wreathed fires spread. Kaz and I were on the beach, threading our way between craters, stacks of supplies, engineers spreading steel gratings over the sand for the heavy stuff to cross to the road, and noncoms yelling at GIs to move inland. We trudged up to the main road and watched as landing craft disgorged more and more men. After being crammed onboard ships for more than thirty hours with hundreds of men who had nothing better to do than play cards, sweat, puke, and pray, they looked excited, like kids on a trip to the shore. They laughed and gabbed, peppering their sergeants with insistent questions.

"Do you think I'll do all right?"

"Can I stick with you?"

"What will you do when we get to Rome?"

"No," a sergeant first class barked at them. "I think you'll piss your pants and run. And don't come near me if you can't keep your head and ass down, you'll just draw fire. You'll never make it as far as Rome, so don't worry about it. Now move your ASTP asses and prove me wrong!"

I watched the GIs following him, the smiles gone from their

faces. I hoped the army had actually taught these kids something about warfare when they went to college.

"Hey Billy!" Phil Einsmann ran up the beach, his only armament a small portable typewriter in a wooden case and his war correspondent's patch on his shoulder. "Where are you fellas headed?"

"We're waiting for a jeep. Looking for a lift?"

"I have no idea where to go, but I'd rather not walk there."

"Here's Major Kearns," Kaz said, as a jeep fought its way against the flow of traffic. I'd gone over my suspicions with Kearns about all the connections with the Third Platoon, Cole, the rag doll, the WP grenade, Inzerillo, and the last murder. I left out the part about my kid brother, and my worry that he might cross paths with Red Heart. He might think I was being overprotective. Maybe so. Maybe it was only coincidence, but it all felt wrong. Someone in the Third Platoon had answers. Father Dare was on my list as well. Einsmann, too, for that matter. He seemed to know more than he'd let on, and cropped up at the damnedest times.

"Boyle, Kaz," Kearns said as he got out of the jeep. Not for the first time, I noticed how people liked Kaz immediately, taking to his nickname, responding to his suave continental charm, not to mention the unstated allure of the mysterious scar down his cheek. A surefire combination. "The outfit you're looking for is headed to Le Ferriere. Father Dare went along with them, since they didn't have a medic."

"Isn't that unusual?" Kaz said. "For a chaplain to go on a combat patrol?"

"From what I've heard, he stays close to the front lines and does a lot of work with the wounded. He's picked up some basic medical knowledge, so he's useful, especially on patrol."

"He's not your average holy Joe," I said. "How do we find them?"

"Go back down this road and turn right just before Nettuno. The road signs are still up. Take the Via Cisterna." Kearns opened a map that showed the village about halfway between the coastline and the Alban Hills.

"What is their mission?" Kaz asked.

"To reconnoiter the village, see if any Germans are there. Le

Ferriere is a crossroads, just south of the canal. It'll be a key position if the Germans move in and put up a fight."

"You see any Germans yet, Major?" Einsmann asked.

"A few prisoners, a few corpses," Kearns said, eyeing Einsmann's correspondent's patch. "There was a small detachment in town, but no organized resistance. Might not be the same up the road. You might want to hang back."

"No organized resistance doesn't get the headlines, Major. I'll stick with these guys and stay out of the way."

"You do that. Boyle, get back to me tonight with a report. Corps HQ is a villa in the Piazza del Mercato in Nettuno. Can't miss it, just a couple of blocks in from the harbor."

"Yes sir," I said. "You need a lift back?"

"No, General Lucas is coming ashore, I'll go back with him. The general and a whole posse of colonels, so find this killer. Whatever you need, let me know. This is going to be hard enough without looking over our shoulder every ten seconds."

A snarling growl of engines rose from seaward, and we all turned to watch another formation of fighters head inland to hunt for German reinforcements. Four aircraft, flying low, turning in a graceful arc that would take them parallel to the beach, not across it.

"Take cover!" I wasn't the first to say it, but I yelled anyway. I grabbed Kaz and pulled him into a ditch with me, looking up at the planes, knowing I shouldn't. I couldn't help myself. It was one of those moments when everything happens fast but you see things with crystal-clear vision, small details blossoming out of a blur, deadly but hypnotic. Bright white lights twinkled from the nose. They looked oddly festive in that split second before the sound caught up and the chatter of cannon and machine-gun fire drove all thoughts but of survival from my mind. Geysers of water sprouted in the surf as the Messerschmitts went for the landing craft and the troops and vehicles piling out of them. They pulled up, split into two pairs, and sped away, ineffectual antiaircraft fire trailing them.

We stood up and dusted ourselves off as a gas tank exploded somewhere down the beach, leaving black smoke belching into the sea air. Yells, shrieks, and curses rose from the men on the beach, and I watched Major Kearns trot toward the landing craft, looking over his shoulder. He was going to have one helluva sore neck before this was over.

"Let's go," I said. Einsmann piled in back and Kaz navigated, holding the folded map in his lap as it flapped in the breeze. We drove through a cluster of pastel-colored buildings facing the water, the morning sun lighting them beautifully, giving even the blackened, smoldering hole in the roof of one of them a lazy, seaside quality.

"Where are all the people?" Einsmann asked as we slowed around a curve. "No one's here. You'd think by now the locals would be out to see all the excitement."

"Perhaps they are still hiding in the cellars," Kaz said.

"Maybe they're all die-hard Fascists," I said.

"Mussolini certainly was popular here," Kaz said. "He ordered the Pontine Marshes drained, and created farmland between the shore and the Alban Hills. His government built new towns and farmhouses, populating them with his supporters. I doubt many of the locals will be lining the streets cheering us on."

"That's good stuff," Einsmann said. "How do you know all this?"

"Kaz knows everything," I said, having found that to be true of most everything I needed to know. Ahead, I saw a cluster of GIs around a farmhouse, and pulled over as one waved me down. They were Rangers, and in the dusty courtyard between the house and the barn, the bodies of two German soldiers were laid out. One Ranger was going through their pockets, handing papers to an officer. The rest of them were gathered around six women, a couple of them young and very pretty, the others maybe their mothers and aunts. They were rubbing their wrists, strands of rope scattered on the ground at their feet.

"What's going on?" I asked. Two Rangers approached, surveying us with suspicious eyes. One American officer, one British officer, and one correspondent in his own ragtag version of a uniform. I didn't blame them for pointing their tommy guns in our general direction.

"We came up the road from Anzio, and found these two Krauts. First ones we saw," a corporal said, spitting out a stream of tobacco juice in their general direction. "Then we heard these ladies hollering inside the barn. From what we can make out, a German officer was bringing a detail this morning to execute them."

"What for?"

"Leaving a restricted area. Seems like anyone left in the coastal zone has to have papers to leave. They took a truck to Rome to buy food on the black market, and almost made it back. The Germans nabbed 'em and were going to shoot them in the morning, once they had an officer on hand."

"Good thing he was delayed. Kaz, ask them about Rome, and how many Germans are between here and there."

Kaz and Einsmann went over to the group, and were soon pulled into a swirl of kisses, embraces, and hands raised to heaven and back to ample breasts in thanks. It looked positively dangerous.

"We're looking for the road to Le Ferriere," I said to the corporal.

"Keep going, right around the bend," he said, pointing to a curve ahead. "Sign is still up. Looks like we caught the Krauts flat-footed. Be careful going up that road, though. By now they gotta have heavy stuff moving in."

"Or maybe that officer and a firing squad."

"Yeah, be nice to turn the tables on the bastards." He spit again, sending another splat of brown juice on the ground, as he looked at the women. "Looks like your Limey pal made out okay for himself."

Kaz returned to the jeep, a young girl on his arm, trailed by the other women, all talking at the same time, mostly to Einsmann.

"I told them he was a famous reporter, and would put their names in the newspaper for their relatives in America to see," Kaz said. "But Gina has something to tell us. *Di'al tenente quello che mi hai detto*," he said, patting her on the arm.

"*Ci sono pochissimi soldati tedeschi a Roma*," Gina said proudly, smiling at Kaz and taking his hand.

"Very few German soldiers in Rome," he translated. "Mostly military police."

"They must have come through the German lines," I said.

"*Hai visto i tedeschi fra qui e Roma?*" Kaz asked her.

She shook her head no and unleashed a torrent of Italian, gesturing toward the two dead Germans.

"None," he said. "They drove to Rome and back and were only caught when three Germans left their post on the beach and came to the farm to look for food. They caught them unloading the truck, and tied them up in the barn. They told them when their officer came in the morning they would be shot. Then one of them drove off in the truck and these unfortunates stayed to guard their prisoners. Gina says the Germans moved most people out of the area, and let only those who were needed to work or farm stay. The penalty for travel without a permit is death."

"Seems like the locals are friendlier than you expected," I said, noticing how Gina had linked her arm with Kaz's.

"Yes, it appears that hunger trumps politics," Kaz said. He tipped his service cap to the women, and kissed Gina on the cheek, which raised a howl among the older ladies, who pulled Gina into their midst. I pulled out chocolate bars from a pack in the jeep, handed them around, and all was forgiven.

"That was a story," Einsmann said, writing in his notebook as the jeep rumbled along. "U.S. Army Rangers rescue Italian beauties from Nazi execution. My editor will love it, the readers will lap it up, and most importantly the army censors will like it. Maybe I can get it out tonight from headquarters."

"If what Gina said was true, that's the big story," I said. "No Germans between here and Rome. I wonder if General Lucas knows."

"You can't go by a story a pretty girl spins for you," Einsmann said. "Not without corroboration. You really think the Germans are dumb enough to leave this whole area undefended?"

"There's times I don't think too highly of our own brass," I said, turning right at an intersection where a faded white road sign pointed to Le Ferriere. "Don't see any reason why they should be any smarter on the other side."

The road was straight and narrow, with low-lying fields on both sides. Kaz pointed out the occasional farmhouse, a two-story stone structure, in the middle of a plowed field. At each one, I expected a machine to open up on us, but there was nothing but silence. We passed a farmer turning his field, and he looked at us with indifference. We were uniforms, and uniforms are bad for farmers. They mean crops churned up by tank treads, houses occupied, food stolen, and that was without the fighting. If General Lucas didn't move quickly, every one of these stone buildings would become a battleground.

I sped up, feeling giddy at how alone we seemed, how strange it was to be driving into enemy territory as if on holiday. On the side of the road ahead, I spotted a vehicle on its side in the ditch. It was a German *Kübelwagen*, a cross between a jeep and a command car, recognizable by the spare tire mounted on the sloped front hood. Kaz had the Thompson submachine gun out before I could even slow down. I pulled over about ten yards short and cut the motor, listening for any sign of movement. Nothing. Kaz and I exchanged glances, nodded, and got out. I motioned for Einsmann to stay put and he was eager to, scrunching down in the backseat, hugging his typewriter to his chest as if it were armor.

Kaz and I each approached a side of the vehicle. The canvas top was down. Bullet holes dotted the windshield and the hood. The driver was half out of his seat, his neck hanging at an odd angle. Another German, probably thrown from the passenger's seat, was on the ground next to him. He'd taken a slug or two in the throat, and the ground drank in his blood. We both made a circuit of the Kübelwagen, looking for evidence of another German. The two dead were enlisted men. Was this the detail heading to execute the women? If so, where was their officer?

Kaz stepped up on the mounded earth beside the drainage ditch that ran along the road. "Billy, come here," he said.

I followed, and saw two more bodies. One was a German officer. I could tell by his shiny boots and the gray-green visor cap lying in the mud. He was on his back, his neck arched up and his mouth wide open. His chest rose and fell with a wheezing sound, his eyes gazing at the sky overhead, as if searching for the way to heaven. One hand gripped a tuft of grass, desperately hanging onto this world. His boot heels had dug into the earth, leaving gouges where he'd flailed, as if running away from death. He had two bullet holes in his gut, powder burns prominent around each one. He'd been left to die slowly, and not that long ago.

"Hey, Fritz," I said, leaning over him. I didn't exactly feel sorry for him, since he probably was on his way to execute those women, but leaving him here to suffer didn't sit right either. His eyes widened, perhaps in fear.

"*Er hat den Amerikaner getötet,*" the Kraut said, grabbing me with his free hand. "*Er hat gemacht!*" A thin pink bubble of blood appeared around his lips, and then burst as he gave a last gasp and died.

"What did he say?" I asked Kaz, as I unclenched his fingers from my sleeve.

"He killed the American. He did it."

"The Kraut? He was confessing?"

"No, those were his exact words. Someone else killed the American. Do you know him?"

I knew the American. He was immediately recognizable by his red hair and tall, lanky frame. Rusty Gates, platoon sergeant. He was laid out neatly, feet together, hands on his chest. A ground sheet covered his body, but the hair was unmistakable. I pulled the cover back and knew for certain. One dog tag was gone. One bullet hole to the heart, powder burns and all.

"Rusty," Einsmann said in a gasp, scaring the hell out of me. I hadn't heard him come up on us, and I swung my arm around, .45 automatic at the ready. "Jesus, don't shoot!" He threw his hands in front of his face.

"Yeah. Sergeant Rusty Gates, Third Platoon. You knew him?"

"Sure. Had a few drinks with him now and then. Met him back in Sicily. He was a solid guy. Think that Kraut officer got the drop on him?"

"Looks like it," I said, drawing the ground sheet back over him. Rusty had seemed like a solid guy. A leader. I'd felt good about Danny being in his platoon, but now, with former supply officer Lieutenant Evans in charge, I wasn't so sure.

"Maybe they shot each other," Einsmann said.

"Not likely," I said. "Probably the Kraut surprised Rusty as he came over the ditch. Dropped him with one shot, then somebody else shot the officer." But as I said it, I saw that things didn't add up. Rusty must have been shot at close range, three or four feet at the most, to leave gunpowder burns. He would have seen the German before he got that close. I looked at the dead officer again. His entry wounds were next to each other, straight on, at the same level you'd hold an M1 at the hip. Just above the belt buckle. *Bang bang*, you're dead, but not right away. "The Kraut must have shot Rusty at close range, then someone else killed him for it."

"Which makes sense," Kaz said. "If the German offered to surrender and instead pulled out his pistol and shot the sergeant."

"Yeah, if it happened that way. Strange, that's all. The guy makes it out of his vehicle after it's ambushed. He didn't run, didn't get more than a dozen yards away. Then he throws his life away to kill one American." I looked at his face. He wasn't young. Maybe thirty-five, forty. He wore a wedding ring. Regular army, not SS. A fanatic, never-surrender Nazi? Maybe. Maybe not.

"He was gut-shot," I said. "Sure to kill him, but not right away. He suffered."

"For his sins, most likely," Kaz said.

I wasn't so sure. We'd heard the story of the Italian women who were to be shot, but I doubted Gates and his men had. Why leave him alive, in pain like that? Who killed the American? Another Kraut? A GI?

"His pistol is gone," Einsmann said. That was obvious. No GI could resist a souvenir, especially with so few Germans around. We went back to the vehicle and searched it, but that had already been done. Two Schmeisser submachine guns had been smashed, and the pockets of the dead searched. We got back in the jeep and started out again, more slowly this time, as I tried to work out in my mind what had happened back there, and what Danny might have seen or done. I didn't like anything I came up with.

A mile or so later, a signpost let us know we were in, then out, of the village of Cossira. It was hard to tell the difference. We came to a fork in the road, and Kaz traced the route we'd taken with his finger, looking around for a landmark or a sign. Drainage ditches, flat fields, and distant hills were all we saw. "This way," he said, pointing to the right fork.

"It's got to be a left," Einsmann said, leaning over Kaz's shoulder, tapping his finger on the map. "We want to be more north."

I looked at the map, and then up at the sun, as if that might give me a clue. "We'll go left," I said. "We can always turn around if it looks wrong."

CHAPTER TWENTY-ONE

"THE SIGN SAYS Carano to the left," I said. "That's right where it should be."

"Sounds right to me," Einsmann said, turning the map around several times, viewing it from every possible angle. The jeep was idling at an intersection. Left was Carano, straight was Velletri, which I knew was up in the Alban Hills. To the right was nothing but emptiness, plowed fields, and damp gullies.

"We should turn around," Kaz said in an exasperated tone. "I said so back at the last turn."

"This feels right," I said, gunning the jeep and taking a hard left. I hoped it was. The road narrowed and became a hard-packed dirt surface. We came to a fork in the road, one weathered sign pointing left to Carano. We went right, on my theory that keeping Carano to our left was the wisest course. It *was* left of Le Ferriere on the map, so logic was on my side. Kaz didn't say a word, satisfying himself with switching off the safety on the Thompson. We drove farther and found another fork in the road. This time, the sign to Carano pointed back the way we'd come. Gianottola was to the left. I couldn't find it on the map, so I went right, for no particular reason, the road curving around a slight rise.

"We should turn around," Kaz said.

"Not yet," I said, unwilling to admit what I was beginning to suspect. That we were lost.

"No, I mean look behind us."

I pulled over and we craned our necks around. The view was stupendous. With all the twists and turns, I hadn't noticed we were slowly climbing. In the distance, the sea shimmered with sunlight. The flat plain of the drained Pontine Marshes was laid out before us, straight roads and canals dividing the ground, stone farmhouses dotting the landscape.

"Okay, we're lost," I said.

"How far have we driven?" Einsmann asked.

"Twenty miles or so, but not in a straight line."

"We haven't seen a single German," Kaz said. "I'm curious as to where they are."

"I'm not so curious I want to find any of them," I said. "Should we go back?"

"I think we should go on," Einsmann said. "Until we hit a main road or town, so we know where we are. Then you can bring back some intelligence."

"And you get an exclusive story, as the intrepid reporter behind the German lines."

"Billy, I don't think we're behind the German lines," Einsmann said. "I'd bet there's no Germans between us and Rome. This could be the biggest story of the war, an invasion that achieves total surprise. Hell, it is a big story, no doubt about it."

"He's right, Billy," Kaz said. "If I can make any sense of this map, we should come to Highway 7 soon."

"The road to Rome, through the Alban Hills?"

"Yes. From the height here, I'd say we are already in the Alban Hills."

"Okay, I'm in," I said, studying the map Kaz was holding. "Velletri, that's on Highway 7, and there was a signpost back a while ago." I waited for one of them to talk me out of it, but Einsmann had an eager grin and Kaz simply nodded, folding the map and cradling the tommy gun like a Chicago gangster. I turned at the intersection headed for Velletri, high up in the Alban Hills, armed with one automatic pistol, a Thompson, and a typewriter.

We saw Velletri, a cluster of buildings on top of a hill, and found a side road to get around it. I didn't want to get caught in a narrow roadway without a clear way out. We found a sign with the number seven, and in a few minutes were on a well-maintained double-lane road. Highway 7, the road to Rome. We were headed due west now, the wooded slopes of the Alban Hills above us and the view to the sea below. We passed small villages, seeing the occasional farm vehicle make its way slowly along the road. No one waved, or seemed to take notice. Perhaps they thought we were Germans and were deliberately ignoring us. Or maybe they knew we were heading into an ambush and couldn't bear to look.

There was no ambush, not at Montecanino, Fontanaccio, or Frattocchie. No traffic either, now that we'd left farm country. The miles were easy, as if we were out for a Sunday drive. I couldn't help but think about Diana, how tantalizingly close I was getting to her. Nothing but the German army somewhere between us.

"This is the old Appian Way," Kaz said. "It was the most important road of the Roman Republic. There are places where the original paving stones can be seen."

"Isn't that the road where the Romans crucified Spartacus?" I asked.

"Yes, and thousands of the slaves who revolted along with him," Kaz answered. "I didn't know you were acquainted with Roman history."

"I have a good memory for when the little guy takes it on the chin. Happens often enough."

"Thousands?" Einsmann said.

"Six thousand, if I remember correctly," Kaz said. "Look, Billy, pull over there." He pointed to a circular stone ruin, close to the road. "It is the tomb of Cecilia Mettela."

"Kaz, the history stuff is interesting, but we can't stop for a tour."

"What is noteworthy about this tomb is that it was built on the highest ground south of Rome. It is on a hill, and I've read that it provides a good view of the city."

I pulled over. The place was huge, a wide tower about thirty feet tall atop a rectangular base of stonework twenty feet high. I saw the possibilities, and grabbed the binoculars. We climbed the stairs and reached the top. One side of the circular wall was crumbling, pieces of stone scattered on the ground below. But the walkway was sturdy enough, and I saw that Kaz had been right. The tomb was on a hill, and from this height, I could see all around us, south to the Alban Hills, and north to Rome. Where Diana was.

I looked through the binoculars, steadying myself against the wall. I could make out buildings, but I wasn't sure what I was looking at. Then, beyond the sea of roofs, I spotted a white dome. St. Peter's, that had to be it. On a hill across the Tiber River. The Vatican, a tiny piece of neutral ground, and most likely home to Diana. I could be there in an hour.

"Vehicle coming down the road," Kaz said. I spotted a U.S. Army jeep, heading out of Rome. "It appears that we are not the first Allied tourists to visit the Eternal City."

"Two of them in the jeep," I said. "Let's flag them down."

We descended and stood in the street, each of us waving one hand and keeping the other on our weapon. The jeep slowed and stopped in front of us, and I could see that the lieutenant in the passenger's seat had his carbine at the ready.

"Who the hell are you?" He looked at us warily, and I realized that we did look like an unlikely unit: one Brit, one Yank, and one war correspondent.

"Lieutenant William Boyle," I answered. "Did you just come from Rome?"

"Damn near. Lieutenant John Cummings, 36th Engineers," he said as he extended his hand. Everybody relaxed as it became apparent we were all on the same side. "What are you doing out here?"

"We got lost, and then decided to keep on going once we saw how close we were. Haven't seen a German between Anzio and here."

"There aren't any. We got close enough to see a few military vehicles crossing a bridge over the Tiber, but it wasn't much. A few trucks and staff cars."

"We should get this news back to HQ," I said, disappointed to hear that he had run across Germans. It would have been a swell surprise for Diana to see me show up for Mass at St. Peter's.

"I was ordered to reconnoiter towards Rome this morning, and we just kept going once we realized no one was in front of us. The Italians didn't even pay us any mind. I don't think word of the invasion has gotten up here. It's a total damn surprise. We've got to get back to report. Want to follow us?"

"That would be excellent," Kaz said. "Otherwise we might get lost and end up in Berlin."

We ate their dust all the way back to the beachhead. Einsmann commented on how quick the return trip was, compared to our back-road journey out. Kaz grinned, but kept his thoughts to himself as he swiveled in his seat, watching for phantom Krauts. It was hard to believe we had all this ground to ourselves.

We pulled into Corps HQ in Nettuno an hour later, parking the jeep in the courtyard of the seaside villa that VI Corps called home. The Piazza del Mercato was a pleasant little square with sycamore trees and a statue of Neptune dead center. Tattered posters of Mussolini fluttered in the breeze from the wall of a bank. A few civilians scuttled by, avoiding eye contact and getting clear of Americans as quickly as they could. I'd been in towns in Sicily and southern Italy where the locals cheered and threw flowers. Here, there was nothing but sullenness and the faded glory of Il Duce looking down at us.

We hadn't found the 3rd Platoon, but I figured we'd come up roses anyway. General Lucas himself would probably give up a colonel or two to find out there were no Germans between here and Rome. Einsmann left to type up his story and get it to the censor before he lost his exclusive. Cummings said he had to submit a report through his regiment, so he left to get it written up so it could work its way through the chain of command. It seemed like a slow process.

"Let's find Major Kearns," I said. "He can get us to Lucas right away."

We entered through heavy wood doors into a spacious home,

with tall windows facing the Mediterranean. It was perched up on a hillside, with a view to the north of Anzio and to the south toward crystal-blue water. The polished wood floors were already scuffed and scraped by countless boots as GIs brought in desks, files, radio gear, and all the other hardware a headquarters can't do without, cases of Scotch included. The place was crawling with brass, and I thought we were about to be thrown out when I saw Kearns, heading down a staircase with General Lucas. The general gripped a corncob pipe in his mouth and held a cane in one hand. I had the uncomfortable thought that I was looking at a man not cut out for this work.

"Lieutenant Boyle," Kearns said, taking notice of me. He explained to Lucas that I was the officer in charge of the Red Heart investigation. "Have you anything to report?"

"Not on the investigation. But we got lost trying to find Le Ferriere, and we ended up right outside of Rome."

"Rome?" Lucas said. "You must really have been lost, Lieutenant. You couldn't have gotten anywhere near Rome."

"We were there, sir," Kaz said. "At the tomb of Cecilia Mettela, on the Appian Way. Highway 7."

"It's true, General. We didn't see a single live German the whole way. From the top of the tomb I could see the dome of St. Peter's."

"Impossible," Lucas said. "We're digging in for a counterattack right now. The old Hun is getting ready to have a go at me. It's a miracle you got back in one piece."

"General," Kearns said, choosing his words carefully. "We haven't seen much activity on our front. Maybe you have achieved total surprise."

"I'm not going to endanger my command because two young lieutenants got lost and managed to drive around the German defenses. I'm glad you fellows had a good ride, but it's hardly what I'd call credible intelligence. Now get some food, and then go out and find that killer. That's your job, not reconnaissance."

"General, we met up with Lieutenant Cummings, 36th Engineers, and drove back with him. He went farther than we did, and he's writing up his report right now. Reconnaissance was his assignment."

"Fine. Then G-2 will evaluate and report to me. Keep up the good work, boys."

And with that, he turned his back on us, leaving a trail of tobacco smoke in his wake. Kearns followed him, and we were alone with the view. A light breeze stirred the curtains, a rich shade of burgundy. The color of blood.

CHAPTER TWENTY-TWO

AFTER OUR ROMAN adventure, we decided to wait until the morning to try for Le Ferriere again. The sun was about to set, and I didn't want a repeat performance with the added bonus of being fired on by our own guys in the dark. So we drew gear and bedrolls from the beachhead supply depot, found a deserted house, and got ourselves a good night's sleep. At first light, we were drinking scalding hot coffee and eating powdered eggs, thanks to the cooks who'd set up their feeding operation overnight. Say whatever you want to say about army food, but when you've got no other choices and the chow is hot, it's a miracle of American ingenuity.

We followed a supply truck headed in our direction, and this time found Le Ferriere. It wasn't much of a place. The ground sloped up slightly from the farmland all around it, and a small church, a factory building, and a few scattered homes made up the whole town. No civilians were in sight, but a battalion headquarters was set up in the factory, and they showed us the Third Platoon position, set up on the right flank, on the low ground a couple of hundred yards out.

We left the jeep and walked, not wanting to draw any attention in case the Germans had gotten observers up in the hills. As we walked over plowed earth already tamped down into a path by GI boots, I grew nervous about seeing Danny. I was worried about him being at the front, but it was the possibility that he was in the same unit as a murderer that really troubled me.

Just as driving a jeep and sending up a cloud of dust could fore-warn the Germans and point out our position, my questioning anyone in this platoon could give away too much of a warning. It hit me that this visit was a lousy idea; if the killer thought we were onto him, he might take it out on Danny.

"Kaz," I said as we neared the position. "We're not here to question anyone. It's just a visit, for me to see Danny. Follow my lead, okay?"

"You're the boss."

I scanned the group of men ahead, most of them busy with entrenching tools. I saw Stump and Flint first, and gave them a wave.

"Hey, kid!" Flint yelled, beckoning to a figure knee-deep in a trench. "You got a visitor."

It was a face I'd recognize anywhere, even wearing a helmet that looked twice the size of his head, steel-rimmed army-issue spectacles, and holding a shovel instead of a book.

"Billy!" Danny ran up to me and looked like he was going to jump into my arms. Then he skidded to a halt, a confused look on his face. He started to raise his right hand in salute, but Flint grabbed him by the wrist.

"Remember what Rusty told you, kid? No salutes up here. Unless you want to point out an officer to a Kraut sniper."

"Sorry, Sarge. I just got confused. It's been so long since I saw my big brother, I forgot he was an officer."

"Let's keep him a live one, Danny boy. No salutes."

"Got it, Sarge," Danny said as Flint grinned and left us to our reunion. "Jeez, Billy, it's good to see you."

"Same here, Danny." I gave him a quick hug, nothing that would embarrass him, followed by a manly clap on the shoulder. "You doing okay?"

"Sure. Don't worry about me. I really lucked out, this platoon is a swell bunch of guys. They told me they'd met you back in Caserta, investigating some officers getting bumped off. What are you doing here?"

"General Lucas couldn't get by without me, so he dragged me along. I heard you were out here, so I decided to pay a social call." I introduced Kaz around, giving his full title and lineage to impress Danny.

"So you're Kaz," he said. "Billy wrote us all about you. I never thought I'd get a chance to meet you in person. What are the odds, huh?"

"Indeed," Kaz said. "A long shot, yes?" Kaz gave me a look and drifted off, chatting with Flint and Stump.

"Danny," I said, draping my arm over his shoulder. "I can't believe you're here. I just heard about the ASTP program being broken up a few days ago."

"It all happened pretty fast," he said. "Mom wasn't too happy about it."

"What about Dad and Uncle Dan?"

"They wanted to cook something up like they did for you, but Mom told them to leave it alone, since it didn't keep you out of trouble. She said I should take my chances, that maybe I'd end up a clerk since I was a college kid. So here I am, in a rifle squad, which is what I wanted in the first place."

"Listen, Danny. You've got to get your head out of the clouds before it gets shot off. This is for real. Keep your head down out here. It's not just a saying. Stay low. And don't panic."

"I won't," he said, moving out from under my grip. "I haven't yet, have I?"

"Okay, simmer down. Just some advice, don't blow a gasket."

"Sorry, big brother. I know you're trying to look out for me, but I'm not ten years old. I've been to college and I've made it through basic training, all without your help."

"This isn't the time to play grown-up, Danny. When the Krauts hit you, it's going to be with a ton of bricks, and they won't care how smart you are. They'll only care about killing you."

"What Krauts?" Danny gestured to the empty fields all around us. It was smart-alecky, the way only a kid brother can be. Half right and totally wrong.

"If you're so smart, tell me the last time in this war when the Germans retreated without a fight? It didn't happen in North

Africa, Sicily, or anywhere else in Italy. It won't happen here. They're going to come down out of those hills with heavy stuff, dollars to doughnuts."

"Now you're the one blowing a gasket, Billy," Danny said, with a grin to show he didn't want to argue anymore. Which he often did when he started to lose an argument, but I let that pass. He was only a kid, after all. "I'll take any tips you can give me on digging foxholes. Take a look at this." He'd been digging a trench, and about two feet down, it was filled with water. "Did you know this used to be the Pontine Marshes, Billy? The water table is only a couple of feet deep."

"Yeah, Mussolini drained them after he made the trains run on time. Kaz told me all about it. Now I have two geniuses on my hands."

"How's them trenches coming along, kid?" Louie ambled over, cigar clenched in his mouth and Thompson at the ready.

"Louie Walla," I said. "Now where is it you're from? Can't recall."

"Funny, Lieutenant," Louie said. "Having a family reunion?" Louie seemed more serious out here. Wary.

"Yeah, came by to check on Danny. He in your squad?"

"Yep, him, Sticks, Wally, and Charlie over there, and a couple of other replacements. I partnered the ASTP boys up with guys who've been around. A little while, at least."

"I'm with Charlie," Danny said. "He's an Apache, can you believe that? And Wally is with Sticks. He's got long legs, that's why they call him that."

"Listen, kid, this gabfest is swell, but get on that shovel. You'll be glad of a hole in the ground soon enough."

"Okay, Sarge," Danny said, frowning and halfheartedly digging into the muddy soil. "You coming back soon, Billy?"

"If I can. And Louie knows what he's talking about, so listen up. You're exposed out here, you need to dig deep, and sit knee-deep in mud if you have to. Got it?"

"Yeah, I got it. Listen, come back soon, we'll catch up, okay?"

"I will." I wanted to hug him again. I wanted to take him with me and find a nice safe job for him in Nettuno. But I didn't. I stuck out my hand, and we shook. I felt like my father, silent and full of knowledge that I wanted to share, but knowing that only experience could pass this lesson on. I turned away, leaving Danny to learn what he had to learn alone, or from strangers. I knew that the more I hung around, the more stubborn he'd get. And that the killer might start playing a new game, if he hadn't already.

"Seems like a good kid," Flint said as I passed his squad, all engaged in the same futile digging.

"That he is. Any sign of the Krauts yet?"

"Nothing. I thought I picked up some movement up in the hills, but it could have been anything." Flint turned his clear blue eyes on me, as if registering my presence for the first time. "What are you doing out here anyway?"

"Just paying a visit to Danny. Nothing much else happening. We had a joyride to Rome yesterday, but since then it's been quiet."

"Rome? Why don't we all go?"

"Good question. General Lucas wasn't impressed."

"You met the old man?"

"Yeah. We're temporarily attached to his headquarters. He thinks it was a fluke that we got through. May have been, since we'd gotten totally lost."

"Did I hear Rome?" Stump said as he joined us.

"Billy drove to Rome yesterday, nearly liberated it himself," Flint said.

"Well, there were three of us, so I have to share the glory. Kaz and Phil Einsmann were with me."

"Phil's here? I thought he was on his way back to London," Flint said.

"Yeah, looking for a story. I doubt the censors will let this one out though. If we get bogged down and it turns out that a reporter and two lieutenants made it to Rome on the first day of the invasion, heads will roll."

"Next time you see Grandpa, tell him we could use some tanks up front," Flint said. "Or at least some antitank guns."

"Is that what you call him?"

"Some guys call him Foxy Grandpa," Stump said.

"Wishful thinking," Flint said. "Listen, Billy, you could do us and Danny a big favor. Talk to Lucas, let him know how exposed we are. We oughta get up in those hills ourselves, or pull back. This is Indian country, and we ain't got a fort."

"I don't talk to him on a regular basis, but I will pass on the sentiment if I bump into him again."

"He's in Anzio?" Stump asked.

"Nettuno, in a nice waterfront villa. No mud."

"Ain't that the way of the world," Flint said, and they all went back to their shovels.

Fifty yards back I found Lieutenant Evans and Father Dare walking in from the village. The padre had a first-aid kit slung over his shoulder and carried a canvas sack full of wool socks. I tried to see him as the killer, dispensing dry socks and then strangling officers. Could a priest forgive himself?

"Lieutenant Boyle," Father Dare said. "I didn't expect to see you again. Still chasing that Red Heart Killer?"

"I wish I was close enough to give chase," I said. "I dropped by to see my kid brother. He's in Louie's squad."

"Yes, I've met him. I try to get to know all the replacements. Sometimes the men ignore them at first." What he was too kind to say was the experienced GIs waited to see if a new kid would live through the first few days. "He certainly looks up to you, doesn't he?"

"I don't know about that," I said.

"You should," Evans put in. "You're all he's talked about since he joined up."

"How'd you make the connection? Boyle isn't an uncommon name."

"I don't know," Father Dare said. "The same name, same Boston accent, someone probably just mentioned you."

"That was all Danny needed to hear," Evans said. "I think we all know your family story by now. Good thing Louie partnered him up with Charlie. He doesn't talk much, so they're a perfect pair."

"Is he really an Apache?" I asked.

"Yes," said Father Dare. "Private Charlie Colorado is a genuine White Mountain Apache. Interesting fellow. I asked him if he wanted any spiritual guidance, and he told me his shaman had taken care of that before he left. Apparently he's protected by Usen, which is what they call their God. The Giver of Life."

"Well, I hope he digs in deep anyway. Usen might be busy elsewhere," I said. "Are you the giver of socks?"

"I am," Father Dare said. "Lieutenant Evans asked me to scrounge some up. There's going to be a lot of wet feet soon, and we have to watch out for trench foot. Clean socks are worth their weight in gold out here."

"Far as I can see, it's our biggest threat so far," Evans said, watching Father Dare as he distributed socks to the men. "After losing Sergeant Gates, we can use a break."

"Yeah, I saw his body by the road yesterday. What happened?"

"Kraut officer got the drop on him. I guess he thought he was surrendering, but the bastard pulled a pistol and shot him in the heart."

"I didn't take Rusty for the careless type, did you?"

"No," Evans said. "I depended on him, he was an old hand, know what I mean?"

"I do. Did you see it happen?"

"No. He had point, and all of a sudden there was a lot of shooting. The car crashed, and by the time I got there, Gates was dead."

"The German was still alive when I got there," I said. "Barely."

"Yeah, well, everyone was upset about Rusty. The Kraut was bawling about something, and no one really gave a damn. I told them to go on, that I was going to put him out of his misery. But I couldn't do it. I fired my pistol into the ground. I didn't want the men to know. I've never killed anyone, and I didn't want the first one to be some poor defenseless bastard. But now I wish I had. I can still hear him talking to me, crying and blubbering."

"You understand German?"

"No. Did he talk to you?"

"No, just curious about what he had to say," I said. No reason to let on that the Kraut was blaming someone else for killing Rusty. Maybe Evans had killed someone before, who knew?

"He did say *Amerikaner* over and over," Evans said. "Maybe he was saying he was sorry. All I know is that I can't get him out of my head."

As Evans spoke, I heard the sound of distant thunder, or at least what always sounded like thunder. Father Dare and I hit the ground. The shrill whistling sound of falling shells came next, and even a rookie like Evans knew what that meant. He went flat as the shells burst, bombarding the village of Le Ferriere. The artillery fire kept up, striking the village over and over. A fireball blossomed up, probably a hit on a fuel truck. Then the shelling widened, explosions reaching the fields all around Le Ferriere, churning up the freshly plowed dirt, sending mud skyward. The barrage crept toward us, and I prayed that Danny would keep his wits about him, dive into a trench and stay put.

The ground shuddered with each hit. I looked across the field to where the squads had been digging in. Shells fell around them, leaving smoking craters as the firing slackened, then stopped.

"Wait," I said as Evans began to get up. He looked at me quizzically until the whine of one last salvo announced itself, hitting Le Ferriere. It was an old trick, waiting to send the last shells over when everyone began sticking their heads out.

I was up, sprinting to the forward position, eyes peeled for Danny and Kaz. I spotted them, and thanked God, Usen, and all the saints I could remember. Next I saw Louie, then Flint and Stump checking on their men as they rose from the ground, wet and muddy.

Something was wrong. Kaz had Danny by the arm, helping him out of the trench. Danny's eyes were wide with terror, and I searched his mud-splattered uniform for signs of blood.

"Danny?" I spoke his name but looked to Kaz.

"He is not hurt, Billy. It is Malcomb, the other ASTP boy. He ran." Kaz pointed to a lifeless body twenty yards out, clothing, skin, blood, and bone shredded by the shrapnel-laced blast.

"I tried to stop him," Danny said. "I tried."

"You would have been killed too," I said. "He panicked. You were smart to stay put."

"I didn't. Charlie grabbed me and held me down," Danny said, his voice shaky as he glanced toward Charlie Colorado, sitting on the edge of the trench. A big guy, bronzed skinned, and quiet.

"Usen," I said.

"I am not the Giver of Life," Charlie said. I begged to differ.

CHAPTER TWENTY-THREE

"HE WAS FROM Princeton," Danny said, as if the aura of the Ivy League should have protected Malcomb from shrapnel and fear. He looked away as Flint helped to roll the body onto a shelter half so it could be carried away. It was a messy, unnatural business. The nuns had taught us that the human form was a sacred vessel, but out here, where artillery fire descended from the heavens, it was a delicate, thin-skinned thing, ready to spill the secrets of life onto the ground. For a soldier on the front lines, nothing is sacred, nothing is hidden, nothing is guaranteed to be his alone. Blood, brains, heart, and muscle are ripped from him, put on display, like his possessions, and carefully searched for the illegal or embarrassing before being boxed up to be sent to loved ones. His gear is divvied up—ammo, socks, food, and cigarettes handed around to squad mates—until finally, with his pockets turned out, his shattered body is covered and carried away. He is useless now, unable to fight, devoid of possessions, weapons, and breath, wrapped in waterproof canvas. This kid was from Princeton. Now he was of Anzio.

"I'm going to get you out of here," I said to Danny, my voice low. I didn't want anyone to hear, not his pals or a suspect. I watched Father Dare rise from giving the last rites, his knees drenched with damp earth and blood.

"No," he said, scrunching his face like he always did when I told him it was time to come for supper. "Leave me alone, Billy. I can do this."

"You can get killed is what you mean. What if Charlie isn't around next time?"

"Billy, if you pull any strings and take me away from the platoon, I will never speak to you again. I mean it. Ever."

"It's only going to get worse, kid. This shelling was just a taste. Are you sure? You don't have to prove yourself to me." But I knew he had to. I wanted to take him by the arm and lead him away from here, but I knew neither of us could live with that.

"Yeah. I'm sure. I couldn't live with myself if I left these guys. It wouldn't be right."

"Okay. I'm just a lowly lieutenant anyway. Probably couldn't pull it off." I jabbed him in the ribs to show there were no hard feelings, and thought about how I could make it happen so it didn't seem to be my doing.

"Thanks, Billy. Maybe the war will be over soon, now that we're so close to Rome. Then we can go back to Boston."

"Sure, Danny. Could happen."

Standing with his hands on his M1, in a muddy uniform and helmet, he looked like a child playing soldier, his wishful thinking nothing but a wistful dream of home. Who was I to burden him with the truth? He'd have more than enough of that in the days to come. It was time for a change of subject.

"Maybe we can get some leave together, paint the town. Have any of the guys mentioned a place in Acerra, name of Bar Raffaele?" I tried to sound like I was just making conversation, suggesting a hot joint.

"Yeah, all the time. Louie said he'd take me there when we got back. You been there, Billy? Is it true what they say, about the girls?"

"It probably is, but it went up in smoke. And if I ever catch you in one of those joints, I'll give you a whupping."

"Hey, I've been around. And even Lieutenant Landry went out with one of the girls there. It can't be that bad."

"Danny, she was a prostitute. He paid for her time, he didn't go out with her. And now he's dead."

"Yeah, I know," Danny said, trying to sound like a nonchalant man of the world. "But Charlie says she was going to give it all up, and wait for Landry. They loved each other. It's sad, kind of like Romeo and Juliet."

"How does Charlie know all this?" I asked, not commenting on Danny's naïve view of the world.

"He used to go all the time, when he was the lieutenant's radioman."

I felt like an idiot. I should have thought to talk to the radioman. He's the one GI in a platoon who spends a lot of time with the platoon leader. He'd hear things, have a sense of his officer that even the sergeants might not.

"Let's go," Louie shouted. "Someone at HQ finally used their noggin. We're goin' into the village, where they got dry cellars. Move out!"

"I gotta go, Billy," Danny said. "Will I see you again?"

"Sure. Maybe tomorrow."

Charlie appeared at Danny's side, moving silently for a big guy carrying two packs of gear. He didn't speak. Next thing I knew, Danny was hugging me with more strength than I'd thought he had. We stayed that way for a moment, and the familiar feel of my brother's grip brought me back to Southie, baseball games on the corner lot, leaves burning in the cool autumn air, and the scent of home. I gripped him even harder, and then we broke off in silent agreement that too much memory might not be a good thing right now.

I watched him move out with Charlie, wondering what secrets the radioman might have been told and what he might have seen. And why had he lost that job? Not that anyone wanted to carry around a heavy radio, much less be a priority target for the enemy. And how much of a coincidence was it that my kid brother was assigned to Landry's platoon and buddied up with Charlie Colorado in the first place?

"You and the Limey officer staying in the village?" Louie asked as we walked along.

"He's Polish, actually, and no, we're leaving."

"No disrespect meant. Just wondering if you needed a place to bunk down."

"Thanks, Louie, but we have beachside accommodations. Too bad they don't have a Bar Raffaele here, eh? Some wine, women, and song would be good about now."

"You can sing all you want, Lieutenant, but the civilians were evacuated from Le Ferriere this morning. Bunch of Italian Carabinieri came in trucks and hauled them away. Guess they knew the place would get plastered."

"I wondered why they were part of all this. Good idea to bring in the local cops. Hey, too bad about Rusty," I said. "Hard to believe that German got the drop on him."

"Can't let your guard down, not for a second. Wasn't like him to, but everyone slips up now and then. That Kraut officer didn't even look like the type."

"What do you mean, the type?"

"You know, a combat officer. He looked soft, not the type to go down guns blazing."

"Must have thought he had a chance," I said. "Why else would he try it?"

"He musta thought he had no other choice. Or maybe he was loco."

"Speaking of strange, how did Danny end up with you? I mean, what are the chances?"

"Truck dumped him and that other ASTP kid off. I got 'em. Simple."

"Rusty assigned them to you?"

"Nothing that official. I was short compared to the other guys, so they were mine."

"You guys worked pretty well together, didn't you?"

"Yeah, with Rusty and Landry in charge, we were a good team. Now, we'll have to wait and see. If Evans don't get his head blown off, he might be all right."

"He got those replacements for you. At least he's looking out for the platoon," I said.

"Naw, they came from Major Arnold direct. Luck of the draw, I guess. But still, Evans ain't the worst we could draw for a second louie."

"Arnold? That your personnel officer?" I felt a twinge of guilt at not telling Louie that Arnold was dead, but I wanted to watch everyone for a reaction. The only guy here who would know Arnold was toes up was the guy who did it.

"Yeah. A souvenir hound, and a real jerk to boot. But at least he sent us a few new guys."

We were close to the village. Acrid black smoke hung in the air from the remnants of a burning truck. The buildings were made of concrete and stonework, and had absorbed the shelling fairly well. The church had taken a direct hit on its roof, and craters gouged out holes in the narrow streets.

"C'mon, double time!" Louie yelled to two men lagging behind us. "See ya, Billy. I want to find a nice deep basement."

I stood beneath a stone archway and watched as Stump and Louie ushered their men into buildings along the perimeter. Flint's squad entered next, and he paused to watch Kaz and Evans behind him, scanning the hills through binoculars, watching for movements or the telltale reflection of the sun off a pair of German binoculars.

"Have a nice chat with the kid brother, Billy?" Flint asked.

"Yeah. Never expected to run into him here," I said as I fell in with him.

"You just happened to be in the neighborhood?" Flint's eyes darted over his men, up to the hills, and to the nearest building. It was small but well built, and covered the entrance to the village. He signaled for his squad to enter.

"I took a little detour. I figured the army is one thing, family is another. You have any brothers?"

"Yeah. My older brother died at Pearl Harbor. I joined up the next day. Got a younger brother myself, he's training to be a fighter pilot."

"Sorry to hear it," I said. "That must have been tough."

"It was. Got everyone riled up, that's for sure. I didn't like leaving my mother and kid brother to run the ranch, but I had to get into the fight. Seemed the only thing to do."

"You're a cowboy?"

"You got to ride a horse to herd cattle, Billy. Guess you could say I am, West Texas born and bred."

"This is a long way from Texas," I said.

"You got that right. Flat like Texas, though. But cold and wet. Can't say I like it much."

I followed Flint into the building, which had been used for storing farm implements. A small engine, maybe from a tractor, was unassembled on a workbench. The place smelled of oil and sweat, but it was dry and had foot-thick walls. Evans glanced in and nodded at Flint, as if he approved.

"How's your new lieutenant coping since Rusty got it?" I asked.

"You heard, huh? Damn shame. I don't know about Evans. He hasn't done anything stupid yet, so we'll see." It wasn't exactly a ringing endorsement.

"Something happen to your radioman? I haven't seen one with Evans."

"We don't have a radio, and haven't been issued a new set. Charlie kicked in the last one, so we're short."

"Why'd he do that?"

"Charlie drinks. A lot. Not often, but when he does, look out. You know how they say Indians can't hold their liquor? Well, no one ever told Charlie. He can drink more than any man I ever met. Stays pretty sober too, on the outside at least. Then he gets to a point where all his meanness comes out, and no matter who you are, best stay out of his way. He's big, strong, and a mean drunk. Took a swing at Landry once."

"And he wasn't court-martialed?"

"Nope. Besides being a mean drunk, Charlie's a damn good soldier. Landry had the MPs lock him up, and it took a pile of them to do it. After the booze wore off, he was all apologetic, and Landry let it pass. Next time, he smashed the radio instead of an officer. I guess Landry knew this little tea party was coming up, and didn't want to lose him."

"Lucky for Danny he didn't."

"Yeah. But if Charlie finds a wine cellar, he'll drink it dry, and then Danny boy better not be in the vicinity. Word of warning, pal." Flint unslung his musette bag and tossed it on the workbench. It fell with a heavy clunk, and the snout of a German pistol poked out where the strap wasn't secured.

"Souvenir?"

"Walther P38," Flint said. "I bought it off Louie after he nailed that Kraut."

"This is the pistol Gates was killed with?"

"It is. It was Louie's by rights, but he didn't want it. I figure if I can get to the rear somebody'll give me good money for it. How about you, Lieutenant?"

"No thanks," I said, but I couldn't stop myself from taking the automatic and feeling the heft of it. The Walther was easy to hold, the reddish-brown grip molded to fit the hand. The peppery smell of gunpowder still lingered over the steel, and I wondered again how Rusty had been caught unawares. "Louie didn't say anything about shooting the German."

"He was pretty upset about the whole thing," Flint said. "We all were."

"Billy," Kaz said from the doorway. "They want us to take two of the wounded back to the aid station. The ambulance is full."

"Okay. Sarge, good luck with the pistol. Maybe try Major Arnold in personnel. I hear he pays top dollar," I said, watching Flint's eyes. No surprise, no flicker of awareness.

"If I get that far back to the rear, I'll have sold it already, but thanks."

The field ambulance had taken the badly wounded already, and the medics were bandaging the last two GIs when we got back to the jeep. Stump was being patched up as well, a medic winding gauze around his forearm.

"Shrapnel nicked me," he said. "Didn't even feel it until I saw the blood."

"Bad luck," I said. "A little worse and you might have been sent home."

"And miss this escorted tour of beautiful Italy? No way. You takin' those guys back? They ain't banged up too bad."

"Yeah. You're not going?"

"I'd be embarrassed with this scratch. Make sure they fix 'em up and get 'em right back to us. I got a feeling we're going to need every man pretty soon."

"It's a long way from Bar Raffaele, isn't it?"

"You got that right, Billy. Paying too much to drink rotgut wine in the sunshine has got it all over this. Them Krauts are gonna keep shelling us until we take those hills up there. All Inzerillo ever did was overcharge us."

"What about that fight, the one Landry and Flint had to pay damages for? What happened? I never heard the whole story."

"I dunno," Stump said, his voice low. "I got a dose of the clap there, you know what I mean? The docs gave me shots and I was out of circulation for a while. Don't spread it around, okay?"

"My lips are sealed," I said. "Any word about replacements?" I asked, thinking that venereal disease made a good motive, for roughing up Inzerillo, at least. Or a good excuse to pretend ignorance. Either way, I wasn't getting anywhere.

"Arnold wouldn't bother to tell us if he had a boatload. Not his style. He only comes around scrounging souvenirs, got a real sideline going for himself. Replacements either show up or they don't."

"That's good to know. I've got a nice SS dagger stashed away."

"Well, see Arnold, he's always buying. I hear he ships the stuff home, got a pal who sells it off. You think rear area guys pay top dollar? It's civilians and 4-Fs who shell out the real dough. Arnold's smart, I give him that. You see him, tell him we need some experienced men, or he might get a Tiger tank for a souvenir, complete with crew."

"Lieutenant?" a medic called to me. "These guys are ready to go."

I wished Stump well and promised him I'd deliver the message to Arnold if I saw him, which I knew was one helluva long shot. The two wounded managed to stay upright as we drove them to battalion aid, where they joined a long line of the walking wounded. German artillery had had a busy day. So had we.

CHAPTER TWENTY-FOUR

IT WAS EASY to get back to the twin towns of Anzio and Nettuno. All we had to do was follow the pillars of smoke. The Luftwaffe had been back, going after transports anchored offshore and the buildup of supplies off the beach. Anzio had been hit hard, first by our own bombardment and now by German bombs. There was even more destruction now than when we'd driven off the beach. I maneuvered the jeep around rubble and burning vehicles, waiting as ambulances barreled by. Everyone seemed to be glancing up, watching for the next wave of attacking aircraft. Near the center of town, a row of houses had been hit, leaving nothing standing but the front facades, doors and windows opening to piles of stone, timber, smashed furniture, and debris. Three women sat at the edge of the ruins, each of them nursing a baby. A few salvaged possessions lay about them. Their clothes and hair were caked with dust, nothing but breast and child, clean and pink.

"Is not war terrible?" Kaz said. "That we should think them the lucky ones?"

I didn't answer.

Back in Nettuno, General Lucas's villa had been renovated, courtesy of the Luftwaffe. There was a gaping hole in the roof, but no sign of an explosion. A GI told us it was from an unexploded bomb, and that Corps staff had moved into a nearby wine cellar for protection. We found Major Kearns in a deep stone basement filled with giant wooden wine casks and thick spiderwebs. A sour smell rose from a dank earthen floor. The place was a full-fledged winery, but had been unused for years. GIs carried desks, tables, map boards, radios, and other gear down a rickety flight of wooden steps.

"Driven underground already, and the casks are empty," Kearns said by way of greeting. "Not the best start for an invasion. What did you find out?"

"Mainly that my kid brother was transferred into Landry's old platoon."

"Life is full of coincidences," Kearns said. "Does it mean anything?"

"I don't believe in coincidence," I said. Dad had always said people mistook cause and effect for coincidence. "If the killer is in that platoon, then he's managed to get one up on me. It's like handing him a hostage. Danny was part of an ASTP group that just landed at Naples. Major Arnold was sending them out to platoons just before he was killed. Now maybe that's a coincidence too, but I doubt it. Everyone knows Arnold was in the souvenir business. It would have been easy to ask him for a favor—like transferring one particular replacement into a certain platoon—in return for a Nazi flag or a pile of soldbuchs." Cause and effect.

"And then kill him?" Kearns said, with a touch of sarcasm.

"It does fit," Kaz said. "Otherwise, Arnold might make a connection, were anything to happen to Billy's brother. And he was the right rank for the killer's next target. It was the perfect opportunity."

"All right," Kearns said. "I'll get Danny transferred out. The division is pushing off in the morning, across the Mussolini Canal. It'll have to wait until after that."

"But sir, he's only a kid," I said, not liking the idea of Danny under fire out on that exposed field.

"There are a lot of kids out there, Boyle. I buy it that it will be better all around to get him out of the platoon, but there's no time to get the paperwork going. Besides, all you need to do is not make a move until after tomorrow morning. That way we won't tip our hand. After the attack, I'll send up the proper paperwork, and it will look completely normal. Now, tell me what else you've got."

"Not much. I spoke to all of them about Major Arnold, but none of them seemed to know he was dead."

"They wouldn't. They were all aboard ship by the time you found him. What else?"

"We confirmed that Lieutenant Landry did have a girl at Inzerillo's place. Seems he wanted her to go straight, but there's no way to confirm that now."

"Boyle, you're not exactly cracking this case wide open," Kearns said.

"I know," I said, not wanting to admit that I was taking time to protect my kid brother. "I just need a little more time to get Danny out so I can press these guys harder."

"So you went easy on them today? Let me guess, you said it was just a social call, to see your brother. Picked up a little gossip, then headed back here to get the kid transferred. Am I close?"

"I had to feel them out, Major. I couldn't even interrogate them properly, since we were under artillery fire for most of the time. They had dead and wounded to deal with too."

"All right, all right. But press them hard next time. Find this guy, before he finds his next victim. I want him brought to justice, and I want it to happen before some Kraut blows his head off. Anything else?"

"Only that Lieutenant Evans is worried about Sergeant Walla," Kaz said. He hadn't mentioned it to me, but between ferrying the wounded and driving through bombed-out ruins, we hadn't had time for much conversation. "He says he's changed since they've come ashore, as if something is worrying him."

"He should be worried," I said, stating the obvious. "Any sane man would be."

"But remember Signora Salvalaggio telling us that Galante and Father Dare dined together, and that they discussed the sergeant?"

"This is Louie Walla from Walla Walla?" Kearns asked. "Seemed like a happy-go-lucky guy to me."

"Yeah, that's him. He did seem different to me today. Less cheery, none of that Walla Walla stuff. I figured he was all business out here, that's all."

"He bears watching," Kearns said, sorting through a pile of maps.

"Louie was the one who plugged that German officer who killed Rusty," I said.

"Rusty Gates got it? Damn, he was a good man," Kearns said as he gave up looking through the maps and rubbed his temples. He looked tired, the exhaustion of too little sleep and too much death.

"I thought so too. Not the kind to let a Kraut fool him either. Apparently the guy was going to surrender but pulled his pistol and shot Rusty. Louie plugged him."

"Listen," said Kearns. "I've been in combat with Rusty. If a Kraut had a pistol in his hands, he would have shot him dead. If it was in his holster and he went for it, Rusty would've put two rounds in his chest before he cleared it. There's no way he would let his guard down."

"Unless the weapon wasn't in the German's hand," Kaz said. "And the German was shot to inflict maximum pain and suffering. Two in the stomach."

"You're saying the Kraut didn't kill Rusty? But why would Louie, even if he is Red Heart?" I said. "What's in it for him, especially in the middle of combat? Eliminating a veteran platoon sergeant increases everyone's chance of getting killed." I needed to question Louie about that. And to see if Evans really had offered to finish off the Kraut.

"It doesn't make sense," Kearns said. "I think we're getting carried away. Focus on what you know. Hopefully the attack tomorrow will keep everyone busy, including the Germans."

It was a hell of a way to run an investigation, right in the middle of an invasion, my kid brother dead center, and hoping that the Germans left our killer alive long enough for us to catch him. It made about as much sense as anything else did.

"Yes sir," I said. "We'll pick up tomorrow, after the attack."

"Good. There's one piece of good news, anyway. Sam Harding is here."

"Colonel Harding?" Kaz asked. "He was still in London when I left."

"He flew in to give a briefing on the situation in Rome and among the Italian partisans. And, I suppose, to check up on your investigation. Sounds like Ike is worried about one of our own bumping off the brass. It's one thing when Jerry does it, but it makes people nervous when they have to keep looking over their shoulder at every GI."

"Where is Harding now?" I asked.

"He's finishing up with Corps G-2. They're located in an old Italian barracks in the Piazza del Mercato, just down the street. Tell him to meet me here when you're done. I'm hoping he brought his usual Irish whiskey."

Kaz and I found the barracks, a thick-walled concrete building that made up in sturdiness what it lacked in looks. A 20-mm anti-aircraft gun was set up in front, and I could see two machine guns on the roof, their barrels pointed skyward. Everyone was going to ground, setting up defenses, protecting themselves. Here, anyway. Up front, Danny's outfit would be attacking in the morning, heading out in the open. It didn't feel right. If headquarters expected the attack to be a success, why weren't they moving up, too? Why go underground just a few hundred yards from the beach? Maybe they had their reasons, but it didn't add up. Like Louie killing Rusty Gates. Like a lot of things.

"Boyle!" The voice was unmistakable. Colonel Sam Harding, my boss. Who worked directly for Uncle Ike, maintaining liaison with the intelligence services of governments-in-exile and our own Office of Strategic Services.

"Sir," I said, standing at a semblance of attention. This wasn't exactly the front lines, but it wasn't good form to point out superior officers to snipers by giving a ramrod-straight salute. It was the kind of thing Harding would appreciate. "It's a surprise to see you here."

"Let's get some chow and you both can update me on your progress." Pure Harding, no nonsense, no time wasted on pleasantries. I could tell he was in a good mood, though. He wasn't wearing a dress uniform, and he was within the sound of enemy shells, with an M1 carbine slung over his shoulder. For a deskbound West Pointer and veteran of the last war, it was close to heaven.

We followed him to the kitchen and had our mess kits filled. The cooks already had their portable stoves in operation, cooking fresh bread, roast beef, and canned vegetables. Danny and his pals were still eating K rations, but Corps HQ was already feeding on the A-ration diet, the same grub you could get at any base back in the States. We were all wearing helmets and carrying weapons, but that was no reason not to eat well.

"Kearns tells me we're up to the queen of hearts," Harding said as soon as we sat at the end of a trestle table, far from the others.

"Major Arnold, personnel officer," I said. I told Harding about Danny and my suspicions about his being placed in Landry's old platoon, and asking Kearns to arrange a transfer. Harding grunted, meaning he didn't disagree but wasn't going to go to bat for me either.

"What have you found out about Landry and Galante?"

"Landry was well liked by his men. He had a soft spot for a prostitute at a joint called Bar Raffaele in Acerra. There was some sort of fracas there and Landry and one of his sergeants, name of Flint, paid off the owner for damages. The owner, Stefano Inzerillo, claimed Landry never paid him anything. But he'd already been beaten to within an inch of his life, and was hiding something from us. We went back to question him again, but someone got there ahead of us and took care of that last inch. Inzerillo burned alive inside his own club."

"No playing card?" Harding asked in between mouthfuls of roast beef. I looked at Kaz, hoping he'd take up the slack so I could eat something, but he shoveled in a forkful of peas and shrugged.

"No. If it's the same guy, he's got one method for officers and another for everyone else." I told him the story of Sergeant Cole, from the incident in Campozillone to the shot to the head in Caserta, not leaving out the rag doll I'd found.

"Pearls?" Harding said in disbelief. Thankfully, Kaz chimed in with the story of Signora Salvalaggio, probably with a bit more history of the Italian monarchy than was necessary, but I didn't mind because it gave me a chance to eat.

"Galante knew about the pearls, and he knew Cole," Harding said. "Perhaps he asked him to look for them."

"That's likely," I said. "He had the run of the palace. But I think the killer knew about the pearls, too, from the way Cole acted. Maybe he was being forced to hand them over."

"Are you certain the murderer is part of Third Platoon?"

"Not certain, but everything points to it. Landry was platoon leader. Cole had been in the platoon; Galante got him transferred out. Arnold sent Danny and another ASTP kid in. They all hung out at Bar Raffaele."

"Sounds reasonable. Do you think this guy has some sort of grudge against officers?" Harding asked.

"It seems he has a grudge against anyone who gets in his way," Kaz said. "But the playing cards are something special. A calling card, so to speak."

"It's interesting that the first body wasn't hidden," I said. "Landry was left in plain view. Behind a tent, but still where anyone could see him. Galante and Arnold were both hidden."

"Are you sure Landry was killed first?" Harding said. I was about to say of course he was, but stopped myself. Why assume that? Not because the killer put the ten of hearts in Landry's pocket and the jack in Galante's.

"Not at all," I said, drawing out the words and thinking it through. "Arnold's body had to be hidden, to give the killer time to get clear of the scene. But the same logic doesn't apply with the first two. If Galante was the first, then the killer had to place his body out of sight—"

"To give him time to murder Landry," Kaz finished for me.

"Right. Which means Landry must have known that the killer was going to see Galante, and had to be silenced."

"Going to see him about the pearls?" Harding offered.

"There's no indication Landry knew about the pearls. There had to be some other reason."

"Simple," Harding said. "He ordered him to." I was about to say that was too simple, but for the second time, I saw something that was so obvious I'd missed it.

"He ordered him to," I repeated, letting it sink in. "But why? For what reason?"

"Doctor Galante specialized in combat fatigue," Kaz said.

"But Galante wasn't seeing anyone from Third Platoon. We checked his records."

"Off the books?" Harding suggested.

"That would work," I said. "The platoon was short on experienced men. If Landry didn't want to lose a veteran soldier, he might ask Galante to talk to him on the QT."

"So, Landry sends a combat fatigue case to Galante. The guy goes off his rocker, kills Galante, then hotfoots it back to the bivouac area to kill Landry," Harding said. "He comes up with the straight flush idea to confuse things, so it isn't obvious that Galante was the real target. It puts Galante in among a group of victims, so we don't see him as the primary victim."

"Then he didn't go off his rocker," I said.

"What?" Kaz and Harding said at the same time.

"It doesn't fit. Who goes off his rocker and then executes a plan like that?"

"Someone crazy enough to murder people," Harding said.

"That's a tough one, Colonel. It sounds logical, but if someone is really crazy, as the law defines it, then he's not responsible for his actions. But these are very well-thought-out actions, up to and including getting Danny in as part of the platoon."

Kaz shook his head. "Then what happened with Galante?"

"Something that was a threat. A serious threat that had to be stopped in its tracks, and covered up with this card business. It has to be related to what happened at Bar Raffaele, which is why Inzerillo had to go."

"Perhaps the killer wanted to be sent home, and Galante refused to give him the diagnosis he needed," Kaz said. "He gets angry, and before he knows it, Galante is dead. Then he has to kill Landry, to keep it all a secret."

"Or maybe it wasn't combat fatigue at all," I said. "Maybe Landry was helping out somebody who had the clap, asking Galante to treat him so it wouldn't go on his record."

"Venereal disease isn't exactly rare," Harding said.

"No, but perhaps a married man would not want it to be known," Kaz said.

"Or a priest," I said, fairly certain that Saint Peter was putting a black mark next to my name for even suggesting it.

"I'm heading over to see Kearns," Harding said. "What's next for you two?"

"I want to find the Carabinieri who came along on this joyride. They may know more than they're telling us about Bar Raffaele."

"Why do you think that?"

"A hunch is all," I said. I didn't want to complicate things by bringing up Luca Amatori's stint at a Fascist concentration camp. That was my leverage, and I needed to keep it to myself. For now.

"Okay," Harding said, rising from the table with his mess kit. "I'll be back tomorrow at 1100 hours. Report to me then. I need to send Ike an update on the situation. You'll find me with Kearns."

That worked fine for me, since I planned an early morning visit to Le Ferriere. I wasn't going to let Danny face the Germans alone, not with an American killer at his back. I knew Harding and Kearns wouldn't be happy with my protecting Danny, or tipping off the killer. But it was my kid brother, so colonels and majors be damned.

CHAPTER TWENTY-FIVE

WE FOUND TENENTE Luca Amatori at the Anzio Carabinieri headquarters, set up in a seaside casino pockmarked with bullet holes from the initial assault.

"Billy, Kaz," he said, rising from his desk, which had originally been a croupier's table. "I am glad to see you both. Is this a social call, or can I be of assistance?"

"We could use your help," I said as I took a seat. Luca's desk was filled with papers, lists of names and addresses from what I could see. An ornate white-and-gold telephone on his desk rang, and he ignored it, nodding to an officer across the room who picked up the call on another phone.

"Has it to do with the killings? The murders in Caserta?"

"Yes. We need some more information on the connection between Bar Raffaele and Lieutenant Landry."

"But I already told you the little I know," Luca said. "And we are quite busy, trying to provide for civil order."

"How many men do you have here?" Kaz asked.

"One hundred and fifty."

"Might not some of them know of Stefano Inzerillo and his bar?" Kaz asked. "Surely some of them visited it for personal reasons, while not on duty, of course."

"I could ask, yes. But as you know, the American military police have jurisdiction in such matters." Luca spread his hands and shrugged, to show how little there was he could do.

"We don't need help with jurisdiction," I said. "I want to know more about the prostitute Landry was involved with, and what happened to her."

"Billy, how can I find a prostitute in Acerra while I am in Anzio?"

"Listen, I know cops, and cops talk about things that are out of the ordinary. Like an American lieutenant trying to talk a prostitute into going straight. It's the kind of naïve thing any veteran cop would get a laugh out of, you know what I mean?"

"Yes, of course. But you must understand, the times are not normal. There are so many Americans, and so many prostitutes. My men come from all over Italy, it is not as if they are all from the area and know everything that goes on. Believe it or not, some of them do not even frequent houses of ill repute."

"It sounds as if you're making excuses," I said. "Is there a reason you don't want to help us?"

"No, not at all. As I told you before, I have only been in the area two months myself. Some of my men even less."

"Maybe you were taking bribes from Inzerillo," I said. "It wouldn't take two months to set that up."

"You have no right to make such an accusation! Are you mad?"

"What, cops in Italy don't take bribes?"

"Why are we even having this discussion?" Luca asked.

"Because we find it hard to believe that an experienced Carabinieri officer would have difficulty with such a simple request," Kaz said.

"Nothing in war is simple," Luca said. "And *I* do not take bribes." He left the implication hanging like a fastball right over the plate.

"But Capitano Renzo Trevisi does?" Kaz said.

"The Capitano grew up outside of Caserta," Luca said. "He knows many people."

"People in Acerra," I said.

"Yes."

"Stefano Inzerillo, for one?"

"I would rather not say. He is my superior officer."

"Luca, I took you for a rookie when we first met. A guy who got a fast promotion, maybe due to the war, but a rookie nonetheless," I said.

"A rook-ee?" he asked, sounding out the word.

"Someone new to the game. I thought the same thing when you came with us to Acerra, to interrogate Inzerillo, since you spilled the beans about Landry being dead."

"Beans?" He looked puzzled.

"Yeah. Don't you watch gangster movies in Italy? That was a rookie move, tipping Inzerillo off, getting him even more nervous than he was. But now I wonder, were you in on it with your capitano? Were you feeding information to Inzerillo and keeping watch on us at the same time?"

"This is ridiculous! You and your American words, they make as much sense as your accusation." He was right, I was making it up as I went along. I didn't think Luca was in cahoots with Trevisi, but I had the feeling he was holding back, and pressure was the best way to find out what.

"Why did a Carabiniere in Acerra call you a Fascist? He said you were a friend of the Nazis."

"I have no idea," Luca said, waving his hand in the air as he looked down at the empty green surface of the croupier's table.

"Was it because of what you did at Rab? At the concentration camp?"

His hand fell from the air, as if a puppet master's string had been cut. "I am not a Fascist," he said, sighing in a way that let us know he'd said it many times before. "I am also not a friend of the Tedeschi. What do you think this has to do with a bordello in Acerra?"

"I think it has something to do with your capitano. He has you under his thumb, and you feel you have to protect him. I'd say Inzerillo was paying him off, and you knew it. You tried to warn Inzerillo that Landry's killer would be coming for him; that's why you blurted out that Landry was dead."

"If it is as you say, then you are wasting your time with me," Luca said. He lit a cigarette, keeping his eyes on the pack, the matches, the ashtray, everything but me.

"No, I don't think so. You don't strike me as a man who likes working for a crooked cop," I said, leaning forward until he had to look me in the eye. "I think you're ashamed of something, and you know that protecting Trevisi is only going to lead to more shame and disgrace. Am I right, Luca?"

Some guys aren't made for lying. Some are. Luca was in between. He put a good face on things, and I'm sure he could lie to a crook or a killer if it meant getting a confession. But something was eating at him, and I knew he wanted to tell all.

"Yes, you are right," he said finally. He took a drag on his cigarette, leaned back and blew smoke at the ceiling. "Capitano Trevisi had business dealings with Inzerillo."

"What kind of dealings?" Kaz asked. Luca only shook his head. It was the same the world over. No cop wants to give up another cop, no matter how dirty. The blue wall of silence.

"That's why he was so glad to offer your services, so you could keep an eye on things?" I said, not asking him a direct question about corruption.

"Yes. He was worried about Inzerillo. He thought there was trouble brewing, even before you came to Caserta."

"Why?"

The truth came easier now. The dam had been broken, and it spilled out. "There was trouble, first with Lieutenant Landry. He threatened to bring in the military police if Inzerillo didn't let one of the girls go."

"I thought Inzerillo didn't run the girls himself."

"He didn't. It was what Ileana told him."

"Ileana? The prostitute Landry fell for?"

"Yes. She told him she needed money to buy her freedom from Inzerillo, that he would not let her go free. Trevisi said it was all a lie, to extort money from the lieutenant who loved her."

"So you lied to us when you said it would be impossible to find her," I said.

"She is gone, that much is true. She fled when she became frightened."

"Frightened by what?"

"One of the soldiers. He threatened to kill her."

"That couldn't have been Landry," I said.

"No, he saw himself as her defender, and she as his Dulcinea." I must have looked puzzled, since he explained. "From *Don Quixote*."

"A simple peasant girl who becomes Don Quixote's idealized woman," Kaz added.

"Oh yeah," I said. I knew that was an old book, but not much more. "So who threatened her?"

"I only know it was a *sergente*. The same one who gave Inzerillo the beating."

"Was it Sergeant Stumpf?" He came down with venereal disease after partaking of the pleasures at Bar Raffaele. That might be a motive for attacking Inzerillo and the girl.

"I do not know. I would tell you if I did."

"Why didn't you tell us before? Why keep this a secret? You knew we were investigating a murder."

"The murder is another matter entirely. I can only say that this sergente asked for Ileana, even knowing Landry was smitten with her. Perhaps there was some problem between them, but I can only guess at that."

"Why did the sergeant threaten her?"

"Because she laughed at him," Luca said, a bitter laugh escaping his lips. "At his failure in lovemaking. He struck her violently and promised to kill her if she breathed a word. Inzerillo heard her screams and tried to intervene, and was beaten for it. I believe the sergeant came back again to hurt him some more."

"And then a third visit, to kill him."

"If it was the same man. All I know is what I heard from Inzerillo himself. A sergeant, and the second time he came with another man, but he would not say who."

"Inzerillo told you it was a sergeant?"

"Yes, but he would say no more. He and Capitano Trevisi both wanted it kept quiet so there would be no trouble with the military police."

"Do you know where the girl is now?"

"No, truly I do not. Trevisi had her taken away to a farm where she could heal. Not that he is kind, but so she can return to work as soon as possible. In another location, of course." Luca ground out his cigarette and stared at the ashes. Finally he looked at us. "I am sorry for lying to you."

"What does Trevisi have on you?" I asked. "Was it something that happened on Rab? What did you do there?"

"I did nothing," Luca said.

CHAPTER TWENTY-SIX

LUCA HAD CLAMMED up tight after that. He'd looked past us, out to sea where the sun was setting and casting a red glow across the horizon. I wondered if he was thinking of the view from the island of Rab, and if he preferred looking out over water to what he'd seen on solid ground.

I'd gotten Kaz on a PT boat shuttling brass between Naples and Anzio, leaving it up to him and his Webley revolver to talk to Trevisi and find Ileana. We needed to know who had beaten her and Inzerillo. That had to be our killer, fixing up loose ends. Maybe Landry was the real target after all, but if so, I couldn't figure out all the red heart stuff. It seemed overly complicated. I was stumped, and our only hope seemed to be that the killer would slip up and leave a clue or two next time. Not the best investigative technique, I'll admit.

Ileana was the key to finding out everything. If she hadn't run off, if she'd talk, and if she wasn't under lock and key in some Naples whorehouse, we had a chance of catching this murderer before he struck again.

But I had another reason for sending Kaz back to Naples. I didn't want him talking me out of heading back to the front in the morning. Someone had to watch over Danny. I might find a clue, but probably not. What I was more likely to find was a lot of lead in the air and bodies on the ground. But I might be able to make sure one of them wasn't Danny's.

Which is why the next morning I was on the road before dawn, driving without lights to Le Ferriere. Grenades in my pockets, extra clips in my ammo belt, Thompson on the seat. The road was packed with vehicles—trucks and ambulances, jeeps crammed with GIs, towed artillery, all strung out on the narrow straight road. If the Luftwaffe paid us a visit after the sun came up, it'd be a shooting gallery. Some of the traffic peeled off onto side roads, but most flowed to the front. Artillery thundered up ahead; outgoing stuff, thank God.

I was half a mile out of Le Ferriere when I noticed that the GIs marching on foot were making better time than I was. And that it was getting light. I didn't want to be a stationary target, so I pulled off the main road, crossing a short bridge over the wide drainage ditch that ran alongside the roadway, and drove down a dirt road until I found a dry spot to pull over. The road was packed with men and vehicles, but out here everything was still. The fields were empty, stubble showing where plants had last been harvested. A few hundred yards away was one of the stone farmhouses that dotted the fields around here, built according to Mussolini's plan. A woman came out of the house and began to hang laundry. White sheets fluttered in the early morning breeze, and the image of domesticity held me for a moment, before I turned to join the column of heavily armed soldiers heading into Le Ferriere.

"Here you go, fellas," a sergeant shouted from the back of an open truck as he tossed out small bundles to each man passing by. "Stick 'em in your pack, they don't weigh much."

"What are these?" I asked as I caught a tightly bound pack of folded white cotton material.

"Mattress cover," he shouted back, not missing a beat as he tossed them to the oncoming men.

"They got mattresses up front?" a skinny kid asked as he stuck the bundle into his pack. Laugher rippled around him, and a corporal by his side shook his head wearily. There were no mattresses waiting in Le Ferriere or beyond, I knew. The Graves Registration Units used them as shrouds for the dead. Usually they carried them to collection points where bodies were left, but they must have been expecting heavy casualties. Some officer who thought less about morale than efficiency probably figured this would save time. A couple of guys tossed the covers by the side of the road, but most kept them, either not knowing what they were for, not caring, or figuring they might get lucky and find some hay to stuff inside. Hell, maybe even a mattress.

As I approached the entrance to the stone wall that encircled the village, a sudden sound pierced my ears, rising above the clatter, clank, and chatter of GIs, the revving of engines, and the crunch of tires on gravel: the shriek of artillery shells. Not the thunderous, sharp sound of our own fire, but the piercing screech of artillery rounds falling toward us. Toward me.

"Incoming!" I yelled at the same moment a few other guys did, and I wasted no time running off the road and leaping face-first onto the flat ground, holding my helmet in place, bracing for the blast that I knew was coming.

The sound shattered the air as the explosions shook the ground and the concussion swept over me, peppering my body with dirt, debris, and who knows what else. The shelling kept on, hitting the village and the roadway precisely. The Germans had this area zeroed in. They knew the column was here, even though we'd come up in the dark and the approach was shielded from their lines by the walled village. I didn't spend much time thinking about that, though. I mainly tried to melt into the ground, praying that I was far enough off the damn road to survive. The ear-splitting crash of each explosion drove everything else from my mind, until there was nothing but the trembling earth beneath and my prayers sent up to the saints.

As quickly as it began, it ended. I moved my limbs, shaking off dirt and making sure everything worked. I was grateful for the silence, until it began to be filled with the groans and cries of the wounded. Smoke roiled from within the village, and wrecks of vehicles littered the road. Men rose from the fields, gazing at those who didn't. A few yards away an arm lay by itself, a gold wedding ring gleaming bright on the still hand. Medics began running out of the village, seeking the wounded, finding plenty. Most of the dead had been caught in the road, slow to react. The words to a prayer ran through my mind: *from thence he shall come to judge the quick and the dead.* I had to get into the village and find Danny, make sure he was still among the quick. As I got to the road, I saw the Graves Registration sergeant, dead, mattress covers smoldering at his feet.

My ears were ringing as I stumbled into Le Ferriere. Rubble spilled out into the street where buildings had taken hits. GIs began to file out of the standing structures, eyes cast to the skies, ears tilted to hear the incoming rounds. Officers formed them up and got them moving, toward the German lines. I passed one building that took a direct hit, the sign for 2nd Battalion HQ blackened but readable.

"Third Platoon, Easy Company?" I asked one lieutenant. "Know where they are?"

"Easy pushed off before dawn. They're out there somewhere," he said, pointing with his thumb to the open fields that led to a wooded rise across the Mussolini Canal. "You might be able to see the advance from the third floor of that factory over there. It's full of brass who came to watch the show."

"I'll give it a try anyway," I said.

"Good luck." He returned to his men, probably knowing that everyone's luck ran out, sooner or later. I climbed the metal steps up the outside wall of the factory, a short, squat concrete building that had a few chunks blown out of it, but was still in one piece. The third floor looked out over the town wall, to the northeast and the waiting Krauts. Inside, a gaggle of officers stood at the far wall, their binoculars trained on the advance. Their helmets and jackets were covered in dust shaken loose from the bombardment, but otherwise they were in good shape. No getting caught out on the open road for them. On a table near the door were thermoses of coffee and a couple bottles of bourbon. A man gets thirsty watching a battle, after all.

A lieutenant turned, probably checking to be sure I wouldn't swipe the booze. It was easy to tell he was an aide to a senior officer. Clean boots, a good shave, and a West Point ring on his finger. He was along to carry the booze and get points for being at the front, so his benefactors in the West Point Protective Association could promote him as soon as possible.

"Can I help you?" he asked.

"Where's Easy Company headed?"

"Battalion HQ could help you. They're down the street."

"They're in pieces. Who's running the show here?"

"Boyle?" It was Harding. He and Kearns detached themselves from the scrum of officers and gave a nod to the aide to let him know I was allowed access to the high and mighty. Ring knockers, we called them, for those big academy graduation rings they flashed around. "What happened to Battalion HQ?"

"Direct hit. If anyone's alive in there, they aren't up to running this attack. You didn't know?"

Neither of them answered, but Kearns was off, taking the aide with him. Maybe the kid would get his boots dirty.

"What are you doing here?" Harding asked.

"Checking on my kid brother," I said. I saw no reason to lie. Harding knew me pretty well, and I thought I had his number. He was a straight shooter, and he responded best to the truth, even when it went against regulations.

"Easy Company, Third Platoon, right?"

"Yes sir. How are they doing?"

He handed me binoculars and eased a major out of the way at the window. "See that track, across the canal?" I did. It was bigger than a path, smaller than a road. Drainage ditches had been dug on both sides, and the piled earth gave a few inches of cover. Small trees and shrubs grew along the ditches, giving some visual cover too. "They headed up there. Two companies on either side, spread out in the fields. The objective is that wooded rise beyond them."

I could make out men crawling in the road and across the fields. Others lay still, dead, or scared out of their wits. Explosions hit the wooded rise, but through the binoculars I could see the deadly sparkle of machine guns sending controlled bursts down into the advancing GIs. It was terrible, that ripping chainsaw sound of the

MG42, a machine gun they called the Bonesaw. It spewed out 1200 rounds per minute, so fast that you couldn't hear the individual shots, just a blur of noise that sounded like heavy fabric tearing. Against that fire I could make out the almost leisurely *rat-tat-tat* of our machine guns, no match for the dug-in German firepower.

"They need smoke, and air cover," I said. "Do you have a radio here?"

"No," Harding said. "The communications gear was in the head-quarters building, and the cloud cover is too low for air support. Hell, we're just here to escort the visiting brass, and to observe." He nearly spit out that last word as he grabbed my arm. "Come on, Boyle. I'll find a way to call in smoke and get more artillery on that hill. You find your brother and his platoon and help them out, then get word back to me. That's what you wanted, right?"

"Yes sir. I'll send a runner back and let you know how far they've gotten." I sprinted down the street, heading for the north gate that opened to the fields and the storm of steel and death my kid brother had plunged into. Danny, who used to follow me everywhere, who got bullied when I wasn't around, who was smarter than I was though I never admitted it, who I'd punched in the arm, hard, more times than I could count—Danny, out there, alone. Meaning with no one he could count on. No family, no Irish, no veteran platoon leader. I jumped smoking craters and debris until I was clear of Le Ferriere. As I descended the slope, I could barely make out the tiny shapes of crawling men amidst the smoke and dust of battle. In the distance, three Sherman tanks made their way along a narrow road across the canal, the first good news of the morning. Bad news caught up with the lead Sherman as it blew up, black smoke churning out of every hatch. The other two tanks reversed, not wanting to roll over another Teller mine or into the sights of a hidden antitank gun. They retreated, I went forward, and I couldn't help thinking they knew what they were doing.

CHAPTER TWENTY-SEVEN

I CAME ACROSS the litter bearers first, hustling the wounded back to aid stations along the canal. Mortar rounds were landing near the closest bridge, so I went into the water, scrambling up the embankment into chaos. Two jeeps, pulling trailers stacked with dead, careened across the field, evading enemy fire so vigorously that the bodies leapt with every jolt, arms and legs bouncing as if they'd come alive. Machine-gun rounds chewed up the fields and zinged over my head, the odd thrum like a hornet buzzing by my ear. White phosphorous rounds began to land to our front, and I knew Harding had managed to get the coordinates to the artillery. Thick white smoke blossomed in the morning air, and I ran until I found the dirt track.

It was crowded with men, prone and pressed tight on either side, up against the cover of the ditch wall. The fields on either side had a gentle rise to them, like a lazy wave about to crest. It was less than a foot high, but when everything clse is dead flat, a fool is damn good cover. That's where the advance on the flanks of the road had stopped. Men had scraped shallow depressions in the soil and rolled into them, protected at least from machine-gun fire. To their rear, a trail of bodies stretched back to the canal.

"Is this Easy Company?" I asked. "Who's in charge?"

"This here's Fox Company, and you better get your damn head

down," a corporal snapped at me. "If you got further use for it, that is." That got a laugh.

"Where is Easy Company?" I stood up, straight as I could. It was crazy, I knew. I'd seen Harding do it a couple of times, taking a chance on stopping a bullet in order to show men he wasn't afraid and they shouldn't be either. I didn't give a damn about morale; I just wanted a straight answer fast. This at least got the corporal's attention.

"Down that way, Lieutenant," he said. "We were supposed to follow them, but we got pinned down. There was supposed to be a smoke screen a long time ago."

"Pinned down, my ass! Where's your officer?"

"Captain's right there," he said, pointing to a medic hunched over a body, bloody compresses scattered on the ground.

"Jesus," I said, and wished that hadn't popped out so loud. I was going to have to do something about morale whether I liked it or not. No one else was left standing. "Lieutenants? Platoon sergeants?"

"Dead. Mortar round caught them in a huddle, havin' themselves a powwow. Captain took us this far, then he took one in the chest. The boys and I took a look and figured this was a good place to hunker down."

"I'm in command now, Corporal. Get up, we're heading up to support Easy Company. You," I said, pointing to a PFC who looked only half scared to death. "You're my runner. Hightail it back to the village and find Colonel Harding. He's either at Battalion HQ or in that factory building on the same street. Tell him the advance is stalled and that I'm taking Fox Company forward to locate Easy. You got that?"

"Harding," he repeated. "The advance is stalled at this point. Fox going forward to find Easy. Who are you?"

"Boyle. Now run there and run back here, fast as you can. Go." I waited for a few long seconds as he stared up at me. If he refused to go, that was it. If I couldn't get one GI to head back, I sure as hell wasn't going to get fifty of them to move up.

"Yes sir," he said, and was off like a jackrabbit.

"Corporal, if you're the ranking noncom, then get your men moving. Follow me."

I didn't look back, and I didn't try to rouse the men. That was his job, and I had no idea if he was up to it. I crouched low, to show them that I wasn't completely insane. I heard the rustle of gear, curses, and the sound of boots on the ground. I broke into a trot, and the sound of men following me into the swirling smoke was the sweetest, most terrible sound of my life. Each death would be on my head.

The sound of mortar fire lessened. The German machine guns slowed their rate of fire, too, sending short bursts into the smoke, hoping for a hit. The *crump* of explosions ahead of us told me Harding had zeroed in on the hill, which would also make the Krauts keep their heads down. I picked up the pace, figuring the less time upright the better my chances were. Visibility was low, but the track was even and easy to follow.

It was then that I tripped. A dead GI lay half in the ditch, half on the track. I went sprawling and fell onto another body, but this one was alive. I lifted myself up and called for a medic. There were none with us.

"Water," he gasped in a raspy voice. I looked closer, and saw he must have been hit by shrapnel. His jacket was shredded and bloody, and one side of his face was torn and blackened. "Water, please."

I unscrewed my canteen and only then did I look at his face; not his wounds, but his face. Steel-rimmed spectacles lay bent and broken by his head. He was a kid, with the same color hair. My hand shook, and I reached for my canteen.

"Danny?"

"Water," the voice said, fainter.

"Danny!" I poured the water on his face, washing away the blood. His eyes bore into mine, beseeching me.

"Water."

It wasn't Danny. I rose and ran, as fast as I could. I couldn't face that wounded kid, I couldn't admit to my fear, to how I felt in my heart at that moment of mistaken identity. It was a cowardly thing to do, to leave him like that, I knew. I told myself someone else would give him water, somebody would be glad for the excuse to hang back. But it was all a lie. I was afraid, that's all. Afraid for Danny and maybe even more afraid for myself. If he died out here, I'd carry that guilt forever.

Now I knew. Now I understood my father. Now I was my father. He'd drummed it into me a million times. *Family comes first.* The Boyles, then the Boston PD, then Ireland. But family first. That's what leaving a dead brother on the battlefield does. That's what finding his brother Frank dead in the trenches of the last war did to him. I felt it in my heart, and it pained me, for all of us.

If I had been alone, I would have wept. But I wasn't, so I barked orders to cover my fears. We were too bunched up, so I got the men spread out, advancing straight down the track and on the flanks. I strained for the sound of our own weapons ahead, but there was too much racket. Not being able to see, it seemed as if the noise was on all sides, surrounding us, echoing in the empty air. They had to be dead ahead, I thought, then wished I'd used a different choice of words.

I felt a breeze at my back. It became a gust, and I could see the smoke drifting past me, coils of misty white churning at my feet, drifting off my shoulders, making for that wooded rise where the enemy waited: their eyes squinted along gun barrels, desperate for a glimpse of us. The cloud cover above had turned dark and swollen, and a salt smell came in with the wind. A storm was brewing, and it was blowing in from behind us, stripping us of the only cover we had.

"Run!" I yelled. "Run!" I prayed they'd heard me, and knew which way. I looked behind me, and could see far enough to know that whatever was left of Fox Company was still with me, and that the smoke wasn't. It blew past me, leaving a clear view to the rear, and at a run I could barely keep up with it. If we didn't find cover or Easy Company, it was going to be a turkey shoot. The guys around me understood, and we all picked up the pace, eyes darting across the revealed landscape, legs pumping, weapons at the ready.

The disappearing smoke revealed a streambed, fifty yards up. GIs waved us by while they watched the smoke roll on, cresting against the wooded rise, breaking like waves on the shore. Thirty yards to go, then twenty, and I could make out the shape of trees. Ten yards, then three long strides and I leapt into the streambed as the MG42s opened up, shredding the air with their terrible mechanical constancy.

"Where the hell have you been?" Evans demanded as I rolled out of the foot-deep water and threw myself against the bank. Bullets clipped the ground above us and zinged overhead, sending clumps of earth flying in the fields where we had been. I knew Evans didn't mean me especially; I wasn't even sure he recognized me.

"Evans, it's me, Billy Boyle. Where's your company commander?" I ached to ask about Danny but I had to focus on the jam we were in.

"Dead. Same with the other two platoon leaders. If this stream wasn't here we'd all be dead. What the hell happened to our support? Why are you here, anyway?"

"Doesn't matter," I said, answering his last question first and giving him points for even thinking of it right now. "HQ took a direct hit in that barrage, got knocked out. There was no one coordinating the attack or calling in artillery."

"We're supposed to have tank support," he said.

"I saw them hit a minefield and take off. I sent a runner back with our position. Maybe he can make it back with orders. You have a radio?"

"No, not even a walkie-talkie. Your brother's okay, last I saw anyway."

"Thanks," I said, letting the relief settle in, then pushing it aside. We all still had to get out of this alive. "Listen, there's something I wanted to ask you—"

"Jesus, Boyle, there's a time and place for everything. Just tell me where the Fox Company CO is."

"Dead, or near so last I saw. Highest rank left seems to be a corporal."

"Jesus Christ."

"No kidding. You're in charge, Evans. What's the situation?"

"We've got good cover right here, couple of hundred yards in either direction. Except for when they drop mortar rounds on us, but they might be running low on ammo. We haven't been hit too hard for a while. Their big stuff sails right over. With the men you brought, we probably have eighty or so effectives, not counting the walking wounded and litter cases. Father Dare and a medic are set up down a ways, with Louie's squad." As if on cue, artillery shells whistled overhead, detonating to our rear, showering us with dirt that rained on our helmets and hunched shoulders.

"Where does this stream lead?" I asked. It wasn't much of a stream, at least not this time of year. Damp gravel fell from the banks, littered in places with torn and bloody bandages. But it was deep enough for cover, and for that it was our Garden of Eden.

"To the left it loops around the woods. To the right to turns south, back to our lines. But we'd be exposed for about three hundred yards. They'd chew us up. And with this wind, more smoke wouldn't last long enough to give us cover."

"Okay, watch for the runner. I'm going to check on the wounded." We both knew I meant Danny. I duckwalked in the cold water until I found Father Dare. He'd found a bit of flat, dry ground next to the bank, and he and a medic were patching guys up as best they could.

"Lieutenant Boyle, was that you who brought the cavalry?" Father Dare asked, as he wound a bandage around the thigh of a GI who grimaced as he did. Once again, I had to wonder, could a murderer soothe the wounded and then kill the living?

"Jeez, Father, can't you give me some morphine? The pain is killing me," the GI said through clenched teeth.

"I could, but then when we get out of here, it might take two fellows to carry you. You'll have to hang on, son. I'm sure the lieutenant here is bringing good news, aren't you, Boyle?"

"Sure. Fox Company's here and we're back in contact with headquarters. They'll be in touch soon. Hang in there," I said, patting the wounded man on the shoulder.

"Easy for you to say," he gasped, but I saw relief flicker across his face. I hoped I wasn't talking through my helmet.

"Shrapnel," Father Dare whispered as we turned away. "Too deep, otherwise I'd cut it out myself. How bad are things, really?"

I told him what happened to headquarters and about Harding taking over, and the losses Fox Company had taken trying to get to them.

"If we'd made this push yesterday, we might have had a chance. But now the Germans are dug in on every piece of high ground within a mile," he said.

"Yeah, and they seemed to know we were coming. They dropped artillery right on the village and the approach road this morning, caught everyone with their pants down."

"It's a real FUBAR situation," Father Dare said, then pointed. "He's down that way, Boyle. Hasn't done anything stupid, so he may be all right."

I thanked him, and went down on my hands and knees until I ran into Louie, leaning against the bank and smoking a cigar, his feet in the water.

"Hey, Louie," I said.

"It's Louie Walla from Walla Walla," he said, with a smile.

"Having fun out here, Louie?"

"Walla from Walla Walla," he finished for me.

"Exactly."

"Well, why not? I'm down to my last stogie, the Krauts got the high ground, what am I gonna do, cry? Not me. I figure this here cigar will drive 'em crazy. Krauts got lousy tobacco, you know? This is my secret weapon." He blew a plume of smoke straight up, letting the stiff breeze take it straight to the Germans.

"We got them right where we want them, Louie Walla from Walla Walla. Where's Danny?"

"Right behind that clump of bushes. Kid ain't half bad for a college boy." He went on puffing, oddly serene, especially compared to how sullen he'd been the last time I saw him.

"Billy!" Danny said, nearly jumping up when he saw me. Charlie Colorado put a stop to that with one hand on his shoulder.

"How's it going, kid?"

"Charlie says he's been in worse spots," Danny said. He leaned against the gravelly bank, loose sand and stones giving way and tumbling down to his boots. His hands gripped his M1, knuckles turning white. He looked away from me, digging his helmet into the earth as if he wanted to burrow into it.

"Don't worry, Danny," I said. "Everyone's scared. But we'll get out of this, believe me."

"I'm not scared. Well, maybe I am, who wouldn't be?"

"Right," I said, sensing that I was missing something.

"Danny is a good shot. He is a warrior today," Charlie said.

"I killed a man, Billy."

I put my hand on his shoulder. There were no words for this moment. Sure, that was what we were here for. Kill or be killed and all that. But when it was your little brother bearing the burden of death, words seemed useless. But I felt I had to come up with something. "The real test is not living or dying, kid. It's killing and living."

"It felt strange," Danny said. "Like I should have felt worse about it. But then I felt bad that I didn't."

"It was his time to die, not yours," Charlie said. "Usen gave you good eyes and a steady hand. He would not want you to turn away from his gifts."

"When did this happen?" I liked it that Usen was watching out for Danny, but I needed to know what was going on in the here and now.

"Not long ago," Danny said. "Flint found a gully that leads up to the hill. We crawled up it and got an angle on the machine gun crew. They were firing into the smoke and didn't see us. I lined up a shot and took it. I got the gunner, saw his helmet fly off. Then they started throwing grenades, and we had to get back."

"Why Flint? Louie's your squad leader."

"Louie is dead," Charlie said.

"No he isn't, I just talked to him."

"Louie is dead," he repeated. "He knows it is his time, and he is waiting. He is dead."

"He is acting strange," Danny said. "Like he doesn't have a care in the world."

"He knows he is free of this earth," Charlie said.

"But why—" I didn't get a chance to finish. Stump crawled up to us, hugging the embankment.

"Sorry to interrupt the reunion, boys. Billy, that runner you sent made it back."

"How'd he get through?"

"He said a Colonel Harding turned him right around, sent him up the streambed in the other direction. Come on."

Danny and I shook hands, putting on a good show for everyone watching, saying "See ya later" like we'd meet up at Kirby's for a beer. I followed Stump. The odd shot rang out from above, but it had turned quiet. I figured the Krauts knew they had us pinned good. If I were in their shoes, I'd hustle up some reinforcements before nightfall, when we had a better chance of pulling out in the dark. Until then, I'd conserve my ammo, just like they were doing.

The PFC was with Evans and Flint, and they were all checking watches. Flint gave a curt nod as he set his watch, all business.

"Boyle," Evans said. "We're moving out in fifteen."

"What's your name?" I asked the PFC. Evans was doing all right, but I wanted to hear exactly what Harding had planned, and this kid was the only one with a clue.

"Kawulicz, Lieutenant. Robert Kawulicz. But they call me Bobby K, on account of the Polack name."

"Okay, Bobby K, I'm going to tell Colonel Harding it's time for corporal's stripes as soon as we get back. Now tell me what he said to you."

"He told me that if I could get to you, I could bring you back. He pointed me down that streambed, and sent a few smoke rounds in. The wind didn't take it like it did above ground. I stayed low, had to crawl in a few places, but they never saw me."

"Good work, Bobby K. You ready to lead us back?"

"Sure as hell don't want to stay here," he said.

"Okay, the smoke is going to hit all over, but mainly on the streambed," Evans said. "So the Germans won't know what we're up to. Stump, go tell Father Dare to get the wounded up front. We don't have much time."

"That's why the wounded should be at the tail of the column," I said, hating how easily the words came.

"No, we have to take care of the wounded, especially the litter cases," Evans said. "That's an order. I'm in command here, not you, Boyle."

"Billy's right," Flint said. Stump nodded his agreement. "The wounded will go as fast as they can, which is slower than the rest of us. Put them up front and you slow down eighty or so men. Say someone drops a litter, and everyone has to wait. The wind could kick up even worse, and suck the smoke right out of that streambed. Then we're all dead men."

"Put the wounded in the rear, they'll make it out almost as quick," Stump said. "Without endangering everyone else."

Evans was silent. He was new to the mathematics of war.

"Time's wasting," Flint said.

"Okay, Okay. Bobby, you're our scout. Flint, take him up front. Have Louie's squad close behind you. Keep an eye on him. Boyle, will you help the medic and Father Dare with the wounded?"

"Yeah, no problem." Evans was learning fast. Why risk one of your own men as tail-end Charlie?

"Send Louie up front, okay?" Flint said. I nodded and crawled off.

"We going back already?" Louie asked when I told him the plan. "I ain't finished my cigar."

"Train's leaving the station, Louie Walla from Walla Walla. Take care of my kid brother, okay?"

"My days of takin' care of people are over," Louie said.

"That's a sergeant's job, isn't it?"

"In this war, a sergeant's job is to get killed or go crazy. Rusty took care of all of us, and look what happened to him. I'm next, I know it."

"Hey, you're not dead yet, are you?" I said, trying to snap him out of it. He looked at me like I was crazy, which didn't surprise me. "You're still breathing, so get your squad up front, and keep them low and quiet."

I told the same thing to Danny and Charlie. Sticks was with them, the tall kid from the squad. I wished them luck. Father Dare and the medic had two litter cases and half a dozen walking wounded. Other men who'd been wounded slightly were already with their squads. The main problem was that we weren't walking, we were crawling.

The wounded guys didn't need much encouragement, not even the GI with shrapnel in his leg. No one wanted to be captured and have to depend on POW medical care. Carrying the litters was tough. We shanghaied one GI to help the medic, and Father Dare and I took the other. We had to duckwalk, holding the litter up to clear the ground. It was easy for the first few awkward steps, then near impossible, until finally spasms of pain were shooting through my arms and thighs.

"You were right, Boyle," Evans said as we halted next to him. "About the wounded."

"You would've figured it out," I said. "We ready?"

"As we can be. Two minutes until the artillery hits the hill and they lay smoke." Eighty men hugged the edge of the bank, all facing the same direction, waiting for the signal. "Good luck," Evans said, and was off, bent low, checking the men. There was going to be no safe place; it was either going to work or it wasn't. I spent the two minutes catching my breath, rubbing my sore thighs, not thinking about Danny in the lead.

The screech of incoming shells was followed instantly by multiple explosions on the wooded hill. The firing continued, keeping the Germans occupied, I hoped. Muted explosions to our rear were followed by plumes of churning white smoke concentrated along our escape route. The line ahead of me shuffled forward, slowly, like a long line of cars when the light changes. We moved, stopped, moved, stopped. I wanted to scream, to tell them to hurry up, but I bit my lip. Low and quiet, I told myself.

Finally we were moving, into the smoke. It was thick enough for us to run bent over, keeping our heads just below the surface. The smoke swirled in places and settled into thick pools in others. The artillery fire on the hill stopped, and for a moment there was nothing but an eerie, empty silence. The small sounds of leather, metal, and gear, boots on muddy soil, and hurried whispers quickly filled the void. Bursts of white phosphorous smoke landed behind us, and for the first time I thought we had a chance.

Machine-gun fire ripped through the air, probing the ditch we'd just left. I felt the air vibrate above me as the rounds searched farther afield, stitching the earth, hoping for flesh.

The line halted. Father Dare, at the front of the litter, nearly collided with the medic. An awful groaning sound rose up ahead of us, and I knew someone had been hit. A stray bullet, I hoped for the rest of us. For the man hit, it made no difference. We laid down the litters and Father Dare gave the other wounded men water. We waited while impatient murmurs ran up and down the line. I was the last man, and felt nothing but the white emptiness of death behind me. I fought the urge to leap out of the streambed and run for it, taking my chances with speed and leaving this ghostly, slow retreat behind.

Minutes passed, and we began shuffling along again. I lost track of time, hunched over, carrying the burden of a badly wounded man, able to see nothing beyond a yard away. The machine-gun fire rose in intensity, and this time it was aimed at us. The Krauts had figured it out, and were spraying the general vicinity with all they had. Clods of dirt kicked up along the bank as we bent further down, our arms heavy with the weight we carried. I had to tilt my head back to see anything, and I could barely make out Father Dare.

The air thrummed with bullets, hundreds of rounds slicing above us, looking for the right angle, the perfect trajectory of bullet and bone.

They found it. Screams tore loose from throats ahead of us, the sounds of men dying. It was like a dam breaking—no more low and quiet, but a footrace as the column sprinted, trying to outrun the Bonesaw, fear taking over where caution had been in control. The bursts kept coming, and I heard Stump coming down the line, telling us to hustle, we were almost there. He stayed with us as we passed bodies being carried out, including Flint with Louie draped over his shoulders, fireman style. Other GIs were carrying wounded between them, and I was too exhausted to even look for Danny. We ran until the streambed curved and brought us out into a field, behind a stone farmhouse. Medics were waiting, and in the swirl of smoke I saw Harding, standing next to a couple of Carabinieri. What were they doing here? We set down the litter, and I collapsed against the wall, my chest heaving, my lungs choking on the smoke, my mind as clouded as the air.

CHAPTER TWENTY-EIGHT

SOMEBODY GAVE ME a canteen and I drank half of its contents down and poured the rest over my head. The damned gray haze was everywhere, and now smoke grenades were tossed out to cover the jeeps coming up for the wounded. I managed to stand, and Harding materialized out of the swirling clouds.

"You okay, Boyle?"

"Yeah, I'm fine. Thanks for getting us out, Colonel."

"I wasn't entirely sure that runner would make it."

"I told him you'd make him a corporal once we got back."

"I'll see to it. Your kid brother okay?"

"I'm pretty sure, but I need to find him."

"Get a move on then. We have a report of Kraut tanks on the other side of that hill. If they decide to hit us now, things could get worse real fast."

Clutching a pair of binoculars, Harding was off to observe the German lines while I went in search of Danny. It was a mass of confusion, the badly wounded waiting for evacuation, the lightly wounded being treated behind the stone farmhouse, as smoke eddied and curled around the building and along the ground. I found Evans trying to sort out his squads from the crowd. He hadn't seen Danny. Dead bodies were laid out, about half a dozen, but I didn't want to look there yet. Flint walked by me, glassy-eyed, working the thousand-yard stare, so I didn't ask him how Louie was doing.

Father Dare was with the medics, looking about ready to pass out himself. He'd seen Stump and his squad, and thought he'd seen Danny and Charlie head down the road to Le Ferriere. I went in that direction as the Krauts lobbed a few mortar shells at us. It was halfhearted, as if they knew we'd pulled a fast one and were only going through the motions, but I jumped into a shell hole until it was over anyway.

When the shelling stopped, I looked up to see I was sharing the hole with Phil Einsmann.

"Hey Billy, helluva mess, isn't it?"

"What are you doing up here, Phil?"

"I was with a party of brass who came up to observe the advance. I snuck away for a closer look and nearly got my head blown off. Were you out there?"

"Yeah. Most of us made it back. Watch out for yourself, Phil. The Krauts aren't going to be looking for that war correspondent's patch on your shoulder."

"I hope I don't get that close. But if I do, look what I won in a poker game last night." He opened his jacket to show me his .45 automatic in a shoulder holster.

"Nice," I said. "For a noncombatant. Ditch that if you're captured."

"Not planning on that either. You going back to the village?"

"After I find my kid brother. Good luck," I said, climbing out the shell hole. I wandered down the road, looking at small clusters of GIs sharing canteens or a smoke, laughing as if they hadn't nearly been killed. Or because.

"Billy!" It was Danny and his pal, leaning against a tree by the side of the road, eating K rations. Canned cheese and biscuits. It actually looked good. I sat down next to him and we just grinned at each other. He gave me a biscuit with cheese and for some reason it seemed like the funniest thing in the world. We both started laughing, and Charlie even joined in, understanding how good it felt to be alive and in the company of someone you cared about.

"I saw Flint carrying Louie out," I said. "Is it bad?"

"Louie is dead," Charlie said.

"I know, but how is he?"

"Billy, Louie is really dead. Sticks too. They both got it in the head," Danny said.

"Jesus," I said. "What a waste." Another round of mortar fire came in, closer this time, leaving no time for mourning. Jeeps with wounded laid out on litters zipped down the road, making for the safety of Le Ferriere. "They're getting closer."

"We had to get out of the smoke," Danny said. "Charlie doesn't like it. He got lost for a while, but I found him."

"It is not a good place to die," Charlie said. "A man's soul would be lost as sure as I was. Louie should have waited for a better place."

Danny raised an eyebrow, not in a mocking way, but in sympathy. It sort of made sense, considering the riverbed was underground and smoke still drifted out of it. It was hard enough for the living to get out, never mind the recently departed.

"The smoke did save our lives," I offered.

"True. But it did not save Louie."

"Hard to argue—" A sharp *crack* cut me off, followed a second later by a massive explosion that engulfed the farmhouse and blew out the back wall where the wounded had been moments ago. Another retort echoed and the roof blew up, sending debris sky high. The force of the blasts was so great that the concussion instantly evaporated the smoke. This wasn't mortar fire, it was high-velocity cannon fire.

"Get back to Le Ferriere," I said to Danny as I ran to the farm-house. As usual, he didn't listen to me, lieutenant or not. I closed in on the scene with him and Charlie on my heels. A section of roof collapsed, and granite stones fell from the weakened rear wall like tears.

"Tigers!" someone yelled, and others took up the call. Every GI thought every German tank was a Tiger tank, but today they had it nailed. Four Tigers, their 88-mm guns pointed straight at us, were trundling across the fields, infantry spread out behind them. Harding had been right: we were sitting ducks, a mass of disorganized men with practically no cover. We had to get back to the village.

"Fall back, fall back!" I yelled, and few needed the encouragement. I saw one Tiger halt, and knew what that meant. "Get down!"

Another shell slammed into the farmhouse, this one bringing down the roof completely, starting a fire inside. Behind the gutted ruin, two GIs were struggling to get up, blood and dust caked on their faces.

"Help these two get to the village," I said, pointing out the wounded men to Danny and Charlie. I searched for Evans, not finding him anywhere, the flames and smoke making it hard to see. The heat drove me back and I stumbled over someone. I knelt and shook the man to check if he was alive. It was Louie. I'd stumbled across the dead, already laid out for Graves Registration. I could see the hit he'd taken, right at the base of the skull. It wasn't pretty. I saw something else, too. Gunshot residue on his neck. Powder burns from a weapon held close to his head.

"Billy, help!" It was Flint, half carrying Evans, whose arm hung limp and dripped blood. Evans looked to be in shock, his mouth half open and eyes wide. "Back there, Stump's hurt."

I stumbled in the direction Flint had indicated, moving against the flow of the last of the dazed GIs making their way to Le Ferriere, my mind reeling. Who had shot Louie at close range, and why? Is that why Louie thought his time was up? Did he see it coming? And did this confirm Louie wasn't the killer? Or did someone take revenge on him? All I knew was that another GI was dead, robbed of his chance for survival. It was a slim chance, but it was all he had in the world.

Two more explosions wracked the earth, and I hit the dirt, feeling debris rain down on me. The clanking of tank treads grew louder, and I rose, shaking off the dust and confusion, willing my body to move faster, to get the hell out before the place was swarming with Krauts, or those tanks got close enough to use their machine guns.

I heard a hacking, choking sound and crawled toward it. I saw two bodies, off to the side of what had been the farmhouse. One was still, the other on his knees, struggling with something wound around his neck, dust and dirt coating his hair and face. I got closer and saw it was Harding. He was pulling at the leather straps of his binoculars, and my mind struggled to understand what I was seeing, to figure out what he was doing. His mouth was open, gasping for air, getting damn little, and I saw the tightly wound straps digging into the skin of his neck. I drew my knife and cut at the leather, knowing we had only seconds before he lost consciousness, the tanks were on us, or both.

The binoculars fell and Harding drew in a wheezing lungful of air. Deep red welts rose on his neck where the strap had gouged his skin. He motioned to Stump, unable to speak. I felt Stump's neck and found a pulse. He had a nasty gash over one eye, and there was a lot of blood, but other than that I didn't see another wound. But what I did see was a king of hearts, crumpled in his clenched fist. I opened his hand and showed it to Harding, although he already had a pretty good idea.

Harding and I draped Stump over our shoulders and dragged him away, the sound of tank treads and German war cries not far behind. We met up with Danny and Charlie outside of Le Ferriere, as our artillery began to pound the area around the farmhouse, ground we had held and given up. They took Stump and we entered the village through the gate where the attack had begun early that morning, and I wondered if the brass had stuck around to watch the retreat of the survivors. Probably not.

An antitank gun was wheeled up and positioned at the gate. All I cared about was getting some peace and quiet to think things through, which was a bit difficult with an artillery barrage sailing over my head and Tiger tanks a half mile down the road. We headed to the aid station, which was doing brisk business. Most of the wounded were being treated outside, with only the most serious cases going inside the small building, one of the few structures in Le Ferriere that had escaped damage. Ambulances pulled up and medics loaded wounded aboard, then returned to the line of men with bloody bandages and dazed looks.

We laid Stump down and Danny began to clean his head wound, washing away blood with water from his canteen and applying sulfa powder. Harding sat on the ground, still not looking all that well. I gave him my canteen and he drank thirstily.

"Can you talk, Colonel?"

"Get ... his ... weapon," he managed to croak out. I took Stump's .45 from his holster as Danny looked at me strangely. I checked the magazine as I sat down next to Harding. There were six rounds, and one in the chamber, meaning one had been fired. I sniffed the barrel. Recently.

"Louie, Danny's squad sergeant, was shot in the back of the head, close range," I said. "Probably when we came under fire in the streambed. With the smoke and the noise, no one would have noticed one more guy going down. Can you tell me what happened to you?"

"Thought I saw vehicles. Used binoculars," Harding said, choking out each word. "Next thing, someone's twisting the strap around my neck. Forced me to the ground. Almost had me, then that Tiger opened up. I blacked out, then you were cutting the strap."

"I found Stump about ten feet from where you were. Did you see who attacked you?" Harding shook his head no, and drank more water. I went over to Stump and checked him again. The cut on his forehead was bad, but that seemed to be his only injury. He was probably hit by a piece of wood or masonry. If it had been shrapnel, he'd have been dead. I went through his pockets as Danny stood back. Nothing unusual.

"What's going on, Billy?" Danny asked. I took the card from my pocket and showed Danny. He whistled. I stowed it away and put my finger to my lips, signaling him to keep quiet about it. Then I brought him over to Harding, who'd managed to stand up.

"Colonel Harding, this is my brother Danny." I was glad Danny didn't play the rookie and try to salute. Harding nodded and stuck out his hand, and they shook.

"Billy has told us a lot about you, Colonel."

"I can only imagine," Harding said, his voice returning but still sounding harsh. "He's mentioned you as well. You hold up all right out there?"

"I think so, sir."

"He did, Colonel, I can vouch for that," I said.

"Good to meet you, son. Take care of yourself. Stay low out there," Harding growled.

"I will, sir. That's just what Billy tells me."

"Danny, see if you can find Lieutenant Evans. Flint probably brought him here."

"Okay, Billy," he said, and he and Charlie began searching the wounded.

"Do we have our killer?" Harding asked.

"Sure looks like it. He had you lined up to be part of his royal flush."

"I was in the wrong place at the right time, for him anyway. I never was so glad to almost be killed by a German 88."

"I don't think he's going anywhere soon, but can you keep an eye on him? I want to find Father Dare." I handed Harding Stump's .45.

"Not a problem," Harding said. "I hear the padre does good work as a medic."

"He does," I said, thinking about the .45 that he carried. Plenty of guys who weren't officially issued automatic pistols, like Father Dare, got them one way or the other. How many of those weapons were out there today, in the smoke? A fair number, but most wouldn't have been fired at all. This fighting hadn't been at close quarters. I stared at Stump's face, cleaned of blood and grime, and wondered why. Why did the killings start, and why did they have to go on?

I asked around and a medic told me he saw Father Dare enter the village church, a few buildings down. I climbed the steps and opened the carved wooden doors, feeling the weight of centuries behind them. The small church had been hit by a shell on the roof, and thick, heavy timbers had fallen in, crushing rows of pews. Father Dare knelt at the altar, his helmet on the floor, his head bowed. He swayed, and it seemed as if he were so lost in prayer that he might lose his balance. I stepped closer, not wanting to interrupt his prayers, but unwilling to let him crack his head against the marble altar. I went to steady him, and only then noticed the pool of blood spreading under his left leg.

"Father," I said, kneeling at his side. Even though he was a rough-and-tumble padre, and we'd dodged bullets together, here in God's house I felt ill at ease, like the altar boy I'd been, unsure of the ways of adults and especially priests. "Are you all right?"

"I am praying, Billy. Praying for God himself to come down and save us. I told him to leave Jesus home, that this was no place for children." He folded his hands in prayer once again, and fell into my arms.

"Shrapnel in his calf," the medic told me after I'd carried Father Dare back. "He must have been bleeding into his boot, and when he knelt down, it all came out."

"Is he going to be okay?"

"He won't be dancing anytime soon, but it should heal up. It's mostly shock that concerns me, losing all that blood. It would have been a lot worse if you hadn't gotten him back here." With that, he went back to tending to the last of the wounded, the less serious cases who'd had to wait.

Danny had found Evans, on a litter, waiting for the next ambulance. His arm and shoulder were heavily bandaged, and an IV drip had been set up on a rifle set in the ground by its bayonet. He looked as white as a sheet.

"Doc said he lost a lot of blood," Danny told me. "Flint saved his life getting here."

"How you doing, Evans?" I asked as I squatted down next to him.

"They gave me enough morphine that I think I'm okay," he said lazily. "But I don't think I am."

"That's a million-dollar wound you got, Lieutenant," Flint said, appearing at Evans's side. "Doc told me himself. You'll live, but you'll do your living back in the States."

"I'm sorry," Evans said. "Sorry to leave you guys so soon. Did we lose many men?"

"It would have been worse without you, Lieutenant," Flint said. "You did real good for your first time out, you can be proud of that."

"Thanks. Tell Louie and Stump so long, okay?"

"Sure," Flint said, barely missing a beat. "Soon as I see them." He walked away, giving me a secretive wink as he passed. No need to burden Evans with the bad news. Danny and Charlie said their good-byes, and I sat next to Evans.

"What was it you wanted to ask me back there?" Evans said, his eyes closing.

"When you were assigned to the supply depot in Acerra, did you ever go the Bar Raffaele?"

"Sure, lots of guys did. But I never . . . you know."

"Never paid for a whore?"

"Right."

"You talked with the girls though," I said.

"Couldn't avoid it," Evans said. His eyes were fully closed now.

"Ever meet a girl named Ileana?"

"Oh yeah, Ileana. A looker." His head nodded off as the morphine took effect. He mumbled something under his breath. ". . . one of the guys . . . wanted . . ."

"What? Who?" But there was no waking him, the drug had taken him far away from this ruined village and the jagged steel buried in his shoulder.

CHAPTER TWENTY-NINE

THE JEEP CAREENED around an antiaircraft emplacement, hitting forty as the driver gunned the engine and sped by a fuel dump, jerrycans stacked ten high for a hundred yards. He was trying to outrun a stick of bombs dropped by a Ju 88, exploding in a ragged line behind us. I held my breath, waiting to be blown to kingdom come if one came close to all that gasoline.

"Listen," I said, grabbing the driver's shoulder from the backseat. "I want to get to the hospital, not be admitted to it. Slow down."

"Not the way it's done, sir," he said, downshifting as he cleared the burning wreckage of a truck and towed artillery piece. "This hospital is set up next to an airfield, ammo dump, supply depot, and most of the ack-ack in the beachhead. It ain't a healthy place to linger, wounded or healthy."

"Why the hell did they put it there?"

"On account of there's nowhere else. You mighta noticed real estate is at a premium around here. I've been ferrying wounded from the aid stations for two days straight, and I've brought guys here and seen 'em hitching a ride back to the line on my next trip. They say it's too damn dangerous."

He slowed as we drove through a gap in the five-foot-high sandbag wall surrounding the field hospital. Rows and rows of tents marked with giant red crosses were set up, the ground between them churned into mud. Engineers were excavating one area, digging in tents so only the canvas roofs were above ground. A field hospital was supposed to be behind the lines, far from enemy fire. This was not a good sign. If the walking wounded started walking away from a field hospital for the relative safety of their foxholes on the front line, something was seriously wrong.

The driver backed up the jeep to an open tent as medical personnel scurried out. Stump was still unconscious, strapped to a litter across the rear of the jeep. By the time the orderlies got Stump off and I had one foot on the ground, the driver had hit twenty, one hand waving good-bye.

"Welcome to Hell's Half Acre, Lieutenant," said a nurse clad in fatigues several sizes too large and GI boots caked in mud. "We'll take good care of your pal, don't worry."

"He's not my pal," I said, pointing to his wrists, tied tight. "He's my prisoner."

"He's my patient, and the rope comes off. I don't care what regulations he broke, he gets treated just like everyone else. Now get out of my way."

"Okay, okay. But I'll be watching. And give me his clothes, I need to search them."

"What'd he do, swipe General Lucas's pipe?"

"He's murdered at least six people." Landry, Galante, Cole, Inzerillo, Arnold. Probably Louie Walla from Walla Walla. Cole was by proxy, but he was a victim just the same.

"You mean six on our side? Who'd want to kill his own kind in this hellhole?"

"Good question," I said. I watched as she checked his eyes and another nurse cut away his clothes, looking for wounds. She called for a doctor as I gathered up Stump's uniform and sat on a cot to check its contents. Like a lot of GIs, Stump fought out of his pockets, not wanting to carry a pack and risk losing it. The medics had made sure to empty out ammo and grenades, but they didn't bother with personal effects.

Cigarettes, a lighter, packs of toilet paper. Chewing gum. A letter from his mother, asking if he'd gotten the mittens she'd knitted him, and reminding him to keep clean and change his socks. It sounded like he was at summer camp, not war. He'd started a letter back to her, saying how swell Naples was, and how their barracks were warm and dry. Odd that a six-time murderer would fib to his mother so she wouldn't worry about him at the front.

Other than a half-eaten Hershey's bar, that was it. No clues. No deck of cards missing the ten through king of hearts.

All I knew was that I was hungry. I ate the rest of the chocolate, and waited.

"Lieutenant," a voice said, from somewhere off in the distance. "Lieutenant?"

"Yeah," I said, waking up with a start. At some point the cot must have reached up and grabbed me, since I was laid out flat.

"The doctor can fill you in now," the nurse said, pointing to a guy in a white operating gown, removing his cotton mask. But I would have recognized him anyway, with that blond hair.

"Doctor Cassidy, right?"

"Boyle! I guess we were both headed to the same place. Did you find that murderer back in Caserta?"

"I think I found him here. The sergeant you just treated."

"No kidding? Did you give him that whack on the head? Nearly did him in."

"No, that was courtesy of a German 88, or at least a piece of a farmhouse that was hit by it."

"He did have some small bits of shrapnel in his legs, but nothing serious," Cassidy said, leading me to another tent that served as the post-op ward. "He's got a pretty severe concussion, but that's it. Not from shrapnel, most likely flying debris, like you said. His helmet must have absorbed most of the blow, otherwise he'd have been a goner."

"Can he be moved?"

"No, we need to watch him for a day or so, in case there's any other damage. We'll know within twenty-four hours."

"Is he awake?"

"In and out. He's got one helluva headache, and is a bit disoriented. Is he really the killer?"

"I found him next to a colonel he was trying to strangle, with this in his hand." I showed Cassidy the crumpled king of hearts.

"A colonel? So he got his major?"

"Yeah, Major Arnold, just before we pulled out."

"Arnold, now he was a piece of work." Cassidy shook his head, his grief at the loss of Arnold easily kept at bay.

"What do you mean by that?" I asked as he opened a canvas flap and we entered a long tent, with wood plank flooring and rows of cots along each side, filled with the wounded, who were bandaged in every possible place.

"Like I told you, he and Schleck didn't believe in combat fatigue. Or I should say, Arnold believed whatever Schleck told him to. And he was a souvenir hound of the worst kind."

"Hey, everyone wants a Luger or an SS dagger," I said, interested in what Cassidy thought the worst kind was.

"Yeah, but with Arnold it was business. He took loot from homes, and collected soldbuchs—you know what they are?"

"Sure. German pay books, with a photo of the soldier."

"Something macabre about that, don't you think? Collecting pictures of dead Krauts? And all that other stuff—caps, medals—he didn't exactly pay top dollar for them. I heard he took them for favors. Not right for an officer. Well, it doesn't matter now. Here's Sergeant Stumpf."

Stump had a thick bandage around his neck, and several on his legs. His eyelids flickered open, then shut. I knelt by his cot.

"Stump, can you hear me?"

"What . . . happened?" His voice was weak and raspy.

"Remember the Tigers at the farmhouse?"

"Yeah. My squad?"

"I don't know," I said. "Can you open your eyes?" He did, and I held up the king of hearts. "Tell me about this."

I watched his eyes blink and his brow furrow, as if he couldn't understand what I was showing him. Then came the sound of artillery, the metal-on-metal screeching sound like hitting the brakes at high speed with pads worn clean away. Every doctor and nurse in the tent instantly covered the wounded with their bodies, leaning over the bandaged men and cradling heads with their arms. I did the same with Stump, just as the first rounds landed—*whump, whump, whump*—close enough to shower the canvas tent with debris that sounded like hail. I felt something burning my back and stood up, swatting at myself.

"Shrapnel," Cassidy said, pulling off my jacket. I noticed small tears in the tent, and one patient dousing his blanket with water. "From that far away, it has lost most of its momentum, but it's red hot." He shook the jacket and a sharp, jagged piece of metal fell out. Another round of artillery echoed across the sky, but was a good distance away. No one paid it any mind, except for one GI, both arms swathed in bandages, who rolled out of his cot and began scratching at the floor, trying to dig into it with damaged hands. Two nurses took his arms as Cassidy raced over with a syringe, jabbing the screaming soldier in the thigh. He went limp, moaning as the nurses lifted him back onto his cot.

"Thanks," Stump said, then pointed to the card I still held. I showed it to him again.

"Some colonel dead?"

"No, no thanks to you. This was in your hands when that German shell knocked you out, as you were strangling Colonel Harding."

"Who? God, my head hurts." He tried to raise his head and check out the rest of his body.

"Bad concussion, a bit of shrapnel in the legs. Nothing to worry about," I said. "It's over, Stump. We got you dead to rights. Found you next to Harding, with that card in your hand. You were trying to strangle him with his binocular strap. Almost had him, too. Then one of the Tigers blasted the farmhouse, and you got hit on the side of the head."

"Harding? The colonel who got us out when we were pinned down?"

"The same."

"Why the hell would I do that? You think I'm Red Heart?" He winced, the effort of speaking painful.

"Why would you have this in your hand?" I held up the king again.

"Dunno. Someone put it there?" His voice was weaker, and his eyes closed.

"That's what they all say, Stump," I said, leaning closer. "Tell me the truth. Why did you kill all those people? What did you have against them? What did you have against Louie?"

"Louie? Jesus, he was my pal. What happened?"

"Bullet in the back of the head, close range. You fire your automatic out there?"

"Of course not, we were never close enough to the Krauts for that."

"It was fired. One round gone. I checked it when I found you."

"Can't be. Louie, who'd want to kill Louie?" he said, struggling to keep his eyes open. "Was a major killed? Who?"

"Yeah. Arnold, the day we left Caserta. You know that."

"No. You mentioned him, said he was alive."

"I just didn't say he was dead. How'd you do it, Stump? Get him alone like that?"

"I didn't," he said. "Why would I?"

"That's what I want to know. Why strangle Harding after he saved our bacon? Why any of them?"

"You said Harding was choked by his binocular straps?"

"Yes. Do you remember?"

"And that you found me holding that card?"

"Yes."

"Lieutenant, my head is scrambled, but even I know you'd need two hands free to strangle a guy. You'd grab and twist those leather straps real tight. Hard to do with a playing card in your hand. That one's a little worn, but it would be badly crumpled if I'd done that. You'd keep it in your pocket until the deed was done. Now leave me alone."

Maybe that made sense. Maybe I should have thought of it. But I wasn't taking any chances. I found an MP and had him cuff Stump to the cot. If he was going anywhere, he'd be dragging an army cot along with him.

I wandered outside, wondering what to do next. I could go back to HQ and see if there was any message from Kaz. I could also check with Kearns about Danny's transfer and see about getting him out of the platoon. It was a dangerous place, with death dealt from both sides of the table. But first I needed some chow. I spotted Cassidy checking charts and asked him where the mess was. He ditched his bloodstained operating gown and said he was buying.

"It's not much on taste, but there's plenty of it," Cassidy said as we filled our mess tins with corned-beef hash and lima beans. The coffee was hot, and there was even sugar, so I couldn't complain.

"Do you get many cases like that fellow who tried to dig a hole in the floor?" I asked after I got most of the grub down.

"We're starting to see them. The artillery bombardment has been getting worse real fast. Most of the wounds we treat are shrapnel. It's the kind of thing that wears on a man."

"But the Third Division is a veteran outfit. Shouldn't it take longer for them to be affected?"

"That's just it, Billy. The Third has been at the sharp end since North Africa. Then Sicily, then the landing at Salerno, where they took a lot of casualties. After that, the Volturno River, and then Cassino. They only had a few weeks' rest before this landing, and now we've got Germans on the high ground shelling us constantly. The replacements don't know what to expect, the veterans do, and I can't tell you which is worse."

"What do you do for them?"

"The GI you saw will be evacuated as soon as a transport is available. He's got a million-dollar wound, both arms riddled with shrapnel, so he's going home. It's the ones without physical wounds I worry about. A short time in a safe rear area is a big help, but there is no safe haven here. Last I heard, the beachhead was only seven miles wide. The Germans can shell us anywhere they want, day or night."

"How do you doctors decide which wounds are the million-dollar variety?"

"It's not an official term, Billy. It's any wound bad enough to get you sent home but not bad enough to be permanently crippling. That guy had severe muscle damage. No way he could heal up well enough to handle a rifle in combat, but with physical therapy he should be okay. Might take a while, so he fits the bill."

"What do you think about these murders? Does a killer like that have to be crazy?"

"Crazy isn't an official term either. Well, to a normal person, yes, someone who commits multiple murders is crazy, since they operate outside the norms of society. But these killings were well thought out, and had a distinctive pattern. The killer eluded capture, until now. These are all signs of intelligent planning. Is that crazy?"

"You sound like a lawyer."

"Goes to show, there are no easy answers when it comes to crazy."

"Take a look at this, and tell me if this sounds like a lunatic murderer," I said, handing Cassidy Stump's unfinished letter to his mother. Cassidy read the letter, nodding a few times. He handed it back.

"I can't say he's not a murderer, based on this. There are many reasons for murder, and plenty of them wouldn't preclude telling your mother a little white lie. He obviously wants her to think he's safe behind the lines, in Naples, since the Anzio landing will be in the news."

"What about the lunatic part?"

"That's harder, Billy. This letter shows genuine concern for another person. I'm just theorizing now, but cold-blooded murders as you've described them demonstrate a total disregard for others. No remorse at all. This letter shows the opposite. He could have not written her, or he could have written her the truth, but instead he took a different tack, making up a story to ease her mind."

"So Stump is normal?"

"Billy, one of the things you learn on a psychiatric ward is that words like normal and insane are essentially worthless. It's what I find fascinating about the human mind."

"That's swell, Doc, but I need answers and I need them now. I've got a lunatic on the loose."

"Well, 'lunatic' is not a precise term, but 'psychopath' is. I think that may be what you're looking for."

"Like I said, crazy."

"A psychotic is crazy, in the conventional sense; they're the ones who hear voices, that sort of thing. But a psychopath is different. You could talk with one and you'd never know it. A true psychopath could write that letter, only if it served a specific purpose and was to his benefit. They're emotional mimics. They don't feel real emotion, but they are great observers, and know when to act normal. But a psychopath wouldn't care about his mother's feelings. He wouldn't even understand what that meant."

"So how can you spot one?"

"It's easy, once they're caught. They're great deniers, sometimes telling such outright lies about their guilt that it's easy to see through them. They usually have a grandiose sense of their own self-worth and capabilities. But otherwise, they can act just like you and me."

"Except that it wouldn't bother them to kill half a dozen people."

"No, it may even be a source of satisfaction for them. Think about it. No conscience, no empathy or understanding of others. They're not good at long-term planning, so they find it easy to act on impulse, and they are highly manipulative, so they can often get away with things."

"But you said this whole thing took planning."

"Yes, but if we're dealing with a psychopath, I doubt he planned everything out first. I'd bet it was an impulse that started the ball rolling. Then the grandiose thinking might kick in. In his own world, he might derive pleasure watching those around him react to his escalating crimes. The more he gets away with, the more powerful he feels."

"It doesn't sound like he'd be a candidate for combat fatigue."

"No. He'd have a sense of self-preservation, but he wouldn't suffer any effects from killing, or seeing his comrades killed. Other than enjoying the spectacle of it all, maybe. Want some more joe?"

"Yeah, thanks," I said, and thought about what Cassidy had said while he refilled our cups. Impulse. The sequence of the first two killings always had bothered me. Now I was sure Landry hadn't been killed first. The playing cards were a trick, a manipulation, to cover up an impulse killing to divert suspicion. Galante had been an immediate threat, and had to be dealt with on the spot. On impulse. I'd bet dollars to doughnuts that Landry knew the killer and Galante were together, so he had to go. Then that grandiose imagination kicks in. Make it look like a guy with a grudge against the chain of command. Get everyone in a tizzy, and watch the fun.

"Would a psychopath enjoy army life?" I asked when Cassidy returned with the coffees.

"Well, you'd have to be crazy to," he said, grinning at his own joke.

"So what would happen if someone told this nutcase he was going to pull him off the line? Send him to a hospital, cure him?"

"You mean a psychiatric hospital? No way. Our hypothetical guy would kill to stay out of one of those."

"He'd prefer to stay in combat? Now that's crazy."

"I'd say in some ways it could be the perfect environment, since there are clear rules and procedures. He could figure out how to manipulate the system easily. But on the other hand, the peacetime army would be too boring. Psychopaths crave stimulation."

"Combat is stimulating."

"Yeah, I see what you mean. I've always said that if you keep men in combat long enough, ninety-eight percent will break down from combat fatigue. The other two percent will be psychopaths."

CHAPTER THIRTY

"WE'RE SHORT ON men, Boyle," Kearns said. "I'm sorry, but Second Battalion has been pulled back into reserve, and that'll have to do. No transfers, not for anybody."

"But sir—"

"Can it, Boyle. If I could I would—we really owe you one. But orders are orders."

"Okay," I said, not liking it one bit, and not certain that I was owed a damn thing yet.

"The provost marshal is taking charge of Sergeant Stumpf as soon as he's discharged from the hospital. Meanwhile we have MPs standing guard. You going back with him?"

"I have to talk to Colonel Harding first, Major. There are a few loose ends I'd like to tie up."

"Be my guest. I'm sure you'll want to visit with your brother for a while."

"Yes sir."

"Well done, Boyle," he said, rising from his desk in the underground wine cellar and extending his hand.

"Thanks. But remember, Stump still denies he's the killer, and we're short on proof."

"I wouldn't expect a mad killer to admit his guilt. And that card and the marks around Sam's neck are proof enough. Not to mention a couple of dozen colonels and generals who aren't asking for body-guards."

Explosions shook the ground above us, loosening dust from the rafters and coating everything in the room with gray grit. Men wore their helmets even here, deep underground. The German bombard-ment was becoming more intense, as the Krauts brought more and more heavy stuff up into the Alban Hills.

I'd stayed with Stump for hours after my talk with Cassidy, just watching, talking a bit, trying to size him up. He was sure of his inno-cence, but worried about the military justice system taking him in and spitting him out. It seemed like a sane way to look at things. They finally gave him something to help him sleep and kicked me out. I'd been dog-tired, and went back to the house where Kaz and I had bunked, only to find everyone sleeping in the cellar. Between a snoring captain and a couple of artillery barrages, I didn't get much sleep.

This morning I'd hoped to get Danny's transfer in the works, but Kearns had put the kibosh on that. At least Danny's outfit had been pulled off the line and put into reserve, which meant a couple of miles between them and the front. Still in artillery range, but then what wasn't?

There were no messages from Kaz, and I couldn't check with him since I didn't know exactly where he was. So I drove back to the field hospital, looking for Lieutenant Evans and Father Dare. I wanted to find out what Evans had been trying to say about Ileana at Bar Raffaele, and I was still curious about the pistol-packing padre. I'd known my share of priests, and while some liked a good game of poker, none of them carried a .45 automatic. Being a man of the cloth could be a good cover for the kind of maniac I was hunting. Like the army, the church gave you a nice set of rules to follow, and it had been my experience that rules were good things to hide behind. Then another talk with Stump. I wanted to look in his eyes and see—what? All that I saw last time we talked was derision at the idea he was the killer. His only proof he wasn't was an uncrumpled playing card. If he wasn't lying, then the real killer was bound to strike again. How sure was I?

Then I'd visit Danny and Flint, and question anyone in the platoon who might have seen a GI with an automatic in his hand during the retreat. What about Flint? If I was right about the killer being in the 3rd Platoon, then he had to be on the list of suspects. But I'd seen him helping Evans out of the smoke. Could he have gone after Harding, then left the job half-finished? Why? If the object was to frame Stump, a dead Harding would have been even better. Could the 88 have interrupted him? But Flint had looked fine, as fine as anyone who'd been through that attack and retreat. If the Tiger had stopped him, he would have shown some effect from the explosion. It didn't make sense.

"Father Dare? He left early this morning," a nurse told me. "Said he had to get back to his unit and be of some use. We wanted to keep him another day or so, but his leg will be all right if he keeps it clean."

"How was he? Was he upset about anything?"

"He just said he didn't want to become a permanent resident of Hell's Half Acre. Can't say I blame him." She consulted a chart and led me to the tent where Evans was resting, a cast encasing his shoulder and arm, bandages wrapped around his head.

"Flint saved my life," Evans said. "I took a load of shrapnel in my shoulder. They told me I would've bled to death if he hadn't pulled me out. There was so much smoke, I'm damn lucky he found me."

"He's the senior noncom now. He's probably in command of the platoon."

"What happened to Louie and Stump? Are they wounded?"

I filled him in on Louie being shot in the head, and Stump being in custody as the Red Heart Killer.

"It's hard to believe. Stump? And why kill Louie? They were buddies. It doesn't add up."

"He's killed whomever he needed to, not just officers. There had to be a reason, I don't think he killed randomly. Is there anything you can think of? Something Louie said or saw that he shouldn't have?"

"Louie spoke to me about believing his time was up," Evans said. "But that was about the war, not these killings. That's how I took it, anyway."

"Were he and Gates close?"

"Yeah, they went back to North Africa. He took Gates's death hard, kept saying he wished he'd been with him, maybe he could have gotten the drop on that officer. Caught out there yesterday, I think he'd given up all hope."

The snarl of aircraft approaching interrupted us, and the crash of bombs down by the sea, a few hundred yards away, signaled the approach of the Luftwaffe, hard at work hitting the ships supplying the beachhead. Our antiaircraft batteries opened up, and the pounding of the guns combined with explosions was deafening. The medical staff grabbed helmets and stood by their patients.

"Can you make it to a shelter?" I asked Evans, yelling into his ear.

"No, takes too long. Best to ride it out. You go."

Now, I had a burning desire to make it home from this war in one piece, and normally at the sound of air-raid sirens I dive head-first into the nearest bomb shelter. But with those nurses, doctors, and orderlies staying put, I felt embarrassed to skedaddle. Dumb, I know. I held my helmet in place with my hands and sat on the floor, pulling my knees up to protect myself. If a bomb hit close by, it would be meaningless, but it gave me something to do.

I felt the vibrations from the bomb hits in the wood flooring, and then a tremendous crash, the cots and me bouncing a couple of times. That was real close, and I was glad that no one tried to dig a tunnel out of there. I would have been tempted to join in.

"Now I know why they call it Hell's Half Acre," I said as the explosions receded.

"I won't miss the place," Evans said. "They say I'll be shipped out to Naples in a few days." He shifted in his cot, trying to get comfortable. His arm was set up, a brace in the cast supporting it.

"Does it hurt?"

"Yeah," he said. "Still got some shrapnel in there. The doc said it would take a few operations to get it all out."

"Hey, a million-dollar wound, congratulations," I said, meaning it. Evans had done all right. But I still had questions for him. "Do you remember when we were talking about Bar Raffaele, right after you were wounded? About the girl, Ileana?"

"I remember Ileana, but I don't recall talking with you about her. They gave me morphine out there, so everything's kind of hazy."

"You started to say something about one of the guys and her, but then you faded away."

"There was a lieutenant who was sweet on her. It was kind of sad, really."

"Could that have been Landry?"

"No idea. I guess so. I didn't know the guy, maybe saw him there a few times. It was just something you talked about, you know? Was she playing him for a sap, or was she going to give up the business? Either way, it'd be tough for him."

"You got that right. Rest up, and enjoy Naples."

"Thanks. You find that killer and end this, okay? There's enough dead bodies here for a lifetime."

I couldn't argue.

Outside, I buttoned my jacket up against the cold wind coming off the sea. The sky was leaden gray, the ground damp, and I felt the chill creep up through my boots. I decided a cup of joe was in order, and headed for the mess tent. I saw that the dug-in tents were finished, set four feet underground and reinforced with sandbags. Litters were being carried down the steps into what looked like an operating room. Not the fanciest hospital, but likely the best north of Naples.

In the mess tent, I spotted Bobby K, wearing his new corporal's stripes.

"Those look good on you, Bobby K," I said, sitting across from him with my coffee. We were at the end of a long trestle table, and I set my Thompson down next to the coffee.

"Thanks, Lieutenant," he said. "I lost sight of you yesterday. Glad you're okay."

"I am. What are you doing here?"

"I was escorting some Kraut prisoners when we got caught in the bombing and had to bring a few of them in to be treated. Soon as they're patched up they're getting loaded on a transport and shipped out. How lucky, huh?"

"No kidding. You're not hurt, right?"

"Nope, just enjoying the privileges of rank. I got three privates watching the wounded prisoners while I sit here. So thanks again. Colonel Harding came through, like you said he would."

"You deserve it, Bobby. You're in reserve with Second Battalion, right?"

"Yeah, we're digging in deep. They've been shelling us pretty bad. We had the POWs in a holding pen but we had to bring them into our shelters. Some of the guys wanted to leave them out there for a taste of their own medicine, but that didn't seem right. Anyway, our captain ordered us to, so that was that."

"So when did they get hit?"

"After it was over. The Kraut observers must have seen the trucks coming in to load them up, 'cause all of a sudden we got plastered. Couple of POWs got killed, but the rest were minor wounds. Minor-when-it-ain't-you kind of minor."

"They seem to be able to zero in pretty well. Spotting a few trucks from up in those hills is a neat trick," I said. I noticed Corporal Kawulicz eyeing my Thompson. He had a carbine leaning against the bench by his leg. "Looking for a Thompson?"

"I tried to get one, but they're hard to come by."

"Why do you want one? That M1 carbine is more accurate."

"Yeah, but it's not like we're target shooting. And they're only .30 caliber rounds. The Thompson has better stopping power with that .45 slug. Corporals are supposed to be issued one, you know."

"Tell you what," I said. "We'll swap." I pushed the submachine toward him and undid my web belt with the extra magazines.

"Really? You sure, Lieutenant?"

"I'm sure." He didn't need much encouragement.

A few minutes later, we walked out of the mess tent, the new corporal proudly sporting his new Thompson submachine gun. I carried the lighter M1 carbine, glad of the reduced weight but still feeling a burden settle onto my shoulders. I was worried about Danny going through the barrages Bob described. How were the Germans hitting us so accurately, so far from the front lines?

We stopped at a tent with a bored private standing guard, and Bobby K stuck his head inside to ask if the prisoners were bandaged up and ready to go.

"Perhaps you can explain this, Corporal," I heard a familiar voice say, and saw Doctor Cassidy emerge from the tent with Bobby in tow. "Billy, didn't expect to see you here again. Are you in charge of this prisoner detail?"

"No, I was just having coffee with the corporal. We're old pals. What's up?"

"Follow me," he said. He took us to another tent and opened the flaps. A sickly smell wafted out and I guessed this was the morgue, or where they stashed the dead if 'morgue' was too fancy a term for a dirt-floor army tent. Several bodies were on the ground, already zipped up in mattress covers. One had only a sheet covering him. "Care to tell me how this happened, Corporal?" He pulled the sheet away to reveal a German officer. His tunic collar was undone, and he wore the distinctive paratrooper's smock.

"*Fallschirmjäger*," I said. His right trouser leg was torn open and his leg swathed in a dirty bandage.

"Right, but he didn't die of his wounds, did he, Corporal?" Cassidy said.

"I don't know, he was limping but seemed okay. Then after the shelling he was out cold. I couldn't find any other wounds, so I brought him here. What's wrong with him?"

"This," I said, pointing to the bruises around his neck.

"And these," Cassidy said, showing the trademark red splotches in the eyes and across the face. "He was strangled, Corporal. What do you know about this?"

"Nothing, sir, honest. We protected these guys from the barrage, brought them into our own shelters. Then we got hit again after the all clear. It was all confused, and we had to make sure no one got away. I loaded this guy in with the wounded and brought him here. That's all I know."

I got a sinking feeling in my stomach. On the paratrooper's sleeve was the camouflage insignia of an *oberst*. German for colonel, two green leaves with three bars underneath. I reached into his tunic pocket, knowing what I would find there.

"The corporal didn't do anything wrong," I said, showing Cassidy the king of hearts. "Take the handcuffs off Stump."

CHAPTER THIRTY-ONE

"A KRAUT? HE'S killed a Kraut?" Heads turned as Major Kearns raised his voice. His worried tone did sound odd, since killing Krauts was our stock-in-trade. Several heads turned among the Corps HQ staff laboring underground.

"Quiet down, Major," Harding said, hustling us off to a far corner of the wine cellar where clerks worked their Smith Coronas. Harding told them to take a break and we sat at the narrow table, typewriters in front of us, army forms and carbon paper scattered about. I'd brought Cassidy along because I thought an expert might explain things better than I could. I still didn't quite get whether this murderer was crazy or not.

"Now calmly and quietly, tell us what happened," Harding said. "I thought you had the killer in custody. Case closed."

"I thought I had," I said, laying the king of hearts found in Stump's hand on the table. The edges were crumpled, but it lay flat. "Until Stump pointed out something I should have picked up. Colonel, you said your assailant used both hands?"

"Yes. He grabbed the binoculars with one and twisted the straps with the other. He pulled back on either side of my neck, so the straps dug into my throat."

"Both hands would have been clenched shut, like this?" I stuck out both hands, mimicking the movement as Harding had described it. When he nodded, I opened my hands and a playing card fell out.

It sat crushed next to the king of hearts, folded in on itself from the pressure of my grip.

"Somebody put that card into Sergeant Stump's hand," Kearns said.

"Yes. I wasn't sure until we found the German colonel. It was by accident, really. A bunch of POWs were wounded in the bombing, and their guards brought in the *Herr Oberst* as well, thinking he might still be alive."

"His tunic hid the bruises," Cassidy said. "When I opened it up, they were clear as day, as well as the petechiae."

"Speak English, Doc," I said.

"Small red marks, burst blood vessels in the eyes and on the face."

"That couldn't be caused by concussion from a bomb blast?" Harding asked.

"No, and a concussion wouldn't leave bruises shaped like thumbs and fingers on his throat. That man was strangled, no doubt about it. He had a leg wound, fairly severe. It would have caused him pain, made it hard to walk, but it wouldn't have killed him."

"Maybe he was unpopular with his men," Kearns suggested.

"He was the only paratrooper in with the bunch," I said. "The others were regular *Wehrmacht*. He couldn't have made enemies that fast."

"So our killer is still on the loose," Harding said. "But it sounds like he may have shot his wad. He failed with me, and now he's reduced to murdering a wounded POW. Hard to see how he could move onto a general after that."

"No, not at all," said Cassidy, shaking his head, as eager as a schoolboy with the right answer. He took one look at Harding's frown and remembered to add "sir."

"Colonel, please listen to Doctor Cassidy. He's studied cases like this, and he has a theory." Harding eased up on the frown and I nodded to Cassidy to continue.

"We are most likely dealing with a genuine psychopath here. Someone who totally lacks empathy for another human being. For him, a person is either a target or a tool, nothing in between. He has a self-centered view of the world, an overblown grandiose imagining of his own importance. For whatever reason, Red Heart has set up this card game, with the goal of filling his royal flush."

"I'd hardly call it a game," Kearns said.

"That's because you're not a psychopath. To him, it *is* a game. High stakes, since it's all about him, but still a game. I know it's hard to grasp, but this is a man who places no value on human life, except as it exists to benefit him."

"So what's your theory?" Harding asked.

"It's important to understand a few things. Psychopaths generally have a need for high levels of stimulation. They are also very clever, manipulative, and versatile. Don't imagine this guy as a drooling sadist; he's a lot smarter than that and very good at covering up what he is. He can observe and copy emotional reactions, but he can never *feel* those emotions. He enjoys humiliating people who trust him. It's one of the behaviors that stimulates him."

"Is that what this whole card game is about?" Harding asked. "Stimulation? Showing us how smart he is?"

"Yes, exactly. And you were onto something when you talked about his failure to kill you. I thought it might knock him off course. Sticking to a long-term plan is not a psychopath's strength. But he rebounded. He found a way, after being thwarted, to kill his colonel."

"And that means what?" Harding said.

"That previously he was following a script. The victims he left his calling card with were all American officers. But now, he's gone from almost being derailed to one card away from filling a royal flush. He probably sees himself as invincible. And he's upped the ante, adding a German to his victims. So I'd bet he'll go after a general for sure, and as soon as possible. Not an American, he's broken that pattern."

"A British general?" Kearns said.

"Unless you got any others around here," Cassidy said. "Italian, French, it wouldn't matter to him. What matters is upping the stakes. I think the POW murder was a desperation move, but one that may have reinvigorated him."

"Wait a minute," Harding said, holding up his hand. "Didn't you just say that sticking to a plan is not what these nutcases do? He's got one helluva plan here."

"I think I know why, sir," I said. "From what the doc told me, being in combat might be a psychopath's dream. Lots of opportunity for killing, legit and otherwise. Arms and ammo. Rules and rank to hide behind."

"As a professional army man, I might take offense at that, Boyle."

"No, it's not the army he likes. It's war. War gives him everything. Death. Stimulation. Belief in his own power. I think something happened in Caserta that put Galante onto him. I was bothered by the order of the murders, but if you think about Galante being the first victim, it makes more sense. The cards were a cover, to confuse us. I think Galante wanted to help this guy. Maybe he told Red Heart he could get him into a hospital, heal him, something like that."

"That would have instantly turned Galante into a target," Cassidy said. "The last thing Red Heart would want to give up would be his freedom to kill."

"So he planted the jack on Galante, then killed Landry? So Landry must have been the one to send him to Galante."

"Exactly. Maybe he noticed something, and sent Red Heart to Galante to be evaluated."

"Why not stop there?" Harding asked.

"Because he'd created a new pattern," Cassidy said. "Remember, this isn't a normal, logical mind at work. He may be addicted. Perhaps killing in combat no longer satisfies him."

"But he also had a reason for each murder. You, Colonel, because you're here to oversee the investigation. Arnold—" I stopped myself. I hadn't thought about Arnold, but there was only one reason I could see. "Arnold, because he paid him off to have my brother transferred into the platoon."

"Are you sure Major Arnold was the type to be bought off?" Harding asked.

"It wouldn't surprise me," Kearns said. "Rumor was he was in the souvenir racket, big time. No one paid it much mind, but I think it was more about loot than souvenirs with him. What do you think the killer's motive was to get your brother in the platoon?"

"Simple," I said. "To use him against me if I got too close. Insurance."

"I don't know if I buy all this," Harding said. "Seems long on theory and short on facts."

"Colonel," Cassidy said. "I observed psychopaths when I was a resident. They're chilling. Some of their stories of cruelty gave me nightmares. Training and arming a psychopath, and giving him permission to kill, well, that's the biggest nightmare of all. Because no matter how many people he kills, it's never enough. He'll never sicken of it. Nothing can ever fill that black hole he has inside. That's why I think he's going to strike again. There's no alternative for him, no going back."

Everyone was silent. These men knew how to fight the enemy, but not how to combat this particular terror. "What about Danny?" I said. "Will you transfer him now?"

"Let's do it another way, Boyle," Harding said. "Let's keep this under our hats. Ship Sergeant Stumpf out and let people think we've got the killer. That will lull this Red Heart character into thinking he's pulled one over on us. You go spend time with your brother. Tell him we're staying a few more days and you're having a reunion. As long as the Germans don't attack, the battalion can stay in reserve. That will give you a chance to watch things."

"What do you have in mind, Colonel?"

"I'm already working on finding a general to use as bait. We'll offer Red Heart a tempting target. We should have somebody here soon."

"Who?" I asked.

"Never mind, just get over there. Bring an entrenching tool, they're digging in deep."

I wondered if the bait was me and my brother. Generals were hard to come by, and the only one I'd seen around here was deep underground, smoking his corncob pipe. I had Kearns sign a supply requisition, and drove my jeep to the quartermaster's tent, where I stocked up on what GIs digging in out in the open really needed. Pickaxes, shovels, blankets, a few cans of meat and vegetable stew, tins of coffee, and a carton of smokes. At least I'd be popular with everyone, with the exception of one lunatic, a lunatic I thought I'd had in custody.

I'd been fooled, and by an expert. In the midst of strangling Harding, a German shell sent them both flying. A near miss that could have killed him. Most guys would have been stunned, groggy, disoriented. Not Red Heart. He quickly found a guy to throw suspicion on, and clocked him one. So who was Red Heart?

I could rule out Evans, not that I'd ever thought him a likely suspect. He'd been in the general area of the first murders, but I doubted he could have attacked Harding with shrapnel in his shoulder, and he was tucked away in Hell's Half Acre when the Kraut paratrooper bought it.

Flint? The last surviving sergeant. But he'd been busy rescuing Evans, under fire, after he brought out Louie's body. It didn't seem to be the kind of thing a psychopath would bother with. Father Dare, with blood in his boot? Maybe he'd gone to that church to pray for forgiveness. Charlie Colorado, lost in the smoke, the radioman I'd already overlooked? Phil Einsmann? Maybe he thought he'd get away clean after the first two, only to have his agency send him right back to Italy. Did he have a nose for news, or murder?

Or Bobby K, who I'd just met, or any of the other guys in the platoon, company, or whole damn VI Corps who I hadn't met yet. Anyone could be Red Heart, but one thing my heart told me was that he was close to Danny. Too close.

CHAPTER THIRTY-TWO

THE BATTALION WAS in reserve in an open field. A pine grove bordered it on the south side, and to the north a paved road cut across it, the roadbed built up about six feet above the soggy ground. GIs were digging in the woods, or along the embankment, carving out caves in the sloped earth. A convoy of trucks carrying replacements and supplies made its way along a dirt track, skirting the customary stone farmhouse in the center of the field. In the midst of these martial preparations, a woman hung her white sheets on a clothesline, domestic chores once again uninterrupted by war.

I saw Charlie Colorado walking along the edge of the embankment, a burlap sack over one shoulder and an M1 over the other. I slowed and asked if he wanted a lift.

"Thanks, Lieutenant," he said, setting the sack down between his legs, the dull clinks signaling full bottles of something alcoholic.

"Having a party?"

"Toasting the dead," he said. "I traded C rations for wine at that farmhouse."

"Hope they like Spam," I said.

"They seemed nervous," Charlie said, glancing back at the woman in the yard. "Maybe they thought I was coming to shoot them. The daughter spoke a little English, and said they hated the Fascists and the Germans."

"Of course."

"It would be foolish to say otherwise to an American soldier with a rifle and C rations to trade."

"Good point," I said, noting that Charlie was pretty sharp. "I heard you were Landry's radioman."

"Yes."

"You went to Bar Raffaele with him?"

"Sometimes. But the owner didn't like me there. Said I drank too much and caused trouble. He was right."

"Did you know Ileana?"

"Everyone knew Ileana," he said, a touch of weariness in his voice.

"Landry fell for her, right?"

"He did. I think she liked him too. She hated working there, most of the girls did. But they had to feed their families, even if it brought them shame."

"She told you that?"

"I could see it, when they thought no one was looking. But there were worse places to work."

"I can imagine. Inzerillo said he had his own doctor for the girls."

"And a priest," Charlie said. "For their shame."

"An Italian?"

"No. Someone who wanted to keep watch on his own sinners."

He clammed up after that, probably thinking he'd said too much. But then again, Charlie Colorado impressed me as a guy who didn't waste a single word.

Ahead of us, trucks disgorged their passengers and handed down supplies to waiting lines of troops. I scanned the sky for enemy aircraft, not wanting to be caught in a line of vehicles during an air raid. Charlie pointed to a section of embankment and I pulled over.

Entrances to the hillside had been scraped out, with shelter halves strung up over the holes, some reinforced with thin wooden planks from ammo and ration cartons. It had a distinctly hobo look about it.

"Billy," Danny said, walking up to the jeep. "You're just in time. Flint's been made Platoon Sergeant. Charlie went to scrounge some vino for a celebration." He looked at the sack Charlie held up and whistled. "You did okay!"

I studied my little brother. He'd already lost that permanently startled look that replacements had. He was at ease, feeling part of the platoon if only because so many had died since he'd joined. Being a survivor meant he was a veteran of sorts, which gave him confidence. The fact that the odds were against him living many more days didn't seem to bother him. For now, he was surrounded by his buddies, toasting their remaining sergeant, celebrating a promotion made necessary by three departed sergeants—two dead, one prisoner.

"Acting Platoon Sergeant," Flint said. "How you doing, Billy? Is it true what they're saying about Stump? He's the Red Heart Killer?"

"Yep. Caught in the act. Denies it, of course, but they all do."

"What's going to happen to him?" Danny asked.

"He's going back to Caserta in irons. Court martial, then firing squad would be my guess."

"Hard to believe," Flint said, shaking his head. "Stump always seemed to be a regular guy."

"Yeah," I said. "The way the doc explained it, that's what guys like him are good at. Anyway, I brought you some decent tools and grub, plus some smokes. Thought I'd spend some more time with Danny before I ship out tomorrow."

"Real shovels," Danny said, obviously tired of digging with a folding entrenching tool.

"Okay," Flint said. "Charlie, stow that vino in my dugout. No one touches it until we give these tools a workout and dig in good and proper. Then we eat and drink."

They unloaded the jeep and got to work, digging wider and deeper. Father Dare came by, and took charge of the extra rations. The meat stew was a new addition, and I figured it would be a welcome relief after meat hash, Spam, ham, and lima beans every day.

"I have a cooking pot I found in the rubble," Father Dare said. "I'll get this heated up for the boys." He took an empty can, punched holes in the bottom with his can opener, and dropped in a couple of heating tabs. Smokeless, the tabs ignited easily and burned hot, long enough to heat a meal. Unfortunately, one pot was going to be enough for this platoon, since it had suffered so many losses.

"Hey, Billy," a voice called from inside a dugout. It was Phil Einsmann, sitting cross-legged in his little cave, pecking away at his portable typewriter set up on a ration box. Above the opening was a wood plank with "Waldorf Hysteria" painted on it.

"That's funny, Phil," I said, pointing to the sign. "What are you up to?"

"Well, I tried to get a story about your killer past the censors, but they wouldn't go for it. Injurious to morale, they said. Ruined my goddamn morale, that's for sure. So I'm doing a piece on the lost company."

"What lost company?"

"Easy Company. I don't want to call it a retreat, since that might not go over well with the censors. But the rescue of a company in a forward position, slipping away from the clutches of the enemy, using the *fossi* to escape, that'll get through and sell papers."

"Fossi?" I was there and I was having trouble following Einsmann's story.

"Italian for ditches. The English call them wadis. Either sounds better than a daring escape through a smoky ditch."

"No argument there. Did you talk to my brother? Make sure you spell his name right."

"Sure did. And that Apache, Charlie. Great stuff. What do you have to say about it, Billy?"

"Talk to this guy," I said, when I noticed Bobby K swinging a pickax not far away. "He ran through enemy fire twice to get messages through, and led everyone out. Earned a battlefield promotion."

"No kidding? He wasn't here an hour ago when I made the rounds."

I walked over to Bobby K and stood with my back to Einsmann. "Bobby K, I'll fill you in later, but have you told anyone about that colonel in the hospital?"

"No, I haven't had a chance. The CO sent me over here, said Third Platoon needed a noncom."

"Keep it between us, all right?"

"Whatever you say."

"Now follow me and I'll make you famous."

I left Bobby K with Einsmann, glad I had a chance to get to him before he spilled the beans about the German colonel. I hadn't expected him to show up in Easy Company, but with the losses in noncoms, it made sense that somebody would be sent to fill in. I wandered over to Father Dare and took a seat on a carton of K rations.

"Do you have your own dugout, Padre? I trust the Lord myself, but I'd rather do it underground."

"God helps those who help themselves, Billy. I've got my own foxhole right over there," he said, pointing behind him with his thumb. "I prefer to dig straight down, not into the side of a hill. Saw two fellows buried alive in Sicily when a shell sent a few tons of dirt sliding over their dugout."

I didn't need to mention that I'd seen what was left of a man in a foxhole at Salerno who took a direct hit from a mortar round. To each his own. "How's your leg?"

"Okay. I got the bandage changed this morning and the nurse said it was fine. I was a little dizzy yesterday, I didn't realize how much blood I'd lost." He dumped a couple of large cans of meat stew into the pot.

"Padre, would you happen to know any chaplains who visited Bar Raffaele in Acerra?"

"Are you asking me to inform on my brethren, Billy?"

"I didn't say they went there for the hookers. Maybe someone thought the men might need some guidance in such a sinful place?"

"Billy, if a chaplain showed up at a joint like that, the men would simply move on to the next disreputable establishment. I told you when we first met, we would not be welcome at such a place."

"What if someone needed help? One of the girls, maybe? Or Lieutenant Landry?"

"Landry was brought up Protestant."

"Interesting, but not an answer."

"I am the chaplain for this unit," Father Dare said. He stirred the pot, staring into the stew as wisps of steam began to drift up. I could tell he was working on a way to explain something to me. "For all the men, Catholics, Protestants, Jews, and even those who do not believe. I've noticed that atheists enjoy talking about religion in a way that believers don't."

"I've noticed that cops and criminals sometimes sound a lot alike. More so than cops and grocers or accountants."

"Exactly. We share a common interest, but one viewed from differing perspectives. That's why Landry and I were friends. He was an agnostic. He believed the unknowable was . . . unknowable. I call it a lack of faith, but that's another matter. We often talked of life and death. He wanted the men to have spiritual solace, but he couldn't partake of it himself. That's why when he asked me to help, I was only too glad."

"Help for him and Ileana."

"Yes. He wanted me to help get permission for them to marry. To testify to her good character."

"To lie for him."

"Can't a woman sin and still be a good woman at heart? Ileana lost her father in the Allied bombing, her brother was killed in Africa, and her mother has succumbed to grief. There are two younger sisters at home, and Ileana did what she had to do to keep them off the streets. There is so much misery in this war, how could I not help alleviate some small part of it?"

"So you didn't think it a lie?"

"What does it matter? They turned Landry down, and now he's dead. I wonder if it's even worth trying to help anymore. What help can I provide against all this killing? It's monstrous, too much for any man to overcome. A priest on a battlefield, I used to think it made sense, great sense. Now it seems pathetic. Anyway, I didn't think Landry and Ileana had anything to do with these killings, and I saw no reason for the authorities to delve into what on paper would sound sordid. Landry's family doesn't need to hear the army's version of what went on between them. Call the boys, will you, the stew's ready," he said, putting a lid on the pot and the conversation.

I stood, heaving a sigh and wondering what would become of Ileana. I put my fingers between my teeth and whistled, signaling that chow was ready. In the distance, two trucks raced toward the stone farmhouse, slamming on their brakes close to the door. Blue-jacketed men spilled out, circling the building. Carabinieri.

"What's going on?" Flint said, pointing to the farmhouse. Just then the shrieking sound of incoming artillery tore at the sky, and men dove in every direction, heading for dugouts, foxholes, any cover at all. I tripped on a shovel and felt myself being pulled underground, strong hands gripping my shoulders. At least a dozen explosions rippled the ground all around us, spraying debris against the soles of my boots as I slithered into the dugout with Flint.

Artillery blasts thundered around us, and I wondered if the GIs caught out in the field had had time to get to cover. Green replacements and trucks filled with ammunition were not a good combination in a barrage. I couldn't think about it long. The shelling kept up, shaking my bones every time a salvo hit close by. Dirt cascaded from above, and my thoughts went to those guys Father Dare knew, buried alive in a dugout like this one. Then I tried not thinking at all, and closed in on myself, knees to my chest, hands on my helmet. The damp, freshly dug soil jumped up at me with every blast, as I felt the impact of each explosion, the concussion traveling through the earth and air, enveloping me, reaching into our hole where the shrapnel couldn't, letting me know that life and death had come down to mere chance, the weight and trajectory of shells alone determining who would walk away and who would remain.

The shelling stopped abruptly and I was left with ringing in my ears and dirt in my mouth. I looked at Flint, and he was already at the entrance, looking out over the open field.

"Jesus," I said as I crawled next to him, neither of us ready to stick our necks out any farther.

"Yeah," he said. "Hell must look like this."

Trucks were wrecked and overturned. Gasoline burned in bright yellow-red plumes, tires in thick, acrid black smoke. Blackened shell holes were strewn in lines across the field, a half dozen in each group, testimony to the accuracy of the German fire. The ground smoldered, an odd smell drifting up, of burnt vegetation, burning rubber and human flesh. Too many men had been caught out in the field, replacements who hadn't learned how to react without thinking or asking questions.

"They had the field zeroed in," Flint said. He crawled out of the dugout and stood. Other men followed his cue. Danny and Charlie, Father Dare, Einsmann, Bobby K, all safe. "Look at the shell holes. This wasn't a random barrage. There were several batteries firing, all hitting within this field."

It didn't make sense. We were in the rear, such as it was. The Germans couldn't have an observation post that could see us, especially behind the roadway embankment. The farmhouse. Carabinieri still surrounded it, and not a single shell had come close. The white sheets still hung on the line.

"You're right," I said. "Just like Le Ferriere. There was a farmhouse there, and a woman hung white sheets on the line. A few minutes later, the shelling hit a column on the road. We were in a blind spot, the Germans shouldn't have been able to see us."

I took off at a run, toward the farmhouse, away from the carnage and the cries of the wounded. I should have stayed and helped, but I told myself I wasn't a medic. I knew I was a coward. I couldn't face the torn bodies, the pleas for help, for mercy, for mother. I ran, glad of the excuse, my palm on the butt of my .45, itching to deliver revenge, or at least blot out the screams for a moment.

Flint was at my heels, and as we closed in on the farmhouse I recognized Luca directing the Carabinieri, who were holding the farmer's wife back as she screamed at him, hands outstretched to heaven one second, beating at her breasts the next. A small girl clung to her skirts, and an older one stood behind her, sullen.

"*Dove la radio è?*" Luca demanded.

"It's the sheets, isn't it?" I said, breathless. The other Carabinieri had turned toward us, weapons at the ready, uncertain if we were a threat or a nuisance. Luca acted as if he expected us.

"Yes, the sheets, the bright white sheets which can be seen at a distance. The signal for the German observers to tune to the frequency assigned to their radio. *Fascisti*," he spat.

"There are others," I said. "I know of one outside Le Ferriere."

"There are many," Luca said. "And we already have visited that farmhouse. Whenever they have a target to report, the wash goes out. We found out about it yesterday, when a neighbor of one family reported them, suspicious of all the laundry being hung. He said they were filthy pigs and doubted they washed once a month, much less every day."

"Have you found their radio?"

"No, and if we do not, we may have to let them go. It could be a coincidence, after all."

"Can we look around?" Flint asked.

Luca gave commands in Italian and one of his men led us inside, where other Carabinieri were ransacking the joint. In the kitchen, two officers had the farmer seated at his kitchen table. He had a stern face, his thick black hair peppered with gray. He wore a work shirt and vest; his hands were rough and callused. On the wall, a rectangular patch of dark wallpaper showed where Mussolini's portrait had probably hung until the invasion.

The Carabinieri were throwing rapid-fire questions at him, to which he shook his head repeatedly. They seemed frustrated. He looked calm and haughty, as if he knew his secret was safe. He was a good actor, but then Mussolini and his bunch were pretty theatrical.

Flint moved closer, edging the officers out of the way. He reached into his pocket, and the farmer flinched. But he pulled out a pack of cigarettes, and the fellow relaxed. Flint offered one, and lit it for him.

"*Nome?*" Flint asked, smiling as he clicked his Zippo shut.

"Frederico Pazzini," he said, giving a slight bow of his head, before taking a deep drag on his Lucky.

Before he could exhale, Flint struck him on the cheekbone with the butt of his .45, hard. Blood spurted onto the table, and Frederico choked on smoke and blood as Flint shook off the two Carabinieri who tried to pull him away. He grabbed Frederico's arm and held it to the table, the muzzle of his automatic pressed into the palm of one callused hand. He thumbed back the hammer, and spoke one word.

"Radio?"

Frederico shook his head, but with fear in his eyes this time. The two officers stepped back, apparently liking what they saw, or at least the fact that someone else was doing it for them. I wondered how far Flint was going to take it. Myself, I was ready to shoot the other hand, images of the dead and wounded still fresh in my mind.

But Flint didn't shoot. He released Frederico, smiled, and shrugged his shoulders. Then he pointed outside, and simply said, "Signora Pazzini." We hadn't taken two steps when Frederico began bawling and pointed to a cupboard near the sink. The officers got down on their knees and pulled out cans of olive oil, tins of flour, and some large bowls. Then they pried up the floorboards, and lifted out a radio. Under one of the dials was the word *Frequenzeinstellung.*

That told us all we needed to know. Flint hit him again, on the other cheekbone, then wiped his .45 with a dishrag, and left. Under the floor, where the radio had been hidden, was the portrait of Il Duce.

The Pazzini family was hauled away in a truck, their little girl in tears at the sight of her father's face. I felt bad for her. I felt bad for the little girls back in the States who'd be crying when they heard their fathers were dead, killed in a field outside Anzio. I felt bad all around.

"What will happen to them?" I asked Luca as he halfheartedly searched through the house.

"They will be sent back to Naples. A trial for the father, perhaps a displaced persons camp for the woman and children."

"He must have been a die-hard Fascist."

"Many of these people are. You know Mussolini settled this area with them. They hate you, and they hate us more for fighting with you." He tossed a pile of books off a chair and sat.

"Must be hard," I said, taking a chair myself.

"At first I looked forward to this assignment. I thought we would be bringing law and justice here. But instead, now that General Lucas is not moving inland, we have received orders to remove all civilians."

"Everyone?"

"Yes. First we have to track down the remaining Fascist spies and make sure they do not escape. Then all nonessential civilians will be shipped back to Naples. The entire Anzio-Nettuno area, evacuated. For their safety, the general said. Because of the bombing."

"He's right, you know. Especially now that the Germans won't have observers in our midst. The shelling is not going to be as accurate. Good news for us, bad news for civilians."

"Yes, yes. But I did not expect to spend this war putting civilians in camps, for both sides, no less."

"It's not quite the same, Luca."

"No, but neither is it combat, where a man can be tested. What shall I tell my children? That I helped run a concentration camp, then worked for a capitano who was corrupt, before evicting thousands of Italians from their homes?"

"What happened, Luca? On Rab?"

"You have to understand, when the camp was first set up, it was to house partisan prisoners. Tito's Yugoslav Partisans fought us and the Germans everywhere. The Nazis and the Fascists treated the Yugoslavian people horribly, shooting civilians without provocation. It quickly descended into bloodthirsty reprisals. The decision was made to remove many of the local Croats and Slovenes and bring in Italians, to repopulate the area. So the camp expanded, with thousands of local civilians, whole families, brought in. Soon we had over fifteen thousand, living in tents. Many grew sick and starved. When the commander of our battalion complained, saying that this mistreatment only drove more people to support the partisans, conditions improved, somewhat." He grew quiet, surveying the wreckage of the living room, one of many he must have seen in his strange career.

"But then?"

"Then the order came for all Yugoslavian Jews to be interned. About three thousand were brought into the camp."

"To be killed?"

"No, no, not at all. We followed the orders of our government, but the army insisted that the Jews be well treated, not as a hostile force. They weren't fighting us; they were only peaceful people who'd been swept up in this madness. So they were put in a separate part of the camp, and provided with what comfort we could give. My commander told me it was the only way to preserve a shred of honor. We had to obey the German commands and the orders from Il Duce, but we could at least do so with some dignity."

"I didn't know, Luca."

"No, and not all camps were the same. In some, Jews were treated terribly. But on Rab, we did what little we could. We were sick of fighting the partisans and all the hatred. It felt good to do something halfway decent."

"What happened?"

"After the fall of Mussolini, orders came from the government that the Jews were to be released. For their own safety, they could remain in the camp voluntarily under our protection. Several hundred left to join the partisans, and many others were taken to partisan-controlled territory. At this point, we had an uneasy truce with the Yugoslavs, and worried more about our former German allies."

"All the Jews got out?" I knew this story wasn't going to have a happy ending.

"No. There were two hundred elderly and sick left in the camp. My battalion was ordered back to Italy after the armistice, and I was in charge of a detachment, which was to close the camp. The last of the Slovene and Croat prisoners were released, and I was trying to find medical care for those Jews who could not travel."

We sat in silence, and I could hear the low murmur of other Carabinieri in the yard and smell their cigarette smoke as they waited for Luca.

"There was none. No transport, no fuel. A German column approached the camp, several hundred men in armored vehicles. We were but a few dozen, with nothing more than rifles. I gave the order. We ran. We ran away, leaving two hundred innocents behind. The Germans took them. I heard later they were sent to a camp in Poland. I expect they are all dead, don't you?"

"Yes, I do." I didn't expect they were dead, I knew it. From Zyklon

B, probably in a place called Auschwitz. It had all been hard to believe when Diana told me Kurt Gerstein's story in Switzerland, which seemed like another world, another time. But here it was, half a continent away. How large was this killing machine, that it would send an armored column to a little island in the Adriatic, and ship two hundred old and sick Jews to Poland? It made no sense. Of course, in a world where people were killed with assembly-line precision, nothing *could* make sense.

"Now you know my shame. I did nothing."

"Once the Germans came, there was nothing you could do. Except die. And then you wouldn't have been a witness. Believe me, I'm a cop, and sooner or later the law appreciates a good witness."

"Perhaps. When the war is over, do you think anyone will care? The graveyards will be full. Who will want to hear the truth? Who will care?"

"The dead," I said. I left Luca in the room staring at the wall. It wasn't my job to absolve him. It wasn't my job to explain that the methodical extermination of Jews and other undesirables could not be stopped by a single Carabiniere, that perhaps it was a small blessing that it was at least remembered. I began to feel the fervor with which Diana had told the story, her need to reveal the secret that burdened her.

I walked back to where the platoon was camped. Graves Registration wandered the field, carrying sacks of mattress covers, stacking the dead like cordwood. Medics treated the lightly wounded as the last of the ambulances trundled off over uneven ground to Hell's Half Acre. The wind stiffened and I felt a cold chill rising from the damp earth.

"Billy, you won't believe this," Danny said as I approached the group. "The meat stew made it. It's still warm. Have some, it's not bad." Danny had indeed passed over a threshold. On a field littered with the dead and injured, he still had his appetite, and celebrated what passed for the luck of the Irish at war: an intact pot of hot stew.

Father Dare ladled some into my mess tin, and I sat on a crate next to Danny. Everyone gathered around the pot and its feeble warmth. Charlie passed a bottle of wine, and it tasted good, sharp on my tongue, warm in my stomach. The living have to take what pleasures they can, from each other and whatever comes their way.

Phil Einsmann had a newspaper and was sharing pages around. "Only two weeks old," he said. "The *Chicago Tribune*."

"Says here Charlie Chaplin is demanding a Second Front now," Flint read.

"They can give him this one," Charlie said, and everyone laughed. Except him. He was serious.

"Coal miners are on strike for more money and decent working conditions," Danny read from another section. "Sure feel bad for them, burrowing underground and all." That got a laugh, and I drank some more wine, happy to be with Danny, happy to be alive.

I flipped through the paper as it was passed around. Nightclub owners in Miami were protesting having to close at midnight to conserve electricity. Business was good. In Michigan, thirteen legislators were arrested on bribery and corruption charges. Business was good there too, until you got caught.

I walked over to Einsmann, and gave him back the paper. "Phil, what do you know about what the Nazis are doing to the Jews?"

"What everybody knows, I guess. They take their property, send them to camps, shoot a lot of them. Why?"

"You ought to talk to Luca Amatori, a lieutenant with the Carabinieri here. He knows what went on in one of the Italian concentration camps."

"No thanks. Not worth my time. The Italians are our allies now. No one wants to air dirty laundry, not when we need them fighting the Germans."

"You've been told that?"

"Not in so many words. But you get the sense of things after enough stories have been squashed. Italian concentration camps? Not what the reading public wants to hear about."

"Ask Luca about clean laundry then. Might be worth your time."

"What's that mean?"

"You're the reporter, you find out," I said as I got up and went back to my seat. Maybe if he got the story about the spies from Luca, he'd ask him about the camp. Maybe not. Maybe Einsmann was busy planning his next murder. Maybe not. Maybe I'd live to see the dawn.

We drank some more. Guys smoked and chatted. No one was trying to kill us. We had warm food and good wine, and deep holes to jump into. Anything beyond those immediate needs was insignificant.

"You sure keep that weapon mighty clean, Padre," Flint said as he opened a letter. Father Dare had his automatic in pieces, cleaning each with a toothbrush.

"Cleanliness is next to Godliness, they say. Letter from home?"

"Yeah," Flint said. "Mail truck had this for me, and a couple for Louie and Rusty. That's it. Sorry, fellas." He looked around at the others, then scanned the single page, before tucking the letter back in the envelope and stowing it away. He shook a cigarette loose from a crumpled pack. "Anyone got a light?"

"I never saw a padre carry a pistol," Bobby K said, tossing Flint a lighter while eyeing Father Dare.

"There's a first time for everything, son," Father Dare said, as he rubbed gun oil on the metal. He cleaned the pieces slowly, handling each like holy relics. When he had it all put back together, he held it between his palms, as if it gave off warmth. "Especially at war, there are many first times."

He sounded weary, and I wondered if the pistol was a temptation, a way out for a man who, in his mind, had failed at whatever good he had tried to do. Or did he worship the weapon, aware of the power it bestowed, so much more immediate than penance? Or maybe the vino had gone to my head.

Einsmann took out his .45 and began cleaning it as well. He had a little trouble taking it apart, not being as adept as Father Dare.

"Geez," Bobby K said. "Watch out, you could shoot someone with that thing." Everybody thought that was hilarious.

"Flint," a captain called as his jeep pulled up. "Your replacements never made it out of the truck. Take a vehicle down to the docks and see what you can find." He scribbled out an order and gave it to Flint.

"Right now, sir?"

"Right now. They won't last long." With that, he was off.

"Okay, let's see what we can find. Danny, you come with me. We'll show these new boys it doesn't take long to become a grizzled veteran. Billy, sorry, but duty calls. Good luck back in Naples." Flint smiled, shook my hand, and walked away, giving Danny and me a minute.

"Be careful," I said, wishing I could take Danny with me.

"I will be. I'm in good hands, Billy. And remember, you were the one who taught me how to fight." We shook hands, even though I wanted to give him a bear hug, which would have embarrassed him. I stopped myself from reminding him that knowing how to bob and weave in the ring was not going to help at Anzio.

I watched Danny and Flint depart, taking a truck that was parked near my jeep. I said my good-byes to the others, reinforcing the story that I was leaving in the morning with Stump in custody. On the way to my jeep, I saw a crumpled envelope on the ground. It was Flint's letter. Had he thrown it away, or had it fallen from his pocket? I was about to give it to Father Dare to hold, when I thought it would be a good excuse to follow Danny down to the docks and see him again, maybe throw some weight around and get some decent replacements for the platoon.

Always looking out for my kid brother, I thought, as I laid my carbine down on the passenger seat and drove off toward the fog that was rolling in from the sea.

CHAPTER THIRTY-THREE

AFTER AN HOUR of looking, I'd given up trying to pick out Danny from among the hundreds of helmeted GIs swarming over the docks. LSTs were arrayed along the waterfront, like open-mouthed whales disgorging modern-day Jonahs. It looked like a major resupply effort, and I figured Stump would be heading back with the wounded on one of these LSTs riding high in the water.

It was almost dark, and I decided to talk with Doc Cassidy again before checking in at headquarters to see if Harding had come up with a general and if Kaz was back yet. Driving to the hospital area, I had to pull over as a line of ambulances came screaming down the road, horns blaring.

Hell's Half Acre was in chaos. The wounded were everywhere, pulled out of ambulances and set in rows, where doctors and nurses checked them, yelling instructions to move this one, leave that one, prep for surgery, all amidst the groans of morphine-addled pain.

"They're all Rangers," I said to a young kid standing next to me.

"Yeah, they tried to infiltrate into Cisterna last night. The Krauts must have known they were coming."

"Looks like they got hit hard pulling out," I said.

"This is the relief force. Two battalions of Rangers made it into Cisterna. Six men made it out," he said in a soft Texas drawl. "Eight hundred good men, half killed, half prisoner, they's saying."

"Jesus," I said, and thought of Father Dare praying to God for help, but asking Him to leave Jesus home. This was no place for kids, but as I looked at this scrawny sergeant, I thought he ought to be still in high school. "How old are you, Sergeant?"

"Nineteen, sir. I mean twenty, twenty years old."

"Don't sweat it, kid. If you're dumb enough to lie about your age to get in the army, I'm not going to get you in hot water. How'd you make sergeant so fast?"

"Guess because sergeants get killed so fast. I've been here since North Africa."

"Looks like the army is robbing the cradle."

"Listen, Lieutenant, just because I look young don't mean you have to insult me," he said. If it weren't for the sweat popping out on his forehead and his fluttering eyelids, I would've bet he was thinking about decking a superior officer.

"Sorry, Sergeant," I said, steadying him before he fell flat on his face. "What are you in for, anyway?"

"Malaria," he croaked. "Give me a hand, will ya?" I helped him back to his tent, and got him off his feet.

"You all right?" I asked as his head hit the pillow.

"Yeah, I'll be out of here soon. Damn malaria hits me now and then. Picked it up in Sicily."

"Want anything?"

"No thanks, Lieutenant. Sorry I mouthed off out there."

"Forget it, kid. The name's Billy Boyle, by the way. From Boston." I gave him my hand.

"Audie Murphy, from Farmersville, Texas. Take care of yourself, Lieutenant." I left him in bed, wondering how he ever got this far, a thin little whip of a kid with a strain of malaria, which I knew had sent stronger men home on a Red Cross ship.

I went back out and looked for Cassidy. The scene had calmed down, and most of the stretcher cases were gone. A few were draped with blankets, those who had died on the way in. A nearby tent was filled with other stretchers, and I watched a medic give a morphine syrette to a Ranger with blood-soaked compresses on his chest. He threw down the empty syrette and ran his fingers through his hair, shaking his head. This was the tent for the not-yet-dead. I walked on.

"Wait for me in the mess tent," Cassidy said when I finally found him. "I have a leg to amputate."

I waited, drinking coffee with sugar, not tasting a thing.

An hour later, Cassidy came in, looking drawn and exhausted. His blond hair was dirty, and there were dark bags under his eyes. "I'm hungry," was all he said. I followed him through the line, accepting frankfurters and beans in my kit, topped off with fresh-baked bread.

"I know I shouldn't be able to eat after all that," Cassidy said as we sat down. "Some guys drink. I eat. Can't help it."

"Those guys were shot up pretty bad," I said.

"They went through hell trying to get to their buddies. Lots of multiple wounds. Two battalions lost, and a third ripped apart trying to rescue them. We only get the worst cases here, you know what I mean? The aid stations and casualty clearing stations take care of the light wounds. And you know what? Most of them want to get up and go right back out there."

He raised a fork to his mouth, his hand trembling. He set it down and gritted his teeth.

"Fuck," he said. "Fuck!" Louder this time, but no one looked. Not uncommon, I guessed. He cupped his hands on the table and took a deep breath. "Too many of them. We were overwhelmed. I shouldn't have had to cut off that leg, but by the time we got him on the table . . ." He shook his head and uncupped his hands. He tried the fork again, and this time his hand was steady, but he still didn't eat. Combat fatigue comes in all forms, I guess.

"Sorry to bother you, Doc," I said, after giving him some time. "Bad timing, but I have a few more questions."

"It's never a good time here," he said. "Ask."

"I need to know what to look for if this guy we're after really is a psychopath. Everything you said points to someone who can act normal, so how can I spot him? I need something to look for, some sign. There's got to be something."

"I'm not sure. The few I knew of were spotted by experts, usually after some violent event that left no doubt. But I'd say the key is what you said about acting normal. It's all an act, so watch for something that takes him by surprise."

"To see how he reacts, like flying off the handle over some little thing."

"That could describe half the guys here. Constant exposure to death can make anyone overreact. Watch for the opposite. Some event that would draw an emotional response from any normal person."

"That's not much to go on, Doc."

"Okay, I'll make it easy on you. Just look for someone without a soul."

"I know a priest who might be able to help with that."

"Father Dare? The padre who was in here with a leg wound?"

"That's him."

"Strange fellow. Didn't want to be separated from his Colt. But he's got a good reputation with the medics and stretcher bearers. He stays up front, helps the wounded."   •

"He says he keeps the automatic to protect the wounded."

"Could be," Cassidy said. "But how much protection would a pistol really provide against machine guns, mortars, tanks and artillery?"

It was a really good question, but what I needed were some really good answers.

THE SUN HAD set, and the going was slow back to headquarters. As I drew close, air-raid sirens began to wail, and the street filled with men running for the shelters. Searchlights blinked on near the harbor and began stabbing at the sky, probing for the shape of German bombers. Flares blossomed in the inky darkness, floating to earth on parachutes, illuminating the town and harbor, creating day from night. Bombs were not going to be far behind. I pulled the jeep over and jumped out, making for a shelter dug out of the earth and covered with a corrugated tin roof. It wouldn't withstand a direct hit, but it would have to do.

There were already about twenty guys crammed inside. I sat near the door, listening to the antiaircraft batteries open up and the *crump* of exploding bombs creeping closer. I hoped Danny was well away from the docks by now; no reason why he shouldn't be. Someone lit a candle, and it gave off a flickering light. I leaned back, settling in for a long wait. I noticed Flint's letter sticking out of my front jacket pocket.

I took it out and looked at the return address. American Red Cross. Why would they be writing to him, from the States? I removed the letter, looking around guiltily, as if anyone in the shelter would know I was reading someone else's mail.

> We regret to inform you that your mother, Abigail Flint, died on December 25, 1943, of injuries sustained from an unknown assailant. Police are investigating and we will provide you with further information as it becomes available. Please accept our sincere condolences.

A chill went through me. Flint's mother had been murdered on Christmas Day, and all he'd done was ask for a light. He'd read the news with no visible emotion. Or if Cassidy was right, with no emotion at all.

CHAPTER THIRTY-FOUR

"I KNOW WHO the killer is," I said. Harding looked up without a trace of surprise. As soon as the all clear sounded I'd gone straight to headquarters and found him with Kearns. "Sir," I added, having been well trained.

"Sergeant Amos Flint," he said. "We're already looking for him."

"How . . . ?"

"Lieutenant Kazimierz has returned from Naples," Harding said. "Good to know you both agree. He's over there, with our general and his driver." He pointed to a far corner of the wine cellar, where Kaz, Big Mike, and Major Charles Cosgrove were huddled around a desk.

It was an unlikely crew. Staff Sergeant Mike Miecznikowski was Polish, like Kaz, but there the resemblance ended. He was over six feet tall, and so broad in the shoulders that he split seams on his uniform regularly. The nickname came naturally. Big Mike was a former Detroit cop who'd become part of our unit after helping us out in Sicily. He got into so much hot water because of it that Harding had to bail him out and take him in.

Major Charles Cosgrove was another story. We'd started off badly when I first came to London, which is a nice way of saying we'd hated each other. Long story. By now, we had both mellowed a bit, and there was a grudging respect between us, which is something for an Irish lad to say about a British intelligence officer from MI5.

"Billy," Kaz said excitedly. "I know who the Red Heart Killer is."

"Amos Flint?"

"I told you he'd figure it out," Big Mike said. "How you doing, Billy?"

"Glad you're here, Big Mike," I said as we shook hands. "When did you get in?"

"A couple of hours ago. First thing I do is pick up Kaz down at the docks off a PT boat from Naples, and he announces the identity of the killer. Looks like the major and I spent twenty-four hours in a Catalina for nothing."

"How are you, Major Cosgrove, or is it General Cosgrove?"

"General Bernard Paget, Commander in Chief, Middle East Command, if you don't mind. Got to bait the hook well, don't we? Paget recently took over as CIC, so it lends a bit of realism to the charade."

"You look the part, General," I said. Cosgrove was kitted out in a nicely tailored dress uniform, with the red lapel patches of a general officer. I wondered when Harding had begun to cook up this scheme, or if maybe Cosgrove had a whole closet full of disguises. "But is this really MI5 territory?" MI5 was charged with counterespionage, catching German spies, not GI killers.

"Personal requests from Winston tend to blur lines of jurisdiction. Colonel Harding asked General Eisenhower, who asked the prime minister, who said by all means. Anything to help get this invasion moving. Winston is not pleased with the progress, or lack thereof, and doesn't wish things to get any worse if this maniac gets close to a real general. So here I am, the sacrificial lamb."

"Don't worry," Big Mike said. "I ain't leaving your side until we got this guy."

"Very good. You make a larger target than even I do," Cosgrove said. Which wasn't the case with most men. Cosgrove had fought in the Boer War and the Great War, but his days of fighting trim were long gone. He was thick-waisted, with a full gray mustache and a limp. Without Big Mike as a bodyguard, he'd be a sitting duck.

"So what did you find out about Flint?" I asked Kaz.

"I found Ileana," he said.

"How?"

"Well, I probably should not return to the Naples area for a while. An officer matching my description is wanted for the theft of penicillin from the hospital at Caserta. I knew I needed something to bargain with, and nothing will make the owner of a bordello talk more than a supply of penicillin for his girls."

"It's practically a public service," Big Mike said.

"Sure it is. So you got someone to talk."

"Yes. Ileana was recovering south of Naples, at a farm. She had been badly beaten. As it turns out, she and Landry really were in love. She rejected him at first, fearing that he would cast her aside. But he persisted, and she came to love him. They had a plan for him to take her away, but they kept up the story of her milking him for money, so Inzerillo would not be suspicious."

"Let me guess," I said. "Landry told Flint."

"Yes. He asked for his help. Instead, Flint went to Bar Raffaele and paid for Ileana's services. He intended to humiliate Landry, to ruin their love. But he could not perform, and Ileana made the mistake of laughing at him. He nearly killed her. He threatened Inzerillo with the same if he said anything, and told Ileana he would kill Landry if she revealed what had happened."

"Then what happened to Inzerillo?"

"Flint's game was not over. He told Landry that Inzerillo had beaten Ileana, so they both went to confront him."

"That was the story about going to pay for damages," I said.

"Yes. Landry demanded to see Ileana, but Inzerillo had already sent her off. Ileana later found out what had happened from one of the girls who had visited her. There was a fight, and that is when Flint beat Inzerillo and threatened to kill him. Apparently Landry managed to stop Flint, who had flown into a bloody rage. Inzerillo escaped, and Ileana's friend heard Landry tell Flint that he would get him help, because he was a good friend and a good soldier. But that he needed help to control himself."

"That was his death sentence," I said. "Landry got Galante to talk with Flint, to treat him off the books, as a favor. Landry knew something big was about to happen, and I'm sure he didn't want to lose a good squad leader."

"Good?" Cosgrove said. "Hardly seems like a good solider."

"An armed man with no remorse. No hesitation, no second thoughts. No soul. He'll never suffer shell shock, combat fatigue, whatever you call it. And a master manipulator to boot. Makes for an effective killer. Landry just didn't understand who he was dealing with. He probably thought Galante could treat him with some pills and sack time."

"But why would Flint care what Galante said? He hadn't murdered anyone yet, and the MPs wouldn't get too worked up over a pimp with a bloody nose," Big Mike said.

"Because Galante understood what Flint really was, and wanted to treat him for it," I guessed. "With all good intentions, he was going to take away the one thing that Flint valued above all else. War. He's like an alkie, or a kleptomaniac, except that instead of booze or theft, he's addicted to killing."

"So he kills this chap Galante, then the lieutenant, if I understand the sequence," Cosgrove said. "But he uses the ruse of the playing cards to reverse the order, to throw off the investigation?"

"Yes, and according to Doc Cassidy, this scheme then took on a life of its own in his mind. Since he failed to kill Harding, switching to a German opened things up for him. Best bet is that he's going to try for an international royal flush,"

"Everybody up to speed?" Harding asked as he joined the group.

"I think so, except for how we're going to pick up Flint."

"You know where his unit is?" Big Mike asked. "Let's go put the cuffs on him."

"Hold on," Harding said. "Boyle, you were with them this afternoon, and they're not going anywhere tonight. I don't want to risk approaching him in the dark. Some trigger-happy GI is likely to think we're enemy infiltrators. Let him be, and we'll go in at dawn, with a couple of supply trucks. It will look completely normal."

"Perhaps we could put this uniform to good use," Cosgrove said. "Why not proceed with the plan? You said you already alerted division headquarters. What could be more normal than carrying on with the inspection? I imagine you'd like some actual proof, wouldn't you?"

"Listen, my kid brother is in Flint's platoon. I don't want to take any chances."

"I think Major Cosgrove is right," Kaz said. "You may put Danny in greater danger by going after Flint directly. If he thinks he is about to be taken, he could try to harm Danny. But if we tempt him with our general, he might be vulnerable."

"That makes sense, Boyle," Harding said. "If he has time to react when he sees you, he could take Danny and others down with him. But if he thinks he's stalking a general, he might go at it alone."

"Why don't I walk over and plug him?" Big Mike said. "He don't know me from Adam. I'm just saying."

"All the same, my good man, I think we should proceed with some attempt at legal proceedings," Cosgrove said. "Which will be more productive if we catch him in the act. All we can charge him with now, with any hope of conviction, is assault on this Ileana girl. There's no evidence against him otherwise."

"Okay," Harding said. "General Paget will inspect the battalion in the reserve area at 0700 hours. I'll pass the word along so Flint will hear about it tonight. Boyle, you need to sit this one out. You'll only spook him."

"I guess so. Sir."

"I still say I should plug him, Sam," Big Mike said.

"Thanks, Big Mike, but I'd rather see you keep those stripes," Harding said. "I had the personnel section pull the files on Landry's platoon, so you and Major Cosgrove can check Flint's photograph, along with others." Harding shoved a pile of folders toward Big Mike, leaving a stack behind. The dead.

"Hey," Big Mike said, opening Flint's file and looking at the army photograph. "This is Flint?"

"Yes," Harding said. "Memorize the face."

"I don't have to. I saw this guy down at the docks, when I was waiting for Kaz. He stood out because he ducked behind a truck, like he'd spotted someone he didn't want to see."

"Was this guy with him?" I pulled Danny's photograph from his file.

"Didn't see him."

"They were both sent down to the docks to pick up replacements. Danny should have been with him."

"Billy, there were hundreds of guys milling around. I could have missed him easy," Big Mike said. He was right. It probably meant nothing. My gut told me otherwise.

CHAPTER THIRTY-FIVE

I WATCHED THE small column leave at 0600, Big Mike at the wheel of a staff car and Cosgrove in back, the red stripe on his service cap proclaiming his general's rank at a glance. A jeep full of MPs provided escort, nothing out of the ordinary for a VIP. Soon after that, Harding, Kearns, and Kaz drove out, an MP sergeant at the wheel. The plan was for them to hang back and observe, waiting for Flint to make his move.

It was a good plan, and it made sense to leave me out of it. Still, I wished I could be there to keep Danny out of trouble. But if all went as planned, I'd have another shot at getting him transferred out, and I had to settle for that.

Military police had set up shop in a municipal building near headquarters. They had coffee brewing and a good cellar in case of an air raid, so I waited there for news from Harding. The MPs had a radio in their vehicle, and would call in as soon as something happened.

The Germans were shelling around the clock, not always a massive barrage, but enough to keep everyone awake and jumpy. Last night had been no exception, and between air-raid sirens, antiaircraft fire, and the Kraut artillery, I hadn't slept much. I was pouring my second cup of joe when a clerk from HQ came in looking for me. I had mail. From Boston. It was over six weeks old, but I was amazed it had even caught up with me.

It was from my mother, of course. Dad might scribble a line or two at the end, but it was always Mom who wrote. She caught me up on family news, cousins getting married, a new baby born to the neighbors, the onset of winter. Then she got to Danny. She had just heard about the ASTP program being cancelled, and was worried about him being sent overseas. Could I ask Uncle Ike about him? See that he got a job in London, perhaps? Stay safe, and watch out for your brother, she said. Both were tall orders in Anzio. Dad wrote about lots of overtime waiting for me at Boston PD, and I thought about all the cash I'd have if the army paid time and a half.

I folded the letter and put it in my shirt pocket. As soon as I had Danny squared away, I'd write. I'd tell her he was safe and sound, doing some boring job at headquarters, sleeping inside under blankets. I hoped it would be true.

I relaxed, listening to the familiar chatter of law enforcement. Gripes, complaints, calls coming in, cops going out. It was early, and with the Carabinieri policing the local populace, there wasn't a lot going on. Until a major burst in to report his jeep stolen. He'd had a .30-caliber machine gun mounted on it, and he wanted it back, now. Never mind that it was pinched yesterday and he'd been too busy to report it, he wanted action now. A pudgy, red-faced guy, he was with the Quartermaster unit that off-loaded supplies in the harbor, and he cursed and hollered until he got an officer to listen to him. I watched the MPs as they turned away, rolling their eyes at the posturing of a supply officer who needed a machine gun on his jeep. I knew the type, and would bet dollars to doughnuts that he'd have a photograph of himself at the wheel, looking as if he were ready for a raid behind enemy lines. It struck me as strange that even while he was doing important work, in constant danger from German shells and bombs, a guy like him had to throw his weight around and try too hard to impress people.

A couple of MPs donned their white helmets and followed the major out while another radioed units with a description and serial number of the jeep. Good luck with that one, boys, I thought. With a day's head start, it could be anywhere, and I doubted any MP worth his salt would search front-line units for a stolen jeep, especially for this loudmouthed major.

An hour passed, and then another. I asked the radioman for the tenth time if there were any messages, and he suggested I get some fresh air. He was a corporal, so he said it nicely, but I got the hint. I walked down to the water and watched landing craft ferry in supplies from Liberty Ships anchored in the bay. Antiaircraft guns pointed their barrels at the sky, swiveling back and forth as they searched for targets. A quiet morning at war, almost peaceful, if you didn't think about all the weapons and rubble about. The water lapping at the rocks along the shore reminded me of Boston, down by the inner harbor. It could be peaceful there, too, until you spotted a dead body bobbing in the swell.

I waited as long as I could, then decided that one of the benefits of being an officer was bothering radiomen whenever you wanted. As I walked up from the seafront, Big Mike pulled up in the staff car, followed by Harding and Kaz.

"He wasn't there, Billy," Big Mike said. He sounded worried, more worried than he should've been. "He's been gone since yesterday."

"Danny as well," Kaz said, as he got out of the jeep. "Neither of them returned to the unit yesterday afternoon, after they drove to the harbor to get replacements."

I felt them all looking at me, waiting for a reaction. I didn't know what to say, or, worse yet, what to do. Flint, loose somewhere in the Anzio beachhead, the sea at his back, the Germans all around, and Danny at his side. I tried not to think about the memory of that floater in Boston harbor as I tried to calculate what Flint's game was.

"Billy," Kaz said, resting his hand on my shoulder. "What should we do?"

"I wish I knew," I said. We trooped inside, and the MPs stood to attention when Cosgrove entered in his general's getup. He quickly waved them off. Harding spread out a map of the beachhead on a table, and marked the front lines with a red pencil.

"The British are on our left flank," he said, drawing an arc from the coast up to Compleone, a northward bulge showing where the British had been attacking toward Rome. In the center, the front was a wavy line from Corano to Sessano, south of Cisterna where the Rangers had been cut to pieces. "This is all Third Division, with supporting elements from the 504th Parachute Regiment."

"Who's holding the right flank?" I asked, pointing to where the Mussolini Canal flowed south to the sea.

"The First Special Service Force," Harding said. "It's a joint U.S.-Canadian volunteer outfit. A commando brigade."

"That's a long stretch of canal for three regiments to cover," Big Mike said.

"German activity is sparse on that flank," Kearns said. "They're covering the approaches to Rome on the north. Besides, these Force men are damn aggressive. The Krauts pulled back a mile or more on the other side to avoid their patrols."

"Is there a general in command?" Kaz asked.

"Yes, Brigadier General Robert Frederick, recently promoted. I doubt anyone could get the drop on him," Kearns said. "Even without hundreds of his men around him, he'd be tough to take. A real fighting general."

"Boyle, what do you suggest?" Harding said.

"Let's have the MPs check the hospitals, in case they got caught in the bombing last night. And send out a bulletin with their names and description to every checkpoint. And to the Carabinieri as well."

"Billy, Flint may have got himself aboard one of the ships. He could be halfway to Naples by now," Big Mike said.

"Danny would never desert," I said. "And if he hasn't turned up, he's still with Flint."

"Sure," Big Mike said, turning his attention to the map, not saying what we all thought. Danny could be dead anywhere, his body hidden under rubble or weighed down and tossed in the harbor.

"Okay, Boyle, I'll get the MPs looking for two men, traveling by truck. I'll contact Naples, and have MPs waiting there. If Flint gets off one of those ships, they'll grab him," Harding said. "Then we'll organize another tour for our general."

"I'm sure it would be possible to board a ship in all the confusion at the docks," Cosgrove said. "But staying hidden, and getting off safely in Naples? I doubt it."

"I agree," Kaz said. "We need to think like this madman. What would he do?"

"And why?" I said. "What does he want?"

"To win the game," Kaz said. "To get his general, fill the royal flush, and beat you, Billy."

"He has Danny," I said. "I'm counting on him keeping him alive until he finds a general to take. Which means he has to have a story, something that would convince Danny to go along with him."

"So boarding a ship to Naples is out. But how many places are there to go within the beachhead?" Kaz said.

"I don't think he'd head for the British sector. A couple of Yanks would stand out. Back to the Third Division front? They'd be nabbed and sent back to their unit," I said. "It doesn't make sense, there's nowhere to go. What does he hope to accomplish?"

"Okay, we gotta slow down and think like detectives," Big Mike said. That wasn't hard for Big Mike; blue flowed in his veins. He still carried his shield from the Detroit Police Department wherever he went. "When's the last time you saw Danny and Flint?"

"Yesterday, mid-afternoon. I brought some supplies out to them; I was supposed to be leaving since we'd found the killer. We took some artillery fire, watched the Carabinieri haul off some Italians, had some chow, and then the company CO told Flint to go down to the docks to grab replacements. The ones for his platoon had been killed in the shelling. It was probably five o'clock by the time they got there."

"How was Flint acting? Like something tipped him off, maybe?" Big Mike said.

"No, he played it cool. He's not a guy who rattles easily."

"So something happened between there and the docks. Something that caused him to skip town with Danny."

"That was about the time I came ashore," Kaz said. "Could he have seen me?"

"What if he did? It wouldn't mean anything to him," Big Mike said.

"Oh no," I said, the sequence of events becoming clear in my mind. "I think I know what it was. Stump. The guy we supposedly had in custody as the killer. Doc Cassidy was going to transfer him to Naples with the wounded. Damn! I'll check with Cassidy, but I bet Stump got on a ship yesterday afternoon."

"And Flint saw him, and knew the jig was up," Big Mike said. "Then he comes up with a story that Danny will buy, and takes off to parts unknown."

"But there are no parts unknown here," Kaz said, pointing at the map. "The beachhead is nothing more than an open-air prison, with the Germans guarding all sides."

"Maybe he's planning a jailbreak," Big Mike said. I stared at the map, trying to put myself in Flint's shoes. "From what Cassidy said, he's pretty committed to going through with this plan. But he also said psychopaths can be impulsive, so it makes sense that he changed course so quickly."

"If he's like most hoodlums, he'll have a new set of wheels in no time," Big Mike said.

"There was a major from the Quartermaster Corps in here earlier. His jeep was stolen yesterday, down by the docks," I said. It fit perfectly. "Big Mike, check with the officer in charge, and find out the time it was taken. If it was around 1600 hours, it was probably Flint. Tell them to approach with caution, that we want the driver and passenger taken alive. There's a mounted .30-caliber machine gun on that jeep, and I don't want any itchy trigger fingers with Danny on board."

"Sure thing, Billy."

"What should we do next?" Kaz asked. I gazed at the map. The right flank, lightly guarded, lightly defended. A wide gap between the Germans and the First Special Service Force. That had to be it.

"We have to tempt him," I said, looking at Cosgrove. "We have to let him think he has a chance to pull it all off. And we have to take him before he does any of it." Once, I might not have cared if Cosgrove got himself killed, but familiarity had bred admiration, so

I wanted to be reasonably certain he didn't end up being a victim. Most of all, I wanted Danny out of Flint's clutches. Trouble was, Flint knew that, and would use it against me.

"Billy, the time checks out," Big Mike said, returning to the table. "The jeep was last seen at 1530 hours. That major left it there for his corporal to pick up, but when the corporal got there, he thought the major had kept it. That's why it wasn't reported right away."

"Okay. They sending it out?"

"Yep, radioing it now to all units, and sending a message to the Carabinieri like you asked. And here's the good news. The major gave them the serial number, VI-37Q-DP-4. The Q identifies it as a Quartermaster vehicle, and the DP means from the Depot Company. It ought to be pretty easy to spot a Quartermaster's jeep with a .30 mounted on it."

"Good work. Now let's catch up with Harding and get this thing rolling." The army believed in doing things big, so each vehicle had its serial number stenciled in white paint on the front bumper. If the MPs kept their eyes open, and Flint stayed on the roads, it was only a matter of time. Big if.

Cosgrove was not going to be very popular. Harding agreed to inform First Special Service Force HQ that a senior general was coming through on an inspection tour, to determine if the unit should be disbanded. It was precisely the kind of news that would spread like wildfire throughout the brigade. If Flint came within earshot of even a single private, odds were he'd hear about it. If I'd guessed right about his plan.

"You sure you want to go through with this, Cosgrove?" Harding asked as our phony general eased himself into the backseat of the staff car. "The Force men are a rough bunch. Between Flint, the Krauts, and them, you won't have a friend within miles."

"Don't worry, Sam," Big Mike said. "I got my .45 automatic, a Winchester Model 12 trench gun, and a .38 police special for backup." Harding permitted a causal familiarity from Big Mike, which no one else would ever dare to try to get away with. Big Mike did it so naturally, I don't think Harding could take offense. Plus, Big Mike knew when to call him 'sir.'

"Where the hell did you get a shotgun?" Harding asked.

"It's not hard when you've got a supply officer desperate to get his fancy jeep back," Big Mike said. "Automatic at my hip, shotgun by my side, revolver in my pocket, and walkie-talkie on the seat. If Major Cosgrove gets killed, you can fire me."

"That's General Paget to you, Sergeant," Cosgrove said. "And if he does get me killed, Harding, break him to private and keep him in the army for life."

"In that case, you're safe as a baby with me," Big Mike said, settling in behind the wheel.

"Remember, the SCR-536 has a range of only a mile. We'll stay close, but don't wander off, or we'll lose you. Check in every thirty minutes."

"Will do." With that they were off.

Their first stop would be Valmontorio, on the coast where the Mussolini Canal ran into the sea. It was the far end of the line that the Force held, and the plan was for Cosgrove to kick up a big stink, so word would spread ahead of him. Kearns had already radioed General Frederick, who agreed to go along with the plan, and let word slip to his staff about an inspection by a British general who thought highly trained units like the FSSF were a waste of resources.

The unit held the canal north up to Sessano, and that was where Luca and his Carabinieri came in. He was there with a truckload of men, supposedly searching for spies. If we needed help, we'd send a radio message and then have reinforcements from another direction. It was a good plan, especially since GIs were used to seeing the blue-uniformed Carabinieri, and tended to ignore them.

The dull *crump* of distant artillery rolled in from the north, and I had the usual thought: glad it's them, not me. We went in the MP office for one last check. No one had reported seeing the missing jeep, no sign of Flint or Danny. By the time we left, the artillery was louder. Closer.

"Why'd you switch to that peashooter?" Harding said as we got into the jeep. He was carrying a Thompson submachine gun. Kaz was armed only with his Webley revolver, but he was pretty good with it and didn't like carrying anything else. Ruined the cut of his uniform, he claimed.

"Traded with a guy who got us out of a scrape," I said. "Besides, it's light, and more accurate than the Thompson."

"Just make sure you shoot him more than once with that," Harding said. "I've seen Krauts take a couple of those slugs and keep running." He was right; compared to the M1 rifle, or the Thompson, the M1 carbine round was small and less powerful. Still, it had its uses.

I drove, Kaz at my side, Harding in the back. We went along the coast road, and watched destroyers cut circles in the bay, smoke pots churning on their fantails, disappearing into the white clouds that they created. All that smoke was camouflage for an incoming convoy, and the German gunners registered their disapproval by sending a few shells after the destroyers, not even getting close but sending up great geysers of blue-and-white foam. The wind kicked up, and dark clouds drifted in from the sea, blowing the smoke in our direction. The water, air, and sky became the same uniform gray, the heavy weather covering the land with an opaque, damp, shivering chill. I steered the jeep around the occasional bomb crater not yet filled in by the engineers, who had round-the-clock work keeping roads, bridges, and airfields functioning.

Where was Danny? What would I do if he were killed out here, not by the Germans, but by a man I'd been sent to track down? How could I tell my mother, or confess my failing to my father? I ached to find Danny, and I prayed as I drove, bargaining with God, offering everything I could think of, frightened that it wasn't God who held Danny's future in his hands, but a homicidal maniac. I'd bargain with him too, if I knew what he wanted, and if it were mine to give.

CHAPTER THIRTY-SIX

"LOOK OUT," KAZ said, leaning forward in his seat. "Slow down, there are shell holes all around."

"Good reason to go faster," Harding said from the backseat, where he'd just finished checking in with Big Mike on the walkie-talkie. I maintained my speed, weaving between the blackened holes, aware of the burned-out wrecks of vehicles on either side of the road. "Looks like the Germans have this area zeroed in. Narrow road, nowhere to go. We'd be sitting ducks if it wasn't for this fog."

The wind had died down, leaving the coast shrouded in mist, making it hard to see where I was going. But if I couldn't see, the Germans up in the hills sure as hell couldn't either, and I was glad not to have a ton of explosive steel raining down on us.

"Stop!" Harding yelled. I braked, and he jumped out, running to an overturned truck, where a body lay sprawled on the ground. All I could think was, please let it not be Danny.

It wasn't. There were bloody compresses on his chest, where medics had worked on him. Other medical debris was scattered around him. There may have been other wounded, so the medics left the corpse behind for Graves Registration.

"False alarm," Harding said.

"Perhaps not," Kaz said, holding the dead man's dog tag. "This says Amos Flint."

"Search him," I said. "We need to find out what name Flint is using." Kaz and I went through his pockets, but Flint must have beaten us to it.

"Nothing," Kaz said. "The man is clever, I must say."

"Save the compliments," Harding said. "The fog is clearing, let's go."

We crossed a wooden bridge and took the road into Valmontorio, a cluster of cinderblock buildings scattered about on either side of the road as it bent north, along the bank of the Mussolini Canal. Every building had been hit. Roofs were gone; the contents of homes tumbled out into the street or were left charred inside gutted structures. It looked like a ghost town.

"Get that goddamn jeep out of sight!" barked a GI who appeared from nowhere. Suddenly men appeared in doorways and at windows. One of them waved us into a spot between two houses and beckoned us to follow inside. "What are you boys doing here?" he said, as if we'd been caught trespassing. At the far end of the room, two GIs were eating their rations, glancing occasionally at the foggy view of the shoreline and canal. A radio sat on a table, along with binoculars and a map of the coast. A rather casual observation post.

"Your rank, soldier?" Harding said, stepping forward so his insignia could be seen.

"Lieutenant George Bodine, First Special Service Force. What can I do for you, Colonel?" He made it sound like a chore to even answer the question.

"Why did you pull us in? Are there Germans close by?"

"No, Colonel, there ain't a live Kraut within a mile of here," Bodine said as the other two men chuckled. "But the fog is about to blow off, and in five minutes you'd be dead if you went up that road. German gunners have been waiting for hours now to spot something."

"It doesn't look like it's clearing," Kaz said, peering out through the glassless window.

"It is. You wait."

"Lieutenant," I said. "We're looking for a sergeant and a private, traveling by jeep most likely, one with a mounted .30 caliber. You see anybody like that?"

"Only visitor here was some loudmouth British general, about an hour ago. Asked a lot of stupid questions and said units like ours were a waste of resources. On some kind of inspection tour or some such bullshit."

"What'd you say to that?" Harding asked.

"Offered to take him out on patrol tonight so he could see what the Krauts' opinion was. He didn't take us up on the offer. You know what they call us out here? Black devils. That's what *they* think of us."

"Why black devils?"

"Because we blacken our faces when we patrol at night. And we leave these calling cards behind, pasted to the foreheads of dead Krauts." He handed Harding a red-and-white sticker, with the arrowhead insignia of the Force, and the words *Das dicke Ende kommt noch.*

"What does that mean?" Harding asked.

"The worst is yet to come," Bodine said, with a smile. "That's why there aren't any Krauts within a mile or so. They began to pull back once we started going out after dark. Now we have to walk farther each night to find any."

"Is this your right flank?"

"Hell no, Colonel. This is the rear area. Most of our guys are across the canal, set up in Sabotino and other towns over there. Nice and snug, not all blown up like this dump. This is where we bring the wounded for transport back to Anzio, and pick up supplies."

"Does HQ know about this?"

"Maybe," Bodine shrugged. "It's a fluid situation."

"Meaning you like being on your own."

"Yes sir. Less interference from the brass, the better. Meaning no offense."

"None taken. You're sure about not seeing our two men pass through?"

"Yeah. Maybe they got hit back at the bridge. The Krauts like to shell that area."

"So I noticed," I said, then heard the shrill whistle that was becoming too familiar. I flinched, and noticed Bodine smiling.

"That's the bridge again," he said. "Must be another supply run. You boys might want to get a move on while the Germans are busy."

We took his advice, heading north along the canal, and damned if the fog didn't clear a few minutes later.

"I guess he knew what he was talking about," I said.

"They recruited a lot of outdoorsmen for that outfit," Harding said. "Lumberjacks, game wardens, fishermen, guys who are used to living rough. They have a sixth sense about the weather."

"Did you believe him about not seeing Flint and Danny?"

Harding shrugged. "Why shouldn't I?"

I glanced at Kaz, wondering if he'd picked up on it. He looked perplexed, and I gave him a minute as I drove down a tree-lined road, hoping the branches gave us some cover from the German observers, or that they wouldn't want to waste all those shells on a single jeep.

"He didn't ask why we were looking for them!" Kaz said, snapping his fingers. "That would be a natural question to ask."

"Yep. Good catch, Kaz. You'll be a detective yet."

"Why didn't you press him then?" Harding said, growling with irritation, at either my lack of follow-up or the fact that he hadn't noticed it. I nodded at Kaz, giving him the go-ahead.

"Because there was only one direction for Flint to go, the same one we are taking. And, assuming Lieutenant Bodine is an honest man, Flint must have fed him some story that made him sympathetic. Something that would appeal to a solider slightly contemptuous of authority."

"Slightly?" Harding said, as he picked up the walkie-talkie for the routine check. "Big Mike, come in. Big Mike, come in."

Big Mike reported in. He and Cosgrove were in Santa Maria, which he said was nothing more than a cluster of farmhouses and chicken coops. Cosgrove was going through his routine, making enemies. Something he seemed to have a flair for. No sign of trouble.

We drove on, slowly, not wanting to overtake them. It began to mist, a fine drizzle that seemed to float in the air rather than fall. I scanned the few buildings that dotted the road, most of them shelled by the Germans, denying us observation posts and a dry place to sleep.

"There, Billy," Kaz said, pointing to a stone farmhouse ahead and to our left. Whenever possible, vehicles anywhere in the beachhead were parked behind buildings to block the view of German observers in the hills. There, tucked in the lee of the farmhouse, was a jeep with a mounted machine gun. The house, set too far back to be an observation post, had not been hit by artillery. It was intact, with a full view over open fields in every direction. A perfect hideout. Kaz was still pointing, and I pressed his arm down.

"Don't," I said, as I carefully maintained my speed. "If Flint is looking, I don't want him to notice anything out of the ordinary." We had him. Now came the hard part. I continued on until a grove of trees masked a turn in the road, and pulled over. "We have to approach on foot," I said. "Very carefully. There's a few rows of trees we can use as cover."

"But this way we don't catch Flint in the act," Kaz said.

"But we get Danny out safely," I said, looking to Harding. He nodded, and we checked weapons, crossed the road, and ducked low as we ran through rows of turnips toward the line of trees. Lemon trees, but my mind wasn't on fruit. It was on getting in and getting Danny out. We needed to go in hard and fast. I was most worried about being in the open, where Flint could see us. That would give him an edge, since he'd have Danny for cover and we'd be exposed. We got near the end of the trees and hunched down.

"I'll take the back door," I said. "Kaz, you follow me. I'll check the jeep. If it's ours, you stay outside and guard it. Make sure Flint doesn't escape if he gets past me. Colonel, wait until you hear me hit the door, then go in the front. Okay?"

"Okay," Harding said. "Low and quiet until we go in."

"And make sure—"

"Yes, we know, Billy. We'll be careful not to shoot Danny."

"Or let Flint get near him. Let's go."

We scuttled to the building, watching the windows for any sign of movement. This was dangerous, too; I wouldn't shoot at a shadow for fear of hitting Danny, but a shadow might not worry about shooting me. We went flat against the rough stone, Harding ready by the door. Kaz and I crouched and went to the rear of the building, hiding behind the jeep. It was splattered with muck, the identification on the bumper hidden by caked-on mud. Flint was a smart one, all right, but his luck was about to run out. I wiped the mud away and saw VI-37Q. It was enough. I nodded to Kaz, gripped my carbine, and made for the door. When I pressed my back against the wall and went for the latch, I noticed the door hadn't been fully closed. I pushed at it with the barrel of my rifle, just a touch, to get a look inside. I needed to signal Harding, and a silent entry wasn't going to do that. Once I got a peek, I'd kick the door and go in like gangbusters.

I didn't get a peek. Instead, I got the muzzle of an M1 Garand in my face.

CHAPTER THIRTY-SEVEN

TWO FORCE MEN pinned me to the wall as two others advanced on Kaz, Thompsons aimed at his head. He wisely laid his revolver on the seat of the jeep. They dragged us both inside, where Harding was seated in the kitchen, disarmed. His colonel's eagle insignia seemed to be buying him a bit more respect than my lieutenant's bars were. A sergeant stood behind him, arms folded, holding a .45 pointed at the floor.

"Who the hell are you?" the sergeant said, to none of us in particular. "*Sprechen Zie Deutsch?*"

"Sergeant, I am Colonel Samuel Harding, of General Eisenhower's staff. These two work for me."

"Yeah, right. Ike's in London last I heard. You tellin' me he sent you down here to sneak up on us? You with that British general snoopin' around? Or have we caught ourselves some Kraut spies?"

"General Eisenhower did send me," I said. "To catch a murderer. Sergeant Amos Flint, last seen driving that jeep outside." I saw the men exchange glances.

"Murder? Who'd he kill?"

"His own lieutenant. A doctor, a captain, a major, a POW, and at least one sergeant from his own platoon. He stole that jeep and we think he's headed into enemy territory. What line did he feed you?"

"Big tall guy? With a skinny kid tagging along?"

"Yeah, that's him," I said. "Hey, if you're sure we're not Germans, how about giving us our weapons back?"

Harding stood and held out his hand. The sergeant gave him his .45 back. Our other weapons were laid on the table.

"They were here earlier this morning. Gave us a story about bein' on the lam from the MPs for slugging some desk jockey who got a bunch of his men killed for nothin'. Seemed believable."

"He's a practiced liar," I said. "Damn good at it, so don't feel bad. He let you have the jeep?"

"We swapped. Had an old Italian ambulance, a Fiat truck, that we used for transporting wounded. Most times, the Krauts don't shell ambulances on their own. But we liked the jeep and that .30 caliber, so we suggested a trade. Thought it might help him blend in."

"Did he say where they were headed?"

"Back to his outfit, he claimed, in Le Ferriere. Said they'd lie low for another day or so until the dust settled, then show up to get the lay of the land."

"How well is the line defended along here?"

"Well, you got the Hermann Goering Panzer Division over there, but they pulled back pretty far. You can cross the canal any time you want and get nothing more than wet feet. It's more of a big drainage ditch than any canal I ever saw."

"You have outposts along the canal?"

"Colonel, our outposts are way across the canal. That's why the Krauts pulled back. They don't like waking up in the morning to find sentries with their throats slit."

"*Das dicke Ende kommt noch,*" Kaz said.

I was sure the calling card that the Force men left behind would appeal to Flint. "Did you give him any of your stickers?"

"Yeah, a souvenir, sorta. He didn't like hearing about that Limey any more than we did. No offense, lieutenant," he said to Kaz. "Seeing as you're Polish."

Kaz, who wore the red shoulder flash that proclaimed Poland on his British uniform, nodded in acceptance.

"We have to get to Big Mike," I said. "Fast."

We hotfooted it out of there, all of us worried about Big Mike and Cosgrove now, not to mention Danny. Flint had a new vehicle, one that gave him an edge. The red cross on the Italian ambulance was like a free pass. GIs would wave him on, the Germans would hold their fire, and Big Mike wouldn't know what hit him.

"Big Mike, come in," Harding said into the walkie-talkie, holding down the press-to-talk switch. "Big Mike, come in." He released the switch. Nothing.

"Keep trying, maybe they're out of range," I said as I started the jeep and pulled out into the road. We were clear of the trees in a few seconds, and I prayed that whatever German up in the hills had his binoculars trained on us couldn't be bothered to call in fire on one measly jeep.

For the second time today, I was wrong. Really wrong. I heard the whistle of incoming shells, and stepped on it. For the third time today, wrong again. The salvo hit just ahead of us, and if I'd pulled over I could have avoided going through it. Bright flashes shuddered against the ground, sending dirt and smoke everywhere, blinding me as I lifted one arm to shield my eyes, holding onto the steering wheel with the other.

The next thing I knew, I had a mouthful of mud. I was in a ditch by the side of the road, a thin rivulet of water soaking me. I tried to get up and clear my head. I saw a blurry figure standing over me, got up on one knee, and blinked my eyes until I could make him out.

"You all right, Colonel?"

"Leg's banged up a little, but I'm fine," he said, taking my arm and helping me up.

"Where's Kaz? What happened?"

"He's looking for the walkie-talkie. We hit a shell hole and rolled the jeep. We're lucky it didn't come down on top of us."

The barrage had stopped, but I heard shelling farther up the road. "That could be Big Mike and Cosgrove getting hit," I said. "Or Flint and Danny."

"The radio is useless," Kaz said, pointing to the jeep on its side in the ditch. The pieces of the walkie-talkie were pinned underneath.

"See if you can get some help to right the jeep," I said, grabbing my carbine. "I'm going up there." I started to run, hearing Harding and Kaz yelling at me to stop, but I couldn't. I couldn't wait by the side of the road like a stranded motorist. I had to move, to get to Danny before everything went wrong. If it hadn't already.

The first thing that went was my helmet. Too damn heavy. Then the canteen from my web belt. I wasn't wearing the ammo bandolier, so all I had was the fifteen rounds loaded in the carbine and my .45 automatic. If that wasn't enough, I was in bigger trouble than I thought. My Parsons jacket went next, and then I settled into a run, remembering track team in high school. Danny used to come watch me practice. I did the hurdles and the long jump. Not all that well, but it had been a hell of a lot easier without combat boots, an automatic flapping on my hip, and an M1 carbine at port arms.

I could see puffs of explosions in the distance, rising above the shrubs and trees that lined the canal. If there were Force men hidden along the canal, they didn't show themselves. From what the GIs we'd met told us, most were on the other side, hiding out until nightfall. I ran, focusing on lifting my legs, getting the most out of each stride, keeping my breathing regular and my eyes on the horizon. Get into the rhythm, Coach used to say. Don't stare at the ground in front of you, it's all the same. Look ahead, to where you want to be.

I ran.

CHAPTER THIRTY-EIGHT

THE EXPLOSIONS AHEAD had ended. The road was deserted. I kept running, my legs aching and my lungs burning. I wondered if a German observer was tracking me through his binoculars, figuring another dogface had gone nuts. Shell-shocked, battle-fatigued, crazy. I ran, remembering Coach's words: *Just because you feel pain, you don't have to stop.* My boots beat a rhythm on the road, and I imagined Danny waiting for me, although all I could see in my mind was a kid in short pants, running through the backyards of our neighborhood.

I stumbled, one boot catching on the pavement, and went head over heels, tucking my chin and rolling until I came up again, running. I was bleeding somewhere on my arm, and one knee felt wobbly, but I focused on picking up my feet and kept going, watching the road ahead.

Then I heard shots. *Pop pop pop*, followed by a *rat-tat-tat*, then a chorus of mayhem as automatic weapons and rifles spat fire, and I picked up the pace, ignoring the searing pain in my lungs, trying to figure out where the fight was. On the right, by the canal. Small explosions thudded, grenades maybe. I was closer to the fight now, and slowed so I could catch my breath and be ready, watching for movement along the canal. I got off the road, double-timing it across a field and into the trees and shrubs lining the bank of the canal, hoping for cover before I was spotted. I worked my way into a patch of dense brush, and stopped, kneeling as I waited for my breathing to get under control. Gasping for air, I parted the bushes and scanned the canal, both directions. Nothing. Then I saw a head pop up across the bank, about fifty yards upstream. More rifle fire sounded, then a submachine gun, probably a Schmeisser MP40.

What was this? A German raid? The Force men said they'd pushed across the canal, but they had a lot of ground to cover, and maybe the Krauts had infiltrated for prisoners. Or revenge, for all those dead sentries. I took a deep breath, the cool air easing the burning in my lungs, and made my way along the riverbank, carbine at the ready, wishing I had my Thompson and a whole lot more ammo.

I heard splashes behind me, and ducked under cover. Footsteps came up the path and I heard snatches of whispered German. Two figures darted past me, and I recognized the camouflage smocks of the Hermann Goering Division. I stepped out onto the path and squeezed off two shots into the back of one of them, then fired two more at the other guy, but I must've missed, because the next thing I saw was a potato-masher grenade sailing through the air in my direction. I ran back down the path, until I heard the explosion behind me, then worked my way into the underbrush and crawled forward. Shouts and cries intermingled with firing, and all I could tell was that up ahead someone was putting up a helluva fight.

I took a chance and crawled out of the underbrush and into the field, running at a crouch along the edge of the farmland, hoping the Germans were too busy with the opposition ahead to worry about where I'd gotten to. I saw the outline of burned-out buildings through the vegetation. The firing was centered on the buildings, and it seemed as if the Germans were trying to flank whoever was inside. I ran faster, closing in on the tree line and the clearing in front of the buildings.

I heard two blasts, and recognized the distinctive booming sound of a shotgun. That had to be Big Mike. Were he and Cosgrove fighting off the Krauts? I scooted forward, staying as low as I could, watching for the familiar helmets and camouflage of Goering's Luftwaffe troopers.

A single German stood up from the undergrowth not ten yards ahead, ready to throw a grenade at one of the houses. I fired my carbine—three, four shots—wanting to be sure he didn't make the throw. He spun around and for a second he looked at me, his mouth open wide in surprise. Then he fell backward, the grenade still in his hand. First came the explosion, then the shrieks. There were others with him, probably hurt but still alive.

I dove into the greenery again, as bullets clipped the leaves over my head. I had their attention now, and I expected another grenade at any moment. I wished I had some of my own. How many times had I fired? Seven, eight? I crawled toward the canal this time, stopping to listen for the telltale rustling of leaves and branches as Germans searched for me. I was near the path, and as I drew myself up into a crouch, I heard a voice.

"Willi?"

"*Ja,*" I answered in a rough whisper. I was rewarded with a hand thrust through branches, clearing a path. I shot him twice, then fired once more in case there was somebody behind him. I backtracked. Four, maybe five shots left.

It grew quiet. Splashes again, but they sounded as if they were heading back across the canal. I went back out into the field, and circled around to the buildings. The first thing I saw was the staff car, then Big Mike on the ground. I froze. Who had been firing? Three dead Germans lay in the clearing, one more at the blown-out door to the ruined home. Shotgun shells were scattered on the ground. I made my way to Big Mike, as silently as I could. His hair was matted with blood, but he hadn't been shot. Maybe grazed, but he was still breathing. I shook him. No response.

CHAPTER THIRTY-NINE

I HEARD A noise in the bushes, rose, and aimed my carbine over the hood of the staff car. I expected Germans, and my mind took a second, maybe two, to understand what my eyes were seeing. It was Danny, pulling at a leather strap twisted tight at his neck. Flint was behind him, shoving him forward, grinning so wide I could see his white teeth gleaming against pink gums. Then I realized what the strap was: the sling of Big Mike's shotgun. The barrel was against Danny's head. Flint's victims ran through my head, and I struggled not to cry out as I calculated my chances. And Danny's. The odds were against both of us, and I felt my stomach drop and my skin go clammy. I aimed at Flint's head, which was mostly hidden behind Danny's. I really didn't know what to do.

"Thank you, Lieutenant Boyle," Flint said, pushing Danny ahead of him. Danny dug in his heels and grabbed at the strap gouging his throat, getting a finger underneath. "You saved our lives. I guess I owe you something."

"Let Danny go," I said. "Then we'll be even."

"Even? No, not after all the trouble you've caused. What the hell did I ever do to deserve meddling lieutenants, huh? First Landry, now you."

"Landry just wanted to help you," I said, knowing that meant nothing to Flint. But I figured he'd kept his grand scheme bottled up so long that he might want to talk. And if he talked, he might make a mistake while he was jabbering.

"Landry was pathetic. Falling for that whore. Can you imagine living with a woman who sold her body to other men? It's disgusting. I did him a favor, and look what he did to me."

"You beat up Inzerillo, and Ileana too. He sent you to Galante, on the QT, to keep you out of trouble. It's my bet Galante wanted to put you in a loony bin, that's why you killed him." I kept my eyes fixed on Danny's, hoping he wouldn't do anything stupid.

"You're smart, too smart for your own good. Yeah, Galante wanted to get me into a psychiatric hospital. Made it sound like going to college. We'd work together and learn new things about the human mind, he told me." Flint's mouth twisted in disdain for the foolishness of Galante's efforts. "I didn't kill him until I had to. He was going to submit paperwork to have me discharged. He shouldn't have done that. It was his own fault."

"Sure, it was all his fault," I said. "Then you cooked up the crazy card scheme to confuse things, right?"

"Crazy? It worked, didn't it?" We were less than ten feet apart. Danny had stopped struggling, his hand limp where he held the strap. "It would have worked perfectly if it wasn't for you getting in the way."

"Like Louie?"

"It was too bad about Louie. I told you that I bought the Walther off him after he shot the Kraut officer. But it was me. I shot Rusty and the Kraut." He said it proudly, his vanity too strong to resist the impulse to brag. Danny struggled, and Flint twisted the strap tighter. I had to keep Flint talking to me to keep his attention off Danny.

"But why Rusty?"

"He irritated me," Flint said. He relaxed his grip on Danny, who gulped air. Danny's eyes widened, as if asking me what I was going to do. I had no idea.

"That's it? What about Louie? I thought you got along with him."

"Louie was okay, but I knew a smart-ass like you would start asking questions about the pistol, so he had to go. Too bad, because you were sniffing around him, figuring him for the killer. I liked that. You screwed up, Boyle. If you'd left things alone, Louie would be alive. Or dead. This *is* war, after all."

"Cole?"

"The bastard killed himself! What, are you going to blame me for every nutcase who takes a nosedive off a building?" Flint shoved Danny closer, his voice rising, his face red with sudden anger. I needed to calm him down.

"Pretty smart, the way you drove him to it, with the doll, always reminding him about that cellar."

"You found the doll, huh? I didn't know your skills extended to rummaging through garbage. Yeah, I had something I wanted and Cole was the guy to find it."

"So Galante told you about the pearls, and you figured out how to find them?" I tried to keep my voice steady, just another guy in awe of his intellect.

"Galante told me they were hidden in the palace. He was big on museums and Italian history. I think he liked the idea of educating me. He even said I could lead a normal life one day. Normal! Can you imagine that? Being one of you faceless creatures, one of the nameless? Not for me."

"Pearls," I said, desperate to keep him talking. "The pearls were for you, right?"

"Bingo! They'd been stolen, Galante said, and hidden in the palace. No one ever found them. I gave Cole all the dope I got from Galante as he figured things out, based on what that old Italian broad told him. Cole and I were going to split the take if he found the pearls."

"He did," I said, doubting he would have lived to collect. "He gave them to me right before he jumped."

"That crooked bastard! He held out on me. Goes to show, you can't trust anyone." He shrugged, as if it made no difference.

"Don't you want the pearls? I could get them for you."

"The pearls! I don't want the goddamn pearls anymore, they're no good to me."

"What, were they for your girl back home, and she dumped you?"

"Drop the rifle, Boyle. Your sidearm too. Then let's go inside, I have a surprise for you."

"Your mother," I said, remembering the letter. "They were for your mother. Then she died, and spoiled all your plans. You were going to bring them home to mother, weren't you?"

Flint's face contorted into a twisted, teeth-crunching snarl. His cheeks went red and he began to tremble. I prayed I hadn't gone too far and was about to speak when I saw movement in the bushes they had just come out of. A flash of camouflage, and then I made out a German, limping on one bloody leg, making for the canal. He turned, Schmeisser in hand, and I fired once, and missed; again, and hit him. He staggered, but he was still up. Then a third shot to the head, and he went down, firing into the ground as his finger involuntarily twitched on the trigger.

I swung the carbine back to Flint, and his face was calm, as if the previous exchange had never happened. How many bullets did I have left? Two? None?

"Thank you again," Flint said, his politeness a knife in my gut.

"Why go through all this, Flint? What's the point, in the middle of a war, for Christ's sake! Why?" I wasn't stalling now, I wanted to know. If he killed Danny, I needed to know.

"Why? Because I can. Because I'm not one of the sheep," Flint said, the last word hissing out between his teeth. "I'm not a man who depends on what's sewn on his sleeve to tell him who he is and what he can do. Or who needs a uniform to run his own world. Your rules, your ranks, your salutes, they mean nothing to me. A street sweeper is the same as a bishop or a general to me. You all play roles and kiss the ass of the player above you, and thank him for the privilege. Why? Because you all make me sick. I'd kill the whole fucking world if I could."

"You're a powerful man, Flint, I can see that," I struggled to keep my words even, to not react to Flint's venom. "So how about a favor, for a kid who doesn't even know what his role is yet? Let Danny go."

"I don't think so. Now, let's go inside, like gentlemen," he said.

"I have a card to play." Flint herded us into the house, me first, Danny between us, the shotgun at Danny's head. I held onto the carbine, not sure how many rounds were left. The first thing I saw was a chair. Communications wire lay on floor, some of it still tied to the armrests. Cosgrove. He'd had Cosgrove tied up in here, but he'd gotten away. Blood stained one of the armrests. Not much, but enough to tell me Cosgrove was hurt.

"Big surprise," I said. Explosions erupted outside, sending a blast of dirt and smoke into the ruined house. We each instinctively went into a crouch, Flint still pressing the shotgun against Danny. "Mortars."

"Just the Krauts covering their retreat," Flint said. "No heavy stuff."

"Let me go, Sarge," Danny managed to croak. Another series of explosions hit, closer to the canal.

"No can do, kid. As a matter of fact, if your brother doesn't find that old Limey general and drag him back in here, I'm gonna redecorate the place with your brains." He looked at me with a smile and raised his eyebrows, daring me to call his bluff. I had my carbine, but there was no chance to get a shot off, and he knew it.

More explosions hit the far end of the house, shaking dust and grit loose from the ceiling and showering us all. We covered our heads, the instinct of the battlefield taking over. A flash of movement caught my eye, and I saw Cosgrove, moving faster than I thought possible, a tire iron in his grasp, which he brought down on the kneeling Flint, smashing into his wrist and breaking his grip on the shotgun, not to mention bones. Flint howled, but kept a firm grip on Danny with his other hand, pulling him up and out of the house, the shotgun wrapped around his neck but hanging free. Another mortar round hit the house square above us, sending timbers crashing down around Cosgrove and me. Cosgrove's face was gray with dust and streaked with bright red, but I could see he was more angry than injured.

"Go," he said, working at a section of roof that had pinned one leg.

Mortar rounds churned the water in the canal, but Flint was headed straight for it, Danny in tow. He was ahead of Danny, keeping him as a shield. In seconds they were in the canal, Flint making his way through the waist-deep water. I heard a German machine gun open up, close by. There were still plenty of them out there. Then, a burst stitched across the water, driving me back. Flint and Danny were up on the other bank now, Danny fighting, punching at Flint with one hand and trying to get a grip on the shotgun with the other. Flint had only one good hand, and he needed it to hold onto Danny, to keep him between us. He kicked Danny twice, and that put an end to his fight.

Rifle fire picked up. Something was happening, but I couldn't focus on it. Flint stood with Danny on the opposite bank, his good arm around his neck. He yelled something, but with more mortar rounds dropping all over, it was lost. I knelt, and braced my arm on my knee, aiming at Flint. I could see his white teeth, his mouth wide, speaking to Danny, his eyes on me all the time. I watched Danny, wondering if Flint would take him, or find a way to kill him. And if Danny got away, how long until a bullet or a bomb caught up to him? How long until he'd be a corpse or a combat fatigue case, unable to control the shakes, his dreams and waking nightmares, his life? I didn't want him serving beefsteak to the brass and diving for cover every time a plate dropped. I didn't want Danny to become one of the faceless crowd of casualties in this war.

I tried to count the number of shots I'd fired. Flint was too far away for the pistol, so it had to be the carbine. Gunfire echoed up and down the canal, louder now, and more explosions hit behind me, the Germans working their mortars overtime. I steadied myself, let out a breath, lined up the target in the sights.

Flint shouted one last time, then pushed Danny down the bank. He stood alone for a moment, silhouetted against the sky. Danny faced away from me, trying to free the shotgun, its strap still twisted around his neck. I had my target. I fired.

And shot my brother.

I WAITED, WATCHING for Flint, but he was gone. So was the machine-gun fire. I tossed the carbine away and ran to Danny, my legs heavy in the brackish water. His right shoulder was bloody, and his eyes dazed. He blinked, as if he thought I might not be real.

"What happened?" He clutched at my arm, wincing in pain. It tore me apart, and I held back the tears I knew would give me away.

"You've been hit. Take it easy, I got you." I took the shotgun from around his neck and hung it from my shoulder. I picked up Danny like I'd done so many times, carrying him in from the backseat of the car, sound asleep, cradled in my arms. His weight was nothing as he rested his head on my chest, grabbing at my shirt with his good arm, his face contorted in pain.

"Am I going to make it, Billy?"

"Don't talk stupid, Danny. You caught some shrapnel in your shoulder, that's all. You'll be fine." I sloshed through the water, watching Cosgrove turn over Big Mike, wadding his jacket under his head for a pillow.

"Flint?" Danny said.

"Yeah," I said. "He got away."

"Why didn't you shoot?"

"I did. I only had one round left, and I missed. What did he say to you?" I laid Danny down, leaning him against the fender of the car, next to Big Mike.

"He said the joker would be waiting for you, downriver."

"That's all?"

"Yeah. He told me that he was granting you a favor, like you asked. Since I hadn't disappointed him."

"You have any idea what that meant?" I pulled open his uniform, sprinkling sulfa on the wound, and applied a compress from the first-aid pack that Cosgrove had retrieved from the car.

"No. I have no idea what anything means." Danny gritted his teeth, grimacing with pain. The bullet was still in there, nestled in a mix of shattered bone and muscle. He needed a hospital, and so did Big Mike.

"How is he?" I asked Cosgrove, who was trying to clean Big Mike's wound with water from a canteen.

"Breathing, is all I can say."

"Thanks for getting the drop on Flint. That was just in time."

"Old trick I learned in Cairo. Tighten your muscles when you're being tied up. When you relax them, you've got a bit of wiggle room. Unfortunate, Flint getting away like that. Jerry should have no trouble bagging him, though, out alone with a broken wrist."

"Yeah," I said, not certain what he'd seen.

"But your brother, he's safe now, isn't he? Banged up, but he's seen the elephant and will live to tell the tale. Not every man here will be able to say the same."

I had nothing to say, nothing left. I felt a tremendous weariness settle in my body. I slumped down next to Danny, as I heard the sound of vehicles pulling to a halt and boots stomping on the ground. Jeeps, an ambulance, even a truck full of Carabinieri. I put my arm around Danny and held him close, his blood sticky and thick. I watched Big Mike, willing him to wake up and shake off the pounding he'd taken. All this suffering, and Flint had gotten away. But I had Danny, and I prayed I'd made the right choice. And that I could live with myself.

Harding, Kaz, and Luca hovered over me, but I couldn't speak, couldn't answer their questions or look into their eyes. Medics pushed them away and took Danny from me. Others picked up Big Mike and put him on a stretcher. Graves Registration men wandered around with the mattress covers, searching for the dead. Finally, someone came for me.

CHAPTER FORTY

"YOUR SERGEANT HAS a subdural hematoma," Doc Cassidy said. "We're prepping him for surgery right now."

We were back at the hospital, in a small tent that had been set aside for our banged-up group. Danny's shoulder was encased in bandages. Cosgrove sported a bandage over his right temple, and for some reason I was on a cot, too. Harding and Kaz sat at a small table by the open flaps.

"Will he be okay?" I asked.

"If he got here fast enough," Cassidy said. "I'll let you know as soon as I can."

"Can I see him?" I asked, sitting up and getting my feet on the floor.

"You stay put, doctor's orders. You were disoriented, in shock when you came in. I want to watch you for another day."

"How long have I been here?" I asked, not remembering the journey here or anything since lights out back at the canal.

"A couple of hours. You don't remember?" Cassidy pushed me back down on the cot and peered into my eyes.

"No, I don't think so. How's Danny?"

"I'm fine, Billy," he said from his cot, a sloppy grin on his face. "Listen to the doctor and lie down."

"Is he?" I asked Cassidy in a whisper. "Is he really fine?"

"He's feeling no pain right now, due to the morphine we gave him. We got the bullet out, but he'll need another operation in Naples. That's a million-dollar wound he's got there."

That was all I needed to hear. I closed my eyes.

Time passed. I must've slept, because I know I dreamed. Of home. Danny, Mom and Dad. Uncle Dan telling stories at the tavern. Walking the beat, playing baseball and mumblety-peg. Sunday dinners. It was all nice until I lost Danny, and I was just a little kid myself, alone in a strange city, and my hands were smeared with blood.

"Billy, what is it, what's wrong?" It was Kaz, seated by my cot.

"Huh?"

"You cried out in your sleep."

"Bad dream, I guess. Where's Danny? How's Big Mike? How long . . . ?"

Kaz answered me, but I fell back asleep, the thought that Doc Cassidy had given me something bubbling up from the tiredness inside me.

It was light outside when I awoke again. I was alone in the tent. I must have slept through the night, I thought, then saw I was wearing pajamas. When the hell did I put these on? I struggled to get up, felt a little dizzy, then lay down for a minute.

"Boyle? Boyle, can you hear me?" It was Doc Cassidy, shaking my arm. I must've dozed off. I opened my eyes, and a lantern was the only light in the tent. How could it be night already?

"Yeah, I hear you. What's going on? Where's Danny?"

"In Naples by now. How are you feeling?"

"Thirsty. Hungry."

"Good," he said, helping me sit up and giving me a glass of water. "I was worried about you."

"I must've been tired. How long have I been out?"

"Forty-eight hours."

"Impossible," I said, although I knew it wasn't.

"I gave you a mild sedative when you came in here. You seemed agitated, in a state of shock. But it shouldn't have knocked you out for two days."

"Big Mike?"

"I don't know. We relieved the pressure on his brain, and Harding got him on a hospital ship headed to Naples, where he can be treated by a specialist."

"What kind of specialist?"

"A brain surgeon. Billy, he didn't wake up. But that doesn't mean he hasn't by now. Your Colonel Harding didn't want to take any chances."

"Danny's doing all right, isn't he?" *Please.*

"That shoulder is going to bother him whenever it rains. After a few months of physical therapy, he'll have at least ninety percent use of it. Could have been worse."

"Yeah. So he's going home?"

"Definitely. He's a lucky kid. He told me about Flint, and how he let him go. And being wounded by shrapnel. Yep, one lucky kid."

"Can I get out of here now?"

"Can you stand?" I got my legs off the cot and stood. Wobbled a bit, but stayed vertical. I looked at Cassidy. "If you can stay upright, you can go," he said.

"What was wrong with me?" I asked as I shuffled around, testing my legs.

"Shock, or to be more accurate, acute stress reaction. Pressure. Exhaustion. Moral dilemma. Guilt."

"What do you mean?"

"Nothing at all. Just words from my psychiatric residency. Here. I saved a souvenir for you." He pressed a small hunk of metal into my hand. "Keep your head down, Boyle."

I waited until he left. I opened my palm and saw the misshapen but unmistakable shape of a .30 slug from an M1 carbine.

HARDING AND KAZ walked on either side of me as we made our way to the mess tent in Hell's Half Acre. I guess they wanted to be sure I didn't fall facedown in the mud.

"We're on a PT boat out of here at 0600 tomorrow," Harding said as we each sat with our mess kits full of hot chow.

"Not soon enough," I said. "I'm sorry Flint got away, Colonel."

"Well, at least he didn't fill his royal flush. We've sent his name to the International Red Cross, in case it shows up on a POW list. Meanwhile, we're looking into anyone who was on that road and was reported missing. We'll figure out whose dog tags he grabbed."

"Any word on Big Mike?" I asked.

"Nothing yet. Your brother is shipping out tomorrow from Naples. Sorry you'll miss him."

"As long as he's going home in one piece, I'm happy."

"Any idea what Flint meant?" Kaz asked. "About a joker down-river?"

"The joker must refer to a card. Maybe he had me tagged for a joker in my pocket. Downriver? No idea. Maybe he meant in the future. Who's to know? So what's next, Colonel?" I said. "After Naples."

"Cosgrove has set something up for us in Brindisi. Then back to London. I hope to God Big Mike is alive and kicking when we get back. How about you, Boyle? Are you all right? That was a helluva nap you took."

"Doc Cassidy said it was a reaction to the sedative he gave me. I guess seeing Danny almost get killed was more of a shock than I thought it was."

"It makes sense," Kaz said.

"Nothing makes sense," I said.

They exchanged looks, and Kaz shrugged, granting me the point. I lifted a cup of coffee, and saw ripples in the black steaming brew. My hand was shaking, so I set it down. Harding and Kaz stared at their food. I tried to look at mine, but all I saw was Danny and his ruined shoulder, Big Mike inert on the ground, the look of surprise on the face of the German with the grenade, and a blur of faceless uniforms, dappled camouflage drenched in blood. Flint, giving me his silhouette on the riverbank, daring me to shoot.

"Billy," Kaz said, his arm reaching toward mine. "Are you all right?"

"Leave me alone," I said, not wanting to lie to Kaz, or tell the truth to Harding. I settled for bitterness instead. I was hungry and I ate, which was simple, unlike everything else that had happened here. I went after my food, not caring what anyone thought, wanting only to fill my belly and get out of the Anzio Bitchhead, which was what the orderly who brought my clothes had called it. I couldn't argue.

PART FOUR

Brindisi, Italy

CHAPTER FORTY-ONE

NEVER ONE TO miss an opportunity to improve relations with our allies, even one that had recently been our enemy, Harding had come up with the idea of returning the pearls Cole had found to the Italian royal family. Me, I had sort of hoped everyone would forget about them, and Kaz and I could do a split once we were back in London, since I'd come to know some fellows there who might be in the market for hot jewels. But Kaz was already rich, so that plan didn't occur to him. Plus, being one of the European nobility, even if from a minor branch of that intertwined family, he felt it was the right thing to do.

The only thing I liked about the whole idea was that Signora Salvalaggio was the one who was going to give them back to the king and queen. It was only right, since she'd practically been accused of the theft, and her whole life had been changed by it. Maybe the king would be so happy to get his mother's pearls back that he'd give her a reward, or a castle, or whatever kings these days had to give.

The only thing that worried me about the whole idea was that Signora Salvalaggio had insisted on bringing Ileana along. She'd taken her under her wing, and since neither had anyone else to take them in, it didn't seem like a bad match. But escorting a former prostitute to see a king just plain made me nervous.

We walked up the stone steps to the Swabian Castle in Brindisi, on the heel of the Italian boot. It was a medieval fortress overlooking the harbor, where King Victor Emmanuel III hung his hat. It would have been hard for him to find a suitable joint any farther from the fighting. Signora Salvalaggio was dressed in her finest black. Ileana wore a long white silk dress that the signora had helped her sew. It showed off her raven-black hair and dark eyes. I didn't comment on the fact that it looked like parachute silk. Shopping was hard in war-torn Italy, after all.

"Remember," Harding had lectured us. "There are over twenty thousand Italian soldiers fighting the Germans right now, and acquitting themselves well. We want more to join them, and we want King Emmanuel to encourage it. He's been supportive, and any little thing we can do to show our appreciation will be good for the war effort. So best behavior, Boyle."

I wanted to ask why he singled me out, but instead I just said, "Yes sir."

The beachhead seemed very far away as we trooped through the ornate rooms of the castle. I'd cleaned myself up, gotten a new dress uniform, and was currently trying to fool myself into believing everything was going to be fine. Danny was on his way home, and he'd have stories to tell. He'd proved himself in combat, and would live to tell his kids about it. Flint was hopefully in a POW cage where he wouldn't be associating with generals, and where, with the help of the International Red Cross, we might find him. What could go wrong?

Nothing. Except that everything already had gone wrong. I was living in a world where shooting your own brother was the logical thing to do. I had known I was going to do it, if the opportunity presented itself, for quite a while. I just hadn't admitted it to myself, even though I knew exactly why I'd swapped for that damn carbine. Now I was having dreams of shooting shadowy men in Luftwaffe camouflage, and as they fell and their faces turned in surprise, they became Danny. All of them. I was no longer afraid for Danny; I was afraid for myself. Would I be able to pull the trigger next time? Be fast enough, quick enough, to act without thinking?

This world had gone mad, and I was part of it. One of the faceless crowd. Flint had been right about that.

I felt a hand on my arm. It was Kaz, and we were already standing in front of the king. How did we get here? I tried to focus, but it was all a lot of Italian mumbo-jumbo. King Victor was a bit short in the legs, and I could barely see the top of his head over Signora Salvalaggio's bent form. Harding had a translator who gave a cleaned-up version of how the pearls were found, and then introduced the signora. She bowed, spoke for a minute, and then motioned to Ileana, who opened her purse, drew out the coiled pearls, and presented them to the king. He said something in a low voice, and nodded to one of his aides, who came and retrieved them. I knew enough Italian to hear him thank Signora Salvalaggio before he turned his back and walked away.

"That was underwhelming," I said. Even Harding didn't disagree, as our small group was left alone in the large room with portraits of long-dead rulers staring down at us.

"I am sure the king will make some gesture," Kaz said once we were outside. Harding and Cosgrove had gone to get the staff car while we waited with the ladies. "Once he understands the value of the necklace."

"His mother draped herself in them," Signora Salvalaggio said. "That family knows the value of pearls like a pig knows mud. I don't want his money. If anyone who is left alive knows of the theft, now they know I and my officer did not do it, God rest his soul. That spineless shrimp can go to hell. His father would be ashamed of what he's done to Italy."

"But it is not fair," said Kaz. "You should have something for all this time under suspicion, not to mention for returning the pearls."

"You are a good man, Baron," she said. "Truly noble, in the real sense of the word. I do not want you to worry about an old woman, or a young one, either." She patted Ileana's arm, who smiled at her with a gentle grace. "So I will tell you a secret." Her fingers worked at the top buttons of her dress, and with a girlish smile showed us a short strand of pearls, which quickly disappeared beneath the folds of black. Ileana giggled as she took the old woman by the arm, guiding her to the car that Harding had just driven to the curb. I laughed, and winked at her as she waited for the door to be opened.

"Kaz," I said, draping my arm around his shoulder, "I don't believe I've felt this good in quite some time. Let's ditch Harding and Cosgrove and find ourselves a bar."

"And toast that grand lady," he said. We were already walking away when a British Army motorcycle skidded to a halt in front of us. The rider approached Cosgrove, who had helped the ladies into the car. He handed him a note, saluted, and roared off. Cosgrove read the note, then handed it to Harding. They both looked at me.

"What?"

"Message from SOE headquarters here in Brindisi. I'd asked them to keep me posted," Cosgrove said. I didn't have to ask about what. Diana worked for the Special Operations Executive, and her mission to Rome had been planned here. She had even adopted an accent from the Brindisi area as part of her cover story.

"Tell me," I said, balanced on a knife edge between two worlds, one with Diana alive, the other too terrible to imagine.

"Miss Seaton has been taken," Cosgrove said, his voice quavering. "The Germans have her."

Epilogue

Pain stabbed at his wrist where the old man had struck. He tucked the useless hand into his shirt, and waited his turn. That bastard had surprised him all right, but not as much as Boyle had. He didn't think Boyle would shoot him in cold blood, not once he'd let Danny go. But shooting his own brother, that took some steel in the spine. He hadn't expected that. It was fun giving him a moment's temptation, and the bonus was watching the shot hit bone, seeing the puff of dust from the hit, sensing Danny's blood in the air.

He hoped Danny had given his brother the message. He couldn't find fault with the kid. He'd fought hard, saved his skin, and hadn't done anything stupid. It pleased him to grant the favor, like a great lord would do for a faithful servant.

Sooner or later, though, they all disappointed him. Rusty Gates, Cole, Landry, they were all the same. Pretending to be pals, then becoming insistent, tedious, demanding, deserving of death. Danny was too young, too new for that. Besides, his plans had to wait. He didn't get his general or Boyle. He still had the ace of hearts and the joker to play. A man had to plan things carefully, not kill everything in sight. Unless the army wanted you to. Downriver, he knew he'd come across a general somewhere. And if he was lucky, Boyle would follow once again. This time, the joker would not get away. The Ace of Hearts would taunt him, remind him of what he'd lost, and of what Flint knew about him. Draw him in deeper. Cain and Abel, in Italy.

The river was everything to Flint. It flowed to the killing sea, and he drifted in it, taking what he needed. Downriver, there would always be more. Downriver, Boyle waited.

"Kommt!" *The guard poked at Flint with his rifle. There were six of them in the room, seated on a bench, guards at either end. There had been seven, but one had gone into the adjacent office and not come out. Flint wasn't worried. He knew they did it to scare them. He let the guard prod him along into the next room.* "Sitzen!"

He sat in the wooden chair facing a German officer seated at a small wooden table, a stack of papers in front of him. His cap lay on the table next to an ashtray full of cigarettes. American cigarettes. He didn't offer one from the pack of Luckies, but lit one for himself.

"We don't get many prisoners from among the criminals on the canal," *the German said. He spoke English well, but carefully, drawing out each syllable, pronouncing prisoners as priz-sun-ers. It took Flint a moment to understand he was referring to the First Special Service Force.*

"Those guys make me nervous," *Flint said with a smile.* *"Can't imagine how you feel."*

"Amusing," *the German said, consulting his paperwork.* *"Sergeant Peter Miller. You are now a guest of the Third Reich, as will be many others from Anzio. How long have you been there?"*

"Listen to me," *Flint said, leaning forward, focusing his gaze on the German's eyes, getting him to see this was more than another of his endless encounters with grubby Americans.* *"I can tell you a whole lot more than how long I've been dodging artillery shells in the beachhead. But first, I need a doctor for my arm. I think my wrist is broken. One of those Force men did it, the bastard."*

"And why did he do that, Sergeant?"

"We got into an argument. I mentioned my family name had been Mueller, and that they had changed it to Miller during the last war, on account of my dad getting beat up for being German. He said he'd deserved it, and one thing led to another."

"Commendable that you defended your father's honor. But foolish that you had your wrist broken."

"The other guy was more foolish. I broke his damn neck. That's why I

took off across the canal." Flint knew he needed a story. He'd been captured minutes after he went across, and this officer probably knew that. Still, it could work to his advantage if he didn't go overboard with the Kraut stuff.

"You killed a comrade?"

"He was no comrade of mine. Those guys think they run everything. I risk my life every day bringing stuff from Nettuno and returning their reports to HQ. You'd think they'd say thanks, but no—"

"Headquarters? What headquarters?"

"General Lucas's headquarters. In Nettuno. Every day I make the trip, and let me tell you, it ain't easy with all that firepower you're throwing at us."

"Tell me about your work at headquarters, Sergeant Miller."

"Here's the deal. I'll spill plenty, once you take care of my arm, and find some officer's uniform for me. I don't want to go to an enlisted man's POW camp. I want medical attention and a promotion. Then we sit and talk, one good German boy to another. Ja?"

"I have another idea. I will have you taken out and shot."

"Hey, suit yourself. Go ahead, and lose the services of a sympathetic German-American who's seen General Lucas every day since he landed." Flint could see the man's eyes flicker, as he calculated what he might gain if the story were true. He knew he could spin tales of HQ long into the night, made up from bits and pieces of gossip, scuttlebutt, and even a bit of truth. Like most GIs he knew which units were where along the line in the beachhead. It might not be news to the Krauts, but it would make the rest of what he told them sound real.

"Very well, Herr Mueller. We will attend to your arm, and find a more suitable identity for you. I take it you do not care how we do so?"

"God's honest truth, I don't give a damn."

Author's Note

Kurt Gerstein, as described by Diana Seaton in Chapter Two, is a real historical figure. As a witness to the gassing at Belzec, he alerted as many religious leaders and foreign diplomats as he could, unfortunately to little effect. Gerstein surrendered to the Allies at the end of the war in 1945, and was initially treated well by his French captors, who allowed him to reside in a hotel in order to write up what became known as the Gerstein Report, documenting his wartime activities. However, he was subsequently transferred to a prison in France and treated as a war criminal. In July 1945, he was found dead in his cell. Whether it was suicide or murder by members of the SS to keep him quiet has never been determined.

Witold Pilecki, whom Kaz describes in Chapter Nineteen, was also a real person. A Polish Army officer, Pilecki deliberately allowed himself to be picked up in a Nazi roundup, knowing he would be sent to Auschwitz. In 1940, he began to smuggle out reports to the Polish Underground. Finally, in 1943, he escaped from Auschwitz and wrote a detailed report on the exterminations being carried out. The report was sent to London by the Underground, which requested arms and assistance for an assault on Auschwitz. The report was either disbelieved or ignored, and nothing was done. After the war, Witold Pilecki resisted the Soviets with as much fervor as he did the Nazis. He began to collect information on Soviet atrocities and executions of former Underground members. In 1948, he was arrested, and after a show trial by the Communist government of Poland, executed.

It was during World War II that the term "thousand-yard stare" was coined. It referred to the unfocused gaze of a battle-weary soldier, who appeared to be looking through the observer to some distant image. During World War II, 1.3 million soldiers were treated for what was then known as battle or combat fatigue, and it is estimated that up to 40 percent of medical discharges were for psychiatric reasons.

Although much had been learned about shell shock—as it was called—during the First World War, the U.S. Army forgot many of those lessons and had to relearn them in the Second World War. In the Mediterranean Theater of Operations, it was not until March 1944 (after the events described in this book) that a psychiatrist was added to the medical staff of each combat division. The term "exhaustion" was used to describe conditions that came to be known as combat or battle fatigue, or later, combat stress reaction, and now post-traumatic stress disorder.

Old Sergeant's Syndrome, as described in this novel, is an actual condition defined by the U.S. Army Medical Department during the Second World War. The syndrome was described in 1949 by Major Raymond Sobel, U.S. Army Medical Corps, in his article *Anxiety-Depressive Reactions After Prolonged Combat Experience—the "Old Sergeant Syndrome"* (*U.S. Army Medical Dept. Bulletin*, 1949, Nov. 9, Suppl.: 137–146).

In a study of men who had broken down in combat, the authors stated that the "question was not, 'Why did they break?', but 'Why did they continue to endure?'" It was in this study that the calculation was made that if left in combat for prolonged periods, 98 percent of soldiers would suffer from symptoms of combat fatigue. The remaining 2 percent would undoubtedly be sociopaths. For details, see: Swank, R. L., and Marchand, W. E. (1946). *Combat Neuroses: Development of Combat Exhaustion. Archives of Neurology and Psychology.*

Audie Murphy makes a brief cameo appearance in this story. Murphy, at seventeen, lied about his age to join the service, and became the most decorated American soldier of the war. Murphy was at Anzio, where he suffered a recurrence of malaria, which is what brought him to Hell's Half Acre. After the war, Murphy suffered from severe depression and insomnia, stating that he remembered the war "as I do a nightmare. A demon seemed to have entered my body."

Murphy became addicted to sleeping pills, which he took to overcome his insomnia. To break himself from their grip, he locked himself in a motel room for a week. After that, he broke what had been a taboo about public discussion of combat fatigue, and became a dedicated spokesperson for veterans, urging the government to provide greater support and to increase the understanding of the emotional impact of combat experiences.

The battle for the Anzio Beachhead is still a matter of debate among military historians. Winston Churchill famously remarked that he "had hoped that we were hurling a wildcat onto the shore, but all we got was a stranded whale." General John Lucas was relieved of his command after a month, and it was not until three months later that Allied divisions finally broke out of the encircled beachhead. What could Lucas have done differently? He knew his forces were inadequate and his orders muddled at best. This was a recipe for disaster, but Lucas went along with an operation he felt was doomed, even as his forces were diminished from the original planned allocations. To be fair to his reputation, many veterans of Anzio say they owe their lives to his caution, and that a more aggressive general might have gambled all and lost.

Acknowledgments

Thanks are due to Edie Lasner for once again graciously reviewing my use of the Italian language. Any errors are certainly due to my transcription in spite of her expertise. My wife, Deborah Mandel, provides constant support and vital feedback in the creation of these stories. My debt to her is profound.

The cover art was inspired by an image taken in Korea, by U.S. Army combat photographer Al Chang, in 1950. The original photograph shows a grief-stricken soldier being comforted upon hearing of the death of a friend. It is a tender, and terrible, picture.